USA TODAY BESTSELLING AUTHOR

DALE MAYER

A Psychic Visions Novel

WHAT IF...

WHAT IF...
Beverly Dale Mayer
Valley Publishing Ltd.

ISBN-13: 978-1-773364-99-5
Print Edition

Books in This Series:

Tuesday's Child
Hide 'n Go Seek
Maddy's Floor
Garden of Sorrow
Knock Knock…
Rare Find
Eyes to the Soul
Now You See Her
Shattered
Into the Abyss
Seeds of Malice
Eye of the Falcon
Itsy-Bitsy Spider
Unmasked
Deep Beneath
From the Ashes
Stroke of Death
Ice Maiden
Snap, Crackle…
What If…
Talking Bones
String of Tears
Inked Forever
Insanity
Soul Legacy
Coveted

Boxed Sets and Bundles
https://geni.us/Bundlepage

About This Book

Detective Abigail Cartwright has earned a reputation for solving weird homicide cases, but, when she's called to a lecture hall at the local university, she faces the oddest one yet. During a What If … lecture, run by soon-to-be-retired Professor Gertrude Milligan, two students died. Without any signs of how or why.

Confused, Abby digs in to solve the mystery, only to find several old cases connect—or do they? Were the two students murdered, or was something else going on?

Professor Leon Wellington is worried about his aunt Gertie. Their personal history was bad enough, but to have two of her favorite students die right in front of her has left her shocked and grieving. How can she not be a prime suspect in this case? Then she goes missing …

When the past collides with the present, the stakes are higher than ever, as a killer realizes how close he is to losing everything …

Sign up to be notified of all Dale's releases here!
https://geni.us/DaleNews

PROLOGUE

GERTRUDE MILLIGAN STRODE down the stairs, studying the empty amphitheater. She was ready for her class, but, as always, she was a few minutes early. She liked to settle into the space alone, before the doors opened. It helped. After all these years, teaching was getting longer and harder, and she just wanted to sit down, have a cup of tea. But this What If? philosophy class was a new one that she enjoyed teaching, and she was here, bright and early.

As she approached the main platform area, she walked to the podium and dumped her paperwork on top of it. She rolled her neck slightly and stretched her shoulders back. She was coming to the end of her reign. She wasn't quite ready to retire, but, at sixty-five, she knew it was time. Giving up her research would bother her the most. She absolutely loved the research. She didn't mind the kids. Some of them were even incredibly intelligent and kept her hopping. They kept her mind going.

And the rest of them were just here because they needed the credits, before they moved on to the rest of their dull, boring lives that had absolutely nothing to do with the *what ifs* in the world, and that was a damn shame.

She walked to the chalkboard, wincing, because of course, nobody had cleared off the last lecture. She quickly took the eraser and wiped down the board, wrote the name of her current lecture at the top, and underneath it wrote WHAT IF? in large bold lettering. Then, just as the doors opened, she turned toward the class. She walked back and forth on the platform, keeping her mind open, thinking about the million things in her day, until slowly the trickle of students came in.

After a glance at her watch, she called out, "Two minutes." And it always seemed like, in that last minute, about half of the class poured in. She frowned at the noisy group. All of them knew her by now. They'd been in her class for at least three months, were reaching the end of the term, and exams were coming up. She was ready, but she didn't think they were.

A class like this was supposed to make them think, to keep them on their toes, and to keep their brains nimble. Instead it seemed to have the opposite effect and put so many of these kids to sleep. As Gertrude looked at some of the older students, they were hardly kids anymore. A couple were under twenty, but most of them were in their early twenties, midtwenties, late twenties. She knew at least one was in her midforties. She even had a couple in their sixties here.

"Time," she called out.

The two students closest to the doors got up, let in a few scrambling students, and then closed and locked the doors. She was strict on that. There were to be no interruptions. If a student couldn't be here on time, they couldn't be allowed to disrupt the rest of her class. She waited a moment for everybody to calm down and to stop shuffling. And then she started.

"Good morning, everyone. Glad to see you could make

it so early." They all cracked a smile. "I know. Lots of final projects, lots of studying for exams to do, as we begin next week. This is our last lecture class, but don't worry. You've come this far, and you'll make it." A twitter of laughter echoed through the group. She smiled. "As always, we're talking *what ifs*. We already discussed in this class: *What if aliens arrived? What if Armageddon happened? What if a Third World War happened?*

"Today, as in some of the other topics, this one will be completely different. We'll discuss psychic phenomena. But not just any psychic phenomenon because, of course, it's a very wide field. There are psychics, and then there are mediums, who don't necessarily consider themselves psychics—like the aura readers, the healers, all kinds of different classifications and groups. But I want to talk about something completely different today because, of course, my mind always thinks in terms of *what if*." She looked around at the class, noting that everybody leaned forward with interest. "Say, for example," she stated, pointing to the row in front, where three females sat together. "Say these three women were targeted."

At that, the trio straightened up, and one asked, "Targeted for what?"

Gertie laughed. "I don't mean *targeted*, targeted. I don't mean to be stalked or with a target on your back or with a gun or something. But let's just say, what if you had a back door into your mind? What if other people had a way to put ideas in your head? What if people could control your thinking? What if people not only controlled your thinking but your actions? Has anybody ever thought about this?"

A couple students put up their hands.

She continued. "And you're thinking more of the movies, aren't you? Like, you know, mind control and other things like that, right?"

They both nodded.

"Right? So think about psychics. Think about energy. Think about people who can heal somebody else just by waving their hands over the surface of an injury and pouring supposedly loving energy into that area. What about people who can stand here and look at you and see your past life all in your energy?" She waved her hand around one of the male students, standing off to the side. "They can check out your history. They can go into something called akashic records—the Book of Life—and see all kinds of stuff.

"And then we have others, energy forms, where people have hooks into each other because, of course, we either love or hate them. These can form at birth, and they can continue right through until your death. Sometimes people say diseases can be caused this way because you're so full of other people's negative energy that you poison your own soul," she murmured. "But what if—now think about this—what if there was a back door to your mind? And somebody else had access to it?"

She looked at the three women, part of her previous example to the class. "I mean, just what if somebody stood up here today, without you even knowing it, and could get into your mind, while you sat here in class? What if that were possible? Now think about it, and then raise your hands and toss out the possibilities of what we could be looking at."

After that, the class discussion was a little slow to start, but then people came up with myriad ideas about how to run countries, how to control somebody's love life, how to gain access to bank accounts, how to control relationships. Gertrude nodded and wrote a lot of them on the board.

"Think bigger. Think Third World War," she suggested. "What if somebody was controlling somebody else from a distance? I mean, just because we have a back door to the mind, does that mean the person has to be sitting right beside you in order to control your mind?" She looked at the trio of students again and asked, "What if the one in the middle could access the two outer women of this group?"

The women just stared at Gertrude, and the one in the center, Carrie, said, "I don't think I like being here."

Gertrude laughed. "Think about it. What if somebody from somewhere else in the world had access because energy"—and she turned to look at the class—"energy ..."

And the class cried out, "Has no boundaries. For energy, there is no life. There is no death. Energy is forever. Energy only transforms. So *what if?*"

By the time the hour-long class was more or less done, it had been a very animated session, and Gertrude was delighted. She readied the last of the homework for her next class. "It's that time, and it's been a pleasure, everybody. Good job. Feel free to take off, to get ready for your exams, and we'll see you next term maybe. If not, have a good life."

And, with that, everybody gathered up their stuff.

Gertrude walked over to the chalkboard, grabbed the eraser, and started clearing off all the notes that she had put there. A small shriek and a weird silence had her turning to look. She asked, "What's the matter?"

While everybody else was still streaming out the doors up at the top, an entire group of people around the front row just stared at Gertrude and then looked at the group of women, still seated there.

"We forgot one *what if,*" said Carrie in the middle, who now stood, her voice high and strained.

"What's that?" Gertie asked.

"What if the back door to the mind could kill someone?"

Gertie shrugged. "Well, if anything else is possible, that is too. Why?" she asked.

Carrie looked at her professor in shock, then turned to the women seated on either side of her. "Because both of them are dead."

CHAPTER 1

DETECTIVE ABIGAIL CARTWRIGHT stood at the top of the amphitheater and studied the layout ahead of her. Her partner was on the way. Forensic technicians were moving silently in their blue suits and booties, and, up at the front, an older lady sat, perched stiffly on a stool. Her energy looked like it had completely drained away, leaving only her ramrod spine to keep her in an upright position. A man stood at her side, with a hand around her upper arm, as if giving her strength. And maybe he was. Abby definitely noted a connection between the two. At that moment her partner, Harvey, stepped up to her side.

"I heard this one is bizarre." Just enough amusement was in Harvey's tone to make her groan.

"Aren't they all?" Abby sighed tiredly, not wanting to even open her other sight. Just the thought brought on a headache. Then the headaches had been getting steadily worse over the last few years—to the point she'd wondered if she needed to change her line of work to ease them back. There'd been a lot of bizarre cases lately. She was ready for a nice simple open-and-shut murder case. Too bad this wouldn't be one. "But they all come down to the same thing though. Somebody killed somebody else, for some reason important only to them. We just have to find out what that reason is, then backtrack it to whoever did it."

Harvey and Abby walked down the wide steps between the rows of seating. There was an odd echo to her steps on the wide wooden stairs. Almost like the sound of the booming inside her head. The huge amphitheater lecture hall sloped down to the small center stage, backed up to a wall, sporting supersize black chalkboards and also whiteboards.

"And yet in this case," he added, "nobody saw anything."

She nodded. "I heard that. That's not exactly news either. The bit of briefing I got was garbled, to say the least."

"Exactly." He motioned toward the two females sitting in the lowest row, facing the podium. "Two dead? That's odd."

"Yes, and the woman sitting right between them is *not* dead and apparently didn't see anything." He looked at her sideways, and she nodded. "Which makes her the likeliest suspect, I know."

"But why would you kill people in front of everybody else, when you'll be the obvious suspect?" He studied the hall. "That makes no sense."

"Because," Abby added, "if nobody saw anything, including the suspect student in the middle, it's pretty damn hard to prove it, isn't it? She's also the one who's the most visible, and, therefore, in a way, the one *least* likely to have done it. She looks like she's completely innocent, yet it's also possible these women were killed to get at her."

"That's another option." He nodded. "I hadn't really considered that."

"As soon as we found out a woman was in the center," she murmured, "I immediately thought, either she's a victim or she's the target." Of course Abby had been wrong before. So keeping an open mind was paramount.

"Interesting." Harvey paused. "Well, this will be one for the books either way."

"Yeah, let's just hope it's not too crazy a case." She was making a name for herself but not in a way that made her comfortable.

"Hey, you're getting well-known for handling crazy."

"But that's the last thing I want to be well-known for," she replied in alarm. "I'd like crazy to disappear."

"Oh, come on. Crazy has no intention of disappearing," he noted cheerfully. "Besides, just think how much less boring our world is, compared to the other detectives."

"I get it," she agreed, "but you know these crazy cases are guaranteed to keep you up at night. Besides, you're the one who gets nightmares over these types of cases."

"Hell." He snorted in disgust. "I haven't slept in forever."

She wanted to make a comment about it because she could smell the booze on his breath but didn't dare. He was pretty sensitive to it, and with good reason. But, at the same time, as long as he was sober and did his job and didn't kill her when he was driving them around one day, she was willing to give him the chance to keep functioning at the level that she needed.

He was her partner, and definitely a bond existed between them, but also a sadness—knowing that he was sliding downhill, out of control, and she could do only so much to help. Particularly when he couldn't or wouldn't see that he had a problem, and he didn't want any help, for sure. They'd worked together for six years now. Since she'd first made detective at the age of twenty-seven. He'd known her for years before. Had even helped her pass her exams and had asked for the partnership. She'd been thrilled.

Abby descended the amphitheater-style lecture room stairs studying the layout of the room. Hard to imagine a double murder could go unnoticed in a full class.

"Did you ever go to school at a place like this?" Harvey asked her.

"I did attend a few classes," she replied quietly.

"What, for philosophy or something like that, wasn't it?"

She nodded slowly, not filling him in on the details.

"And why did you quit?"

"You know why I quit," she said. "I found law enforcement and went there instead." She'd been trying to get into the academy at the time but exploring options—in case she didn't make it in.

"Oh, right."

Although she still hadn't found all the answers to her parents' deaths, when she was just a child of eight, it had set her on the path of justice. She suspected that, at this point, there was no walking away. She periodically entertained the idea that she would do something different one of these days, but it never seemed to happen.

Recently she'd solved a couple really weird cases, so now all the weird cases automatically seemed to come to her. And she was okay with that, except that she knew she was crossing some lines in terms of what the world would accept for answers, and that made it tough to deal with. How did you give a victim's family answers that dealt with psychics and energy work? Not that she was a pro at any of that. In truth she was a rookie, and her skills, no matter how hard she tried, never improved.

Stefan would tell her that she had the ability to do so much more, but she'd blocked it. Sometimes she'd like to block Stefan. Then he'd been with her longer than Harvey.

Stefan, always a nag in the background. She almost smiled at that, knowing he likely heard her.

Calling Stefan a friend seemed to cross a line, but he was one and had helped her on a few odd cases that didn't follow normal patterns, as they'd been beyond odd. The department heads hadn't been happy, but in the end, cases solved, they'd swallowed their chagrin and had quickly moved on. She shouldn't be held responsible for that, but, of course, she was. Life was just like that. People were just like that. And that gave her absolutely no other place to go really, except down the rabbit hole of weirdness. She shrugged; she was good with having her own niche in which to work her magic, and she would keep putting away criminals, as long as they kept coming onto her radar.

She reached the lower front section, where the two victims still sat. Abby walked up to stand in front of them. Both were female, young, blonde, and pretty. Just something about them had a sisterly look, not in a biological sense, but like sisters in kind. They both were well dressed and looked like they would be best friends, and that was something Abby would check early on, as well as their relationship with the woman who had sat between them. Something else common to both women was no physical sign of how they died. No mess, no blood, no visible injuries. No defensive wounds either. They both looked like they'd just fallen asleep. Their eyes were closed, and they sat upright. Their energy ... was already gone.

Hearing more footsteps, she shook her head, then turned to study the coroner, who was coming down the stairs.

"What have you got for me today?" he snapped.

"Two dead within the last couple hours. They apparently died during a lecture."

He looked at her in surprise. "What do you mean?"

"They were in the middle of a philosophy lecture," she explained. "When everybody got up to leave, these two didn't move. The woman sitting between them found out both women were dead."

"Two of them?" he asked, his voice rising.

"Two of them," Abby repeated, with a nod, "yes."

He shook his head. "What are the chances I'll find this is a murder-suicide?"

She stared at him in surprise. "I don't know. That's for you to tell me. But I hadn't considered that."

He snorted at that. "Like you don't know half the time before I even have the chance to say anything. So, any guesses on this one?" he asked Abby, his tone sharp, as he studied her.

"I wish I did," she stated calmly, "but, honest to God, not a whole lot to go on here."

He nodded. "So, it'll mostly be the lab that gives us the answers we need, I'd wager."

"Maybe." She hesitated. "It's a weird one though."

"Right"—he pointedly stared at her—"but that is your domain."

She laughed at that. Too many people would say that, despite keeping her energy work to herself. Too bad she didn't have the ability to look at a crime scene like this and see the answers. No. Which was too bad. However, she could tell if someone was lying… if they were having a good day… a shitty day, or if they were hiding something. Other than that her abilities were pretty much useless. Hence Stefan saying she could do so much more if it weren't for her wall …

"I keep hearing that," she replied, "but I'm not sure anybody's domain covers this kind of weird."

"Yours does, and you'll find out who did it." The coroner waved her away. "Go off and do your job and leave me to do mine."

She nodded and stepped back. Dr. Henshaw liked space, disliked being crowded, and, although he would ask a lot of questions, he really hated if you jumped to conclusions, especially when he hadn't had a chance to provide any evidence. Assumptions would piss him off. A lesson she'd learned early on. And, of course, that made her a favorite—if any of the detectives could be considered as such—because Henshaw had no tolerance for anyone who couldn't hold their own. She was well-known for holding her own, only that often came under the label of being abrasive to some, and to still others, bitchy.

She didn't care what anyone called her, as long as they got out of her way when she had work to do. Kind of like Henshaw himself, actually. She watched as he stepped up, took a closer look at the victims, and muttered, as he started his exams. Abby waited quietly, listening, but hearing absolutely nothing more than what she'd already expected.

She turned to look at the older woman, still sitting on a stool at the front of the stage. Still hovering close was a large man in a suit, now bending over to speak with the professor. Abby walked closer. "Dr. Gertrude Milligan? I'm Detective Abigail Cartwright." She held up her badge.

The woman looked up with a start, as if she'd zoned out. "Yes, yes." She tried to stand. "That's me. Everyone just calls me Gertrude."

"Okay, please sit down," Abby said. "I just need to ask you a few more questions."

The older woman sagged onto her stool. "What happened to them?"

"I don't know," Abby replied. "The coroner is here now. He'll find out."

"Yes, of course." Dr. Milligan shook her head. "I don't mean to be foolish."

"It's not foolish," Abby stated calmly. "We all want answers. Now can you tell me what you saw?"

The older woman immediately turned her palms up. "I would if I could," she cried out, her voice cracking. "I'm not sure if I saw anything."

"Explain, please?"

Gertrude went through what happened before and during the class, including all the discussions they had. She had just turned to clean off the chalkboard at the end of the lecture, and everyone started to get up and leave.

"That's when the commotion started, and Carrie, the girl in the middle, screamed. I turned around to see several people standing and staring at these three women in the front row. When Carrie said both her classmates were dead, I walked over to check, as did several of the students. We checked for a pulse but found nothing and called for help."

"How many were in your class?"

"I can give you a class list," she offered, "but we don't have a sign-in sheet, and I don't take roll, so I can't confirm everybody who was here."

At that, Abby winced. "Do you have any cameras in here?"

"No." She shook her head. "Not in here. Should be some in the hallway though."

"Fine, we'll run those." Abby wrote down a note, as she quickly surveyed the amphitheater. "We'll contact the university and see where I can access the camera footage."

Abby nodded to herself, turned back to Gertrude, and looked at the man standing beside her. "And who are you?"

"Leon Wellington." His lazy drawling voice made her look at him a moment longer than was necessary. "Gertie is my aunt, and I'm a prof here on campus as well."

That startled her. The last thing he looked like was a university professor. He had that lean grace, almost like a model who had learned his poses, getting them right each and every time, but, beyond that single point, she didn't think anything else was model-like about this man; he was more panther-like. Predatory. "And when did you happen on the scene?"

"She called me," he replied smoothly, "and said she needed help."

"Why did she need help?" she asked.

Gertrude spoke up. "Because it was my class, because I'd sustained a shock, because …" She waved her hand. "I hardly need to explain any more than that. Leon is my only family, and I knew he would be here close by to support me."

"Good enough," Abby stated calmly, as she turned her gaze from Leon to Gertrude. "What can you tell me about these two students?"

"They were best friends," she explained. "They always sat together and were always giggling. Sometimes it would get irritating because I wasn't sure if they were paying any attention to the class, in favor of the boy in the next seat." She shook her head. "They were boy crazy, like so many women of this age."

"Right. Do you know if they had boyfriends?"

She shrugged, frowning. "No. I don't know anything about their personal lives."

"What was your own relationship with the women?"

"Excellent. Both were sweethearts. Not sure they were particularly worried about an education, but they were always fun to have in my class," she said warmly, only to suddenly remember they were dead and teared up again. "Let me just say, it was a pleasure to have them in the class."

"What about other friends they might have had?"

"That's a question you should put to the woman who sat between them, Carrie. They always sat together, the three of them."

"Did you see anybody else sitting close to them?" Abby asked.

"No." This time such bewilderment was in Gertrude's voice that Abby believed she was telling the truth. "I don't know if they chose to take some drugs and kill themselves while they were here or if they accidentally overdosed somehow. I can't imagine anybody was close enough to kill them," she stated, "and they weren't necessarily the kind who would cause such hatred to get themselves killed over."

"It doesn't take much," Abby noted, "particularly if they're both beautiful and if potentially a male were involved."

Gertrude looked at her in surprise, then understanding slowly dawned. "Well, I suppose that's possible," she replied, "but I really don't appreciate if somebody did this intentionally in my classroom."

"I don't think anybody would appreciate that," Abby stated. "Do you have any contact information for the students? And you mentioned a list."

"Yes, we can get all that from the registrar." She gave Abby a wave of her hand. "I don't have anything to do with their private lives."

"Do they ever do any extra classes, any tutorials with

you? Have you had any contact with them outside the classroom?"

Immediately she shook her head again, "No. None. I see them when they come in for class, and, when they leave, they leave. That's it."

"And yet you don't always see them when they leave either, do you?" she asked.

Gertrude stared at her in confusion.

"You said you were cleaning off the board."

"Yes, yes, of course," she agreed, "but I do that every time, for the classes coming in after us. It's only common courtesy."

"Good," Abby noted. "So then nothing was out of the ordinary. There was no change in routine, and nothing seemed different today?"

"Nothing, absolutely nothing. Except …" At that, her nephew squeezed her shoulder.

"Except what?"

Her voice grew thin, as she answered, "Except for today's topic."

"What was that?"

"Well, the class is on philosophy, and we were discussing *what ifs*. Like *what if* there were an Armageddon, *what if* we, you know, had a Third World War, *what if* we were invaded by aliens, things like that." She paused. "The discussion went on to include psychic phenomenon as well, and, in listing more *what if* scenarios, I asked, 'What if there was a back door to their minds? What if somebody could access your brain and make you do things? How would life look then?'"

Abby's heart froze, and she wanted to retreat a step. But she didn't dare. Because that would just bring more attention her way. And, damn it, for this being another weird case. It had psychic bullshit written all over it. Hopefully the coroner would find something tangible to take it off that *strange* list. But, casting a side glance at the two dead women, Abby knew in her heart of hearts that it wouldn't be that simple. "Interesting choice of a class topic," she noted quietly.

"Yes, it sparks a lot of ideas from the students. Though I'd never done that particular *what if* question before. Brainstorming these topics has long been a part of my presentation and not outside the realm of anything else I would have done on another topic."

"So, you're saying, you've never asked *that* particular question before?" she asked curiously.

"No, never."

Abby stared out and around, wondering if that had any importance for this crazy day. She pulled out her notebook and wrote down a few notes.

At that, Leon asked, "Detective, does that matter?"

"Does what matter?" she asked.

"The subject my aunt was teaching today."

"Well, we wouldn't like to think so," she replied, "but the fact that it's different means that it's noteworthy. It's just one more thing in a long chain of events that makes it a different scenario. Is it important? I have no way of knowing yet."

And she wouldn't explain it to him, even if she did. This was definitely a hands-off investigation, and she didn't care who didn't like it. Except there was something about him … She took a peek at his energy, but, outside of being upset—and that tracked through his energy blending with Dr. Milligan's energy—he appeared to be telling the truth. Although a hint of darkness was in his aura. Trauma from the past perhaps?

Boom went the pain in her head. Gasping slightly, she shut down her inner gaze and turned toward the tearful professor.

"I would like to be kept in the loop," Leon said smoothly, as if sensing her boundaries on this case.

She looked at him blandly. "I'm sorry. That's not our protocol."

He just nodded quietly.

But something about that gaze was deep, dark, and penetrating. She shook her head. More to shake off the odd connection between them. "You, of course, can talk to the police commissioner, but that won't be something I'll be bringing up with him, and I can't have you interfering with my case in any way," she warned.

He stared at her. "In what way could I interfere?"

"I have no idea." She studied him. "I just want to let it be known straight up front that no interference will be tolerated."

He smiled, as if he'd heard it all before and had half expected it. Well, maybe not expected it but wasn't surprised to hear it. "Interesting," he murmured, "but taken under consideration."

"Good. She turned to look around at the forensics team. "We'll be here for a few hours, and I'll need to contact you again with more questions," she stated, looking at the professor.

Gertrude nodded. "Is it possible I could leave now?"

"Yes, absolutely, as long as I have your contact information, so we can follow up later." And, with that, Abby took down Gertrude's phone number and her address, and then Abby stepped back, looked at Leon. "What about you?"

"What about me?" he asked helpfully. "Do you want my

contact information too?"

Something almost personal and private was in that tone of voice, but it sounded false, like he was hiding something.

Keeping her tone even, she agreed. "That would be good, in case we had trouble reaching your aunt."

He gave it without issue. Something odd was in his mannerisms, but she couldn't place it. Personal, almost intimate, yet different. So weird. Then he helped his aunt, as they both left the room.

Her partner walked down the stairs and looked at her. "What was that?"

"What was what?" she asked, turning to face Harvey.

"Whatever is going on between the two of you."

She noted an odd look in his eyes, as he watched her closely. "I'm not sure anything is," she answered quietly, knowing how well Harvey knew her. "Why?"

"Oh, he was making a play for you. I just don't know why."

"What? Meaning, I'm so ugly that nobody would be bothered?" she asked humorously.

"No. We all know that you're gorgeous. But you also keep your private life very separate from work. But, of course, that guy doesn't know it." Harvey leaned closer. "But he gave it a try anyway. Bet he tries again too."

"Hopefully not," she stated cheerfully. "Then I wouldn't have to smack him down. Can't say I enjoy that part."

LEON ASSISTED GERTIE, as he'd called her for decades, out of the building. "I want to take you straight home," he murmured. She tried to rally, but he saw the stiffness sliding out of her spine. "This isn't one of those times when you have to be strong."

"It's a bad day." Her voice quivered. "Those poor women."

"There's still a chance it was natural causes."

She sent him a sharp look, before snapping, "I'm not a fool."

"No, you're not," he murmured quietly. "I've never thought that."

"You didn't tell her what you teach here?"

"She'll find out soon enough. She'd had it with me already, it seemed, so ..." He just shrugged. His specialty was criminal law, but he also taught a class on mythical and paranormal events. His criminal background had him lending a hand in local cases, whenever the police needed a consultant.

"Be interesting if they asked you to consult with her. She seemed to take a dislike to you."

"I don't know about that." He'd found her fascinating, so he hoped that hadn't been her reaction.

"God, I still can't believe that happened." Gertie reached up her bony hand to gently push back a wisp of hair off her face. "Those poor women."

He studied her hand carefully. She was shaking, her arm only slightly uncoordinated but heavy. "Will you be all right at home?"

Immediately she stiffened, outraged. "Of course I will. I had nothing to do with what happened to those women in the first place. Now that I've answered the questions the police have, it's up to them to sort this out."

He admired that sense of calm and righteousness. It never really worked out so well for him, but, in her world, a spinster all her life, it had held her in good stead in getting through those years when everybody thought she should have been married, the years where she had wished she had been married, the years where she had desperately wanted children but had never found a partner.

Not that she ever admitted all that. Yet Leon felt he knew Gertie well enough to make those assumptions and for them to be valid. A lot of disappointments had filled his aunt's life. Although she was a hard person to get close to, she was essentially a good person inside, but she hid behind a stiff, crusty exterior. Still, he understood how the disappointments had rocked her over the years.

He drove them carefully through town, before pulling up in front of her brownstone. "Do you want me to come in?"

"No, of course not." She unbuckled her seat belt. "I'm totally fine."

"You may well be," he replied, "but that doesn't mean you always have to be so strong."

"Of course I do." She widened her eyes, as she looked at him in surprise. "There's no other way to be. You know that."

He winced. "Well, it would be nice to think that you didn't have to be that way all the time."

"Nonsense. This life is what you make it." She unlocked the car door, stepped out, looked back at him. "Don't you go worrying about me now. I'll be fine." And, with that, she slammed the car door. With her back ramrod straight, she strode up to her front door.

He watched her carefully, looking for any break in that facade she always put up, but she appeared to be holding steady. He sighed as he put his car in gear, then pulled back out into the traffic. He returned to the university because he was overwhelmed in paperwork. But one of the things that he really didn't enjoy was to leave her like this, if she needed somebody. The trouble is, she was one of those people who always made a point of never needing anybody, which made it frustrating to lend her a helping hand.

Just the two of them were left in the family, and he thought it likely that she did allow him into her life more than anybody else, if there had been anybody else. But he didn't even know that for sure. She had always been difficult to get along with. It was her way or the highway. He had no trouble with Gertie, but he understood who she was and where she was coming from. Not everybody was willing to go that extra mile and give her a little bit more leeway.

Back in his own parking spot at the university, he hopped out and headed toward his office. As it happened, he crossed paths with the same detective again.

She looked at him, then frowned, as if trying to remember where she'd seen him, and then her face cleared. "Did you get your aunt home okay?"

He nodded. "Yes, but she's pretty shaken up."

"Of course," she said gently. "It's been a shock for her."

"You're right." Leon searched for her partner, off to the side on the phone. "I guess the investigation will take a few days."

"We'll be lucky if it's done by then," she stated quietly. "Sometimes it can take a whole lot more."

"Isn't that the truth," he muttered. He smiled, as he stepped past her. "Good luck with your hunting, Detective."

Her eyebrows shot up at that, and he felt her eyes boring into the back of his head, as he headed for his office. But he didn't give her any more clarification. It was a fairly well-known phrase in the military and in law enforcement. He had joined the military at eighteen, did a tour, then moved into law enforcement at twenty-two, before adding fifteen years on the force and then moving on again.

Now, as a professor for the last two years, he was thirty-nine, and the years had seemed to disappear so quickly for him. He imagined that was probably how his aunt felt as well. Time just flew by when you were busy. He smiled, thinking about it.

Still, he'd been almost married once, and that had been enough for him, at least for now, but he had to admit something about that detective intrigued him. An age-old weariness was in her gaze, as if she'd seen more than she'd ever expected to see in this lifetime. But also a naughty humor, as if to say, "Well, here we go again. Let's see what we find this time." He wondered at that dichotomy. It was unusual in one so young, but then, as he thought about it, maybe she wasn't as young as he'd first thought. She had that hard edge of experience.

He headed toward his office, then looked up to see a line of students waiting outside. He groaned. "What's going on here?"

The students moved toward him.

One said, "I have a few questions."

Another one stepped up. "I have questions on the exams coming up."

He stared at them. "And yet you all seem to be here at once. Why is that?"

They shrugged.

"More for moral support," one of the younger women explained. "After the murders today, we're all a little shook up."

He winced at that. "If it was murder, yes, but we don't

know yet. Come on in." He opened up his door and stepped inside, while the six students filed in behind him. He walked around the corner of his desk and stood facing them. "What's going on?"

"Nothing," one woman replied cheerfully. "I just, you know, had some questions."

He raised his eyebrows. "Real questions?"

"Of course." She nodded. "About the exams."

"Well, I'm not answering any questions about the exams," he stated immediately. "I told you that in class."

"But everybody gives us extra help when it comes to the exams," she protested.

"Not everyone does," he said, "and I certainly won't. You're expected to have paid attention in class."

"Maybe," she agreed, "but I still don't understand some factors."

"Well, if you have a specific question about a factor that you don't understand, that's a different story. But, if you're asking for insight into what the exams could be about, I gave you that information already. So you're out of luck if you're looking for more." He turned to the next one. "And you?"

She said, "I'm with her."

"And you?"

By the time he had addressed all the students' concerns, and they had left, he felt a little more tired than he should be. But it seemed like, no matter what year, what group, a portion of the student body always looked to step in closer to get a little bit more information, a little bit more insight into what the exams would bring. Extra insight that the other students didn't need or want.

It happened every time, but he still found it wearying. No matter how many times he told them that he wasn't giving them more information, it seemed like they needed to be told over and over again, hoping he would say it in a different way, so they would glean that little bit more. But it wouldn't happen. He'd been at this just long enough to understand the behaviors of his students.

Finally he got up and closed his briefcase, taking work home yet again, and he headed out the office door. He gave a last fleeting thought about the two dead women in the amphitheater, hoping that, by now, the families had been notified, and the bodies removed. It would take time to absorb the news, then find the way forward. The university's reputation was one of the big concerns. They didn't need any more bad press. There had been just enough trouble with cheating scandals and other rumors flying around that they had hoped for a few clean years without any bad press.

Unfortunately this would be the kind of bad press the university could not escape from.

CHAPTER 2

ABBY WALKED INTO the small university staff room, where the one student—who'd been sitting between the two dead women—had been sequestered. But instead of looking like she might have recovered slightly over the last hour or more sitting here, she actually appeared catatonic. Abby looked around to see if she was alone or if somebody was with her, but Abby saw no sign of anyone, outside of the policewoman standing off to the side. Abby immediately walked over, sat down, and picked up the girl's cold hands.

"Carrie, are you okay? I'm Detective Abigail Cartwright. I'm sorry you had to wait so long."

Carrie slowly lifted her head and looked up, her eyes huge wells of pain, and whispered, "I didn't have anything to do with this."

"Good, I'm glad to hear that," Abby replied, "but I still need to ask you some questions."

The woman's eyes filled with tears. "I didn't see anything," she said. "But how could that have happened? How could I have been sitting right there and not seen anything? Two people, my two best friends at that, are dead. They died right in front of me, and I didn't notice anything. How is that possible?"

"I don't know." Abby studied Carrie. "What did you see?" The young woman had been traumatized by the day's events, and she'd be lucky to remember anything. However, nothing was off about her energy; it was full of pain and grief, as to be expected. Abby immediately shut down that part of her vision, trying to head off the oncoming headache before it grabbed hold.

"I saw the professor. It was an interesting class. I was paying attention to her."

"Why did you sit in that place, in that particular seat?"

"I always do." She looked at Abby in confusion. "The three of us always do."

"You always sit at the front of the class?"

"We do if we like the class," she added. "If it's one we're likely to want to skip out on, we sit at the back, so that our leaving won't be so obvious and disturb people."

That made sense. Abby pressed her point a little further. "In the time that you were sitting there, did anybody else come and join your row?"

She looked at her in surprise. "I don't think so, but I wasn't paying attention to anything but the professor."

"But you weren't paying attention to the prof the whole time, were you?"

"Enough," she said. "I didn't really see anything happen around me. Plus I was in the middle, so wouldn't I have noticed?"

"Did anybody come and talk to the two women?"

She shook her head. "Not that I know of."

"So, it was a completely routine class?" Abby asked.

"Routine, except that they're dead," Carrie wailed.

"I get that," Abby said, "and that's why I'm asking the questions I'm asking. We have to find out what happened."

"And I don't know what could have happened," she murmured. "All I can think of is that maybe they had food poisoning or something."

"Interesting option. Did the coffee taste okay? Did they complain of feeling sick? Did you guys eat before class?"

She nodded. "We stopped at the little cafeteria round the corner from class. It's in the same building, and there was no line outside, so we went up and got coffee."

"All three of you?"

Carrie nodded. "All three of us got coffee. It's kind of a routine for us."

"Okay, did you get anything to eat with it?"

She stopped, looked at her in confusion, then her face cleared. "No." She shook her head. "We didn't. We just drank our coffee."

Abby made a note of that on her notepad to check out the coffee.

"Yeah, at least I didn't notice anything different. But, you know, I just drank mine, almost by habit. They weren't complaining either."

Abby winced at that coffee comment because she was guilty of the same thing. You pick up a wonderful coffee, and then you just get so busy that you don't even get a chance to enjoy it. You sense that it went down the hatch, but not in the way where you actually appreciated it. "What about your friends? Did they have any enemies? Any arguments? Stalkers? Recent breakups that turned ugly? Anything to say someone might have done this?"

"No," Carrie whispered. "I've been sitting here thinking about it, and there's nothing. Neither had any recent boyfriends. It was always the two of them and then me. I was on the outside. Friends with both but not part of their duo. Not everyone loved them, but, in all the years I've known them, and that's over ten now, I've never seen anyone actively dislike them.”

“Okay.” Abby nudged Carrie back to the day’s events. “Is there anything else you can tell me about what went on today? Was anybody acting oddly, anybody being difficult, giving the prof a hard time or causing a disruption?”

She shook her head. “No, we were really engaged in the class today. It was kind of a fun one, something to make us, the whole class, sit up and think.” Carrie sighed. “Honestly I don’t even know what to say. We’ve really enjoyed the class, and I was sorry it was coming to an end.”

“So, you had no problems with the professor?”

“No, none at all. She’s been really good,” she stated. “I’ve always heard rumors that she can be hard to deal with and a tough grader, and maybe that’s fair, but honestly the class was more interesting than most. And, early on, I knew I would see it through, even if it meant a lower grade than other classes.”

“Do you think anybody held a grudge against her? Like, was anybody openly upset about the marks that she gave?”

The young woman stared at her. “I have no idea,” She shrugged. “Our scores are always posted by student number on the board outside, so nobody knows who got what. It’s a common system. Your marks are your marks, and you either do the work and get better marks, or you don’t do the work, and you don’t.” She shook her head. “I honestly don’t have a clue who got what.”

“Okay, but if somebody did get a low grade, have you seen any animosity toward the professor, anybody causing issues during class, anybody being disruptive or yelling at her?”

She shook her head. “No, of course not, besides”— confused, she frowned—“what’s that got to do with my friends?"

"I don't know," Abby murmured. "Nothing perhaps, but, because it was a classroom scenario, we have to check everything."

Carrie nodded, as if understanding, but clearly she didn't have a clue.

Abby asked, "Are you a local?"

"No." Carrie gave a quick headshake. "I'm living on campus, but I'm actually from Montana."

Abby wrote that down. "And you'll be staying here now?"

"Well, I have to. I have other classes and projects I have to finish, final exams to take."

But Carrie had a blankness to her tone, as if she just couldn't begin to understand how much work she had left to do or how she would possibly do it now. Abby nodded. "You might want to talk to your counselors here. I'm sure some assistance is available for you to deal with the loss of your friends."

Carrie nodded, as if she understood that, but still lacking a look of comprehension.

Abby stood. "Do you have anybody here to take you home?"

"Home?" She looked up at her. "I live around the corner."

"How long have you been sitting here in this room?"

"I don't know. One of the police officers told me to come in here and wait, until somebody came to talk to me."

"You were waiting for me." Again the other woman just nodded blankly. "Come on. Let's get you back to your room."

Obediently the other woman stood.

"Do you have somebody to stay with you tonight?"

Carrie shook her head. "No. If you mean friends, well, you've taken my friends to the morgue." At that declaration, her eyes filled with tears, and she sobbed noisily.

Abby sighed, gathered the young woman into her arms, and held her close. When she showed signs of calming down, Abby said, "Come on. Let's get you back to your place. I wish somebody could stay with you tonight though."

"Me too," she whispered, "but there isn't anybody."

"What about family?"

"I don't know." She hesitated. "My mom's at home, but she looks after my brother. He's disabled. I can't expect her to just pick up and come here to look after me. Besides she's a couple hours' drive away."

"No, of course not. How about going home for the holidays, so you could maybe put some of this behind you."

"I was supposed to go away with my friends." She started crying yet again.

Grabbing her up, keeping her moving, Abby headed outside, where several police officers were. She quickly explained what the problem was, and one of the other women walked over and took Carrie's arm.

"We're from victim services," she explained to Abby. "We'll take care of her."

With relief, Abby handed her off. She wanted to tell the girl to not leave town because Abby still might have questions, but that would have gone unheard. This young lady, so caught up in her own grief, wasn't even cognizant of what was going on around her, and it would be a while before the full import set in of how her life had been devastated. Abby watched as the woman was led to a car and driven away.

As she stood here, pondering her next move, Harvey

stepped up.

"Hey, I wondered where you were."

She looked at him, gave him a weak smile. "Finding lots of dead ends. How about you?"

"More dead ends, although we'll have to talk to the professor again. I did get the video cameras from the hallway, and it does show a ton of students coming in and out all day. We'll have to double-check to see if any of them she doesn't know were allowed inside."

"Right, we can do that first."

"I can do that, if you've got something else you want to do," Harvey offered.

"What I want to do," she grumbled, "is figure out what the hell happened. Unfortunately it feels like we'll need the coroner's report for a cause of death first. At least we have a very good idea of the time of death."

"Were the women seen talking to each other during the class?"

She nodded. "Yes, other students are confirming that. We're still going through a whole list of interviewees yet," she noted. "That room over there is full, but I've got four uniforms helping with those."

Harvey pointed down the hallway. "Since the prof already left, I'll confirm with her later. For now, I'll go double-check the witnesses—getting photos and contact info—so I can check that against the video cam feeds of all these students caught on the film."

"Good enough. Let me know if there are any abnormalities." Abby watched as Harvey walked away and then turned to an adjacent large lecture hall, where everybody who'd attended Gertrude's class were still being held for questioning, but not at the crime scene.

It shouldn't take very long to run through the questions they had. It was more a case of getting all the contact information and making sure that people would be around in case the detectives had further questions.

At the full lecture hall of people to be questioned, Abby did her part by taking photos, getting contact info, asking the standard witness questions. By the end of it, she stepped out and compared notes with the other police officers.

"Great. It looks like nobody saw anything, nobody heard anything. Nothing," she said in exasperation. The others nodded in agreement. "But we're also missing dozens of statements from students who could possibly help."

One officer added, "According to the students I interviewed, the two victims just died as they were sitting there, and nobody was close to them. They saw no sign that they were struggling, no evidence of sickness, no infected wounds, no shots, nothing like that of any kind."

Another uniformed cop spoke up. "Which, if you'd seen the bodies—I don't know if you did—but I saw no evidence or sign of foul play at all. It's as if both hearts just stopped at the same time."

Abby shook her head. "You know what? It would be a far reach for *one* young person to have died like that," Abby stated, "though it's possible. But for two of them?"

The other cops all nodded.

"We'll get these reports written up," the one stated, "and send them in tonight."

"That would be good." Abby stood here, staring thoughtfully at Gertrude's lecture hall. "I wonder if it's possible for anybody to make it into this lecture hall and not be seen." She entered Gertrude's classroom and scanned the amphitheater and all the seats leading downward. She noted entrances were on both sides of the lecture podium, and also double doors were here at the top of the theater seating, where the students came in and out.

"We can put it to a test," one of the cops suggested. "I'll stay here at the top, and somebody can come in from both sides down there, and we'll see if I can see them."

She nodded. "Let's do that—one pair at a time—just to make sure that we're not thinking something happened in full view of the whole class, when it might not be as exposed as we think."

With the others helping her, she took a position in front of the seating, where the professor would have been, and two cops went up to the topmost desks and stood there, while two others entered the amphitheater from the bottom entrances. They were both coming in and out, as Abby acted as she thought the professor would have. As she pretended to be writing on the board, turning around every once in a while to talk to the imaginary class, she caught sight of both of them moving about.

Now the topmost pair tried it, with the other pair on watch, and Abby playing prof. One crawled along the edge smoothly and carefully, and the second one entered the first row, heading toward where the women were. Abby didn't see that one. When he popped up beside the dead women— soon to be transported out of here—she stared at him.

"Oh, now that's interesting. I did not see you there. You came down or came through when I had my back turned." She frowned. "So potentially, that's one avenue." She asked the two cops nearest her. "Did anybody see him make it down here?"

They both shook their heads.

"Well, at least we have one avenue where an assailant

could have come in," she said.

"But that would mean that the other girl should have seen it."

"If she was seeing anything. She told me that she was paying attention to the professor."

"Or was she sleeping?" one of them suggested.

Abby frowned at that. "That's something we'll have to figure out too, won't we? What are the chances that she was napping and that somebody knew she would be napping. Well, she won't be napping unless somebody gave her something." Scratching her head, Abby thought out loud. "All three coffee cups were grabbed and have been taken by forensics. Let's find out if any drugs were in one of them. And how would the killer know that these three women would be there today?"

"They would have to know beforehand, would have to plan by watching the students' daily patterns," one officer suggested. "These women would have to set up a precedence of attending all classes."

"Which they probably have, where this course is concerned. The prof is known to be tough, and, if you don't show up to her class, she doesn't give you much leeway on the marks," Abby murmured.

"In that case," one of the officers said, "it's pretty well guaranteed that the women would be here."

"Right. Let me check this out myself." She walked to the two areas where the two officers had snuck in.

One officer asked, "Do we have any security on these doors or any cameras outside that would show us if somebody had come in or not?"

She brought out her notepad and checked. "Harvey's collected camera footage already. I'll have him particularly check out these side routes though." Thanking the officers, she turned and left, thinking about heading over to the morgue.

As she stepped outside into the evening, she looked up to see a light dusting of rain coming toward her. She sighed. "More rain." She muttered to the heavens above, "We could really use a break, you know?" Checking her watch, she shook her head. *Eleven o'clock? How did it get to be so late so fast?* "Screw that. I'm going home." She needed to catch a few hours of sleep and knew that the coroner wouldn't have anything on these deaths in the next little bit. Unfortunately, as much as she might want to think this case was a top priority, it just wasn't happening. If they were lucky, the two women would be on tap for tomorrow, but, barring that, it could be a couple days before they got there. It all depended on the caseload the coroner's office had.

She always liked to think that her cases came first, but it just was a fact of life that, in a busy morgue, there was always another case ahead of you. Sometimes a half-dozen cases. Still, she also knew that this one was out of the ordinary and would get the coroner's interest piqued, so he would get going on it as soon as he could. Unless something was simple about it, and *simple* was a whole different story. If so, it would also mean that she was overlooking something.

It was possible, though not necessarily likely, that somebody could have snuck in and killed one girl, but could he have accessed the second girl on the other side of Carrie, even if she were sleeping? And while Carrie denied sleeping, someone had gotten to these women during that class.

How else could it have happened? No ideas came to mind, but that didn't mean that, in her tired fugue state, other options weren't there, just waiting for her to be clear-minded enough to see them.

She stepped out to the parking lot and entered her vehicle, and headed home. As soon as she walked up the steps to her small townhome, she opened the door and stepped inside, happy to see Migolo stretched out on top of his cat tree. He meowed at her. Abby shook the rain off her coat and hung it up on the hook, kicked off her boots, dropped her purse, closed the locks, and armed the security system, all before walking over and scratching the stretched-out furry belly.

"Hey, baby. I know you didn't get dinner tonight, did you?" She gave him a cuddle, scooping him off the cat tree, and walking into the kitchen. Dinner seemed like a long time ago for her too—she wasn't even sure she had eaten. Matter of fact, she was pretty damn sure she hadn't. She always kept a stack of power bars in her purse for that reason. They were for nutritional value, to keep her functioning, not for their savory taste by any means. She scooped up a can of cat food, opened it, and gave it to Migolo.

She walked to the fridge and realized it was way too late to eat. But found an open bottle of red wine. She pulled it out, poured herself a glass, walked through the living room and straight upstairs to her bedroom, where she turned on the fireplace—just to take the evening chill off her room— put down the glass of wine, and got ready for bed.

Propped up in bed a few minutes later, with the wine at her side, she turned on her laptop to check the news. And, of course, her case was headline news: Two Women Dead During Class. Abby always wondered how the media outlets knew these things were actually happening, since not too many people should have been talking about this, but, with that many students, there would be a lot of talking. She shook her head.

And a ton of media was around this, period. The biggest thing is the fact that nobody knew if it was foul play. She just couldn't see how it could be anything but murder. One death from natural causes maybe, but two? That was much further out of the realm of possibilities. But she'd seen some pretty strange things in her life, so she would withhold judgment until they could determine the facts. She just hoped that, maybe, somewhere along the line, somebody would give them answers because otherwise this would be just a bad deal from start to finish. She tossed off the rest of her wine, closed down the laptop, and crashed.

CHAPTER 3

WHEN ABBY WOKE the next morning, and not because Migolo was stretched across her back, it was seven o'clock. She'd had what should have been enough sleep, but, because she'd worked so late, her body was sore and tired. And the ever-present threat of a migraine loomed in the background. Moving gently, so Migolo slid, as only a feline can, off her back, Abby shifted off the bed, headed for the shower, only feeling marginally better as she stepped out, soaking wet. Then she worked hard to get her shoulder-length hair to dry off somewhat and to get dressed, before heading downstairs for coffee and some desperately needed food. Her phone went off while she was frying eggs. She glanced at her Caller ID, frowned, and then answered it. "Morning, Harvey. What's up?"

"Hey, you okay? You sound worn out. Bad night again?"

"I hardly feel like I got any sleep last night. Not to mention not getting to bed until late."

"I don't think the families got any sleep at all."

"Great, thanks. That just makes me feel even worse," she muttered. "Do you have a reason for bugging me so early?"

He laughed. "Always."

She smiled. "Well, I'm just making breakfast, so either speak up or it can wait."

"Well, I'm just coming up to your front door. Do you

have extra coffee?"

She groaned. "Of course I do, but, one of these days, you'll have to take care of your own breakfast."

"Well, I could, but I'm forever doing errands for you."

She laughed at that. "It's called *your job.*" Not technically true but he loved doing them, so that worked out well for her.

Sure enough, moments later she heard a knock on her door. She stood, hit the End button on her phone, then walked to the front door and checked to make sure it was him. She disarmed the security system and threw open the deadbolt. Her history would never make her blasé about security. "Come on in."

As he walked into the kitchen, he sniffed the air. "Eggs too, huh? I didn't get time to eat." He looked at the toast and eggs on her plate.

She sighed. "Go ahead, sit down, and eat. I'll make some more."

He looked at her. "Oh no, that's okay."

She waved at him. "Don't even play this game with me. Just eat and get on with it, will ya?"

He didn't even argue. As he snatched up the fork, sat down with a big grin, he said, "Thanks!"

She smiled at the older man's enthusiasm. "Did you get around to the professor's last night?"

"I couldn't even get in to see her," he admitted.

She stopped and stared.

He shrugged. "She wasn't answering the door, and, when I contacted her nephew, he thought she'd probably taken sleeping pills and gone to sleep."

"Well, we'll start there this morning then."

"Just remember, boss. Other people deal with stress in

different ways." He used the nickname he'd been using for years—but shouldn't do because she wasn't his boss. They were partners, and he was her senior by fifteen years.

"I know. I know, but I need people available for answers."

"Maybe so," he agreed, "but other people would probably say they needed to step away from all this, in order to keep their sanity."

She knew he was right; it was just frustrating. "We'll start there this morning," she repeated. "We did most of the interviews last night, but nobody saw anything. The rest of the students will be tracked down today, but I'm not holding out hope. But here's what was interesting. After my interviews with one roomful of students, with the four cops helping me over there, we set up a scenario to see if anybody could have stepped inside the doors, murdered those two, and slipped out without half the class seeing them."

"And what was the verdict?"

"Well, it was possible"—she tilted her head—"just not very likely. The professor must have been fully immersed in what she was doing up there, like writing on the board or conversing with someone intently. And everybody at the back would have had to be looking at their own stuff, instead of at the door. In our scenario, the guy managed to get to the location by crawling in along the floor to the first set of rows."

"Which would then imply that the women themselves wouldn't have seen him and neither would anybody else," Harvey noted.

Abby scrambled more eggs and tossed them into the pan. "And, even if he had gotten to the one victim, how would he have gotten around Carrie to get to the second victim?"

He stopped, looked at her, and then nodded. "So, either that's not how it happened, or somebody is not telling the truth."

"Or somebody wasn't even there or wasn't aware or stepped out before the doors were locked or something."

"And, of course, they won't consider even the tiniest bit of information as major."

"And we're still conjecturing here," she stated, "because we have no idea how these women died."

"But they did die in a classroom discussing *what if* scenarios. Spooky timing. What kind of a lecture is that anyway?"

"Philosophy, and, in this case, they were doing a whole series on it." Abby paused. "The idea is to make you think, like, out of the box, contemplating some of the things that nobody ever wants to contemplate, hoping that people come up with ideas."

"Interesting," he murmured. "So, in this case, what if somebody had access to your mind?"

She nodded. "And that's an interesting scenario in itself because, in a case like this, with a weird death, you immediately want to know if somebody could kill someone that way. Especially considering that two women are dead and by a invisible means."

He looked at her in surprise. She nodded. He shivered. "That is just creepy. Damn spine-chilling."

"Maybe." She shrugged. "But it's also a very interesting adjunct to our murders. And what if somebody was trying to make it look like that?"

"You mean, versus actually doing something like that?" he asked drily.

She looked at him in surprise. "Do you believe in that stuff?"

"Well, I know you sure as hell do," he replied. "You deal with woo-woo stuff all the time."

"Well, I've dealt with some pretty crazy serial killers," she admitted. "But something like this? Not so much."

"But what's the difference? The last one was a psychic, who was murdered for her messages."

"Sure, but that murder was committed by a very earthly presence. If killing someone by accessing the back doors of their mind were even possible," she stated, "I'd love for somebody to explain it to me. And talk about opening up a whole new headache."

"Hey, those kinds of headaches are what we specialize in." He gave her a fat smile. "Besides, you live with headaches. How is yours this morning?"

"Fine"—even though it was far from it—"besides, the other cases were all charlatans, making it look like something like that."

"Right. At least that's the official department line."

As she sat down with her eggs, she thought about it. "I want to go through those tapes that you saw last night."

"I didn't see anything, but you might."

She didn't say anything to that. Her instincts were better than most, and, when it came to sussing out suspects, she was pretty damn good at it. She also didn't have reason to look at anybody in particular, so she was throwing a wide net, hopefully catching something. "We have to sort out motives. Why those two women?" But, of course, Abby was jumping the gun, assuming they were murdered. She winced. "I can't see a way for it to be anything but murder. I mean, how else do you see two women die in exactly the same way?"

"Were they sisters by any chance, so shared genetics, or did they meet in some medical support group because they had health conditions?" he asked.

"Waiting on the coroner," she said glumly. They finished off breakfast, and she stood. "I'll head to the office. I've got to start doing a history on everybody who was in that room."

"That will take a while."

She nodded.

"Unless you want to come along to see the professor," he offered, with a shrug.

"I could." She thought about it. "Okay, so I'll come with you, and then we'll head into the office and split up the attendee list, and I'll go through the videos."

"Good enough."

With that, they stepped outside. She frowned. "But we have both vehicles here."

"Not a problem," he said cheerfully. "I'll ride with you." She rolled her eyes at that. "I have no problem at all with you paying for gas."

"Of course not," she muttered. But they both hopped into her car and headed for the professor's brownstone. Abby checked her watch. "We never checked to see what her schedule was, to see if she'd be teaching today."

"No," he agreed, "and it's only eight-fifteen, and, unless she had an eight o'clock lecture or something, then she would be here."

Abby headed up the stairs, knocked on the brownstone door, and waited. When there was no answer, she pulled out her phone and called the woman's cell phone number and again nothing. Frowning, she phoned the nephew. "Hi." She identified herself on the phone. "We're trying to locate your aunt."

"She should be home," he replied, yawning.

Maybe she'd woken him up. "Well, we're standing outside the front door, and there's no answer, and she's not answering her cell phone."

"I'm on my way to the university," he stated, sounding more alert. "I'll swing by and meet you there."

She turned to look at Harvey. "Leon is coming here."

He raised his eyebrows. "*Leon?*"

She shrugged, just managing to hold back the flush of heat rising up her neck at instinctively using Leon's first name. "That's his name."

"You rarely use first names."

"Hardly an issue," she declared flatly.

They stood here waiting, barely talking, her mind churning with all kinds of ideas on what might have happened with the aunt, while seriously hoping it was nothing.

But, when the nephew arrived, he looked at her with a frown on his face, as he pulled out his keys to unlock Gertrude's door. "I presume you think something's happened."

"I don't know," she said, "but we need to talk to her. We have video of everybody entering the lecture hall and want her to take a look to see if they all were her students."

He nodded. "That would be the fastest way of finding that out, wouldn't it?"

"You would think so," she replied.

He walked in the front door and called out, "Gertie?" No answer. "Just a sec." And he raced up the stairs, calling out. A moment later, he reappeared on the landing, shrugged, coming downstairs again. "She's not here."

She frowned at him. "Would she have gone anywhere else?"

"Back to the university. She practically lives there."

"Any reason why she wouldn't be answering her cell phone?"

"There could be all kinds of reasons, as you well know," he said testily. "Maybe she doesn't want to talk to you, or she turned it off because too many people were calling her. Or maybe she forgot to charge it, or she forgot it at home."

At that, she pulled out her phone and quickly phoned the same number. But she heard no phone ringing in the house.

He shrugged, as he joined her. "So she's probably at the university."

"Where does she park her vehicle?"

"Lots of time she walks or takes a cab. She has a vehicle, and it would be parked in the back." He led the way to the kitchen door and pointed outside to a detached garage. "She doesn't normally drive though, so the car is probably out there."

"But she can drive?"

He nodded. "Oh yes, she has a license."

Noting all of that, Abby walked down to the garage and looked in through the window. "Looks like an older Mercedes."

"That's hers. It's a maroon color."

She nodded, as she turned to walk back. She looked over at Harvey. "I guess we'll return to the university then." Turning to Leon, she asked, "Does your aunt have any special haunts?"

"No, but she does have friends on campus, so it wouldn't be out of line to consider that she's spending a moment, having coffee with someone. It would have been a tough night for her."

Back in Abby's car, she and Harvey made the fast trip to the university. As she got out, she headed in the direction of the professor's office.

"Do you think she's dead?" Harvey asked.

"God, I hope not," she murmured quietly, as they walked through the halls, filled with students mingling and rushing from one end to the other. "But, if we don't find her, we'll have to consider the alternative."

"Which is?"

"That maybe she couldn't show up for her day at the office."

He looked at her sharply, but she shrugged. "Hey, this is a long way from being an open-and-shut case. Anything and everything is still on the table."

As they got to the professor's office, she knocked. When there was no answer, she tested the door, but it was locked. As she turned, she saw Leon coming toward them. He frowned, as she nodded at the door. "It's locked."

"I have a key."

"Wow." She stared at him intently. "Is that normal?"

"For me and my aunt, yes," he replied. "Lots of times she's forgotten things, and I'd still been at work, and she's asked me to pick it up here and drop it off on my way home."

On the surface that made a lot of sense, but, at the same time, she just wasn't so sure. He quickly unlocked the door and let her in. She walked around and felt some relief, knowing that nobody was here. She looked up at Leon. "Can you tell if she was here anytime recently?"

He wandered the small space. "Everything is always like

this." He raised both hands in disgust. "She's the only person I know whose desk is always absolutely pristine. Her files are always very orderly, everything exactly as you'd always want it to be. I've tried myself, really tried, yet somehow I can never achieve the same thing."

"It does show a very strict and disciplined mind-set."

"True," he murmured. "But don't get me wrong, Detective. She's also a very warm and caring person."

"The two aren't mutually exclusive," she noted, "but the need to have her desk like this? It usually shows a need to have control in her life."

He studied her carefully. "That's an interesting assessment."

She shrugged. "So where is she likely to be right now?"

"That's what I was hoping to find out when I got here," he replied. "Normally she would be right here. But she isn't, so I don't know what to tell you."

"Fine. We'll do our best to track her down. Does she have any favorite places, like a summer getaway cabin or something? Does she have any place that she would go to get away from all this?"

"This is it… the university," he said, with his arms spread out. "This is her passion. She lives and breathes it."

"No partner ever? No children? Other siblings?"

He shook his head. "A fiancé who died but no children. And, my parents, both her sister and her brother-in-law died decades ago."

She nodded quietly.

"What is it you're thinking, Detective?"

"Actually I'm worried," she said bluntly. "Two of her students were murdered, and I don't know if any of it is connected to her. I would like to have her safe and sound here in front of me, so I don't have to worry about where she's gone or if somebody else has found her."

At that, his gaze narrowed, as he studied her intently. "You're thinking that her life might be in danger?"

"I'm thinking that anything is possible," she snapped. "Including that."

"I did talk to her last night, after I dropped her off. She sounded fine, told me that she was tired and that she would have an early night."

"An early night could mean an early waking up"—she looked around—"particularly for somebody of this mind frame."

"Maybe she wanted to come in and get some work done, particularly if she would normally work in the evenings," Harvey suggested. "Last night wasn't conducive for it, so it would make sense that she would come in here to catch up."

She frowned at that and turned toward Leon. "You have no idea where she is, correct?"

He shook his head. "I have no idea, and now I'm getting worried myself. I checked with the friends I mentioned and neither had heard from her."

Abby said, "I think I'll go over to the dean's office." When she saw Leon hesitate, she looked at him and asked, "Any reason not to?"

"No, but while you're there, you should ask him about some not-so-nice letters she'd received."

Her eyebrows shot up. "You didn't mention this last night."

"Last night we weren't talking about my aunt," he replied quietly. "We were talking about students from her lecture hall."

Point to him for that one. "Well, if you can think of anything that's connected to your aunt—anything unpleasant, criminal or otherwise related—I'd like to hear about it. So, tell me about these letters."

"There's just been a letter writer over the last few years who has given her grief," he explained. "I don't have all the details. She's always tried to just toss it off as no big deal. They weren't threatening in any way, more like angry at her teaching style."

"And that might be true," she said, "but, under the circumstances, it still bears consideration. Sometimes these letter-writing types are harmless, and sometimes they can be dangerous."

He nodded. "I agree with you there. That was always my experience in the industry as well."

At that, she stopped and looked at him. "What do you mean?"

"I was on the force for fifteen years. I now teach criminology here."

"Why here?"

"Partly because my aunt is aging, and it's just the two of us," he said quietly. "Partly because I enjoy being in a university atmosphere."

"Are you still in law enforcement at all?"

His lips quirked. "Yes. I work as a consultant."

"I knew I'd heard your name before."

His eyebrows shot up at that. "Interesting. I normally consult with the FBI."

"Right." She nodded. "Are you the one who specializes in cults?"

"I wouldn't say that I *intentionally* specialize in cults," he answered quietly, "but I have been brought in on quite a few cult-related cases, yes."

"Right, that's probably why they all seem to think you're a specialist. Just because you've helped them on a case or two." She shook her head. "I'm in the same boat. People put me on these woo-woo cases, whatever the hell that means, and suddenly I'm a specialist too."

At that, he stopped, stared. "Woo-woo?"

"Of course it's a perfectly legal term," she stated, with a straight face. But her eyes twinkled.

He smiled. "A sense of humor, I like that."

"It's what keeps us sane, isn't it?" Just enough challenge was in her voice that she waited for his response.

LEON NODDED QUIETLY. "It is exactly that. It's a tough-enough job at the best of times. It's rather brutal, especially when there are a lot of strange cases. These deaths affect everybody."

"I don't know of a case that I haven't been affected by." She shoved her hands into the pockets of her jeans.

Leon looked over at her partner, who seemed more like a lap dog than anything. Except that intelligence beamed from behind those thick glasses. His mind was probably sharp too and his experience ... priceless. "I don't know where my aunt is. But now you've got me very worried."

She nodded. "Well, if you think of any place where she might be or if you hear from her, let me know." With that, she handed him her business card then strolled out of the office ahead of them.

Leon wanted to say more but wasn't even sure what he could do. He did want to be involved in the case, but he also knew he'd get smacked down. He'd had way too many cases of his own in the past, where friends and family of the victims wanted to get involved, and he had had to stop them. The last thing you wanted was somebody getting involved that you would have to look after.

She didn't know that he was perfectly capable of taking care of himself, and she also didn't care. She wasn't looking for his help; she was looking for answers, and, if he didn't have one, she didn't have any time for him. Well, good enough, he could track down his aunt just as well as she could. Hopefully better.

The trouble was, he wasn't exactly sure where to start because Gertrude rarely disappeared. She had only once before. She had ended a relationship with an old friend, who she'd been going out with for probably eight or nine years. When they broke up, she just up and disappeared one day. If anything, this could be a similar scenario, but he couldn't remember how he'd gotten hold of her back then. He wasn't even sure he had. He was pretty certain it was a case of waiting until she showed up again.

But, in this case, that was just dangerous because the detective was right. Whatever was going on, they didn't have any answers yet, and more questions made it dangerous for everybody involved. The last thing Leon wanted was for his aunt to get hurt. He brought out his phone and quickly called her number yet again. "Hey, it's Leon. Please call me."

This time, he would keep calling, reaching out. Also he physically checked back at her place again, at noon, to see if she was there. By the end of the day, he'd checked in on the phone four or five more times. The dean had already called to ask Leon if he knew where his aunt was because she'd missed lectures, and, at this point in time, he had no answers for anybody. But he was much more worried because now it looked like she'd disappeared.

The question was, had she gone on her own or had someone taken her?

CHAPTER 4

IT HAD BEEN another long day, nearing that forty-eight-hour deadline, where the leads grew cold. Abby had finished going through the video camera images, looking at every one of the students who came and left the professor's class, checking out each of their faces, matching them when they left—or trying to. Many she couldn't identify—with heads down, some with baseball caps, others in sunglasses. Some came in hordes; some had snuck out early before the doors were locked and didn't have a clue what was going on. Those who had skipped Gertrude's class yesterday could still be even more students they had missed interviewing. Abby and Harvey and the four cops had interviewed most of the others yesterday, who had been in shock, had been rounded up outside the scene of the crime, where they could be questioned. She had understood the students' reactions. So far, she was just dealing with frustration.

When the captain approached her desk, she looked up in surprise. "Captain, what can I do for you?"

"How about a few answers?"

"If I had some, I'd give them to you immediately," she said, "but, in this case, I don't have anything to offer."

"What about the coroner?"

"Still waiting on him, and that's adding to the frustration."

"He's usually faster."

She nodded. "Yeah, he usually is, but, so far, there's nothing. He's likely waiting on tox."

"That could take weeks."

"It can, but he's rush ordering, so hopefully that will help."

"Fine." He turned and stormed off again, but that was the captain. He liked to be kept informed at the highest level, yet not bogged down by details.

Just then her phone rang again. She looked down, picked it up, and greeted the coroner. "Hey, what have you got?"

"What I've got is a whole lot of nothing," he snapped, "as you well know."

"I don't know anything at the moment," she murmured, her heart sinking.

"I'm assuming, from what I saw of the crime scene, you had nothing there to trace or to track down. But how the hell did two people die right in front of a whole classroom, without anybody noticing?"

"That's what I'm dealing with," she said. "Yet I haven't even started opening up the histories of every student there, and, of course, we have no motive for the crime yet either."

"And nobody's stepped up and admitted they did it, I presume?"

"No, not at all." Abby smiled. "Wouldn't that make our day?"

"Well, it's never happened so far," he murmured, "so I highly doubt that it will this time."

"No, it won't, but I guess we can keep hoping."

"Yeah, well, you can keep hoping," he added, "but I don't have anything. There's absolutely zero visible cause of death. No internal hemorrhage, no heart attack, no aneurism, no anything. So, the only thing I've got is that tox screen still to come."

"How long?"

"I'm doing a run on a bunch of simple possibilities, which will get back to us in a couple days, but, other than that"—he sighed—"I don't have anything, until the rest comes in, and that could be a week or two. I did check stomach contents. Coffee with cream and sugar for both victims. The rest will have to wait."

Abby winced at that. "So, we can't even say if it's a homicide at this point."

"I can't yet, no."

"So, it's indeterminate. That's great," she muttered. "Because anybody, if they had a hand in doing this, just succeeded in getting away with murder."

"No," he argued, "because we will get to the bottom of it. I just don't have any answers for you yet." And, with that, he hung up.

Immediately she threw down the phone.

Harvey walked in at that moment, looked over at her. "And?"

"And nothing," she replied. "Unknown cause of death, tox screen still pending. Their hearts just stopped."

"Shit, but it's not like we really were expecting anything different."

"Maybe not." Abby's heart sank at that expectation already. "The families are expecting answers."

"Yeah," Harvey agreed, "but we can't be concerned about the families, when we're still figuring out how to help the victims."

Abby tried to throw off her mood, but it was hard.

"When you think about it, we have nothing but the two victims."

"Right. So, we must assume that there was foul play of some kind, and that somehow, somewhere along the line, we will get the answers we need." He lost his smile.

"We always get the answers." She stared at him, hating that this might be heading down the psychic pathways again. But this was something she'd never seen before.

Stefan whispered in her head, *Neither have I.* Then he was gone.

"It just doesn't always happen the way we want it to." Abby shook her head.

"Isn't that the truth," Harvey muttered. "You know they'll expect something out of you."

"Of course they will." Abby's stomach sank. "Too bad I have no answers."

"Woo-woo strikes again." Harvey grinned.

"Which doesn't help at all," she snapped. "I'd rather be sitting here, staring down the barrel of something completely different."

"Let's hope we do soon."

She nodded. "Any word on the aunt?"

"Nothing," he replied. "I took another look at her brownstone, but I found absolutely no sign of an attack. No sign she had a visitor. Nothing."

She nodded. "It looks like she packed up and left."

"And, under the circumstances," he added, "that's suspicious as hell."

"Yeah, but in which way?" she asked, staring at him. "Do you really see her killing two students in the middle of her class? Because, if that's the case, why those two? Why in front of everyone?" She paused. "Did we ever get those letters the dean was supposed to send?"

"No, he said it would take some time to gather them."

"Are there that many?" she asked.

"If felt more like a brush-off to me. He didn't even want to agree to give them to me in the first place."

She looked at him in surprise. "Why not?"

"I guess she's had a colorful life."

At that, she frowned. "How colorful?"

"We're about to find out. But the dean didn't seem to think that this was knowledge that should be made public."

"I don't have any intention of making it public. But, if somebody had anything to do with our dead students, we need to know, and we need to know now."

BY THE END of the day, Leon was more than worried about Gertie. Her voicemail was now full, and he could no longer leave messages. He found no sign anybody had shown up in her office all day, and, according to the dean, she hadn't called in to reschedule classes. Leon was on his way to her house yet again, hoping to find something. To think of her just disappearing like that wasn't totally out of character, but it was scary as hell, especially when in conjunction with the two deaths in her classroom. It was a connection that nobody would overlook.

He took her front steps two at a time and knocked hard, then quickly unlocked it. Stepping over the threshold, he met a gloomy silence inside, and he swore. He took his time and searched through all of the lower part of the house, but everything was the same. Her last cup used—he couldn't even remember when he'd seen a soaking dish before—sat full of water in the sink. But none of her many other dishes were out of place. He opened the dishwasher to find it empty, but then he'd brought her home in the evening, when she hadn't even cooked. If she'd been home all day, she would have put the dishes away in the morning and never would have been home again to have filled it.

Hating the way his thoughts were going, he searched all through the house, even checking in the space where the utilities were and then headed to the bedrooms. Two bedrooms and two bathrooms were upstairs. He did a thorough search but found absolutely nothing, neither any indication that his aunt had slept in her bed. That was a problem with Gertrude being as neat and as tidy as she was because her bed was perfectly made, as if she hadn't slept in it, but he also knew it would be perfectly made even if she *had* slept in it because she always got up and made it just like this again. He also found no sign of her monster purse she packed everywhere.

"Gertie, where are you?" he murmured. He tried to think about who else she might have contacted over this traumatic event. He finally came up with one friend Gertie might have reached out to. It took a moment to find the number. He quickly dialed, and, when a woman's voice answered, he identified himself. "I'm looking for my aunt. Have you seen her?"

"No," she replied. "I told her to come here and to spend a few days, but she declined, saying she was fine."

"So, she's not there with you?" he asked, his heart sinking.

"No." Then she stopped and asked, "Can't you find her?"

"No, not at all."

"Oh my, where would she have gone?"

"Well, that's what we don't know," he murmured. "And I really, really, *really* wish I could find that out."

"Of course. I'd hoped she'd come here."

"Any idea where she would have gone?"

She cried out, "No, none. It's not like her to leave at all."

"I know it's hard enough to get her to leave her house but to leave the university too? That's very unusual."

"And very suspicious," she suggested. "I wouldn't just say *unusual*. This is scary. What could have happened to her?"

"I know she was pretty upset." He added, "I mean, after all, two women in her class died."

"Yes, she called and told me about that."

"Did she say anything else in that phone call? Because it sounds like you may well have been the last one to talk to her, before she did whatever she was planning on doing."

"No, she didn't say anything. And now you've got me really wondering what could possibly have happened."

"Okay, I'm still holding out hope that she's disappeared somewhere for a couple days to get her head on straight. The cops were asking her a lot of questions, and she was struggling to answer some of them, and I know that's been a real problem."

"Well, you know that her memory has really gotten a lot worse."

"I know," he noted quietly. "I'm glad she told you about it."

"Well, she didn't originally," she said. "Only after I started bugging her did she came clean about her condition and how it had worsened."

"Yes, and I know that she's really bothered by it. I mean, anybody who has spent their life in academia, with their intellect such a big part of their identity, to know they are getting Alzheimer's and will slowly lose everything has got to be awful."

"Well, I can't imagine."

"I know," he agreed, "and that's one of the reasons why I'm wondering if she just took off for a bit."

"You don't think that maybe she's gotten lost somewhere, do you? I've heard of spontaneous cases of rapid-onset Alzheimer's."

"I haven't," he noted, with surprise.

"It's usually due to trauma or stress."

He winced at that. "Great. So, this definitely qualifies. If you do hear from her, could you please contact me? I'm really worried."

"Oh, I am too. I'll definitely call you if I hear anything." And she disconnected their call.

Leon had to be happy with that. He took one last look around Gertie's place and then, into the silence of the night, called out, "Gertie, where are you?"

And, of course, with no answer, he slowly let himself out of his aunt's brownstone and headed back to his car.

CHAPTER 5

ABBY WALKED INTO the station the next morning and headed into her office. Her mind buzzed with possibilities because, so far, there was absolutely nothing. The most interesting thing they had learned was that Gertrude had disappeared. There'd been no sign of her, and she hadn't returned to her home since she'd been brought home the night of the murders.

After dropping off her notepad and purse, Abby walked to the water cooler area and put on a pot of coffee. It was early; she was the first one here. And then, taking a stack of the files for each of the students researched from Gertie's class, Abby sat down and opened up a notepad. She was most interested in the two dead students at the moment. It was easy to say they led a blameless life.

One was twenty-seven; one was almost twenty-six, both blonde. She studied their files in amazement because Harvey had gathered a lot of similarities. Both had boob implants; both had nose jobs done, and both had Botox to enhance their lips. She stared at the images of them. "Not only do you two look alike," she noted, "but it seems that you've gone to great lengths to make sure of it."

And what was the appeal of that? They weren't sisters, according to their last names, although Abby would have to get DNA results to make sure, but she had no good reason to go down that pathway.

Were they just best friends who were getting sucked into an *Oh wait. You did it. I should do it too* scenario? Abby needed to contact both of the families again, now that they'd had another day to settle down. She needed to see if they had thought of or discovered anything helpful.

They'd been interviewed right at the beginning, but, of course, nobody ever had answers right off the bat. Everybody's too shocked. And you can ask all the questions you want that first time, but it never really does any good. She picked up the phone to call the mother of Samantha, one of the two dead women. When Abby identified herself, the woman started crying again. "I'm so sorry," Abby explained, "but I really need to ask you some more questions."

"I don't have any answers. I just want Sammie back," she wailed. "Besides, I don't like talking on the phone."

"I can be at your place in a couple minutes."

The woman hesitated, then Abby added, "Please. We're doing our best to find out what happened to your daughter."

She groaned. "Fine. My husband's gone to work, though I don't know how he can even think about working with all this," she spat into the phone.

Hearing the note of despair and anger in her voice, Abby winced. "I'll be right there."

She ignored the fresh pot of coffee, knowing that the rest of the team would come in and immediately take advantage of it. She hopped up, grabbed her purse, and headed out. She was even in before Harvey today, and she wasn't worried about waiting for him either; she just needed to get some answers. She had to get something up on a whiteboard that would make sense. So far, nothing did.

As she drove to the house, she arrived to find the woman

standing on the porch. Abby quickly parked and exited her vehicle, heading toward Sammie's mom.

Hesitating, the woman then stepped back. "Come in."

Abby stepped inside, smiled at her. "Thank you for seeing me. I'm sorry to be calling so early."

She shrugged. "It doesn't matter. I have no purpose anymore. Sammie was my everything."

"Was Sammie an only child?"

"No," she said, then "Yes." right after that.

Abby looked at her and asked, "Which is it?"

"We're part of a blended family," she explained. "Sammie was mine, and my husband has two daughters."

"Got it." Abby nodded. "That explains the comment."

"It doesn't matter if it's a blended family or not," she murmured.

Abby nodded in agreement. "Understood. What about her friends? Did she have a regular group of them?"

"What about them?" she asked. "She had so many girlfriends."

"But she had a couple special ones, right?"

She nodded. "Sure, one in particular. That was Aimee. The other victim."

But she spoke of Aimee with a less-than-friendly tone. "And did you have a problem with that victim? With Aimee?"

"Only that I didn't approve of her," she replied. "If anyone did something to get the two of them killed, it would be Aimee."

"Why is that?"

"She was never happy about anything. She always wanted more. Something different. She was one of those who was always fixing her body," she snapped. "It was surgery for this, surgery for that. And she got my Sammie into it as well. Before we knew it, Sammie was so busy doing all these surgeries that she didn't even look like herself anymore."

"You think that was because of Aimee?"

"I know it was." She shrugged. "Sammie told me that Aimee was the one showing her how to become a better person."

"A better person or a prettier person?"

"My daughter was beautiful," she said, her tone harsh.

"Absolutely," Abby backtracked quickly. "I'm not disputing that. I'm just trying to figure out what her mental state was in regard to her friend."

"Her friend was a mess," she snapped. "She didn't have the same happy home life that Sammie did."

"So, why do you think that she was doing the surgeries?"

"Well, to make herself look prettier," she said in surprise. "Isn't that why they all do it?"

Walking carefully around this big minefield ahead of her, Abby said, "Yes, that's what I'm asking. Do you think that's also why Sammie did it?"

She glared at her. "My daughter was beautiful," she repeated. "She didn't need to do anything."

"And I agree with you." Yet Abby wasn't giving an inch. "But I do need to understand why she was doing these kinds of surgeries."

"Because of that bitch," she snapped. "It was all about her."

"Sammie was doing it because of Aimee?"

The woman stiffened. "Sammie loved Aimee, wanted to be like her. Sammie always thought Aimee was right about everything. Perfect in all ways. And if Aimee said jump, Sammie would jump. I've never seen anything like it."

Not exactly sure where she was going with this, Abby asked, "Do you agree with that?" She hesitated, and then when the mother wouldn't talk anymore, Abby leaned forward and asked, "Did you agree to all the cosmetic surgeries?"

"My Sammie was beautiful. She didn't need to do anything. But there was no talking to my daughter." She bawled again, big noisy cries for a life lost.

"I'm sorry," Abby said, "and I'm so sorry for your loss."

As she escaped to her vehicle, Abby had to wonder about a relationship where the two dead women had bonded over cosmetic surgery. She doubted that was a first. And it was sad that their mind-set would be there, but Abby wasn't terribly surprised by it. Young women often grow up with a poor body image, and, by the time they were adults, they could throw off whatever parental guidance and restrictions there had been and do whatever they wanted to do. And, in this case, obviously as adults, they had chosen to do things that these parents were not happy about.

Abby wondered if the stepfather even understood anything about the stepdaughter's relationship with Aimee or if that was something that Sammie kept secret. Abby should have asked Sammie's mom about that. Frowning, Abby thought about going back in, then realized it would have to wait until the next round. Was it that important? She didn't know, unless they ended up suspecting that the stepfather might have had something to do with the murders.

But would he have killed his own stepdaughter? It certainly wasn't out of the realm of possibility; they'd seen it happen time and time again for a multitude of reasons. It just depended on where the stepfather fit into this, if he fit into this at all. Frowning, she stood outside her car, as she thought about it, and turned to look back to see the mother standing on the porch, her hands crossed over her chest. There was something about her energy… Abby quickly walked back over. "Did your husband know about the relationship between Aimee and Sammie? About all the surgeries?"

She nodded slowly. "Yes."

But something in her tone made Abby wonder. "How did he feel about it?"

The woman glared at her. "He had nothing to do with this."

"I didn't say he did," she clarified in a mild tone, "but you're not answering my question."

"You're just digging up sore spots," she wailed. "We have enough of those."

"Well, then you need to tell me the answer to that question, or I'll have to go to your husband's place of work and ask him directly."

At that, the woman's face paled. "Don't do that. He only found out about Aimee's strange influence over Sammie a few weeks ago. There's been a lot of upset recently."

"Interesting. And I gather he wasn't happy?"

She shook her head. "No, he was furious. At me for allowing it and even more for hiding what she was doing from him," she muttered, as she stared off in the distance. "And, like me, he blamed her *friend* Aimee."

At that strong emphasis on the word *friend*, Abby clearly understood who was getting the blame for this. They were conveniently forgetting that, just as her daughter had been adult enough to sign up for cosmetic surgeries without parental permission, she'd also been old enough to choose the friends she wanted, without asking for parental permission.

Nodding at the woman, Abby got back into her vehicle and drove back to the station.

LEON WANDERED THROUGH the house yet again.

"Damn it, Aunt Gertrude, where are you?" he snapped. But there was no answer today, just as there hadn't been any last night either. He didn't know if he should be terrified that something had happened to her or angry that she'd taken off without a word, into the world of silence that she could handle much better than most people. If she would at least just let him know in some way that she was safe, it would be a whole different story. But, of course, she hadn't. She was doing nothing to make anybody feel better about her actions, including her beloved university. And that was even more disturbing.

Leon knew the cops were worried that either she was involved and had taken off or wasn't involved and had possibly become a victim herself. He couldn't even look at it that way; yet, with the police training and experience he had, no way could he ignore it.

The trouble was, as he wandered through Gertie's house, careful to not touch anything, he found no signs of violence. No signs she had been taken by force. No signs that she had been coerced to leave. He stared outside her bedroom window and down onto the small backyard.

The garage was at the back, connected to the house via one walkway, with a little bit of grass that his aunt had taken out and replaced with one of those fake grasses, so she didn't have to look after it. She was never here anyway, according to her, so why have something she had to maintain? She hadn't had a problem with it, but now he realized that it meant no tracks, no nothing. It didn't matter if it rained or not; there wouldn't be any tracks left behind. And that just made it harder to find out anything or to get any answers right now.

Upset and angry at himself, he picked up his phone and contacted the detective. When she answered, her voice was distracted. "Detective, it's Leon. Have you had any leads on my aunt's disappearance?"

"We don't even have a missing person's report yet," she noted. "And, if you want to file one, you'll need to come in and fill one out."

"But I don't even know if she's missing for sure." He winced at that because, of course, he knew that.

"We want to talk to her, and, of course, her timing is suspicious."

"She didn't have anything to do with this," he stated instantly.

"Everybody keeps telling me that. However, until we get answers, we don't know who has anything to do with anything. And I need to have people available to talk to, so I can get those answers," she replied in exasperation.

"I do understand that." He stared at the backyard. "I'm in her brownstone right now, but I haven't found anything to point where she may have gone."

"And yet neither did we see any sign that she left under duress."

"I agree with you there." He pushed the hair off his forehead. "And I do have a heavy criminology background, so I do understand how this works."

"Then you should also know that, if you're planning on reporting her as a missing person, you need to come and open up a file."

"Yes, of course. This is the first time I've been on the other side. I hadn't realized just how disconcerting it can be."

Her voice softened. "When you're on the victim's side of things, it can be very difficult."

"Very," he murmured. "I've found myself not even knowing what to do."

"You wait for us to get answers."

"What answers?" he snapped. "You're trying to get answers on a lot of things right now. And, so far, none of the answers are coming together."

"Well, that's because people are disappearing," she snapped back. "And it's pretty hard to get answers when nothing's there."

He agreed with that, but, at the same time—and probably because of his own frustration with everything going on around him—he didn't want to listen to reason. "Well, I'm hoping that you'll put my aunt's case in the forefront, if for no other reason than a potential connection to your case."

"It's not that we'll ignore that your aunt isn't around," she noted. "That won't happen, but we also have to consider the fact that she may have disappeared on her own."

"And I can tell you that she wouldn't have. Not without letting someone know."

"You can tell me that all you want," she replied, that same exasperation rising, "but that's not helpful. You haven't given us any idea where she might have gone on her own. You tell me that it's only the two of you and that you're very close, and yet we have no answers."

"No, I get it, fine. I'll dig into my aunt's history a little bit more." Not that he wanted to open old wounds, but he would, if it was warranted.

"And what would that tell you?" she asked curiously.

"I have no idea. There are tragic events in her past that she didn't like to talk about, and I don't know if that's part of it."

"Well, if it's interesting and pertinent, please let us know," she said. "The bottom line is, I have two dead young women, and, so far, we haven't got any answers."

"Were you able to verify they were murdered?" he asked. "Maybe all of this had nothing to do with it. Maybe my aunt took off because she felt she was a terrible instructor and should have seen something more. You guys are really good at throwing on the guilt."

"*You guys?*" she asked in a hard voice.

He winced at that. "I know. You're right. I did plenty of that myself."

"That's the problem with being on the other side," she snapped. "You don't get to just forget what all of this is about. It's about the victims."

"But you haven't told me if the forensics has come back and if it's being declared a homicide."

"I haven't told you squat," she said, "and I won't." And, with that, she hung up.

He groaned, stared down at the phone. "You know what, Detective? I don't blame you, but still I really do blame you," he snapped. "Would it be so hard to be human?"

But, of course, his own training reared its head. "Wow, Leon. If you've got a problem, you need to deal with it yourself."

With that, he headed to his aunt's home office. So far, he had avoided getting into any of her obviously personal stuff, thinking she would be back any time. She had gone away every once in a while, for a spa day or a date or just to get away on weekends, where she'd booked a few nights at a couple favorite haunts. But he'd already made phone calls to the two places he knew she typically went to, and she wasn't registered there. Did it mean that she wasn't there? No, of course not. She could have registered under another name. But why would she? And, if she would register under another name, why would she go to a place where people would know her? Unless, of course, she was meeting somebody.

With those thoughts churning in his head, he raced to her office, sat down at her desk, and found the drawers were locked. "Well, enough of that crap," he muttered. "I don't know why you feel like you need to keep all of these locked, but, if you disappear on us, and we have no idea where you are, you don't get to keep secrets."

And, with that, he quickly pulled out a couple tools from his pocket and picked the lock. His old skills were something he kept sharp, never knowing when he might need them. As soon as it was picked, he pulled it open and whistled because one drawer was stuffed with money.

"Good God." He stared at it. There had to be twenty, even thirty thousand dollars in there, all tossed in casually, not stacked nice and neat. Completely opposite to Gertie's normal OCD behavior. He didn't touch it, didn't thumb through it, even though he had gloves on, but all he could think about was what possible reason she could have for having that kind of money sitting here. He knew that she definitely distrusted the banks but to this extent? He didn't even know what to think anymore.

He carefully went to the next set of drawers and then the next. He found no more money, thankfully, but several big folders. He pulled out the top one and took a careful look.

One contained case files. He stared at them for a long moment. One in particular drew his attention. It was about his parents. He studied it, wondering how and why Gertie would have anything like this. What possible reason could she have for having the old case files investigating the deaths of his parents?

The fact that his parents were murdered was something he had always tried not to delve into. But obviously his aunt had more than a passing interest in their cases. But then it was her sister, and maybe that was why. Maybe she couldn't let go of her own loss. That made sense to a certain extent. Nobody really dealt with loss or had any experience to deal with it until it happened; then you had to react without anything, really, to go on.

He opened the file hesitantly. It wasn't anything he wanted to get into. That was a whole set of memories he didn't want to open up; yet he felt compelled to sit here and to look at it, even though it was the last thing he wanted to do. He shook his head.

"What are you up to, Gertie?" he murmured, hoping against hope that the answer was absolutely nothing, and that this was just a product of her need to try to get answers. His aunt was all about searching for answers. All about crossing the *T*s, dotting the *I*s, and, more important, understanding why something had happened, so she could move on. But the fact that these files were sitting here still in her drawer maybe meant that she hadn't gotten anywhere in that department.

He sat back, frowning, as he studied the dreary thick folder in front of him.

He would take it with him. He knew he would, but he wasn't at all sure what the detective would say about it. He frowned and then picked up the phone and called her.

"You again?" she said in exasperation.

"Yes. I don't know if it means anything, but I got into my aunt's office drawers here at the house that were locked."

"And?" Her voice sharpened. "Any idea where she's gone?"

"No," he replied quietly, "and I'm not sure that anybody would know she had this because it would certainly be a reason why they would kill her."

"Had what?"

"She's got a substantial amount of cash here," he admitted. "I'm quite surprised at the amount."

"Like how much?"

"I didn't disturb it, but I'm guessing somewhere in the range of thirty thousand, if not more, sitting here in one of the locked file drawers."

"Interesting. Does she really hate banks or something?"

"Yes, actually," he admitted. "She does."

"So, I presume that's what you're thinking is the problem, or is something else going on here?"

"I don't know," he said. "A bunch of folders are in the other drawers. I'm just starting to go through it."

"Hang on. I'm coming."

"I can send you digital copies instead," he muttered.

"No," she snapped. "I'm coming."

"Fine. Get here fast then because I have to return to class soon."

"I'm already on my way," she replied. "I'm just changing directions right now. Be there in ten."

He hung up the phone, then stared at the picture of his aunt and her sister, his mother, on the desk.

"Gertie, did you disappear on purpose?" he murmured

to the empty room, wishing like hell he had answers. These kinds of things had to be the worst. No answers, nothing but suspicions, with no clear direction to go. But, if Gertie had left on her own and expected to be gone a long time, surely she would have taken this money with her. The fact that she hadn't meant that either she was expecting to come back or—his mind filled in the blank—she wasn't expecting to need it wherever she went. And that, for the first time, brought up a possibility he had no wish to consider.

Yet how could he not?

What were the chances his aunt had committed suicide?

CHAPTER 6

A BBY PARKED OUT in front of the brownstone, raced up the steps, knocking on the front door and stepping inside without waiting for him. "Leon, are you here?"

"Back here," he called.

She followed his voice, closing the front door behind her and heading to the office. She stepped inside, looked around, and nodded. "It's what you'd expect her to have for an office, isn't it?"

"She was a good person," he said.

"*Was?*"

He winced. "I don't know. I don't know what to think now. Come here and take a look at this." He pulled open the one drawer, and she whistled.

"Wow. That's a lot of cash here."

"I know, and these drawers are full of files, including this one." He pointed to the big thick file atop the desk.

"What are they files of?"

He looked up, took a deep breath, and said, "Old murder cases."

She looked at him in surprise, her eyebrows slowly raising. "Ones that have been solved?"

"Two separate cases, two different deaths. Both a long time ago."

"Come on. What's the deal?"

"My parents were murdered," he said bluntly. "First my father, then my mother, and hers was a very difficult case. My aunt never accepted the verdict and kept looking. As far as Gertie was concerned, the accused had nothing to do with it."

"Interesting." She studied him carefully. "What do you think?"

"I think she's right," he said bluntly. "I made my protests known to the detectives handling the case at the time. Nothing like having your own family caught up in something like this where you can't get answers, and you're not allowed to verify any of their information to make sure they're on the right track," he explained. "Let's just say it was a really difficult time for my aunt. It was her only sister, her only family, and she never believed the end result."

"So what do you think she was doing about it?"

"Well, based on this, either she might have been still investigating or was just keeping it open, thinking that maybe this wasn't quite the way that it happened."

"You said there was more. What are the other cases?"

"I'm just looking through it now, but I think she considers them all connected."

"Connected to the murder of your parents?"

"Yes." Leon nodded. "I think that's exactly what it is. I think she's been investigating somebody, or multiple somebodies, thinking that they might have been the killer."

"And she never mentioned this to you at all?" she asked incredulously.

He shook his head. "No, and I probably would have told her to let it be," he admitted. "Like I said, it was a very difficult time back then, and, as much as I wanted to believe they had caught the killer, I also haven't been convinced."

"So, she would have kept this thought alive, whereas you were prepared to move on."

"I was prepared to move on, as long as nothing else popped up, suggesting we shouldn't," he murmured. "We had several arguments about it, but obviously she wasn't deterred."

"Fine," Abby said, "in that case, since it might be connected to my case or to your case, we'll have to open up an investigation."

"I'd appreciate it if you would," he replied, his face drawn.

She studied the fine lines on his face for a moment. "Have you had any sleep?"

"Does anybody ever have any sleep in a scenario like this?"

For him, of course, this situation was an ugly reminder of the murder of his own parents. "Do you suspect foul play here with your aunt?"

"I don't know," he replied quietly. "What I don't understand, if it isn't, is why she wouldn't have said something to me. You have to understand, Detective. We were close. She wouldn't take off like this. The only thing that makes sense is an accident, or Alzheimer's, or something along that line. I can't imagine any other possibility."

"You keep saying that, and you keep using past tense, which is disturbing."

"And I get that." He reached up to massage the back of his neck. "It feels like it's past tense."

She heard the emotions in his voice, choking him. "Listen. We won't go there just yet," she explained briskly, "but obviously I'll need to take a look at the rest of this." She waved him away from the chair.

He nodded and stepped back, as she snapped on a pair of gloves and sat down, flipping open the file. She winced when she saw some of the photos. "How did Gertrude get copies of all these?"

"I don't know," he said honestly. "I haven't even seen all of these, and I tried hard to get a copy of the file and hit a brick wall, until I was on the force myself."

"Do you think there was anything dishonest about the investigation?"

He stared at her in surprise. "I had no reason to think so."

She nodded. "But, as a detective, you would have had a good idea if they were doing their job."

"Oh, I think they were doing their job and wanted to get it closed quickly."

She nodded again. "We get a bad name if we don't and a bad name if we do."

"Isn't that the truth," he muttered.

"Is that why you left the force?"

"No," he said, but something was in his voice.

She turned to face him. "This really isn't the time to hide what you're feeling."

"I went into internal affairs."

She froze and then let out a heavy breath. "Not an easy path."

"No."

"And your decision to investigate dirty cops had nothing to do with the murder of your parents?"

"Yes, it did," he replied, "but I didn't do anything about it right away. I stayed in the same department for another couple years, but it did weigh on me when I saw somebody, who was on my parents' case, take possession of drugs in lieu of hauling somebody into the station."

She just sat back and stared. After a long moment, she asked, "Did you bring that one down?"

He nodded slowly. "I did."

She grabbed a piece of paper and a pen. "I need some names, dates, case files, the whole works."

"I have the IA case all on my computer."

"Even after the fact?" she asked, raising her gaze to him.

"I kept all the public notices, news bulletins, newspaper articles, things like that."

"Why?"

"It was important that the dirty cop be brought down."

"And, at that time, did you ask to have his cases reopened?"

"I did, but he had a very good closure rate, and it was suggested that shouldn't happen."

She frowned at that. "I guess that happens, doesn't it? Once you start doing that, there's no end to how many cases have to be looked at."

"That's true," he said, "and I don't know how many he was fair and honest with or how many he might have screwed over."

"Right. What did he have to say?"

"Nothing worth repeating."

"In other words, fairly foul for you, I'd say. Yeah, he wouldn't have held back. Nobody likes cop chasers."

"Nobody likes dirty cops either."

She nodded. "I get it, but that's a tough spot to put yourself in."

"It was, but what will you do when you actually see it happen in front of you?"

She frowned at that. "It's never happened to me, thankfully. So, I wasn't put on the spot, where I had to make that kind of a decision."

"No, but I was," he said quietly. "And I made that decision."

She nodded. "You have to be commended then, for making a choice like that, and I'm sure it wasn't easy."

"Not easy at all."

"I suppose you have a decent success rate after that one case, don't you?"

"How do you know?" he asked but in such a dry tone that she laughed.

"Well, I'll obviously do an investigation into you as well," she replied. "But what I don't know is how or if any of this relates to the two dead students," she noted forcibly, glaring at him. "Are you doing this on purpose?"

"Doing what?" he asked.

"Piling up my desk to confuse the main issue. Is there anything you can think of in any of the cases you closed? I'll have to take another look at any that might be related to your aunt or could be related to this case that's currently on my docket."

He shook his head. "Honestly I don't know."

"Honestly you don't know or honestly no?"

He gave her a smile. "You're the one who's into the woo-woo stuff."

"We already went over that one." She glared at him, wishing she had a way to deal with woo-woo cases on her own. Leon's energy was open and honest. But she didn't have Stefan's abilities to look deeper.

Almost immediately Stefan whispered in her mind, *But you could have.*

"Speaking of woo-woo stuff, I knew a psychic who consulted on a few of my cases. There was one case in particular ..."

She rolled her eyes at that, tossed the pen down on the desk, and asked, "And?"

"He was of the opinion that abilities were out there that could do an awful lot more than people knew and that we would all be petrified if we had any idea just how much somebody could get away with."

"Like what?" And just her luck he'd worked with a psychic.

"Like murder," he said, "and leaving no trace."

She sucked in her breath. "And who is this person?"

"Stefan Kronos. The case he helped with was a long time ago. The suspect has also passed on, so the case was never solved."

"*Great*," she muttered. Of course Leon had spoken to Stefan before. "I want all those case files. I want to know everything there is to know about your parents' murders and whatever other cases your aunt has collected here. But, damn it, this will all take me away from the current case."

"And yet it might not," he said, "especially if they are connected."

She looked at him. "And it might not," she admitted. "Well, at least now I've got a good idea what I'll do for the next ten or twelve hours," she snapped. She stood, picked up the thick files. "I'll get forensics over here." She took photos of the files. "You see that I'm taking them, right?"

"I do," he said. "I can help you sort through them."

"Not a good idea." When he glared at her, she shrugged. "You know as well as I do that it's not a good idea."

"I left my fate in the hands of the cops last time. I can't do that again."

She stopped, glared at him. "Why not?"

"Because that's what happened." He waved his hands at the files she held. "I lost my faith in the system, all because of crooked cops."

"Well, I'm not crooked," she said, "and all I'm trying to do here is solve a problem."

"I get that. I really do, but I need you to let me in on this."

"That's nice, but it's too damn bad. You don't get that choice."

WHEN ABBY GOT up to leave his aunt's house, her arms full, he followed her to the front door, closing the door as he walked out.

"Are you going home?" she asked, turning toward him.

He looked at her in surprise. "Yes. I was just thinking that, but I need to cancel my classes this afternoon." With that, he pulled out his phone and contacted the dean.

She had stepped aside to give him privacy, but now she was beside him again. "What's at your house?"

"I have some files that my aunt gave me a long time ago. I'll go through them and see just what they are."

"Is there a reason you didn't look at them before?"

"Yes. They were all related to my parents. Don't worry, Detective. I already feel guilty enough right now, with Gertie gone."

She nodded. "That's kind of a given. I guess the question is whether there's any justification for it or not."

He snorted. "She's missing, isn't she?"

"If she is, why haven't you filed a report yet?" She continued, not giving him much time to answer. "I'll let you know if I have any more questions." And, with that, she opened the passenger seat of her car and dumped the stack of folders on it. She turned to look back at him. "Forensics is on the way."

"Right. I'll leave the front door unlocked then."

He stood here, watching as she got into the driver's seat and drove away. It was unsettling being in the victim's role yet again. Had his aunt really stirred up something by keeping track of all these people, all these potential suspects? He hated to think so, but he also knew that she was meticulous about keeping digital copies of documents and would likely have information on her computer.

Matter of fact, he was pretty damn sure that he could open it up and check on some of the names he'd filed away in his distant memory, hoping to never revisit again. At least that was what he had thought at the time. Now he wondered how much Gertie had continued to do on the case, poking and prodding around.

As he got home to his own place, his phone rang. He looked down to see a number he didn't know. "Hello?" he answered, as he unlocked the door.

"Hey, my name is Anthony Kolbassa. I'm a private detective working for your aunt."

He stiffened. "And?"

Anthony hesitated. "She said if I couldn't get a hold of her to contact you."

"When did she tell you this?" He couldn't believe this was the first he was hearing about this.

"I've been working with her off and on for the last couple years," he replied. "I've tried for the last two days to contact her, but I'm not having any luck."

"Yeah, neither am I," Leon said quietly. "I think we need

to meet, so you can bring me up to date. What the hell was she into?"

"Honestly, she was still investigating her sister's murder. And she was damn sure it was related to several other cases."

"The police just took copies of the folders she had in her office," he said, "but I think I have a bunch in digital form."

"Oh, I have a whole lot more to send you. I'd just as soon not bring the cops into it, if we don't have to, at least not yet."

"Well, if my aunt has gone missing because of this, I have to. I'm hoping she's still alive, but there is no way to know."

"In this case, I suspect not," Anthony stated. "She was very good about contacting me."

"Yes, but there was an upsetting incident at the university," Leon murmured. "It would make sense for her to disappear a day or two."

"You mean, the two dead women?"

"She told you about that?"

"Yes, right after she got home that day."

"When can we meet?" Leon asked.

"It needs to be now," the private detective said. "And time is of the essence, if she's truly gone missing."

"No cell service, her phone's just been turned off. Her vehicle is still parked at home. No sign of her at the office, at her house, and she made no arrangements for her classes," Leon replied in exasperation. "We have no way to track her movements. I dropped her off after that very upsetting day at the university. She said she was fine, then headed inside."

"Did you go into the brownstone with her?"

"No, I didn't. I started to, but she objected." He reached up to rub his head. "And believe me. I feel guilty enough about that already. The only thing about it is the fact that I found no sign that she was forced out of the house or anything."

"That's something," Anthony said. "Where are you?"

"At home."

"I'll be over immediately," Anthony replied. "I do have some files and some information."

Leon ended the call, immediately wondering if he should say something to the detective. He'd have been pissed if nobody contacted him in a similar situation. He groaned and pulled out his phone. When she answered, her voice was snappy.

"I know you're already pissed," he noted, "and the last thing you need is more on my aunt, but apparently she's had a private detective for the last couple years. He's called me to meet with him, having being told by my aunt that, if he ever couldn't reach her, or if something happened to her, to contact me."

The detective let out a noisy breath. "Wow, she was definitely into something."

"She was, indeed."

"When are you meeting the detective?"

"He's on his way over to my house now."

"I'll be there in five." She hung up on him.

He winced at that, since the PI had said no cops. But that wasn't really an option, when they were looking to find his aunt. He put on coffee, while he waited. The detective arrived first.

Abby looked at him in surprise. "Where is he?"

"He's on his way still. He also told me not to involve the cops."

"That's nice. This is why we end up with so many problems."

"Hey, I called you," he said.

Just then they heard the sound of a vehicle driving up. She stood in the living room and took a look. "Interesting."

"What?"

"He's driving a Mercedes."

"Well, I don't imagine he's just scraping by, if he's any good at his job anyway."

"Is that what the money in the drawer was for?"

"I'm afraid it may be," he admitted, "but I don't have any way to know that."

She nodded quietly. "Well, let's see what he has to say."

He hesitated.

"Go ahead and just introduce me as a detective. We'll see how he reacts."

Shrugging, he said, "He probably won't like it at all."

"Too damn bad. I'm a little tired of people yanking my chain, especially while time is running out on your aunt."

"I know," he said, heading to meet the private detective, who was approaching Leon's front door with a large briefcase. "Hey. So, what was my aunt getting you to do?" he asked, as the PI stepped in the door. He shut the door behind him, as Anthony turned to look at him.

"Well, she told me that you pretty well dismissed everything that she had to say."

"No. It wasn't that I dismissed it"—knowing it was a lie—"but there was only so much that I could handle, when she brought it up to me a while back."

"She said that you have a nose for it and that you'd gone after the one avenue you could, and she would pursue the avenue that she could. But, in all honesty, I've been hunting down leads for years and found nothing. Every name she gave me, I came up with a solid alibi, or they were dead or something to knock them off the list. At this point, she still wants answers, but I don't have any to give."

"What avenue was that?" Abby asked, standing behind the PI.

He turned, his eyebrows shooting up at Abby, glaring at him.

"Sorry," Leon said. "This is Detective Abigail, Abby—"

The private detective hissed.

"Don't bother arguing with me," Abby said. "We're trying to find his aunt, so any information you have that would be helpful, I need to know."

"You haven't given a damn all these last years."

"Well, that's an interesting accusation," she said, "considering that I'd never met or spoken to her prior to the deaths of her students at the university just days ago. And now that you've brought in the university, I have to consider that it might be related to my other case."

"I don't know if it's related or not," the private detective said, "but it's a shit show, one way or the other." He walked over to the dining room table, laid down his briefcase. "I made copies of everything. It's all here." He looked over at Leon. "You shouldn't have brought the cops in on it."

"Why is that?"

"Because I suspect a cop is involved." He popped open his briefcase. "Only I don't know which one."

"In that case, I doubly want to know," she snapped at him.

"And so do I," Leon said.

"Too bad. I don't give a shit what you guys want. I'm only concerned about my client, and, as she's not here right now, the only one calling the shots is me. If you want any other information, you can pay me for it." He dropped copies of the files on the table, then walked out without another word.

CHAPTER 7

ABBY WALKED TO the table, pocketing the card from the private detective, Leon already sorting the stack of files. "He's got an attitude," she noted. She hadn't checked out his energy. It had been a shitty day, and her reserves were already low. In all honestly, she hadn't even thought of it. Damn. Next time.

Leon looked at her briefly. "We all do when we're under stress."

"True enough." She grabbed the closest file and read the name. "Is it the same person suspected of all of these deaths?"

"I was hoping for a summary. Shit."

"Did you find the digital files you were talking about?" she asked him.

"I haven't had a chance to do anything," he snapped. "I had just walked in when the PI called."

"Interesting timing." She struggled to keep her temper in check, but the thought of another case—and a huge one at that—being connected to her current one was frustrating. This material needed to be gone through, and that would take time—time they didn't have to waste, if this ended up not connected. That the PI didn't find anything on Gertrude's family's murders she was digging into helped. Yet how could Abby dismiss these files without at least going through them?

"He'd been trying to get a hold of my aunt," Leon explained. "He last spoke to her when she called him, right after I dropped her off on the same day the two women died. She told him about them."

"So, he is the last one who spoke to her?" she asked sharply.

Leon nodded. "I think so. I spoke to a friend of hers, who also heard from her about that same time."

"Interesting," she murmured.

"The PI was looking into a lot of issues for her and has been doing so for a long time. That's even more disturbing, in my opinion."

"What? That you didn't know about it or that she was doing it regardless?" she asked.

Leon walked over to the window, rubbing his face before he spoke. "That she was still fully invested and working toward the resolution of something that I had walked away from."

"Guilt again, huh?"

"No, not so much guilt." He sighed. "Well, maybe. If we find out that she's been killed because of something from that investigation, then probably." He raised both his hands and swung around to face Abby. "What do you want me to say? At the moment I'm worried about my aunt and trying to come up with a way to get back into the investigation."

"Well, apparently you have a way now," she replied, "because all of this will have to be gone through."

"What's that, an olive branch?"

"No, I'll be taking all this with me."

He swore.

"It pertains to my case and is my evidence," she snapped.

"You don't have time to go through it. You just said so."

"Which is why we'll do it right now," she replied. "If you want copies of stuff, you need to make them yourself." He immediately snatched up the first folder. "I'll get busy scanning then."

"Good. I'll sit here and take notes while you do that, and then I'm out of here. And I don't have much time, so do it fast."

"Got it." He took a deep breath, headed to the copier, and started scanning. By the time he got to the next folder and the next, he was hungry. "I know that you have to head off and do your own stuff," he noted, "but I'll order in some food."

She looked up, briefly interested. "Depending on what you're ordering, I'll get something too."

"I was just thinking about some of the big sandwiches from the deli."

"I'll have some too then. It'll be a long night."

"You're not going to bed?"

"I'll crash when I run out of steam." She studied the paperwork in front of her. Even as he watched, she reached out and scrubbed her face.

"It looks to me like you need a break now."

"You got any coffee?"

"Actually I do. I made it, while waiting on the PI, then forgot all about it."

She hopped up and walked with him into the kitchen, where he poured coffee for both of them. She took it and took a sip. "I don't have a large enough notepad. Do you have anything? I should have brought my laptop."

"Well, if you want, we can use my laptop to take down notes," he offered readily enough, "and then send out copies for both of us."

And that's what they did. She agreed on the simplest of paths right now. "How about that order for food?" she asked.

He laughed. "I'll call right now."

Hearing him placing an order, she looked up, smiled briefly. "Not trying to be a bitch."

"Got it, oh ye of little talk," he said.

"Talk happens when there's time for it. Right now, we have a missing woman."

He appreciated the fact that she was working on his aunt's case but knew that she also had to work on the murder of the two women too. "I don't understand how it could be related." He took a drink of coffee. "Yet timing-wise I don't see how it can't be."

"I know." Abby nodded. "That was my thought too. Which is why I'm here right now. And, if I get to the bottom of this and find out I've wasted all these hours, I'll be pissed. But it's a pathway I have to check out."

"Agreed." Leon continued to scan in all the evidence. By the time he was done, she sat here, munching away on a sandwich, a frown on her face.

"You look like you found something."

"Well, I found something, but I have no idea what."

"So tell me."

"We've got this guy here." She pointed at the file before her. "He's been arrested, suspected of murder, questioned about a murder, but again there's no evidence, so I'm not sure why your aunt's on his case."

"Who is it?"

"Tony Esparazzo."

"Oh. Well, that's because he's the nephew of the guy who supposedly killed my mother. Gertie always thought that the guy who went to jail for it had agreed to go in

Tony's place."

"What was the relationship?"

"Tony was Michael Esparazzo's nephew, and Michael didn't believe his nephew had done it."

"Meaning that Michael did believe Tony did it but wanted to keep him out of prison, so Michael took the fall for Tony."

"That's what was suspected at the time, yes. No proof, mind you. The cop doing the investigation said that, as long as somebody went to jail for it, he was good with it. And did a half-ass job closing it."

"Ouch," she said.

"I'm of the opinion, and I'm sure you'll agree, that it should be the right person who goes to jail. Particularly when we suspected that Tony continued to kill. I went after the detective, and apparently my aunt went after the nephew."

"But the nephew is where?"

Leon held up a summary sheet. "He's been taken off the suspect list after due diligence. Apparently he had a solid alibi. He was in prison. Confessed to a different murder." He sighed. "According to the PI there are no viable suspects. What's even more depressing is this is the first I've realized that Gertie was doing all this."

"So you said." She nodded.

"And I mean it, Detective."

"I get that. I'm getting tired and a bit punchy. Sorry." She reached up and gently massaged her temples.

He watched her searching her pockets. "Missing your pain pills?"

She looked at him in surprise. "I get migraines but left my pills on my desk." She rubbed her temples again. "Back to this guy. Interesting that he confessed. Then again, if they had him dead to rights, it would go easier on him at sentencing time."

"Or they browbeat the confession out of him. Hate to say it, but I've seen that a time or two as well."

"The problem with a confession—regardless of how it's obtained—is then the cops don't look any further," she noted quietly, "and unfortunately that happens too often."

He looked up at her, smiled. "What's this, Detective? A softening in the attitude?"

"Hell no," she declared, "but you've brought me more work than I'll likely solve anytime soon. So it's all about prioritization right now. I've got a missing woman, and we've got two dead students."

At that reminder, he immediately sat back down again to look at the files.

"The women worry me," he replied, "but we can't help them. I'm hoping we can save my aunt."

"Of course, and both should happen." She sighed, shaking her head. "I don't know what happened to the women, or how, and I want to make sure that it doesn't happen again."

CHAPTER 8

A FTER A TORTURED night the phone woke Abby the next morning. The voice on the line and the information waiting for her didn't help. Her heart sinking, she listened to Dr. Henshaw talk. "What do you mean no cause of death?"

"I'm telling you, from one moment to the next, they were alive, and then they were dead," the coroner barked over the phone. "I don't have anything else to tell you. No narcotics were in their systems. We're still waiting on results for other classes of drugs, but we can detect absolutely nothing. For whatever reason, those two women just up and died."

"Good God," Abby murmured. "How will I tell the parents that?" And it also meant she'd be forced to step outside the box again. Something that made her headaches so much worse.

His voice softened. "Believe me. I'm not happy about it myself. There's no reason for two healthy young people to up and die."

"You did confirm they were healthy?"

"Yes, I do know how to do my job."

She winced at that, shifting in bed and pulling Migolo onto her lap for a cuddle. "I'm not questioning that. I'm questioning this can happen in someone so young. Two someones."

"I'm doing a hell of a lot of that myself."

She heard the aggravation in his voice. "I get it," she noted heavily. "I hate mysteries like this."

"Hey, this is right up your alley. This is woo-woo in a big way."

She winced at that. "Yeah, it's all about the *what ifs* in this case."

"The *what ifs* are important. If you come across any more information, I can keep looking," he said. "Obviously I'm waiting on the rest of the tests, but I'm not holding my breath. Hopefully something will come up as a definitive answer, but, at this moment, I don't know what that could be. The worst for all of us is when we have an unknown cause of death in two healthy individuals."

"And how will you put it down?"

"I can't even tell you it's foul play." And, with that, he hung up.

And that was the crux of the matter because, if foul play wasn't involved, she couldn't justify more time on this case. She had other cases sitting on her desk too. And the time that she had right now would come to a quick end, if she didn't have any plausible reason to keep the investigation open.

Arriving at the office, with all the new files from Leon dumped on her desk, she looked around to find Harvey right in front of her. She stepped back, shook her head. "When the hell did you get here?"

"A while ago." He smiled broadly. "What the hell, so the coroner's got nothing?"

"As in zilch," she replied. "Two supposedly healthy young females died at the same time, at the same place, at the same moment. That is bizarre." She rubbed her temples.

"Headache worse?"

"Yeah, left my pills here. It hasn't gone to a full-blown migraine yet, so I'm hoping I caught it in time."

"Good." Then he smirked. "Your reputation is growing."

"Well, it's about to tank," she snapped, "because I've got nothing on this."

"Not yet, but you will."

"And I don't know how I'll find anything to go with it. But I've got a ton of other stuff now too." She pointed at the mountain of paperwork atop her desk. "I'll need your help."

"Of course," he said. "Why the hell didn't you call me about any of these last night?"

"Because it was late, and I was trying to get my mind wrapped around it. Besides, didn't you have that kid's soccer game?"

His face softened. "Yeah, we did. It was a hell of a deal."

"Good. Come on." She dumped half of the files on his arms, and then she picked up the others. "Let's go find an empty interview room."

"Maybe we should bring some more people in on this one," he suggested, as he followed her down a hall.

"If we can get it, fine, but you know the captain will say we've got like another twenty-four hours, and then we'll move on."

"That sucks, doesn't it?"

She found a storage room, full of boxes, but the table was big and empty. She dropped her armload there. "Particularly when we don't have anything that says foul play, yet how can it not be?"

"I don't get that." Harvey dropped his stack on the opposite end of the table.

"Neither do I." She sighed heavily. "But you also know that it won't matter what we say. Results count, and, if we don't get them, this will go cold."

"Well, you mean it will as far as everybody else is concerned, but I know you. You'll hack away at it."

"I don't have much of a choice, do I?" She cocked her head at him, looking at him sideways. "These cases get to you."

"I know," he agreed. "They get to me too, just not as much as they get to you. Maybe it's decades of experience," he added, with a paternal smile. "With luck, you will get there too."

She shook her head, plopped down in a seat near her stack. "I still don't know how you can throw it off like that."

"I have to. Otherwise it's just takes me somewhere I don't want to go." Harvey took his seat as well.

"Sometimes I think I'm already there."

"Sometimes I think you are too," he said in a serious tone.

She smiled. "But people like you keep me sane, you know."

"Ha. I don't think I keep anybody sane."

"Well, as long as you keep yourself sane, then we're doing something right."

They'd been working together for a long time, and, although he gave off the impression of being more of a dopey sidekick, his brain was sharp, and he picked up things that other people missed—a lot. People looked down on him because of his easygoing laid-back joking manner, but Abby wasn't fooled. She'd seen him in action too many times, and she definitely needed his help now.

And more than just reminding her about her pills and to drink more water or to eat.

"There's so much information to filter through," she noted, as she opened the topmost file. "This case just got very complicated."

"Which case is that?" the captain asked, standing right in front of her.

She turned and frowned at him. He frowned right back. She raised both hands. "This one. The two dead kids at the university."

"I already talked to the coroner myself," he stated. "Seriously, their hearts stopped? And that's all he can say? Absolutely no known cause of death?"

"I know," she replied. "They just up and died. But I don't get how that happens."

"Well, that's because you're not God," he snapped.

She glared at him. "Don't bring religion into this. Those women didn't have to die that day."

"And for me to believe that, you'll have to bring me some proof. For all we know, the multiple cosmetic surgeries were too much for them, like they tried to look and live alike."

"Exactly, but because no foul play is attached, budget comes into play, right, Captain?"

He nodded. "In other words, you're out of time, so move fast."

She groaned as the captain left, and she turned around, facing Harvey. "I hope he doesn't think that we're not doing anything at times like this," she muttered. "How can he when we're surrounded by files?"

"You know it's just him trying to roar. He always needs a target."

"Well, I wish he wouldn't always choose me," she said. "It makes me feel even worse."

"It does make you try harder too though, doesn't it?"

"Maybe," she admitted. "I hate to think so though."

"It doesn't matter. Let's just carry on doing what we do best."

"I like that." She pointed at her stack of files on the table. "Now let me give you a bit of a rundown." And she went over all that she had learned from Leon and the PI and these files to date.

When she was done, he sat back and looked at her. "You found out all this last night?"

"Yeah, late last night, and I should get a copy of the other digital files, the old ones that Gertrude kept but had given copies to Leon." When her phone buzzed, she glanced at it, nodded. "Yes, that's them. I'm sending them to you right now."

"Jesus." Harvey checked his phone.

"Don't even start on me," she said. "You should have seen me, trying to get my head wrapped around all this last night. And the fact that the private eye wasn't exactly cooperative didn't help. But what does any of this tell us? Nothing. The PI couldn't find anything but likely stirred up a mess of worms while looking. I'll call him in a bit and see if he found anything or anyone who might have hated Gertrude enough to take her out."

"I think that's actually a requirement of the job." Harvey grinned at his own humor. "PIs always hate us."

She groaned. "That's such BS. We're here to solve two murders and to find a missing person, and there really shouldn't be any of that nonsense. Now several cold cases are connected too by the very nature that they exist. So we have loads to consider. Too bad more people aren't willing to talk."

"Sure," Harvey noted, "but you know for a fact that there will always be a group of people who hate cops. Just the sight of us gets their backs up immediately."

"Sure, but, when we get a case that's got a body, then we have to look into that."

"So, this other professor, this *Leeeon?*" he said on a teasing drawl.

"Yeah, what about him?" she muttered.

"He's been called in as a consultant on a couple police cases."

She looked up, frowned. "Yeah, he mentioned something about that."

"I thought he was a professor of criminology, which he is," he added, "and he teaches a lot of criminology courses, but he has a second degree in mythology."

She sat back and stared at her partner. "Wow." She shook her head. "I didn't see that coming."

"Interesting combination. You two should be perfect together."

"Don't even go there," she snapped, again focusing on the files in front of her.

"Hey, girl, it's time you went there, if not once but a few times," her partner said in exasperation. "Let off a little steam, burn off a little of that energy, and find a reason to live again."

"Sex?" Her eyebrows shot up. "It's a fun activity, but why the hell would you want to do it with anybody a second time?"

He shook his head. "You're just afraid of commitment."

"Not afraid of it." She rolled her eyes. "Terrified! Why

the hell would you want to hook up with anybody in this world? Do you know how many killers and strangers I meet who look and act normal, but who are absolutely off the wall?"

"Not all guys are like that," he admonished.

"No, but I've not run into many deemed a *poster child* for Man of the Year either."

"Hey, look. Most of the men in your life are dead or murderers," he snapped back. "And the rest of us are taken."

"Exactly," she agreed, with a beaming smile. "All the good ones are gone. Now can we get to work?"

He let her get away with it, which was good because that was an old argument between them and had become a big running joke. But sometimes she could sense his need to push the issue a little bit more each and every time. He'd been very happily married, once a long time ago, and often said he'd remarry if he found another perfect woman, like his first wife. Although he hadn't yet, he was happy to try women out in the meantime.

She just tried to keep him off her back. She hadn't had a long relationship in quite a while, and, though it bothered her sometimes, usually she realized what a lucky escape she'd had. Every time she got into an ugly case that involved husbands killing their wives, it just reminded Abby that, while not all men in the world were bad and destined for prison, man, oh man, once you made a bad judgment, it was pretty hard to trust again. She knew that from experience.

But she didn't give Harvey the details of her past, and she didn't ask him for details of his, and that's the way they liked it. At least most of the time, until he got too pushy. "I just need a couple uninterrupted hours to get through all these, without being brought onto other cases."

"And that's not likely to happen," said a man, his voice calm, from the hallway.

She looked up in surprise to see one of her coworkers, Chase. "Why is that?" she asked, scowling.

"Because we have a DB."

She groaned. "Can't you guys take that one?"

"Well, we would, except for one thing."

She stopped and stared blankly at the wall in front of her. "And what is that?"

"Because your name was in the vic's wallet. And so were the names of the missing professor and her nephew."

"No, no, no, no," she said. "I don't want to hear that at all."

"Male, midforties, driving a newer model Mercedes."

Her heart hitched. "Oh no, please no." She shook her head, her heart sinking. "Please tell me it's not the private detective."

He nodded slowly. "Yeah, looks like a private eye."

She groaned and looked over at Harvey. "Now this will really take over."

"Yeah, and the problem with that then is the two women end up sliding down in our caseload."

"Not because of lack of trying," she muttered.

"I know." Harvey stood and collected the files. "But definitely because of a lack of any opportunity to go in any one direction."

And the trouble was, he was right. They had just too many avenues to consider, and nothing was bearing fruit, except for the fact that this other case supposedly was related. She hated to think another death might break the case wide open, but ... On that note, she got back to her desk, dumped everything onto her desk. Then she picked up her phone and called Leon.

When it went to his voicemail, she left him a text message instead, not wanting anybody to hear her, asking Leon to go through the PI's files to see what dirty cops he suspected could be the one involved in all these murders, and grabbed her purse and her jacket to find Harvey already at the door, waiting for her. "You know, one of these days," she said, "we'll actually have a chance to work on a case—and just one case at a time."

"In your dreams," he replied. "Murder never takes a holiday."

LEON WAVED THE students from the classroom and sat down heavily. He was still trying to contact his aunt, even though he knew it was completely useless at this point, but he had that compulsion to keep trying. The fact that her phone was dead—or at least not even accepting voice messages anymore—he presumed that nobody had located it. But had the cops even tried?

He hated always doubting everything they were doing, but it was really damn hard not to. He'd seen too much of the lying, cheating, even incompetence during his years in internal affairs. Still, he was surprised to see a voice message on his phone from the detective. As he listened to it, he frowned, then walked over to his computer to see if he could access any of the files that he had at home. He had some of them here in his office at the university and had left a lot of it on a storage device at home.

With that in mind, he grabbed his jacket and headed out. As he drove home, he took another pass by his aunt's place again, hoping against hope that maybe something would have changed. But it all looked completely the same.

From there, he headed to his home office and, before even getting himself a beer, sat down to see if he could find the information the detective was looking for. It was here somewhere, but it had been years since he'd dug into it, and he hadn't really kept up much of a filing system, so he wasn't exactly sure where he would find it.

When his phone rang again, and he saw that it was her, he groaned as he answered it. "I'm looking for the information," he snapped. "You haven't given me much of a chance to find it."

"Well, right now we're outta time." Heavy fatigue filled her voice.

He immediately straightened. "What do you mean?"

"Your aunt's private eye is dead."

"What?"

"Murdered, or at least I'll assume so."

"What do you mean, you assume? How was he killed?"

"There's not a mark on him," she snapped.

He hissed ever-so-slowly, the breath escaping in a long slow slide of air. "Jesus."

"Yeah, you want to talk to me about that a little bit? You said that there was another case the PI was working for Gertrude?"

"Yes, I don't remember all the details though. And I'm working on finding it."

"Work faster. I'll be here for a few more hours."

"Where's here?" he asked.

"At the PI's car. He's parked outside his house, sitting in the front seat of his vehicle."

Leon really hadn't wanted to go in this direction, but he couldn't see how to avoid it now. "I know someone who could explain this. A psychic who often consults with law enforcement might help, and I know that you're pretty black-and-white, but sometimes you can't see things out there."

"Well, I'm looking at it right now." Anger was in her voice.

And he couldn't really blame her, but it would also make her hard to approach.

"I'm looking at a dead guy, who does not have a single mark on him, who looks like he just went from one breath to the next, had a heart attack, and died."

"Well, he certainly could have had a heart attack," he noted.

"Well, I've got to tell you, and this isn't for sharing, but neither of the two women in that classroom of your aunt's had any evident cause of death. From one moment to the next, two healthy women were just gone."

"Crap."

"No heart attacks, no infections, no tox, no drugs, no overdose, no nothing."

"That's not possible," he said in bewilderment.

"Well, how do you think I feel about your case now?"

"Actually that makes about as much sense as any other thing," he replied, "but I can see that it's not something you want to entertain."

"Hell, nobody wants to entertain that," she snapped. "Just think about it. We have enough causes of death in this world, without having something show up that's invisible."

"I get that, but it is some of what I do and what Stefan Kronos does. It's my mythology-cult degree that brings me to consult on those types of cases."

"You seem to have an eclectic history that I wasn't aware

of. I didn't realize you taught mythology."

"Yes."

"I thought you were in criminology."

"I am, and I have consulted with the police on several cases," he explained, "and I do have a degree in criminology, although it's not something I advertise."

"Interesting," she murmured. "Yet why the mythology?"

"I find it fascinating, I think the kids like it, and I present a unique bent to it."

"Well, you need to present something unique now," she stated, "because this is looking beyond suspicious."

"Oh, I didn't do anything," he replied, his tone turning cool.

"Maybe not, but you're about the only one I know who has anything to say on the matter."

"Well, I don't have to say anything at all, if it makes you happier."

"Nothing will make me happy right now, so get used to it," she snapped.

"Look. Call Stefan. He might help. He was a big help on the cases we were both brought in on. You said so yourself."

She pinched the bridge of her nose, trying to calm down. "I need to solve these cases and not have any more dead bodies show up."

"And what about the missing one?" he asked, his voice hard. "Does my aunt's disappearance not even register?"

"It registers," she retorted. "But who's got any insight into where and how she's gone? Her phone is just off. There's no sign of it."

"Right, and the last time she used it?"

"As far as we can tell, in her brownstone, not long after she arrived home that night."

"Which lines up with what the private detective told me, who's now dead."

"Yes, and yet it doesn't line up with anything else."

"Which is really shitty," he murmured.

"Yeah, you think? Knowing Gertrude's OCD habits, and her continuing desire for the PI to dig up information, she must have a file, specifically on potential suspects that the PI has pulled together. See if you can find that PI file among Gertrude's copies, please." And, with that, she hung up.

CHAPTER 9

"I'LL CANVASS THE neighborhood," Abby told Harvey, feeling anger, frustration—hell, even fear crouching in her. Then she could blame Stefan on the last one.

"No, we will do it together," Harvey argued.

She looked at him gratefully. "We can split it."

"No." Harvey shook his head. "Since we've got some killer out there who doesn't leave any marks, we need to stick together."

"I don't know why they would go after the PI."

"Depends on what the meetings between him and Gertrude were like."

"That was my thought too," she noted, "but really nothing is anywhere to give us a clue as to where to go."

"Which is why we start canvassing."

They started at the end of the block and made their way up, asking everybody when they had last seen the private investigator, how long they had noticed his car on the road, and anything else that came to mind, based on their responses. That was the detectives' same basic line of inquiry each time, and, when they made it down both sides of the street, Abby shook her head. "I don't think he was here very long."

"He has a GPS on the car, so we'll find out easily enough."

"Yeah, if we can track that backward," she agreed, "let's

get forensics on it. Maybe we can find out where his last stop was before here."

"That might help."

When they returned to the vehicle, forensic techs still worked on it. Abby stepped over and asked one about it, who nodded. "I'll pull the data for you."

As she waited, the tech headed back inside the vehicle. "Forensics makes life a lot easier," she noted.

"It does, except when it's making things a lot harder." Harvey laughed at his own humor.

She snorted, as she nodded, because a lot of truth was in that statement. Soon the technician came back over.

"Okay, I've downloaded the information off it, and here is the address of the last place he stopped."

She stiffened as she read the address. "Seriously?"

"Do you know it?" the forensic tech asked.

"Yes, it's the address of our missing person."

"Wow, maybe they're connected," he suggested.

"I don't think there's any *maybe* about it," she snapped, then she turned to Harvey. "Next stop is Professor Gertrude Milligan's place."

"Good. Wouldn't it be nice if we found her sitting there, having a cup of tea, wondering what all the fuss was about?"

Abby shook her head. "I would be ecstatic if that were the case," she replied, "but somehow ..."

"I know, but you've got to stay positive."

"Says you. This is just a shit show from start to finish."

"You're unhappy because you can't make progress in any specific direction," he noted. "Maybe time to call in your psychic specialist. I never got a chance to meet him."

"Not happening," she said. Stefan brought on her headaches in a big way.

I don't have to be there, as you well know, he whispered through her brain, triggering another migraine to threaten her balance. Instinctively she shoved him out of her mind and slammed the psychic door, only barely stopping the ripples from taking over her body.

"Too late," she told Harvey. "I already feel like somebody out there is laughing at us."

"Yeah, that wouldn't be the first time either," he muttered, as they got into her car. She drove back to Gertrude's home and parked out front.

"Did you even consider that you might have been the last one to speak to the PI?"

She stared at him. "What do you mean?"

"We don't know how long he's been dead," he explained. "For all you know, he left this place last night."

"Yeah, but we spoke to him at Leon's place."

"You were at Leon's house?" he asked, his eyebrows elevated, and then he grinned. "I think I approve."

"Don't bother," she snapped. "He was meeting the private investigator there, so I came over at the same time."

"So, the PI came over here to Gertrude's place afterward."

"Apparently." She frowned. "You know what? Leon found a ton of money in her file drawer. I don't know if he came back for that or not."

"Well, I suggest we go find out." Harvey hopped out of the vehicle. "What kind of money are we talking about?"

"Didn't count it. I saw him look at the desk again before we left, but it was a lot of money," she admitted. "Easily thirty thousand."

"Wow, what does it take for somebody to put that kind of money in an office drawer?"

"I wondered if that was how she was paying for the private investigator."

"She still had to get the money from somewhere."

She nodded slowly. "She could be taking out a few thousand every month for it."

"I'll run a check on her bank accounts," Harvey noted.

"I already did a cursory one," she said, "just looking to see if ATMs have been utilized since her disappearance. The answer was no."

"Well, I'll do a deeper check because she's getting that money from somewhere."

"She should be making good money at the university. So she set something aside, paycheck to paycheck."

"Well, you hope so, but, in this case, I'm not so sure."

When they walked into the brownstone, she headed straight to the home office. "Well, he didn't disturb anything if he was in here."

"That seems to be the MO right now, doesn't it? Absolutely no evidence, no sign of anybody having trespassed anywhere."

"I know." Abby sat down at the desk. "It was in this drawer here."

"Well, pop it open then." It was locked of course; she looked up at him, and he shrugged. "You know how to fix that." She had it open in seconds. And he whistled when he took a look. "Wow. That's all just sitting here?"

She nodded. "It is, indeed." She slowly closed the drawer again and checked out the others, but, as Leon had pulled out all the files from those drawers, they were pretty empty. "Okay, so why did the private eye come back?"

Harvey shrugged. "Could be any reason, maybe just to check for himself that she wasn't here. Maybe he was doing one final check in his own head that maybe she wasn't missing but had actually returned home, and he would find her having that proverbial cup of tea." He paused. "Funny how we all see her as a slightly eccentric innocent little old lady, isn't it?"

"Yep, it sure is. And that's good acting on her part because think about it. That's not somebody who hires a private detective and keeps him on salary for the last what? Two years? All to look into the murder of your sister from a good ten or fifteen years earlier. I don't even have the dates in my head," Abby noted. "We need to get a good timeline going."

"What about the other murder?"

She stopped, looked at him. "What do you mean, the other murder?"

"Well, when I ran a check on Leon, I found out Leon's mother was murdered a few years back, but his father was murdered even before then."

She slowly sat back into the office chair. "What? He spoke of his parents' murders, and he might have mentioned that they were separate events but the importance of that skipped by me."

"Two separate murders, two separate time frames," Harvey stated, "but there was one common denominator."

She nodded grimly. "Leon and his aunt."

LEON PROBABLY SHOULDN'T have even mentioned it. He still couldn't find the case number of the file he remembered. But he was even struggling to find all the information that his aunt had sent him. He sat at his home office desk, puzzled, wondering what was going on, when he spied one of the locked cupboards off to the side.

He got up, quickly unlocked it, and, with relief, found the hard drives that he'd placed there many years ago. He pulled them out, connected them to his computer and started sorting. In the second one he found the material he wanted. He sent off a copy to the detective.

Then he sat down to take a closer look at the data himself. There was very little on it, as in very, very little. It was depressing. As he sat here, his phone buzzed. He looked over, saw the call was from another prof at the university, a good friend. "Hey, Tommy. How are you doing?"

"I'm fine. How are you holding up? I heard your aunt's gone missing."

"I'm sure it's all over the university by now."

"It is." Tommy's tone was … comfortable.

Something about Tommy was just staid. He wore the same four different shirts in a rotation every Monday through Thursday, the days that he worked at the university. They were getting a little threadbare; but, when they got too threadbare, he'd go out and buy four more. He taught history, and generally people would say his lectures were as dry as the dust, which was the foundation of his course. But he was a good man at heart and always had been there in times of trouble.

"Do the police have any idea what happened?"

"No," Leon said, "and neither do I. Not a whole lot to even go on because she's an adult and could have left on her own."

"Right. I guess they generally don't do much about missing persons of an adult age, especially if nobody has found any signs of foul play."

"Exactly, and they haven't," Leon answered quietly.

"Her place looks untouched, as it always does."

"But everything about her is always so perfect," Tommy noted. "Nothing's out of place. Never a coffee stain on her desk. I mean, her clothing is always impeccable," he noted in complete bewilderment, not understanding how anybody could be that way.

"Just no sign of her having done anything. Her car is there, but then she almost never drove it. She wasn't much for traveling that way."

"What about going away with friends?"

"It's possible," Leon agreed. "That's the problem. We just don't know. Her phone isn't responding, and it apparently hasn't been used in a few days."

"So that's a little concerning."

"Right, but remember the time that she forgot to charge it for days?"

"Oh, yeah," Tommy replied. "I do remember that. Everybody wondered what happened to her the last time."

"Right, she didn't know her schedule had been changed, so she didn't know she was supposed to be anywhere at a specific time, and, when she didn't show up, all hell broke loose because people thought that she had disappeared."

"Which is what will happen if you started putting out that alert again now."

"Right, nothing like crying wolf to have everybody look at you sideways and say, *Yeah, so where is she this time?*"

"And the trouble is, it wasn't her fault last time either," Tommy noted.

"No, it certainly wasn't." Leon groaned. "But I don't know what to do anymore. I've tried all the avenues I know."

"In that case it's just a matter of waiting."

"How long?" he asked quietly. "How long before something bad happens, and I realize I should have done something a long time ago, but now it's too late, and the unthinkable has happened?"

"If that's the case," Tommy replied gently, "chances are it's already happened."

He winced at that. "I know." Leon sighed. "I'm just trying not to think about that option."

"It's not an option, but it is something that you do have to consider," Tommy murmured. "Your aunt is a good person, but she did have a tendency to get some people a little riled."

"Just some people," he noted in a wry tone. "She was a good person though."

"The best," Tommy said stoutly. "We'll hold on to hope that she's out there and just enjoying a holiday, like she was last time."

"Wouldn't that be nice," Leon replied.

When Tommy hung up, Leon got back to his search, studying all the digital files in front of him, but it was getting to be a bit more than he cared to look at. When his phone rang again, he half expected it to be Tommy again, but, as he looked, it was a number he didn't know. He picked it up, frowning. "Hello?"

He heard almost nothing but a weird clicking staticky sound coming through the phone.

He stared at it. "Hello, hello." Then he called out, "Gertie, is that you?"

There was a weird whisper on the air, almost like a *yes*.

"Gertie, where are you? What's wrong? Do you need help?"

But then there was nothing but silence. He slowly hung up the phone and stared at it, waiting for her to call again. If she were stuck somewhere without cell phone service, that would explain the static. When it rang again, he picked it up, but this time nobody was on the other end at all.

Frustrated, he slammed it back down. "Try again. Please, Gertie, please."

But the phone remained silent.

CHAPTER 10

ABBY STARED AT the information in front of her. Why hadn't Leon said anything? Her hand reached for the phone, not even thinking to check the time. When she got Leon on the other end, his voice was groggy, as if she'd pulled him awake from sleep. She checked the time and winced. "Sorry. I didn't check the time."

"What time is it?" he asked, his voice sleepy, trying to wake up.

"It's two in the morning."

There was a moment of silence. "You woke me up at two in the morning?"

She apologized again. Just because she was a workaholic that didn't mean everyone was. She should have checked the time, damn it. Almost as if Migolo could read her mind, he opened one eye and stared at her in surprise. Then closed it and went back to sleep. "I didn't check the time."

"Well, now that you've woken me, let's hope you have a good reason."

"I don't know if it's a good reason or not, but I needed to ask you something."

"What?" he snapped. "Let's get this over with, so I can get back to sleep. Some of us have to go to work tomorrow."

"And I said I'm sorry."

"And you keep saying you're sorry is just pissing me off

even more."

She was at the point of saying sorry again when she realized it and managed to hold it back. "I didn't realize when you talked about your parents' being murdered that you actually were talking about two separate events. Is that right?"

"I assumed you had investigated me already and knew the details."

"Well, I hadn't, so it was a bit of a shock when I found out."

"And when was that?"

"Earlier this evening."

"So, you're calling me just now about that?"

"No." She took a deep breath. "I'm looking into your aunt's history."

"That would be fun. She's the Mary Poppins of all of us."

"And yet you know she was engaged way back when?"

"I know somebody was in her life way back when, yes. What difference does that make?"

"Are you aware that he was murdered?"

There was a shocked gasp at the other end of the phone. "What are you talking about?"

"Did she ever mention him?"

"No. But you have to understand that my aunt is sixty-five-plus, maybe even sixty-seven now," he corrected, "and that relationship would have been when she was about twenty."

"Yes. Her fiancé was shot to death on the side of the road."

"And what has that got to do with anything now?"

"I don't know if it has anything to do with anything.

But it might explain her fascination with what happened to her sister, and why she couldn't let it go."

"Was his murder solved? Who did it?"

"No," she replied quietly, "it's a cold case."

"Well, that would explain some of her mistrust of the police."

"I don't know about *mistrust*," she added, "but potentially why she had to keep investigating because she felt like the police wouldn't get the answers that she needed."

"That sounds very possible, considering what she's been through," he noted.

"I know." Abby took a breath and continued. "So, you didn't know anything about it?"

"No, I didn't know anything about it. Why?"

"I'm trying to see if anything is connected. An awful lot of deaths have happened around her."

"Maybe," Leon acknowledged.

"And you don't know of anybody who may have had a grudge against her?"

"Did you check with the dean? For the letters and all?"

"They're pulling anything that they have, but I haven't gotten anything from him yet."

"She had a couple students who were pretty ugly and a couple parents. But nothing that I would consider this level of dangerous."

"What kind of threats?"

He hesitated and then said, "I don't have any proof of this. I just know what she told me, and typically that's not very much, only the bits and pieces."

"Please stop stalling. Just tell me."

"I understand one threatened to kill her, and another threatened to kill himself. They were usually about grades, though one was somebody who was hung up on her and wanted to go out with her."

"Interesting," she murmured.

"She had a lot of foes, but she had a lot of supporters too."

"I'm not criticizing her in any way," she explained. "I'm trying to understand who your aunt was, so I can figure out what's going on here."

He didn't respond, not sure of what to say.

"Do you happen to know a Dr. Brisko?"

"The plastic surgeon?" he asked in surprise.

"Yes." She stared at the phone in shock. She'd just tossed out the question on a whim. "What do you know about him?"

"Nothing."

"But you know his name," she pressed.

"Yes. My aunt actually went to see him."

"Bingo," she said softly.

"*Bingo* what? Is he involved in this somehow?"

"That's something we still have to figure out, but both of the students who died had gone to him for multiple surgeries."

"What? Why?" he asked. "They were young and beautiful."

"But apparently they didn't believe so."

"Both of them?"

"Yes, it was part of the weird relationship they had."

He sighed. "I can see that. Women are particularly vulnerable and often bond over things like that."

"Well, I don't understand it myself," she said tiredly. "I'm meeting with the good doctor tomorrow morning."

"I'd like to come."

"That's nice," she quipped, "but it's not happening."

"Well, it was worth a try."

"Go back to sleep."

"How am I supposed to do that now?" he asked in exasperation.

"Well, it's still early, so you might get a few more hours."

"If you hadn't called, I would have gotten lots of sleep. But now that you have, how am I supposed to shut off my mind?"

"I don't know, but give it a try." And, with that, she hung up.

She really was sorry for having woken him up. She surveyed the papers she had printed up that surrounded her on the bed. Somehow Migolo was half covered in loose pages now.

It was pretty damn frustrating because so many pieces were here, and it was like a great big jigsaw puzzle. She couldn't tell if it was all from the same puzzle or whether several boxes of puzzle pieces had gotten mixed up. And that was one of the hardest parts.

It was difficult to focus on one thing, when so many others were there. Did the aunt's case even have anything to do with the two students? If Abby could at least get rid of one of these issues, she could work on the next one. But, so far, nothing was cooperating the way it needed to.

She picked up her notepad on the multiple murders and wrote down more of her notes, starting back with the murder of Gertrude's fiancé. The fact that it was a cold case also made it very suspicious. How far back did revenge go? She knew very well that they went all the way back as far as you could remember. She shook her head at that.

Three murders, just around Gertrude alone, long before her students' deaths. Her fiancé, her sister, her brother-in-law. All three separate events and committed at different times. What were the odds of that happening?

GOING BACK TO sleep was an impossibility at this point. The detective should have known that. Leon was actually quite pissed about the whole thing. And yet not because she had at least called him. Sad state that was, if getting woken up in the middle of the night made him happy.

He got up, grabbed his notepad and laptop, and started working himself. He was going through all the various places that he had known his aunt to have ever visited in the past. Only as he was running down ideas, having made a few phone calls where the time change worked, he still came up with nothing. Then his phone rang again. He answered it. This time it was the same static. He leaned forward. "Gertie, is that you?"

There was a weird *yes* in the background.

"Where are you?" he asked. "I can't hear you well enough."

There was more static, and then she spoke. "What if?"

"What if what? What are you talking about?"

And then Gertie was gone again. He quickly dialed the detective. He took perverse pleasure in hearing her sleepy voice. "Ha, it's my turn to wake you up."

"What's the matter?" she asked, immediately sounding wide awake.

"I just heard from my aunt," he said, his voice jubilant.

"What? Oh, thank God. That's perfect. That's great. Where is she?"

"I don't know. The call was full of static, and all I could get from her was that it was her, then she mentioned *what if*."

"What?"

"I don't know for sure," he replied in frustration. "I got a phone call earlier, and I thought it was possibly her, but I couldn't tell, and it just cut out again."

"And you didn't mention it to me?"

"Well, number one," he snapped, "you woke me up when I was sound asleep, so it was hardly at the top of my mind. And number two, it's not as if I could confirm that static was her. You probably would have just told me that, when she calls again, let you know if it was really her."

"Yes, you're probably right." She let out a big yawn that he could sympathize with. "So, can you go get her?"

"Did you hear me? She literally just confirmed it was her, and, when I asked her what happened and where she was, so I could come and get her, she said something about *what if*, then hung up."

"Okay, so I guess I'm brain dead here at the moment. What does that mean?"

"How would I know? You're the one who wanted to know if anything happens."

He wanted to hang up, and she knew it. "Wait, wait. Wasn't that the name of the lecture?"

"What lecture?"

"The lecture that she was giving when the two students died."

He stopped, frowned. "Yes, it was. But what did she mean?"

"I don't know," Abby said, her voice grim, "but it's another damn connection that means nothing."

"Or," he said quietly, "it means everything."

"Well, stay by your phone and see if she can get through again because we sure as hell need more than ghostly visits in the night." And she hung up on him.

He stared down at the phone and had to agree. "Come on, Gertie. Try again, please."

The worst thing was thinking that maybe she was out there struggling and needing help, and here he was perfectly willing and capable but had no idea where to go to get her, no way to track her phone. Or was there? He immediately called the detective back. When she grumbled into the phone, he asked, "Can you track her phone?"

"Just a minute. I'll need a few minutes to get my brain turned on for that. I'll call you back." And, with that, she hung up on him. Again.

But this time at least he knew he had her attention, and it was a sign of the fact that she was so tired that she hadn't had the idea herself. He waited, leaning against the headboard, studying everything in front of him, but his stomach was in knots, as he waited for word on his aunt.

When the detective called back, her voice was brisk. "Her phone hasn't been turned on."

"What?" he cried out. "How's that possible?"

"Presumably she used a different phone," she suggested. "But her phone, the number that you gave us, hasn't been turned on. Let's verify the number." And she read it off to him.

"Yes, that's it," he confirmed.

"Well, that number has not been turned on."

"Shit. Now what?"

"Now we wait," she said. "We wait. That's all we can do. Work what we have and wait."

She hung up on him again.

CHAPTER 11

ABBY WOKE UP the next morning, the ever-present headache threatening as usual. On top of that was an unusual grogginess. Apparently she'd slept through her alarm. But then she'd been up how many times in the night with Leon? Too bad it was all work related. Then again, until this case was solved, he needed to keep firmly away from her. Too bad, as he was one of the most interesting men she'd met in a long time. She pushed that thought away. *Later.*

After a quick cuddle with Migolo, Abby dragged herself out of bed and into the shower, where she turned it on as hot as she could stand it, then turned it on cold as soon as she was done. Shivering, but now fully awake, she stepped out, dried off, and got dressed quickly. As she was putting on coffee, she checked the time and realized she didn't even have time for that. She grabbed her briefcase, loading up all the files still spread out on her bed and now the floor.

"What a way to start the morning," she grumbled.

Even as she headed to the front door, the doorbell rang. Groaning, she pulled it open to see Harvey there.

"Hey, what's up?" he asked, looking at her.

"I had a shitty night."

"Ha. Join the club."

"You too?"

He nodded. "The girlfriend and I had a nasty fight."

"Ah, sorry to hear that."

"What was your problem? Headache again? If so, you need to get to a specialist. Those things are getting worse."

"No, I worked late. Then I woke up Leon with some questions. I finally got to sleep, then apparently Gertrude called him on the phone."

Harvey stood stock-still in shock. "Wow, that's great news. I was beginning to wonder if she was alive."

"It is great," she agreed, "but it also sounds like she's in trouble. The static was so bad that he couldn't hear anything."

"Couldn't hear anything but he knew it was her?" He shook his head at that.

"She did confirm it was her. It was clear enough for him to hear a simple yes. But she also said something about *what if.*"

"What if what?" Harvey asked, looking at her, puzzled. "This case, instead of becoming clearer, gets weirder."

She shrugged, as she got into his car. "Glad we're taking your car. I'm too tired to drive."

"Yeah, I figured it was my turn."

"It sure as hell is. Besides, mine is out of gas."

"I can handle driving today."

"Good. I'll remind you of that next time you try to save on gas by riding with me."

Chuckling, he said, "Noted. But what's that *what if* deal?" He paused. "The topic of that class was What If." He stopped and stared at her.

She waved at him. "Come on. Get driving."

He turned on the car engine and pulled out into traffic. "That's right. It was, wasn't it? I remember thinking it was an odd name for a class."

"I liked it actually," she noted. "I'm very much some-body who always had questions. And those kinds of questions are right up my alley."

"I get that, but do you think that's what Gertrude meant?"

"I don't know, but that's all we have. Oh, she wasn't using her phone. Hers is still off."

"Great, that doesn't help much."

"No, it sure as hell doesn't," she replied. "So, after all that, it was pretty hard to get back to sleep again."

He pulled up to an intersection and waited for the traffic to clear, so he could turn left. "So you and Leon are getting pretty close, huh?" he asked, with a sideways glance.

"Don't even start with me."

"Too late," he replied cheerfully.

"Well, you can stop anytime. Oh, and I also found out something else." She tried to change the subject.

"What?"

"I found out that the aunt's fiancé, way back when—and I mean, way the hell back when, like thirty, no, closer to forty years ago—was murdered."

"What?"

She nodded. "Right. Isn't that just enough to blow your mind?"

"But that's bizarre. How can anybody have that much bad luck?"

"Yeah, that's three murders," she repeated, "her fiancé, her sister, and her brother-in-law."

"I don't know," Harvey said. "That's just ..."

"I know." Abby nodded her head. "Freaky, isn't it?"

"Talk about bad luck. I mean, just think about it. That's an awful lot of people to lose."

"It is, indeed," she agreed. "I'll pull the cold case file to see if anything's there."

"Are you really thinking that Gertrude had something to do with it? Although, as she's the common denominator on all three cases, both in her distant past and also in her current present, you have to wonder how could she *not* be involved?"

"I know, but now she could be in trouble too. I'm not thinking anything at the moment. And, until I get some damn coffee, my brain won't function properly anyway. But something has to connect all three of our cases."

At the office, she headed for the coffeepot, poured herself a big one, emptied the pot into a second cup for Harvey, and walked to her desk. "I want that cold case pulled, and I want to compare all three of the murders to see if there were any similarities."

He nodded. "Will do. I suggest we set it up on a whiteboard in one of the conference rooms."

"Find one that's got some time and space," she noted, "and we'll see if we can get this mess organized. With just so many floating pieces, I'm getting cross-eyed, thinking about it."

"It's all good. We'll get there."

She smiled. "I know." Now if only she really believed that. She would have to contact Stefan soon.

And you know I'm here, when you're ready. But you could also solve this case on your own, if you'd pull down that damn wall, Stefan whispered in her mind.

As they headed toward the conference room, the captain stopped her. "Update?"

"I'll have something pretty quick," she replied. "The nephew seems to have received a phone call from his aunt during the night. It was terribly staticky, and all he got was it was her and something about *what if.*"

"What the hell does that mean?" the captain asked.

"Well, that's the problem. We don't really know, but what I can tell you is What If is also the name of the lecture she was giving when the two students died."

At that, the captain stiffened. "Seriously?"

"Yes. Also, the aunt's fiancé was murdered like forty years ago," she added.

He stopped and stared. "*Seriously?*"

She laughed. "I know. Harvey and I have been talking about it this morning, thinking about what bad luck one person can have, where three people in her immediate world were murdered and also another three people in her distant past were also murdered."

"You know what that is."

She did. "I know. It's a connection."

He nodded. "And you better get to the bottom of it, fast."

In the conference room, she felt that spark that signaled something was moving, something was happening, and maybe something she could actually bite her teeth into. At least she hoped so. But, as they studied the murder board, even ninety minutes later, with as many of the details that they had pulled up on all the various cases, she looked over at Harvey and sighed. "Not a fucking thing connects them but her."

He shook his head. "I can't find anything. We've got a bullet. We've got what looks like an attack on the father, and then the mother we don't really have anything on."

"Well, we have blunt force trauma," she stated. "If that's nothing, then we have the two students, with absolutely zero forensics, in the lecture hall."

"Right, so how does any of that have anything to do with the other?"

They sat here and studied the board in front of them, and she felt the depression weighing her down. "There's got to be something," she murmured. "How could all of these be unrelated?" Just then her phone rang again. She looked down at the screen, and it was Leon. "Did she call again?" she asked immediately.

"No. And I'm at the university right now."

"And?"

"I was talking to a couple other people—you know, asking around to see if anybody knew where she might have been, what she might have done. Apparently one of the other lady profs here knew her quite well and said that Gertie might have gone off with a friend. Apparently she had somebody show up—a few days before she disappeared— somebody from years ago that she hadn't seen in a long time."

"Is that something she would normally do?" Abby asked.

"No," he said. "However, if it was an old friend, somebody she'd kept in touch with, then maybe she was just excited and decided to go out for dinner or something."

"Did they say how long ago?"

"Well, that was the funny thing. She made it sound like it was a long time ago, like from before she started teaching."

"When would that have been?"

"Thirty-plus years ago," he replied reluctantly.

She stared at her phone. "As in, when her fiancé was murdered?"

"Yeah, within a decade of that. I don't have dates in my head, but I thought she was in the university, working on her master's degree about that time, but it could have been her graduate studies or her bachelor's. I'm really not sure. That would be around the same time frame."

"Maybe, but why wouldn't she have told you that on the phone?"

"I'm suspecting because she can't. Maybe it's the friend's phone that she used, and then it subsequently died. Maybe they've run into trouble and are out in the middle of nowhere. I don't know." Leon paused. "It's already something that I wouldn't have expected of her, and, to get these weird phone calls, it's just putting my nerves on edge."

"Of course it is," she said immediately. "I'll add that information to the file. If your contact can remember a name or any details about who this person might be, if that person was picking her up or something, it would be helpful."

"I'll go back and talk to her again," he offered.

"Wait. Can you give me her name and number? I'll have to talk to her myself at some point."

He quickly gave her the name. "Emilia Tristen."

"What does she teach?"

"English. Do you still want me to go and talk to her?"

"Yes, that would be great, and I'll follow up with a call when I get a chance."

"Okay, fine."

"By the way, did you come up with anything in your esoteric studies that would cover any of these events?" she asked in a half joking manner.

"I've been racking my brains over this," Leon admitted, "but honestly, I'll have to say no. Except you need to contact Stefan Kronos."

"I was kidding." And no, she wasn't ready for Stefan.

"You might have been kidding," he said quietly, "but I'm not." And, with that, he hung up.

"One thing about this …" Abby stared at the wall in front of her a few moments later.

"What's that?"

"It's progression."

He looked at her in surprise.

"What are you talking about?"

"We've got a bullet. We've got a knifing. We've got blunt force trauma."

"But that's backward. Usually we see this progressing from their fist to a knife to a gun. So, he's aging and just trying out new methods, and you're thinking it's the same killer in these old murders? Someone paid or is still paying for the fiancé's death? So was that a wrong conviction?"

She shook her head. "I'm not saying that, but you know what? If you lived in a really bad area of town, where there were lots of gang fights, then knifing would be the common thing. And I guess that, if murder was something that you saw on a regular basis, maybe blunt force trauma would be a regular thing as well. But what are the chances that all three were different? And then you add in the two students …"

"I'm not sure you even know what you're saying," Harvey said.

"It just seems so odd that every one of these is a different method," she stated tiredly. "Hell, never mind. I'm not making any sense at all."

She picked up the phone and dialed the phone number that Leon had given her earlier. "Hello, Professor Tristen," Abby said, identifying herself. "I understand that you have information that could possibly relate to Gertrude's mystery disappearance."

"Potentially," the other woman replied in a hearty voice. "But I know she wouldn't like us talking about her private life."

"I get that, but, if she's in trouble, we would very much like to help her out."

"And if she's not?"

"Then we'd leave her to it." Abby rolled her eyes at Harvey, who was grinning at her. "From the phone calls, we're assuming that she needs help of some kind."

"Well, in that case," she added immediately, "she just said that she heard from somebody out of the blue, somebody she used to care for a great deal, and she was really surprised to hear that they were in town."

"And did she give any indication of the gender of this person?"

"From the way she was acting, I assumed it was a man," the other woman relayed in a happy voice. "And surely you can understand that."

Abby winced at the tone in her voice, as if to say, surely the detective was female enough to understand something as obvious as that. "Did she give you a name, a time frame? Was this person picking her up? Did she say anything about going home to get changed, anything along that line?"

"No, she mentioned something earlier, before all the cacophony in the classroom, and I knew it would be that night. But, for all I know, she might have canceled it because of the two women. That was such a terrible thing for her. I was really hoping that somebody would have sent a grief counselor over to help her out. You know that we do that for the students, but what about for us?" She was warming to a topic that was obviously very dear to her heart. "I mean, it's hardly fair that, as staff, we don't get the same care and consideration that the other students and the families of the bereaved get."

"I'm sure that's something you should take up with the dean," she mentioned quietly.

"As if he'd listen," she snapped. "If it'll cost money, it won't happen."

"Well, that's just the way it goes sometimes," she added. "If you think of anything else in that conversation that would be helpful, we'd appreciate hearing from you."

"Oh, I don't know why it's a problem in the first place. Surely she's entitled to go off and to have a few minutes to herself."

"Of course she is, but it's really poor timing right now, and we would like to hear from her, to know that she's safe. That's all. A quick phone call to say she's safe."

"Fine. If she contacts me, I'll have her do that. Or at least I'll ask her to do that," she said, with a half laugh. "You don't tell Gertrude to do anything."

"Of course not. I am waiting to hear from the dean about this," she added, "but maybe you would know. Is there anybody who holds a grudge against her? Has she ever spoken to you about anyone?"

"No, not at all. She didn't make friends easily, and that was a bit of a problem for some people," she said, with a sniff.

"So, in other words, there were ruffled feathers, but nobody in particular you could pinpoint as being difficult?"

"Exactly."

"What about the two students? Did you know them?"

"One was in one of my classes," she noted. "The other one was not."

"And what did you think of that?"

"Wow, the poor child is dead," she replied in outrage. "That's hardly a question to ask."

"Yes, I know that," Abby said, reaching for some patience. "And that's why I'm trying to investigate the death, to see if there was foul play involved."

"Well, I don't know how there *couldn't* be foul play," she declared. "It's not like two children will die at the same time, in the same class, for no other reason."

"And yet so far," Abby explained, "the coroner hasn't come up with a cause of death."

"Well, that just means the killer is smarter than you are," she replied in a snappy voice.

"Perhaps you can answer the question," Abby said, again striving for patience.

"I don't know anything about her. She was a good child. She showed up for class, did her work. She was not an A student, but I wasn't really expecting her to go very far."

"Why is that?"

"Because I don't think she cared one whit. She was more concerned about looking after herself. I think she was in the market for a husband."

"At the university?"

"Of course. A lot of the women do that. They check out who's being successful, who's going somewhere, who'll have money, who's got family money, and they set themselves up to go after them."

"Do you know of anybody she might have gone after?"

"No, not at all, but that doesn't mean a whole lot. No, certainly not." And then she hung up.

Abby turned back, looked at Harvey. "Some of these women ... Prof Tristen acted like these women were in junior high or something."

"They're quite stuck in a different age, aren't they?"

"Absolutely."

He added, "By the way, while you were gone, the coroner called."

"And?" She looked up at Harvey.

"He's working on the private detective."

"Oh, thank God. Please have something." Abby dialed the coroner and immediately heard his voice on the other end. "Please tell me that you have something concrete for this one."

"No can do, and it's making me damn pissed."

"What do you mean, no?" she wailed.

"No definable cause of death. It's like he sat there in the vehicle, and, from one moment to the next, he died."

"No coronary, no asphyxiation, no CO_2 suffocation, no heart attack? Nothing?" she asked, sounding a bit frantic.

"No," he said, his voice heavy, "nothing." He stopped for a moment. "You need to catch this guy."

"What do you mean, *catch this guy*?" she asked. "So far you haven't given me anything to go on."

"I know. That's why you've got to catch him. Because he's found a way to kill people that I don't understand. We need to stop him before he does it again."

"If you're right, it's got to be the cause of death for all three of them."

"These three deaths are like nothing I've ever seen, so, yes. That's your connection," he said. "Work it until you find out who did this. I've seen a lot in my career, but I've never seen anything like this." And, with that, he hung up.

She looked over at Harvey, who was just shaking his head.

"What the hell? How is that even possible?"

"I don't know," Abby admitted, "but that's our linking case right there. It means it's foul play for the women as well."

He nodded slowly. "Will the coroner revise his report?"

"I would think so. He'll have to call it homicide from unknown causes."

"Great, and how are we supposed to tell the families that?"

"I don't know, Harvey," she murmured. "I just don't know."

WHEN LEON WALKED into his office at the university, Emilia stood there, glaring at him. "What was I supposed to do?" he asked. "*Not* tell the police about the phone call?"

"Your aunt will be terribly upset," she replied stiffly. "Justifiably so."

"And I would be totally okay to apologize to my aunt until I'm blue in my face, if only she were standing right here in front of me," he explained gently. "But the problem is, right now we have no idea where she is, and I don't know if she is okay or not."

At that, Emelia's voice softened. "That's the only reason that I spoke to the police."

"Well, I appreciate that you did." Leon pulled his hair off his face.

"You need a haircut," she noted.

He laughed. "That's the least of my worries right now. I need for my aunt to come home."

"Right. I forget that it's just the two of you, isn't it?"

He nodded. "There is just the two of us, which is why this makes no sense."

"Well, it does if she's fallen in love again," she said, with a twittering laugh.

He looked at her. "Do you really think *that* was the kind of relationship she had with whomever this was? I mean, especially after all this time?"

"What I can tell you," she said, "is that she was really excited about it."

"So potentially, an old beau," he murmured.

"Exactly, and more power to her, if you ask me," she stated. "Gertrude works too hard. She never takes a break. That woman needs to live a little bit."

"That's true," he agreed, "and I'll be more than happy if that's what this is all about."

After she left, Leon sat at his desk, wishing the day was already over, only to look up and see the dean staring at him. "Problems, Harry?"

"You mean, other than the actual ones that we're dealing with right now?" he asked in a tired voice.

"You sound like I feel. I was up half the night working on the case, talking to the detectives. Trying to find my aunt, trying to figure out what's going on at the university."

"Well, I'd be happy to have somebody tell me what was going on here," he said in a tight voice. "We can't afford the bad press of having our students dying in the midst of a lecture."

"I know it," he agreed, "and I'm not spreading anything, but there's no way to keep these deaths quiet."

"It was an accident of some kind, I'm sure," the dean stated, with a wave of his hand. "We need it to die down."

"Feels like we've been saying that for a long time."

"We probably have been," he admitted. "It's just so very upsetting."

"I hear you. I'm dealing with it myself."

"Yes, and that's another problem. Gertrude's not here to

do her last lectures, and we have exams coming up. Thankfully your aunt has always been one to have her exams ready ahead of time."

"What do you want from me?"

He frowned. "I don't have anybody who can take her class."

Leon heard the plea coming in Harry's voice. "You need me to step in?"

"If you could, it's just for today."

"Well, I can step in to give an explanation, then send them on their merry way with signups for the exams," he said. "At least the term's over, so it's not like it'll interrupt anything."

"Yes, if you can do that, that'll be great," he said, "and don't give out too much information."

"I wasn't planning on giving out very much at all," he replied, "but they are students of hers, and they deserve something."

"Yes, yes, but just, you know, watch it."

And Leon knew what Harry meant.

As he watched his boss walk away, Leon knew it was basically a case of *Don't tell them anything, and try to keep everybody happy.* Like that would happen. His aunt, despite her quirks, was well loved by her students. At least those who were interested in her topics.

And as he walked into her lecture hall, he heard murmuring going on around him. He held up a hand. "Obviously I'm not Gertrude," he said. "I am Gertrude's nephew and a professor here myself. At the moment, she is not able to finish off the term, and, as this is your last lecture anyway, it's not a big deal. We'll just spend a few minutes going over the exams, making sure you're prepped and ready, and then you can go."

He knew that not one of them would argue about that. He had yet to see a student upset about a class being canceled. Too often they were screaming with joy and racing to get the hell out of there.

As it was, this one was a little bit different because obviously rumors had been circulating.

"Do we have any information," asked one of the young women, "about Sammie and Aimee?"

He shook his head. "No, I haven't had an update from the police on that."

"Is any of this connected to why your aunt's not here?" somebody shouted from the back.

He looked to the back to see a young man sitting there, nervously twiddling with his glasses.

"Not as far as I know," he admitted. "But again the investigation is ongoing, and I can't speak about it." And that seemed to satisfy them. It was a standard pat answer that really meant nothing, but it gave him something to say. He watched as the rest of the class got up and moved on out.

Except for the one young man who had asked the earlier question. He came down to speak to Leon. "Are you sure your aunt's okay?"

"Why are you asking?" he asked.

"Because I heard a rumor that she disappeared."

"Interesting. The rumor mill is always pretty busy, isn't it?"

"And it's often very accurate," he replied.

"Well, I don't know what to tell you," Leon said. "I'm not free to speak about any of this."

"Of course not," the student replied, shaking his head. "I just really don't want anything bad to have happened to her."

"Neither do I," Leon said. "Neither do I."

With that, the young man seemed to be somewhat satisfied, and he turned and raced out. Leon should have gotten the young man's name. He pulled out his aunt's roster on the computer to see who was always attending, and took a painstakingly slow twenty minutes to go through it before he finally found that student's picture online as part of his student file. His name was Bruneau. Leon shook his head at that. "That's not the name I would have given you."

But then, when a baby is born, it's not as if they knew what he would look like when he hit late teens and early twenties. But, in this case, he was pimply-faced, looked like he was a bookworm or a gaming geek, someone who never got out into the sun much. It wasn't a criticism; it was just an observation that the name seemed totally out of character.

Then again, did he look like a Leon himself?

CHAPTER 12

W HEN ABBY WOKE up the next morning, that sense of defeat sent added pressure that she needed to do something, that something needed to break. Abby would have to ask Stefan for help, likely triggering a massive migraine. But it couldn't be helped. Still, she had a few things to check first. But, so far, there was absolutely nothing. She planned to go to the coroner's office first thing this morning, on the off chance that she saw for herself that nothing was, indeed, there.

As she dressed, she wondered about the argument she would have with Dr. Henshaw. It wasn't all that usual to attend autopsies, and she had certainly missed out on this one but hadn't realized the importance of it. But obviously something magical was going on, magical in a black magic kind of way. As she approached the coroner's office, he happened to be standing there, staring at the papers in his hands.

When he looked up and saw her, his eyebrows went up. "To what do I owe this visit?"

"I'm hoping against hope that I can look at the body myself and that you found something that you haven't told me about."

He shook his head.

"I'm getting desperate here."

"You and me both," he snapped. "I've never in my life seen anything like this, and now I have three cases."

"I am going back in today to sort out and see if anything at all connects the three families. I have yet to connect with the plastic surgeon, but it doesn't apply to the PI, although I do have inquiries into it."

"Let me know. He might not have been a patient. You might want to consider the fact that he could have been investigating another patient or something."

She looked at him in surprise. "You know what? That's not a bad point. I know the PI worked for Gertrude for a long time, but that doesn't mean she was his only client."

"Most likely she was one of a dozen, if not fifty," he guessed. "They have to make a living somehow, and one client won't do that."

"No." She thoughtfully considered that. "I'll head over there and ask the good doctor myself." She checked her watch. "He's not returning my calls."

"You do that. And let me know."

"Right. Tit for tat?"

"If I had anything to give you," he said regretfully, "I would. But I don't have a damn thing. And believe me. It's pissing me off as much as it's pissing you off."

"I get it." She gave him a grim smile.

"I hope so, because this isn't funny for any of us."

"Nope." She shook her head. "We're all struggling with it. I keep thinking about the families. How do I tell them, *Foul play but nobody knows how or why or in what manner?*"

"I know," he agreed, "and it's not even so much foul play, but we should note it."

"I know. I know. It's undetermined causes."

"Exactly."

And, with that, she took her leave and drove straight over to the plastic surgeon's office. When she walked in, one of the receptionists looked up, smiled. "May I have your name, please? You have an appointment, right?"

"I'm here to see Dr. Brisko," she noted, holding up her shield.

The receptionist frowned. "I'm sorry. He's got a full slate of patients today. He doesn't have time to see anybody not on his schedule."

"Well, it doesn't matter if he has time or not," she snapped briskly, her voice rising, "I'll see him. So we can either do this now, or he can take a break and come down to the station and talk to me there."

"He really doesn't have time," she repeated worriedly.

"Well, he'll have to make time, as he's not returning my calls. I'm out of time and patience."

At that, another woman stepped forward. "Let me go talk to him."

"Why don't you just show me where his door is," Abby said, getting irritated at the balking. "I could have been out of here already by now, but for all of this squawking about something that I'll do whether you like it or not."

The other woman stiffened. "We're just trying to do our jobs."

"And you're making great gatekeepers," Abby replied, "but it's not helping his cause. It's just pissing me off and making me more irritated than I already am."

"That's not our fault," the first woman squawked.

She glared at her. "I will see him, whether you allow me to or not." She went around the front desk, heading toward the back.

"What's the matter?" A door opened, and a middle-aged

man with just a little bit of white tucked around his ears stepped forward. "What's all the noise about?" he asked his two front desk employees. "You know how I feel about that in my front office." He turned to look at Abby, approaching him, and glared. "Are you the one causing all this?"

"You're damn right I am," she said, holding up her badge. "You aren't answering my calls. They were hindering me from speaking with you. So it'll either be here, right now, or you'll come down to the station and see me."

His eyebrows shot up. "What on earth?" He looked at his watch. "I've got like five minutes."

"Good. If everybody stopped wasting my time, that five minutes would probably be enough."

He immediately turned and strolled into a private room. She followed, as he turned around. She looked at the door pointedly, and he said, "Go ahead and shut it then." Once shut, he asked, "What's this all about?"

"A couple of your patients," she replied, then named the two women.

He frowned, as he thought about it for a moment. "The two girlfriends who were best friends since forever and wanted to have all this work done." He nodded, with an eye roll.

That was the first indication Abby had that he hadn't necessarily been fully on board with all that either. "Why did they want to have surgery?"

"Why does anybody want to have cosmetic surgery?" he asked. "Because they were constantly thinking something was wrong with them. It doesn't matter what you tell them or how much you try to discourage them, they want it done, and, if they don't get it done by you, they'll go somewhere else."

She stared at him a moment. "They both had multiple sets of surgeries?"

"Nose jobs and Botox, although most people don't consider that surgery as much as a procedure," he noted. "One had an eye lift already because she had a droopy lid, and there were several other things. Breast enlargements maybe," he guessed and, after a moment, added, "Yes, they both had breast implants."

"And did you try to discourage them?"

"Of course I did," he replied. "As far as I'm concerned, there should be a law against anybody under thirty getting this kind of surgery, but I'd be out of business if that were the case."

"Did you feel confident they were psychologically ready for this cosmetic surgery?"

"Well, the one certainly was. She'd been dying to have a surgery since forever. The other one? I don't think it was her wish, as much as she was trying to keep up with the girlfriend. Did I approve? No, of course not. Did I try to talk her out of it? Yes," he said. "But obviously I won't kill my business, and they're adults. So they can do whatever the hell they want to do. What's this got to do with you though? Are they threatening me with a lawsuit or something?" he asked in alarm.

"No, there won't be any lawsuits, at least not from them," she said, "with a caveat."

"So, what's this about?" he snapped.

"They're dead."

He stared at her in surprise. "What do you mean, they're dead?"

"Both of them are dead."

"What happened? A car accident or what?"

"No, they were sitting in a lecture hall, and then, from one minute to the next, they both died."

"That's not possible." He glared at her, as if she'd made that all up.

"Well, that's what the coroner is saying too, at the moment. So we're looking at anything in their history that might have caused this."

"Whoa, whoa, whoa." He held up his hands, as if to stop her. "They haven't been in my office in months. I had nothing to do with this."

"I know that, and not once did I say that we were looking at you for causing their deaths."

"No, but you're here," he replied. "That's enough. If anybody else sees you and makes that connection, my business would be toast."

"Well, it's a good thing I'm here, nice and early then, isn't it? Most of your adoring fans won't even be awake yet."

He just frowned. "No reason to get ugly."

"Look. I'm trying to solve what happened to these two women," she snapped, "and I just need you to be cooperative enough for us to understand what's going on."

"Well, I want to understand too. The last thing we did was breast implants, and they were both doing very well. They both healed perfectly," he noted. "I was really happy with the way both came out."

"Okay, that helps. What about Gertrude Milligan? Do you know her? Do you happen to know Anthony Kolbassa?" She named the private investigator.

He shook his head. "Neither name sounds familiar. Hold on." He typed something into his computer. "Ah, she came for a consult on a facelift. My opinion was she didn't need one yet. She had great shape and bones. I suggested a few minor tucks in a year or so, if she wasn't doing some-thing new to knock off a few years but she never came back."

"And Anthony?" She repeated his last name too.

"Him?" the doctor spat. "I know of him, but I don't know him personally or professionally."

"So how do you know him?" she asked curiously.

"My wife hired him to follow me around. She decided I was cheating, and she wanted proof."

"Ah." Abby stared at him. "And were you?"

"No, of course not, but my wife has a problem, and she's been accusing me of cheating on her for the last twenty-odd years. I told her that, if she didn't stop, I would turn around and do exactly what she was accusing me of. Do you know what it's like to be followed and to know your every move is being tracked all the time? Always constantly afraid that I'm cheating on her." He shook his head. "Absolute crap is what it is." He sighed. "I never met him though."

"You know I'll have to talk to your wife."

"*Great.* That'll just make her even more paranoid."

"Well, if you haven't done anything wrong—"

"I haven't," he snapped, "but it doesn't matter what I say. She doesn't believe me. She's been like this forever."

"Interesting." Abby stood, as she stepped out of the room. "Well, that's all for now, though I may need to ask you some questions again."

"Talk to my women up front. I'll tell them to let you through, but please avoid coming back here if you can."

"If you would return my calls," she stated, "I won't have to."

With a bright smile she walked out to the reception area. It always made her day a little better when she got to ruin somebody else's day who so deserved it. Not that Abby was a bitch, but some people just refused to cooperate, and Abby didn't give a shit if her presence gave them a problem or not.

As she walked out, she smiled at the ladies. "Thanks. Next time you're supposed to let me through without all the backtalk," she said, as she left.

She headed outside and saw a street vendor selling coffee. She snagged a cup from him, only to see fresh pretzels sitting off to the side. She grabbed one of those too.

She walked over to the closest bench and plunked herself down. She could have gone straight back to the office, but sitting out here in the fresh air and contemplating what she had learned was just a whole lot easier on her psyche.

Here was another connection between all these victims. None of it made sense yet, but it was another thread to pull. And that made for fascinating contemplation. She was just downing her pretzel, when her phone rang. She looked to see it was Leon. "What's up?"

"That's what I would ask you," he said. "I was hoping you had some answers."

"And I was hoping you had talked to your aunt again."

"Well, it hasn't happened, and I don't know if it will," he murmured. "I'm worried that was a call for help, and I couldn't get enough information to help her."

"It's possible," she said, "but still nothing you can do about it."

"I know, but that doesn't make me feel any better."

"No, and I understand that. But there is only so much I can do to help if we don't have any place to look. I don't have the man-hours to send people all over the place," she added. "We know for a fact her phone is not traceable and her vehicle is still sitting there at home. It hasn't been driven anywhere, so I don't know what I'm supposed to do."

"Nothing but wait for a lead, I know," he said, with a heavy voice. "Where are you?" he asked. "I can hear street sounds."

"How very observant of you," she noted on a laugh. "I'm sitting on a street corner, with a cup of coffee, trying to put this crazy puzzle together."

"Whereabouts? A good pretzel place is downtown."

"I know," she replied, with a mouthful. "I'm chewing on one."

"Damn, I can practically taste it. I want one."

"Too damn bad. I'm not heading in your direction for a delivery either."

"Never crossed my mind, Detective, but, if you wanted to, that would sure be nice."

"Like I said, not happening. I'm going in the opposite direction."

"Yeah, whose cage will you rattle this time?"

"Somebody who's already got a very suspicious nature apparently. So this should be fun."

And, with that, she hung up, stood, and dropped her pretzel wrapper into the garbage beside her, then headed to her car. She wasn't kidding. When it came to people who were paranoid, it was always a delicate balance between saying something that would set them off and saying something that would unleash the information you wanted. In this case, she suspected it would go badly, but she had to see for herself.

She wondered why the good doctor stayed with his wife. And was she really as paranoid as he described? Well, Abby would find out one way or the other soon enough, and she drove in that direction.

Arriving at the address Dr. Brisko had given her, she

walked up to the front door and knocked hard on the ornate dark mahogany wood. When there was no answer, she did it again. She heard noises inside, but it appeared they were otherwise occupied or were deliberately choosing not to come to the door. That would just piss her off. She stepped back out, looked up, and yelled, "Hello, hello." Finally an irate face peered in the window above.

"What do you want?" asked the woman.

"To talk to you," Abby yelled, studying the partially hidden flushed face.

"Well, I don't want whatever you're selling, so go the hell away."

"I'm not selling anything." Abby held up her badge.

The woman gasped. "What? Why are you here?"

"Well, you and your partner can come on down here and let me talk to you."

At that, the woman disappeared, and Abby heard voices. She realized the good doctor had been cuckolded. That's why the wife was so paranoid because she was actually doing what she was accusing him of. She shook her head at the duplicity of people and waited for the woman to open the door.

When Mrs. Brisko did, she was pulling her ruffled hair into a bun at the back with a scrunchie, as she tried for a smile.

"Come in, come in," she said, "and I'm alone. You were wrong."

"No, I wasn't wrong," Abby corrected her. "You and your lover were up there, which is especially interesting since you're constantly accusing your husband of cheating on you."

The woman stared at her in shock. "Oh my God, oh my

God. Does he know?"

"Well, I sure as hell hope you'll be the first one to tell him. Otherwise that'll be something I get to do—with great pleasure, I might add."

She shook her head. "You can't. You just can't," she squeaked out.

"Why not?" Abby asked in a hard voice. "You make his life miserable, with all these accusations and private investigators for years, it seems, and then you cheat behind his back?"

"But, if he divorces me, I'll have nothing." With that, she wailed.

"Good God." Abby shut the front door with a hard *bang.* "Maybe you should have thought about that before you actually had an affair."

At that, heavy steps came down the stairs, and Abby looked up to see a man she'd never seen before, sheepishly coming into the room.

"She's right, you know," he told Mrs. Brisko. "You've been making his life pretty damn miserable."

"Of course I have. It's the only way to keep him from suspecting."

"Wow, that's nice," Abby said, then turned toward the woman's lover. "And you are a party to that too."

The man shrugged. "I'm not here for the long haul. I'm only here for a good time."

At that, the other woman cried out, "That's not fair. We've been together forever."

"Good God," he said. "We're only together as long as it's fun. Remember? That was our agreement."

"I know. I know." She pleaded with him, "Don't leave me, please."

"This is not my sin, so you go do whatever atonement you need to," he said, "but don't bother calling me until you've got it sorted out. I don't do drama." And, with that, he turned and walked toward the door.

Abby laughed. "You don't do drama, and yet you're in the middle of this?"

At the doorway, he turned, looked at her. "I have a few rules. I don't give a shit about married women because if they'll cheat, they'll cheat, whether it's with me or somebody else, but I will not do drama. And I will not get involved in the middle of it."

"Interesting rule," Abby noted. "What's your name by the way?"

He hesitated, looked at her, and asked, "What difference does it make?"

"Well, I'm involved in a murder investigation," she added, "so it makes a lot of difference to me."

His eyebrows shot up. "What?"

"You heard me. So whether you like it or not, you're involved in drama. You just broke your first rule."

He shook his head and started to panic. "No, no, no, no. That can't be."

"*Several* murders, in fact," she noted, "so I'll need your contact information and your name."

He looked over at Mrs. Brisko, still staring at him in shock. "You damn bitch. I told you that I would never get involved in this crap."

"I know. I know," she agreed. "I don't know what the detective is talking about. I didn't have anything to do with this."

"Do with what?" Abby turned to look at her. "You sound like you do understand what's going on here."

The woman immediately shook her head. "No, no, I don't. I don't know anything," she wailed, again facing her lover. "She just arrived at my door. You saw that."

"Yeah, I did," he said, his voice hard. "Regardless we're done. You go tell that husband of yours, or I will." With that, he turned toward Abby and handed over his card. "This is me. I'm a salesman."

"Yeah, and what are you selling?" she asked, with a smirk.

He glared at her. "Not that."

"Sounds like you are. Sounds like you're making a hell of a success of it too. Is a medical supplies salesman another word for *gigolo* these days? Or maybe you're selling dildos?"

He glared. "It's got nothing to do with my work."

"Yeah, I wonder if your boss knows anything about what you do while you're on the clock."

"I work on commission," he stated stiffly. "So it's none of their business." He glared at her. "It's none of yours either."

She shrugged. "I don't care what kind of an asshole you are in real life, but the minute you cross into one of my cases," she snapped, her voice going equally hard, "you become my business. I don't give a shit what you say. I'll do what I need to do to find the answers I need."

"I don't know what the hell you're talking about," he said. "Right now, I wish I'd never even laid my eyes on this bitch. But, if it's not me, believe me, another bull will be riding her in no time. That's just what she is. Somebody else pays the bills, and she has a good time at their expense."

"*Nice*," Abby said. "Stay in town, won't you?"

"Always," he replied sardonically and walked out the door, without another word at the doc's whimpering wife on the couch.

Abby glared at the cheating wife. "That was pleasant."

"You didn't have to show up this morning," she cried out.

"No, I didn't, but, on the other hand, you didn't have to be a cheating wife." At that, a hard gasp came from the hallway, and Abby looked up to see Dr. Brisko standing there. "Oh, did you not know?" she asked. "Your wife's lover just left."

He turned in shock and stared at the woman he married, who burst into tears even harder than before.

"I really wouldn't listen to that caterwauling," Abby suggested, "because lover boy's still in his vehicle out in front here."

At that, Dr. Brisko raced forward, took a look out the living room window, and back at his wife. "Seriously? That's Ron."

She nodded. "I know. It's Ron."

"How long has this been going on?" he asked.

And Abby could tell from his voice that he was devastated.

"It just started," the wife tried to explain.

"No, it didn't," Abby refuted, her arms across her chest, bored. "Nice to know that you'll lie right now. I'll be taking good notes of whether I can trust anything else that comes out of your mouth."

"You! It's all your fault," the woman snapped. "You didn't have to come here this morning."

"Wow, on the other hand," Abby pointed out, "look at how much good it's done. I just came to ask some questions and instead find you in bed with your lover. And, by the way, it was your husband who gave me this address."

The wife turned to look at him in shock. "What? You are responsible for this?"

"Well, it's a murder investigation, and one of the people who is dead happens to be the private investigator you set on me to make my life miserable," her husband explained. "And here I find out that you're the one who's screwing around." And then he stopped and, in a small voice, he asked, "Is this the only one?"

Immediately she nodded like a puppy. "Yes, yes, it is. It's the only mistake I made."

He looked over at the detective, and Abby shook her head. "Not according to lover boy. Ron's just one in a long stream of many," she repeated. "Apparently you go to work, and so does she, but she works on her back. Free of charge."

LEON TAUGHT CLASSES throughout the day, his heart heavy. Every time his phone rang, he was sure it would be his aunt, and, even when it wasn't ringing, he kept checking to see if he got a text message or something. But there was nothing. Most of his students were leaving today and wouldn't be attending more classes, as they were heading into exams. Now final reports were being handed in, but essentially it was wind-down time. He had his exams ready to go, and he would be supervising a couple of them, depending on how the schedule worked.

He didn't have the years at the university that his aunt did. Normally she wouldn't have to even show up, but she was the kind of person who would show up anyway because she abhorred cheating of any kind. He smiled at that; she might not have been easy to get along with, but you always knew where you stood with her. She was exactly as she seemed. Maybe a bit hard around the edges, but she always came with purpose.

As he walked toward his office, readying to leave for the day, the dean called to him.

"Hey, any news?"

Leon shook his head. "Nope, nothing on any of it."

"Rumors have it that you heard from Gertrude."

"Well, rumors have that I thought I heard something, but she couldn't get through, so I don't know if it was her or not." He shrugged. "If she could call me, and I heard clearly enough, I could say for sure that it was her." He wasn't sure why he was backtracking from saying he heard from her, but everybody was jumping on him about it, and he didn't know what to say. "I hope it was her. Let's put it that way."

"Well, I do too," he agreed. "I can't imagine replacing her at this stage."

And, of course, that's all he was concerned about—the university's responsibility to the students. "It might be a little hard to get a replacement prof. I can see that," Leon agreed with a nod.

"Don't even talk like that," the dean replied in horror. "Your aunt's been a mainstay here, and we could always count on her."

"Well, you can always count on her, until you can't," he noted, "but that's hardly her fault."

"No, no, I get that." The dean waved his hand. "I didn't mean to sound ungrateful. Your aunt's been a godsend all these years. She's not been any bit of trouble, unlike some of the profs." He sent a glaring look down the hallway and walked off in a huff.

Leon didn't even need to turn to see who he was talking about because it could have been several profs that he didn't like either. But that was okay; that's just the way life was. He returned to his office, unlocked it, stepped inside, and sat down in his chair. Almost immediately his phone rang. He grabbed it. "Hello." This time, it still showed no number, no ID at all, but, as he waited, he heard the static again. "Gertrude? Gertie, is that you?"

"Yes."

And this time it was a little bit clearer, a little more distinct. "Thank God. Are you all right?"

There was a weird silence, and then she said, "I don't know."

"What do you mean, you don't know? Do you need help? Where are you? Tell me where you are, and I'll come get you."

There was an odd metallic echo in the room.

"I can't talk long," she replied in a hushed voice. "You have to check out *what if.*"

"Check out what about it?" he cried out. "You said something about that last time. What does that mean?"

"It's connected," she said. "I don't know how. I don't know why, but it's connected."

"Look. I know you left with somebody. Where did you go? Who picked you up?"

"I can't talk long," she repeated, her voice getting faint. Static kicked in.

"Are you a prisoner?" he cried out in concern. "Do you need help?"

"It's too late for that," she said sadly. After a moment, then she added, "Call him."

"Call who?" he asked.

"Call the man from before. Regarding your mother's death." And, with that, she was gone.

He stared down at his phone in shock. "Call who?" he whispered. "What the hell," he roared. He got up, paced around. Who the hell was she telling him to call? Something to do with his mother's death?

He shook his head, as he walked around and around and around. Finally he turned and cried out, "Who the hell am I supposed to call, damn it!"

When his phone rang again, he looked at it in frustration. The ID read Private Caller. "Hello," he answered.

"If you would stop screaming," the man said, "I might help."

He stared down at the phone. "What the hell are you talking about?"

The man groaned. "You know that it'd be so much easier if I could get past this stage and have people not freak out, but I don't have time for this shit."

"What are you talking about?"

"Your aunt called me," he replied, "and she wants me to talk to you."

"You heard from her too?" he asked excitedly. "I just got off the phone with her, but she didn't sound okay. I'm trying to find out where she is, and she wouldn't tell me."

"That's because she doesn't know," he said quietly.

"What do you mean, she doesn't know?"

"Your aunt has no idea where she is. She doesn't know what she can do, what she can't do. The fact that she's even communicating is a feat in itself."

"I don't understand," Leon said. "Why is everything like talking in Chinese all a sudden? I don't understand why it's not clear. What the hell is going on?"

He took a long slow deep breath. "Look. This will be a bit of a shock."

"You think? I'm past the point of being worried about shocks," he snapped. "I want some answers. Who are you?"

"And I have one answer that you won't like."

"What's that?" Leon sat down at his desk, exhausted.

"I am Stefan Kronos. We've spoken before."

Stefan Kronos? Why hadn't his name come up as one of Leon's Contacts then? Instead it read Private Caller, so maybe Stefan had a new phone. "What is going on? Just tell me, dammit," he spat in a tight voice.

"Look," Stefan said. "I'm sorry to tell you this, but your aunt is dead, and she was contacting you and me from the other side."

CHAPTER 13

AFTER LEAVING THE doctor and his wife in a full-blown spewing temper fit, after which she was hoping the doc would kick his cheating wife out of the house, Abby got back into her vehicle and returned to the station. Now she was more tired and fed up than anything.

As she walked in, Harvey looked up at her, smiled. "Hey, I've been looking into the case files that our PI had been working on."

"Good," she said. "Hopefully he found something other than a cheating wife?"

Harvey looked at her in surprise, clearly confused. "A cheating wife?"

"Don't worry about it. It was more of a nuisance than anything. What did you find?"

"Well, he's the one who supplied a lot of the information on the sister's murder," Harvey noted. "He's been running a full investigation into it but can't get any information to satisfy his client. He's even made notes in here, like, 'No answers. Yet saying nothing found will *not* get us paid, but there's really not a whole lot to find.' He's got personal notes about her being fairly aggressive and determined to find answers. Although maybe not any longer."

"No." She nodded. "Particularly as there have been phone calls to Leon—so she's no longer a missing person—

but her absence isn't helping us close the cases. What else did you find?"

"I looked into a bunch of the PI's cases. We do have a couple divorces happening now because of the work he did, and he does have a couple companies grateful for the job he did on tracking employee theft and things like that, but nothing really hard-core. Nothing popped."

"Right, what about relationships? Did he have any?"

"Not in the last few years that I can see," he noted. "He was married. His wife left him, saying that he was never around, except to get drunk and fall asleep on the couch, and was more interested in his cases than in her."

Abby winced at that. "That's got to be a hard thing to hear."

"Particularly when he was the one pulling in the income, since the wife wasn't working at the time. Of course, now with the separation, she's back at work."

"Interesting." Abby shook her head. "I just wonder if any happy marriages are out there."

"Oh no, you don't. You don't get to ride the *Why bother? All relationships end up in the sewer* train."

"No, of course not," she said, with an eye roll. "How about completely miffed and unamused about people's propensity for lying?"

"Hey, that's just the reality in the world we're living in right now."

"But it doesn't have to be," she argued. "Is everybody a cheater? Does everybody break their vows? Is everybody just out for themselves?"

"Sometimes. And certainly in some of the people we live and work with, yes," he agreed, "but it's not everybody."

"So, I just have a skewed view of humanity because of

the people I work and live with, is that it?"

"I think it's mostly the cases that we have to work," he murmured gently. "When you think about it, it's not as if we're dealing with the most honorable, ethical, trustworthy types."

"No." She shook her head. "That's a definite no. So nothing with the PI, yet he's got the same manner of death as the two students."

"Exactly. Did you find out anything at the plastic surgeon's office?"

"Only that his wife's a lying piece of shit." She tiredly sank into her chair, then explained what had happened that morning.

He listened, and his jaw dropped, as she explained what she found at the house. "Seriously?"

"Yeah. She's been bending over clear throughout her marriage, just not with her husband." Abby reached for her cup of coffee and took a sip. "Meanwhile, constantly having him followed, accusing him of what she was actually doing." She sighed. "And I did talk to the coroner. He has absolutely nothing on these deaths that are helpful."

"No, so far, we don't have any connection either."

"Well, we've got connections," she clarified. "We've got the manner of death. We've got the same plastic surgeon, even the same PI involved. And there's got to be more. If we've got that much, there has to be more."

"Not really," he said. "We have to consider the fact that, you know, he's the only private investigator in the local area, so it makes sense for the wife to use him. He's also one of the cheapest, and that would be important too. So he could be a complete anomaly."

"Maybe." She hesitated. "We need something."

"Well, we might need something, but we sure don't have it."

"No, we don't." She shook her head. "I know the other thing is possible that he just up and died too. The heart can just stop working, and that would make more sense in his case than it would in the other two."

"Right, and what about the women? Have you gotten anywhere on that investigation?"

"I've still got to check in on a couple students who left earlier that day. Plus, more were home sick that we didn't get a chance to talk to." She stood. "I think I'll go do that now. We need to cross all the *T*s, dot all *I*s, before the next murder happens, and we're taken off this one."

"Of course we wouldn't be taken off it."

"No, but our attention would be, particularly if we don't have any avenue to pursue."

"What about Leon?"

"Well, he keeps getting phone calls, although I don't know about recently, from his aunt," she said, "and that's enough to keep him thinking that maybe she's okay and is actually on her way home from wherever the hell she is." At that, her phone rang. She groaned, looked down at it. "Oh, speak of the devil."

"Hey," Harvey said, "I know this is a private conversation. Let me just, you know, go down and talk with the guys for a few minutes. Use your charm. He sounds like a good guy. Besides, he's into you. You don't have many of those."

She glared at him, then at the phone, as she sat down. "Leon, what's up?"

"I'm going crazy," he stated flatly. "That's all there is to it."

"Oh, great," she replied, exasperated. "Like I need that

shit."

"Stefan Kronos? Can you bring him on board?"

Wincing, she'd been trying to ignore this name. "Not sure. Nobody here likes the public to think that the department couldn't solve a case with just traditional solid police work, so they've turned to a psychic—even if the psychic was valid enough to help out."

"Well, if the psychic can help, why don't you use him?" he asked, his tone getting irritated.

"Look. You called me about this," she reminded him. "I don't know what your problem is, but I'm busy. So, either you've got something valuable to say to me or you don't—in which case I'll hang up right now."

"Wait," he shouted.

"What?" she snapped, her temper flowing freely. What was it about this man that set her off so much? It was easy to blame it on her cases, but that wouldn't be the whole truth. In truth she liked him. That just made her fight against the attraction harder. Not only did he push buttons she had no time or energy for right now but he was connected to one of the weirdest cases she'd seen.

"I had another phone call from my aunt."

"Oh, good news." She settled back. "Why didn't you say that from the beginning?"

"Because it's not that easy." He then went on to explain what Gertie had said.

"Back to that damn class again."

"I know," he agreed, "but it gets crazier. While I was sitting there, trying to figure out what man she was talking about regarding my mother's murder, I got a phone call."

"Yeah, who was it this time?" She pinched the bridge of her nose. "Look. I'm not trying to be snappy, but I haven't had much sleep. I'm very short-tempered and short on patience."

"So am I," he replied. "Are you sitting down?"

"Yes, I'm sitting down. What?"

"Stefan Kronos called me."

She froze. "Seriously?"

"Yes, seriously. I didn't even believe it was him at first. He said my aunt called him, so he'd call me."

"Jesus Christ." She pinched the bridge of her nose even harder, almost bringing tears to her eyes.

"I know. Not what I expected either."

"You don't get anything that you expect when you deal with Stefan."

"So, you do know him? Regardless he knew you."

"Yes, I had to consult with him on a couple cases." She hesitated; knowing Stefan could open a ton of issues she didn't want to deal with right now. "What did he say?"

"He said my aunt's dead."

Silence. "Ah, crap." She did know Stefan; he was bang on with most issues, so, if he said Gertrude was dead, Abby was inclined to believe him. "And do you believe him?"

"According to him, my aunt is trying to talk to me, and I'm not getting the message."

"Well, that's no surprise, given she's possibly dead." There was a note of humor in her voice. Not that it was terribly appropriate, but anything that would push away this whole psychic thing would make her feel more comfortable. Except her headache was starting to boom, even just at Stefan's name coming up.

"He said you're very psychic yourself, but then you keep all these walls up to keep the dead out."

"Well, if you knew the dead were walking into your

walls, wouldn't you put up thicker ones?"

There was silence in the other end. "Detective, have you ever talked to the dead?" he asked.

"No. Have you?"

"Well, according to Stefan, I have. Apparently it's she who's been calling me on the phone, and the reason for the static is because she's dead."

"So they have really shitty cell service?" She snickered.

"Stefan told me that she was murdered."

"*Great.* Did she very kindly tell you by whom or how or where she happens to be, so we could put some of this to rest?"

"Stefan said that's not the way they operate."

"Yeah, I know that's not how they operate"—she groaned—"which is one of the reasons why I don't like even bringing up that subject because they never give you any straight answers. They just give you a whole lot more shit to deal with."

He gave a strangled laugh. "Sounds like you really have dealt with some of these things before."

"I have, and none of it has been very satisfactory."

"Stefan told me that he helped you close a case. Is that correct?"

"Yes," she replied cautiously, "depending on what you mean by *helped close.*"

"Are you always this cagey?"

"Did you hear what you just phoned me about?" she asked. "So, if you don't have anything to help me with," she snapped, "why are we even talking?"

"Because Stefan says it's important that you open up."

"Open up to what?" she murmured.

"He said that he told you that you needed to open up, or

some of these deaths wouldn't stop." His voice lowered, he asked, "Have you seen this killer before?"

"No," she replied, "in all honesty, neither have I seen anything like this type of death. So I don't know what Stefan's talking about." Of course she was lying; even now her headache boomed at the thought of taking down her wall.

"He said that killers change. They grow. They improve, and what they can do is hide from the common people by cloaking themselves."

"Cloaking themselves," she murmured.

"Yeah, that's the term he used. But he did seem to be grasping around, trying to find a term to make it something that I could understand."

"So often when you talk to Stefan, he's way over your head anyway," she remarked tiredly.

"Well, he seemed to think that it was really important that you deal with some issues in order to stop whatever is going on."

"He said that?"

"Yes, although he didn't specifically say that it was related to my aunt."

"Damn good thing because that's not happening." And, with that, she hung up. Then she sat here, trembling for a very long time, more grateful than she expected to be that Harvey had taken off to give her some privacy. Who knew she would need it just to regain her composure?

"Damn it, Stefan," she muttered. "What have you gotten me into?"

And there he was again, in her head, just like last time.

The same damn thing as always, Stefan murmured. *Murder.*

"I don't know anything about this murder."

No, but you could if you wanted to.

"Damn it, that's not fair. You know how much pain this causes me."

Nothing is fair about this, he said, his voice harsh in her ear. *And your wall is causing this.*

"Which is why I walked away and slammed that door shut."

Yeah? So you tell me… How closed is that door now?

LEON WALKED INTO the police station, asking to see Abby. The woman at the front desk made a phone call and then looked up. "She's not in the station."

He frowned. "Damn it."

The woman shrugged. "I can have you leave a name and number, and I'll get the message to her."

He turned. "Don't bother. I'll just phone her."

He headed back outside again. He stood here, his hands in his pockets, studying the damp, wet weather. Nothing quite like Seattle for bringing in some rain, when it should have been hot and sunny. He strolled back to the parking lot. Almost at his vehicle, he looked up to see Abby running toward the station's front door to beat the oncoming rain.

He called out her name, but she didn't hear him. He increased his pace and raced after her. He called her with a shout, just as she was opening the door. She turned to look up and saw him. Immediately she frowned. He matched her frown with a deeper and darker one of his own.

"What do you want?" she asked grumpily.

He chuckled. "Are you always this cranky?" Then he noted the man at her side, her partner, Harvey.

"Yep, she absolutely is," Harvey said. "Abby, I'll go on in. I'll talk to you in a bit." And he went inside.

She looked at the retreating man and then at Leon. "Why are you here?"

"Because you didn't answer me about Stefan. Did you talk to him?"

She opened her mouth and then snapped it closed.

"You did, didn't you?" He was so damn happy to hear that.

She glared at him. "What's it to you?"

"Look. We need to talk," he said, "and I don't think outside in the pouring rain is really a good idea."

At the word *pouring rain*, she looked up at the gray sky and groaned. "I almost made it inside dry."

"Well, we can do it here, if you want." He looked at the alcove that was the entrance to the station. "Or we can go grab a coffee."

She hesitated and then nodded. "Fine, let's go grab coffee. A little coffee shop is around the corner."

"It's likely to be busy."

"It might be," she muttered, "but we might get lucky, maybe not."

As they walked over, she looked at him. "You don't seem too upset about what Stefan told you."

"I remembered the last conversations I had had with him—after my aunt paid him to contact her dead sister, my mother."

"Did it work?"

Leon nodded. "It did. Stefan wasn't happy about doing it, but, like today, he called me afterward and said that my mother told me to move on and to live my life and to stop going down this pathway."

"That sounds like a mother," she noted.

He nodded. "Yes, that would definitely be her. We were very close. It gave me a certain measure of satisfaction to know that she was safe over there, whatever *there* was. But it was still very difficult in so many ways."

"Of course," she replied quietly. "It would bring up all of the horrible memories of losing her all over again."

"Exactly."

"Did Stefan give you any help as to who killed her?"

"No, and my mother couldn't tell us either. Apparently that's common."

CHAPTER 14

"IF I WERE murdered, and someone contacted me on the other side, I would tell," Abby said bluntly.

That startled a laugh out of Leon. They'd reached the café. He stepped forward to open the door. "Maybe, but then you're a special case."

She shrugged at that, as she walked inside. "I've just seen too much injustice in the world," she murmured. "I would like very much to see somebody pay the price."

"But do they ever really?" he asked.

"I'm not getting into a discussion on justice and the merits of our penal system."

"No, we need to focus on Stefan."

"We really don't." She winced, then spied a table in the back.

"I'll grab two coffees." By the time he reached her again, he picked up the conversation without missing a beat. "Why don't you want to work with him?"

Reaching for her coffee, she quickly took a sip. "It's not that easy."

"He told me that you have certain abilities."

Abby snorted. "I think he says that about everybody."

"Really?" He was obviously surprised at her answer.

She nodded. "Yes, it seemed like, every time I met him, he was telling me that."

"Well, he didn't say anything to me about having abilities."

"No, but I wouldn't be at all surprised if he does the next time though."

"And do people really have abilities, or is it just him?"

"I would say he's special," she stated succinctly.

"Is that the only time you've ever worked with him?"

"There were a couple cases." She shrugged. "And, yes, he was very instrumental in bringing the cases to a successful close, but he was very unsettling to work with."

"Ah." Leon nodded. "I can see that. I remember being quite shocked at just how much he knew."

"Yes, and that's just a minor part of it too." She shook her head. "He knows stuff that you never expected to think about anyone else knowing," she murmured. "And to know that somebody else could look at you and see that stuff, it's very unnerving."

"But he can help?"

"What do you want me to say?" she asked. "If your aunt is truly dead—and I'm very sorry to hear that—but, if it's true, what is it that we're trying to do here? If I don't have a location of the body, with no idea who killed her, I don't really have very much to go on."

Leon slouched into his chair and nodded. "And I get that, but Stefan also seemed to think that you could stop a particular killer."

"Yeah, he was adamant about this four years ago and then again two years ago," she noted, "but that doesn't mean this has anything to do with me."

"*This?*" Leon immediately jumped on her wording. "You said 'this,' like you knew what he meant. Do you think whatever's going on is related?"

"I have no idea." She glared at him. "You just spoke to Stefan yourself. Why don't you ask *him* more questions?"

"I would, but basically he told me to talk to you."

"Of course he did." She rolled her eyes. "He has his ways of sending me people who he wants me to speak with, to convince me that I should be doing more."

"Doing more?"

"Yes, doing more, along *his line.*"

"So, you can do stuff like that?"

"I don't know that I can do anything," she backtracked immediately.

"No, no, no, obviously something is here that we have to get to the root of."

"No," she stated, speaking succinctly. "Nothing is here to get to the root of."

"Look. He said something else. Stefan made it sound like you were in danger."

She frowned, then shook her head. "What do you want me to do? Wake up one morning and just do something psychic? That's hardly even feasible." When he hesitated, she added, "It's not like I can turn on a switch or say some magical little rhyming spell out into the universe and start to see stuff. No. It's not like that. Stefan talks about me having walls? You have walls too," she pointed out, "but do you know how to pull them down?"

He shook his head slowly. "I guess it is a bit far-fetched to expect you to know how to do something instantly, isn't it?"

"It is. And it's the same for him. He expects me to do something I don't know how to do. I don't know what to do about it and would mostly just like it to all go away. Matter of fact, it's literally a huge headache for me."

"He seems to think a killer is out there."

"Do you how many killers I deal with on a regular basis?"

"Fine." He winced. "So maybe that's not the best example."

"Back then," she said, "I spent a lot of time thinking about it, racked with guilt over it all, but I couldn't fix it last time, and I'll not fix it next time. Some of this is just beyond human understanding." She rolled her shoulders to ease some tension.

"You look exhausted."

"I am tired. I don't have any answers to give the families. I don't know if whoever killed your aunt is connected to these two students, but it sure would have been nice if somebody would have asked that question when they were busy talking to her."

He winced, then sat back. "I'm sorry to say that I didn't even think of it."

"Of course, because your focus is your aunt, but I don't have that luxury. I have two dead students, and I have a dead private investigator, and they all have families."

He nodded slowly. "I'm sorry. I seem to be taking up a lot more of your time. I didn't really mean to."

"No, you did mean it, and it's all right. I get it."

"No." He shook his head. "You don't. Yes, I know that it sounds like it's all part and parcel of the business at hand." He hesitated and then figured, what the hell, and added, "But I also really like you, and I find myself drawn to you."

"You're not drawn to me," she corrected. "You're drawn to the answers you're hoping I have. And the idea that, once you get them from me, you can move on with your life, putting all this behind you. Including me."

"You don't know me that well, Detective," he said, with a smile.

"Agreed. I don't know you that well," she replied immediately, "but some things are universal. And that is one of them."

"Do you often let people walk in to take you out for coffee or have relationships because you are a part of the case?"

"I nip it in the bud right off because that's just a no."

"Because of what is expected of a police officer or because you don't want to have anything to do with anybody who is part of the case?"

"It'd be pretty damn hard to find anybody in this world who's not involved in somebody's case, somewhere," she noted. "And I would never make a distinction on that, if I cared enough to get involved with somebody. But it's not a smart thing to do right now. It splits my focus, and I can't have that. Plus, I don't want to cause any rift in the station by having a relationship with somebody involved in a case."

"Is that because I could be a suspect?"

"We're all suspects in some way or another," she said bluntly. "In this case, you have an alibi, but it's still your aunt, and you do still benefit from her death."

"In what way?" he asked in surprise.

She stared at him. "Are you not aware of her will?"

He thought about it and then nodded. "There is just the two of us, so I suppose she would leave me whatever she has to leave me, but I hardly think that's worth killing her over."

She looked at him in surprise. "*You* might not," she murmured, "but an awful lot of people would kill for a hell of a lot less, and then there's that beautiful brownstone she owns. And what about that cash drawer she's got stuffed to the brim?"

"I still don't get it," he muttered. "And you're right. I wish I had asked more questions."

"Ha, it's never that easy and won't be the next time, if there is another time either. When she gets through to Stefan, and she gets a chance to talk, it won't be about that either. Maybe if you went to meet him, you might have somebody actually contact her, and you can ask a few questions yourself. But, when they come through with the burning need to come through, like she just did, it's for something completely different—usually messages of love and forgiveness for family members."

"Sounds like you really do understand."

"I don't have much choice," she said tiredly.

"You want to tell me about it?"

"No, I really don't."

At that, Stefan burst into her brain. *It's a good time to tell him.*

"No," she snapped. And then she realized she'd said that out loud. She glared at Leon. "I have to go back to the station."

He leaned forward, grabbed her hand, and asked in a low whisper, "Is that Stefan?"

She sat back. "Does he talk to you like that too?"

"No, but he told me that he can talk to some people in their minds, without warning sometimes."

"You must have really had a heart-to-heart with him."

"Well," Leon added, "you and I do have a lot of interests in common. And I think Stefan was trying to give me a heads-up on you more than anything."

"A psychic matchmaker? Yeah, that sounds like him too," she snapped. "And, yes, it's him, speaking in my head, and he drives me nuts because it makes me look crazy."

"Not to me," he said.

"Well, then you are an anomaly because almost anybody else listening to me would say that I was a nutjob—and I'm not playing that game."

It's not a game, Stefan snapped in her ear. *This has gone on long enough. People are dying.*

She glared again at Leon. "I have to go."

"You could at least tell me what he was saying."

"No, that I cannot do." And, with that, she raced away.

LEON WATCHED HER escape. Abby had picked up her pace and was flat-out running across the street to get away from him, which just added to the fascination of who she was. Stefan had said an awful lot more that Leon hadn't shared, but basically she was in danger, and she had the ability to stop something, but she refused to listen. She had good reason for refusing to listen, Stefan shared, but he couldn't let it go, and he couldn't stand the thought of seeing her killed or other people die, all because she was being stubborn.

Hell, Leon wanted to be stubborn himself. It had been a hell of a blow to hear Stefan say that his aunt was dead. But to even consider that she'd used his phone to communicate with Leon just blew him away. It was also devastating. But, as much as it was devastating, he'd already known when Stefan told him; at least he'd already suspected. The phone calls had been very strange, but, as soon as Stefan said it, Leon understood.

Who the hell needed to find out that their only living relative was dead? Murdered even? Gertie had been a great woman, and it would be a hell of a mess to clean up. But somehow they needed to find her body, so he could put her to rest in the plot right beside her sister in the family crypt.

A space for him was there as well, but he wasn't too bothered where he ended up. It was such a weird feeling to think that he was all alone. He was an orphan of the world right now, not a place he ever expected to be, not when he grew up with a father, a mother, and an aunt. But here he was, the last of them all. He shook his head at that, got up, thanked the woman with a smile, and stepped outside.

He wouldn't get a hold of Abby anytime soon. That was obvious; she would just pull back farther and try to avoid him even more. He understood it, but, at the same time, it made him sad.

He couldn't imagine what the guilt was like, particularly if somebody had died because of her inability to open up that aspect of her subconscious.

In his family, he had been more of the opinion that they should leave well enough alone, instead of contacting Stefan over his mother's death. He had certainly believed everything that Stefan had said back then, but it hadn't changed the outcome. It hadn't changed anything; that was the part that really bothered Leon. Even though people on the other side apparently could talk, and his mother was there, whatever *there* meant, it didn't change the fact that she wasn't here.

She wasn't in this world. She wasn't someplace that Leon had the ability to touch her and to hold her and to tell her it would be okay. Because, of course, it wouldn't be okay anymore. His family lived with the pain. His family lived with the fear. His family lived with the shock of sudden death, and not only sudden death but knowing that it was at another person's hand. It had changed their lives forever.

Gertie became harder and more bitter.

Leon himself had closed up, becoming much less open to the world around him. Of course, inside, he frantically studied everything he possibly could about the dark side because now a whole new field had opened up, and he was desperate to learn more. But just learning about it wasn't the same as actually experiencing it, like he had.

It was almost terrifying to think that so much was out there in the world than he had ever known was possible. And it's something down the crazy pathway that he was currently on, and he didn't regret it because he'd had a first-time experience with Stefan. And speaking to his mom meant that there really was life after death. The fact that his aunt had now been murdered on top of his mother, his father, and apparently Gertie's fiancé, was just horrifying.

At the same time, he knew that they would all be together. That was the one thought that made him smile.

"Gertie, is Mom there? Are you holding her hand, like you said you would?" he murmured to the world around him. Because really he got an awful lot of comfort in knowing that there was life after death. A couple businessmen walked by, looked at him strangely, and hurried past. He just smiled.

They didn't know what he knew.

CHAPTER 15

ABBY RACED INTO her office, only to see the guys grinning at her as she walked in. She glared and sat down at her desk. Eyebrows shot up, and she ignored them because nobody really understood. Not like she did. They didn't understand the intricacies of what she'd been through and what Stefan was pushing her to do. Not to mention the simple fact that she didn't have a clue how to even do it.

And then there was Leon.

In her head Stefan whispered, *But I can show you.*

She shook her head, desperate not to say a word out loud that would make her look like she was absolutely losing it. The job was everything to her. It was her heart and soul, her driving need to help people in this world. And in the other. He whispered yet again. She glared hard around her, but thankfully nobody was close by. She whispered back at him, "Stop it. I don't want to be sanctioned for being crazy."

Well, if we could do something about these murders, he said, *I wouldn't have to bug you.*

And, with that, she firmly closed the door to her mind, shutting him out. Somehow she'd managed to learn how to do that, without too much trouble, but nothing else.

On impulse, she checked her emails but found nothing really important. She got the lab test back from the coroner, but, as she read that, nothing was there, no cause of death, just *Subject died of unknown causes.* She swore at that because that was the last hope of finding something not *woo-wooish* about this whole damn thing. She went through the rest of her emails, took care of some of the business that had to be done today, and realized that she owed a visit to the private investigator's ex-wife. But maybe Abby could get by with just a phone call. She dug out the information and quickly dialed. When the woman answered, she explained who she was.

"*Huh*," she said, "I knew that job would kill him one day, if the alcohol didn't."

"We don't know for sure it was the job or the alcohol that killed him," Abby clarified. "He was found dead in his car."

"Well, that's almost divine justice too," she noted sadly. "He and that classic Mercedes of his were inseparable. He was in it all the time."

"Well, it was part of his job, wasn't it?"

"Of course. That's one way to look at it."

"Did you have any contact with him in the last forty-eight hours?"

"No. He and I haven't talked for at least a couple months."

"So, no sign of a reconciliation?"

"Good God, no, I was done with that."

"Got it. Do you know if he had any enemies? Given his line of work and all?"

"He probably has dozens of them," she stated. "He was working for that one crazy professor and had been for years. I know he was frustrated with her because he could only find so much information, and it didn't seem to matter what he found. It wasn't enough."

"Well, I think an awful lot of desperate people are out there, looking for answers," Abby stated, trying for a moderate approach.

"Yes, I imagine there are. I know myself, after living with a private investigator, I would never hire one."

"Why is that? Do you think he didn't do the job justice?"

"Oh no, I think he did, but I don't think any of the answers he found brought people any happiness," she explained quietly. "They were always looking to find cheaters or criminals of some kind. So, getting the answers might have helped in one way, but it made people very sad and angry at the same time. When I left him, I swore I would deal with sunshine and roses for a change, instead of all the negatives in his life. All he had were clients looking to find people doing something wrong, like spouses who wandered or employees who stole. I didn't want to live in that world anymore. He couldn't understand it because, to him, it's how he made his living, and, in a way, it was what he lived for."

"Well, without the one, he couldn't have done the other," Abby said.

She replied, "And I get that. I really do. But he didn't understand how I needed to see something good in life too and not all the negative that he kept bringing home every day."

"Did he talk to you about his cases?"

"Somewhat," she replied carelessly. "I told him that I didn't want to listen, that it wasn't anything I ever wanted to hear."

"No, not if that's what you've been trying to avoid."

"And again, he didn't get that," she murmured.

"Do you have any children?"

"No, I didn't want any, and neither did he. He was never home, and I wouldn't raise them on my own," she declared. "So, with that not being an issue, when it came time to separate, it became a very easy thing to do."

"Of course," Abby agreed. "Then it's just about splitting up the possessions."

"And all he wanted was a couple of his favorite chairs and enough furniture to fill an apartment. That was it. So I took the rest, with no money between us. We just split everything down the center, and that was fine."

"Do you work?"

"Yes, I'm a lab tech. And, no, I don't know anything about the cases he was working on. Again it's not something I want to know."

Something was sad about that, yet, at the same time, Abby could understand how the woman might have felt. Abby herself didn't feel that way, but she saw that for somebody who didn't want to lean into the darker side of life, then sharing her life with a private eye would be difficult. That woman had a choice, but Abby knew she did not. This work is what she did, and just the thought of quitting or doing something different made her heart stop. She knew that leaving this work would put her on the path to a slow death. Trying to do something different would eventually kill her.

"Good enough. Thanks for talking to me." And, with that, she wrote off the ex-wife. Just as she was about to end the conversation, the other woman asked, "When can I have his body?"

Abby stopped, looked at the phone in surprise. "Will you handle the funeral arrangements?"

"We're separated but not divorced."

At that, something prickled in the back of her mind. "Meaning you'll inherit everything."

The other woman gave her a flat-out reply. "Yes, that's exactly what it means. Do I need his half of our assets? No. Would I have killed him for his half? No, but thank you so much for reminding me what a harsh world we live in."

Abby shook her head. "Nobody needs to be reminded of that. I deal with this stuff day in and day out. As for when you can have his body, I don't know yet. Definitely not for a few days." And, with that, she hung up.

Her mind was buzzing, yet all of it ending up in threads that went nowhere. As she looked up, Harvey sat in front of the huge timeline they'd set up with all the different cases posted.

"I don't know how they could possibly all be related," he said, turning to look at Abby.

"Well, I just talked to the private detective's wife, and I'm not sure either." She sighed. "Although she did say that he'd been working for Gertrude for a long time."

"So, you've been talking to Stefan again, huh?"

She nodded. "Yeah, I spoke to him." Well, it was a partial truth.

"About the last case?"

"No," she murmured, "about this one."

He just gave her another stare.

She shook her head. "So, what do you want me to say? It seems like the woo-woo shit is happening again."

"Oh, crap," Harvey said. "I was really looking forward to a nice clean bloodbath."

"And I agree with you, but guess why Leon now believes his aunt is dead?"

"Stefan?"

She nodded. "Apparently it was Gertrude on the phone, trying to get through to Leon, but the reason she couldn't get through to him because of all that static was because… wait for it,"—she looked at Harvey, raised her eyebrows, and very dramatically added—"she was calling from the other side."

He looked at her for a long moment, and then the corner of his lips twitched once, then again, and he burst out laughing. "Wow, since when can ghosts use technology?"

"According to Stefan, it's not all that unusual," she muttered. "But, man, it sure pushes my buttons to even think about it."

Harvey was still laughing when he finally managed to get up. "That just defies everything."

"I know. I'm not too impressed with it either." She eyed her phone suspiciously. "Have you ever wondered how many people are on the other side, waiting in line to use a stupid phone to contact somebody here?"

"Nope, and I really don't want to."

"Neither do I, but now that Stefan has put that idea in my head, I can't let it go."

He chuckled. "Yeah, and every time the phone rings, you'll be wondering who it is and where they may be calling from."

"Exactly." She glared at him. "I get that you think this is hilarious, but it also means that she's dead, and we don't have a body."

"Well, it means that Stefan thinks she's dead, but, until we have a body, we can't confirm that."

"I know." She raised both hands. "But, as we learned through our last case, everything with Stefan has a way of turning out the way we don't want it to and exactly how he says it will be."

"I know, and that's pretty freaky," he agreed. "As soon as you said his name, I knew we were right back into the same old mess, though we didn't have to deal with very much of it back then."

"No, it closed pretty quickly. And that was partly because of Stefan's help."

He nodded. "And that is also what gave you that reputation too."

"A reputation I don't want." She stared at him.

"I don't think reputations are ever what anybody wants." He gave her half a smile. "It's just something that happens because of what you do."

"I didn't do anything."

"And again, I don't think that matters much."

"Fine. Let's just get this one closed fast then, too," she said, "and we can move on to something normal."

"Or maybe not because you seem to have this bent for woo-woo."

"Stop saying that," she said crossly.

"Hey, I'm only calling it like it is. Especially when you consider that now the damn phone lines are b-b-bugged."

For whatever reason, he was particularly tickled by his own joke, which he seemed to think was absolutely hilarious, and it sent him off in a fit of gasping laughter again. By the time she heard a voice over the din, she turned to see the captain standing there, glaring at her.

She shook her head. "Honestly, we're just letting off steam."

"Except for one thing," her captain said. "I heard mention of Stefan Kronos."

She winced. "Yes, that is true."

"I thought I made it clear that you weren't supposed to contact him without going through me first," he snapped. "That is not something we want this department to have a reputation for."

"I get that," she muttered, "the problem is, I didn't contact him."

He looked at her in surprise. "Well, who did then?"

She sent a sideways look at Harvey, but he was still giggling too hard to be of any help.

"Stefan contacted me and Leon."

The captain shook his head slowly. "Oh, no. No, no, no. We're not doing that again."

"Oh, I get it," she agreed, "but I'm not sure what you expect me to do about it. What do you think he had to say? It was all about these victims." She pointed at her whiteboard. "Well, mostly about one in particular."

"Which one?" he asked, studying the board.

"The professor."

He looked at her, at the board. "What? What do you mean the professor? I thought her nephew had heard from her."

"Yes, he did." Then she took a deep breath. "According to Stefan, the phone calls were from her, but she was calling from … the other side."

The captain stared at her; then his face went stark white. Afterward he turned without another word and walked out.

She wanted to do the same thing, but that option wasn't exactly there for her. She looked over at Harvey, who had finally gotten his hilarity under control.

"Wow, he took that well."

"You think?" Abby shook her head. "I think he just

wants this to go away."

"And you know the way to make this go away," Harvey said, "is to solve it."

"Agreed, so let's get at it." She rolled her neck sideways. "We've got a lot of work ahead of us."

"Well, the first thing would be to find the body."

"And that means we need to track her last movements. So let's get camera footage from the university, see who this person back in her life might be, and where Gertrude may have gone. That will give us some idea of what we're potentially looking for."

"Do you think she might be still on the campus?"

"I don't know. If you think about it, the last place that we know where she was is when Leon dropped her off at home. After that we don't know. She would supposedly then meet this person from her past."

"And do you think that person from the past is related to her fiancé?"

"I don't know," she replied quietly. "Really no way to tell."

As she was about to request the video footage that she needed, her phone rang. Troubled, she stared at it for a long moment, but saw it was Leon. She picked it up, answered. "What do you want?"

"Wow, nice way to greet a person," he said quietly.

"Yeah, well, everybody's pretty unsettled right about now."

"That goes double for me too."

"Why? What happened?"

"I got into some of the files at my aunt's place, and she was going on and on about being guilty about something and afraid that her sister paid the price."

"Well, if so, it explains why she kept the PI on the case for so long."

"Maybe, but, at the same time," Leon added, "Stefan made it very clear that the dead don't blame her."

"That doesn't mean she doesn't blame herself. And, if she were involved in anything that got her sister murdered, then maybe she was looking for that killer and hoping to find justice."

"Maybe." Leon paused. "I don't know. It's really hard to understand all this."

"Can you send me whatever you have for files?"

"Yeah, I already did. I copied them over to you as soon as I saw them."

"Good." Then she yawned.

"Yawning already, Detective?"

"Well, some of us didn't get much sleep last night," she snapped.

He chuckled. "Depending on how you say that, it could be a good thing."

"Well, it's not in this case. Now if there's nothing else," she snapped, "I'm hanging up. I have work to do."

"Are you always this prickly?"

"Yes." She hung up, then immediately felt bad and quickly sent him a text. **No, just a really shitty night.**

But he should know. He's the one who woke her up.

He responded with a happy face, and then he ruined it with another text. **Dinner?**

She stared at it for a long time, until Harvey came over and asked, "What the hell's going on? You're looking at your phone like a ghost is about to climb through it."

She glared at him. "Not funny."

"Actually I think it is. I don't know how believable it is,

but it's definitely funny."

As she continued to glare at the text on her phone, Harvey came up behind her, read the message over her shoulder, and said, "Jeez, put the poor guy out of his misery and say yes already." He snatched the phone from her hand and typed it in and hit Send. Angry, she reached up and pulled her phone from his fist. But he shook his head. "You know you want to."

"I'll hardly get involved with somebody who's a suspect."

He stopped, gave her a direct look, and repeated, "Suspect?"

"His aunt is dead." She added a wave of her hand. "And he works on the campus where the two students died. Of course we have to consider him as a suspect."

"No, you don't. He has an alibi for the two women. He was teaching his own class, with three-hundred-plus students. So, he's not connected with that. He's not connected with the PI either."

"Well, he could have been the last one to see him alive."

"Maybe, but we also can't place him at the scene where this PI guy was killed in his car."

"I know," she admitted, "but an awful lot of threads don't make any sense. It's a little premature to take him off the suspect list."

"And yet you already have," he pointed out.

She glared at him. "No, I haven't."

"Yes. You have."

"Besides, it doesn't matter. I could always put him right back on again," she replied, "but, if I get involved with him, that becomes much harder and more complicated to do."

"Not for you." He shook his head. "If anybody can keep their head on straight with cases like this, it's you."

"That's not exactly a compliment," she muttered. Her phone buzzed, and she looked down to see that he would pick her up at 8:00 p.m.

"Now look what you've done," she muttered, flashing her phone screen in front of her partner's grinning face. Then knowing she had a slim chance for a way out of this, she wrote back. **Unless I'm called back to work.**

His response came back immediately. **Naturally.**

She raised both hands in frustration. "He's just too understanding."

"Doesn't have to be that way," Harvey noted. "I'm sure you'll find out that he's got warts, just like every other male. You always find a way to push them out of your life sooner or later."

"I do not," she replied crossly.

"The hell you don't. Look. Don't get mad at me for simply stating the truth."

"It's only the truth as *you* see it."

"Of course." He raised his eyebrows. "That's all any of us can see."

"Unless you're Stefan, apparently. Can you believe it? The damn phone used by dead people." She was still thunderstruck by all that.

Even when Harvey nodded, he added, "I know. It just pushes the bizarre into a whole new realm, doesn't it?"

"It sure does."

"What's our next step?"

"We have zero forensics," she noted, "on any of the vics. We don't even have a body in the professor's case, so we need to put a great big question mark up there."

He got up and tacked up a question mark that he had obviously predrawn.

She looked at him.

"Hey, I knew what you would say." He shrugged. "I haven't worked with you for this long without learning how your mind works."

"What the hell is the motive in all these killings? If these deaths are connected, why would anybody go after the students?"

"If it's connected to the professor, then maybe to get back at her."

"Get back at her how? Why would killing two students get back at her?"

"Maybe she refused to cooperate over something. Maybe she knew something. Maybe she was digging into something that she had been warned away from."

"That could work." She frowned. "But why those two students?"

"Opportunity," he guessed. "They were in the front though, so why so public?"

"Because it happened right in front of her?" Abby nodded. "Would make Gertrude feel bad, guilty even. But remember? Another student was between them. What about her?"

"I don't know what to say about that. She's still pretty shaken up."

"Well, if you'd just missed death by a heartbeat, wouldn't you be?" She didn't expect an answer from Harvey. "Particularly when the third student hadn't been sleeping during the event. So how the hell did anybody get past her?"

"Woo-woo," he started to say.

Abby glared at him. "Unless we're looking for killers on the other side now," she replied, "that shit's not funny."

"That shit is our way of surviving how unfunny this really is," he corrected. "And don't you forget it. Maybe killers *are* on the other side."

She groaned. "I know. I know. I know. But just to even contemplate that somebody out there on another plane of existence is killing our people is ..." And she stopped. "I don't even know what it is, besides completely wrong."

"Just because it's wrong doesn't mean it's not happening."

"I get that, but, if so, what are we supposed to do about it?"

"We're supposed to find these killers—on this side or the other, wherever the hell they are—because that's the job."

"And sometimes the job sucks."

"Not sometimes. All the time."

She looked at him in surprise. "Really?"

He shrugged. "Kinda getting a little fed up with it myself."

"I don't know." She shook her head. "That just seems like a defeatist attitude right now."

"Well, it is a little bit more interesting," he admitted. "A while back I was definitely ready to quit, but we got into that woo-woo case, closed it really fast, and now we have this one."

"So, now you're finding it fascinating because psychics are involved?"

"Hey, you know that I've always been interested, since those cases way back when and since I found out my grandma had the sight. I loved reading about those cases. I was hooked, even as a teen."

"I know." She rubbed her temples. "You were supposed to retire at some point, weren't you? You've been around since those cases happened, but you don't mention them."

"Nope, not over thirty years," he stated. "The cases were just enough years apart that there wasn't any connection in my head. Besides, the first happened almost before you were born, and it was years later before you were even a cop."

"If you weren't working the later cases, and given your sleepless nights with your nightmares, why'd you deal with them?"

"We often learn from other people's cases just because you never know when information might be of further value, but I don't remember these first three from like five decades ago." He studied the board and shook his head. "You know what? That's something that's been pissing me off too because it's like, as soon as the case is over and done, it's out of my mind."

"That is simply self-preservation," she said, "I mean, if you keep all that shit in your head, you'll go crazy."

"Who's to say I'm not crazy already." He gave her a bland smile and hopped up. "I'll go put on some coffee."

"If you're lucky, a pot has already been made."

"Naw, I'm never that lucky." And he walked out.

She studied the board and wondered what the hell she was even doing next. They had checked the witnesses. They had checked everybody in the immediate lives of the students, even other friends, and the PI and the plastic surgeon. She frowned. They hadn't checked the other professors connected to either Gertrude or to the two dead students. Was there any other connection to the PI? Something had to be there; she was just missing it.

Frustrated, she got up, walked back to her desk, sat down, and started to run searches. Something had to pop, and she was bound and determined to not leave the office until she found something. Then she checked her phone and remembered she had a dinner date tonight. "Crap," she muttered out loud. "Well, if he thinks I'm dressing up, he's wrong. I don't have time for that shit."

LEON WAS REALLY surprised when she had agreed to dinner, so he had followed up immediately, hoping that she wouldn't back out. But, even as he drove toward her place at 8:00 p.m., he wondered if she would find an excuse and not be there. He wouldn't put it past her, but he was hoping that she wouldn't. When he got there, he was surprised to see lights on. He hopped out, headed toward the front steps, and knocked on the door. When she opened it, he saw the fatigue and the huge dark circles under her eyes. Immediately he offered, "We could order in, if you're too tired to go out."

She looked up at him, and he saw her thinking about it. Finally she shook her head. "No, let's go out. Maybe it'll help to shake some of this into better shape."

Feeling the same sense of frustration within her that he had, he nodded. "Let's go." He led the way to his car, glad that she hadn't dressed up. A little café was around the corner that he really loved. It offered more of a home-cooked meal than anything—just a mom-and-pop operation—but sometimes those were the best. When he pulled up in front, she looked at him.

"I've never been here."

"Just simple home-cooked food."

"I don't even remember when I had that last," she said, stifling a yawn.

"Well, let's go in and get you a hot meal, and maybe you can get an early night."

"That would be good for a change," she muttered.

He led the way, getting a little more concerned the closer she got to the front door because she was obviously exhausted. "You should have canceled."

"No, I wouldn't give you the chance to think that's what I was doing."

"But, if you're tired, you're tired."

"Sure, tired is one thing, but this level of tired is a whole different thing. It won't go away with a good night's sleep."

CHAPTER 16

ONCE INSIDE THE restaurant, Leon and Abby were seated in the back. As they sat down, Abby looked up at the waitress and asked, "May I have a glass of white wine, please?" The waitress immediately nodded and disappeared into the back.

"That should put you to sleep."

"Hopefully it'll help me sleep through the night," she said, stifling yet another yawn.

He looked at her in concern. "Seriously, we can just go back."

"I haven't eaten. I need some food."

"Did you have a chance to look at the email I sent you or no?"

She stared at him in surprise, pulled out her phone, and checked her email. "I got interrupted and forgot about it," she admitted. "Things have been really busy.

"Not to mention confusing and chaotic," he added, with a nod. "Makes sense."

"That might make sense, but nothing else does."

"You'll put it all together," he said.

"How do you figure that?" she murmured, staring at him. "If anybody should be pissed off and upset, it's you. Not only have neither of your parents' cases been satisfactorily closed but we've made no real progress on your aunt's."

"I was concerned about that at the beginning, but, like I said, I've learned to let go of a lot."

"Some of this stuff there is no letting go of." She slowly shook her head. "I mean, if you think about the number of murders that go on in the city all the time, it's just heartbreaking."

"But you have a good reputation for closing cases." She looked at him in surprise. He nodded. "Hey, I did my homework."

She shrugged. "Doesn't matter how much homework you do. Every case is different. The clock starts running as soon as we get the call. We're expected to solve them all, but too often there just isn't enough information to solve them. Does Gertrude's disappearance have anything to do with the first case?"

"Her fiancé, you mean?"

"Yes, I keep coming back to that. That one professor said Gertrude was meeting somebody. Somebody out of the blue, who had shown up from her past."

"Yeah, and I don't have a clue who that was."

"I did call to double-check, but she hadn't remembered anything new or different. Just the fact that she was sure it was a male, which she was excited for Gertrude about, yet that your aunt was uncertain about seeing him again. Both worried and uncertain—definitely not excited."

He looked at her in surprise. "Uncertain?"

"Yes. As in, definitely someone she knew but maybe not sure what they wanted to see her about again."

"Interesting." Leon settled back in his chair. "I can't think of who that would be. She's avoided most men."

"Well, maybe having her fiancé killed way back when affected her ability to trust again. I don't know." Abby shrugged. "Maybe she just never found anybody special."

"Maybe. Or maybe she was waiting for this guy to show up. That's one of the reasons I sent you that file."

"So, what's in the file?" she asked. "I'll take a look at it tonight."

"No, you won't. You're too tired."

"I need to look through it," she said, "unless you can give me the highlights."

He smiled. "It's about Gertie's history. It's about her fiancé. It's about the suspicion of who killed him back then."

"Does she identify a motive?"

"Yeah, the motive is her."

Abby stared at him in surprise. Just then the waitress returned with her wine and menus. "I don't understand."

"We'll talk about it in a minute," Leon stated.

Caught unprepared to order, she grabbed the menu. Helping her out, he ordered roast beef with all the fixings. She thought about that, nodded. "I'll have that too." As soon as the waitress disappeared, she leaned forward. "Okay, tell me more."

"Gertie details a love triangle, and she figured it was her ex-boyfriend—a man she'd broken up with a couple months before going out with her eventual fiancé. She blames her fiancé's murder on this ex, not the guy who did time for it. And the ex shows up afterward, trying to woo her back. This ex had swept her off her feet, but, in her notes, she eventually realizes he wasn't the angel that he professed to be. He had a dark side."

"What kind of a dark side?"

"He was into the occult, voodoo, cults. He was into anything and everything. And back then, don't forget. All kinds of physical things upset people, such as tattoos. He had skull tattoos on his body. He had witchcraft signs as tattoos."

"Now that does not in any way fit with the image I have of a potential partner for your aunt."

"I know, right?" He shook his head. "However, she had pictures to prove it."

"And she didn't want anything to do with him after her fiancé died?"

"She indicated she was really torn on how to handle the situation, as he'd been hovering around, acting like he really cared. When her ex took a job several states over, he asked her to go with him. When she refused, he took off, and she hadn't seen him since."

"Did you happen to check her emails to see if she had had any recent contact with him?"

"I didn't." He frowned. "But I will now that you mention it."

"Maybe that's the man who was coming back into town. I need his name, so I can track him down."

It wasn't long before their dinner arrived. She stared at the huge plate in surprise. "Wow, I wasn't expecting anywhere near this much food," she murmured, after the waitress left.

"Like I said, it's a bit of a gem."

She nodded and tucked in. He watched as she started at one end and worked her way through the entire plate. He was quite surprised to see that she could eat it all. He remained quiet as they both ate. She looked up, smiled. "I was really hungry."

"Clearly you needed it, so I'm doubly glad that you didn't cancel on me."

"I thought about it," she admitted, "multiple times."

"I know, but you still have to eat."

She chuckled. "Plus, I got the rundown on that file that I didn't review." She shook her head. "It bothers me though and makes me worry about what else is falling through the cracks. I'm really busy, sure, but I should have at least glanced through it."

"Cut yourself a little slack. I get that we have an awful lot of deaths happening," he noted, "but it feels like there isn't the same anxiety anymore because my aunt obviously isn't coming back."

"And yet Stefan could be wrong."

"He could be, but it doesn't feel to me like she's coming back."

"I'm sorry," she said. "That's a tough way to go through life."

"What about you? Do you have family?"

She smiled and shook her head. "No, I was a foster kid. After being in that system and watching so many of the other kids, who I knew would wind up in juvie or jail, I decided I didn't want to be like them. I went in the opposite direction."

He looked at her in surprise. "Wow, that is a big deal, considering the environment you were in."

"It doesn't have to be though," she murmured. "When you think about it, we all make choices about which way we want to go in life, and this was what I wanted to do."

"And clearly it's where you belong. I'm thrilled for you actually."

"I don't know. Sometimes it just seems like none of it is important."

"That's the fatigue talking. The job you do is very important."

"Well, I can tell you that my captain isn't too happy that

Stefan might be on this case. That kind of publicity is the last thing the department needs. I'm hoping we can keep it quiet, but I don't know how."

"I hear you there. The dean is beside himself, and not out of concern for my aunt or those students. Still," he agreed, "you're right. If we can track down this guy my aunt was meeting, we might finally get to the bottom of it."

She nodded. "Maybe. We still can't explain how these deaths are happening though. Or that whole *what if* thing your aunt mentioned."

"Well, that What If topic was the lecture for that day. We had talked about it before she presented it to the university as a potential lecture thread. We discussed all the different things in life that people talk about, and the *what ifs* that arise, like, what if something were to happen, how would they handle it? Most people don't even think about it. But what if we did have aliens arrive? How would the world, our government, or other governments handle it? How would each individual person handle it? What would we do in a case like that?"

"So, the discussion she was actually facilitating in class was …" And her voice trailed off.

He nodded. "What if there were a back door to our minds."

"Meaning that other people could access our minds?"

"Yes, exactly."

"So, mind control is killing them? Or what?"

"Well, that was the thing. Many ideas surfaced. Some people thought such a thing would allow people to control what the other person did. Maybe it would make them say things that they wouldn't normally say. Maybe it would change the way they thought about something. But, if you consider that the brain is the center of a working human, then having anybody else have access to that space in our head could change everything about us. What if somebody could access, you know, one of our government leaders and have him do something dangerous, and, if anybody tried to stop him, then just access their brains too?"

"In other words, if this were possible, it's not a technology or a skill set we would want the enemy to have."

"It's not a skill set or an ability we would want *anybody* to have, as far as I'm concerned," Leon said. "I'm sure that people would say that hypnosis is one step in that direction."

She frowned at that. "We didn't check to see if anybody was doing hypnosis, did we?"

He laughed. "I don't know, did you?"

She flushed. "Sorry," she murmured. "I keep forgetting that you're not part of the team, so you're not up on the research."

"Well, it sounds like maybe you should check into something like that. Even if only to prove that something like that was impossible."

"Meaning, like the back door to the mind could actually be through the front door or through something like hypnosis?"

"Well, it came out in class. I have her notes on it. And considering the fact that two students would end up dead in Gertie's class, as far as the students are concerned, there was something to what she said. I don't believe it myself and I have spoken to my aunt in the past and she didn't give hypnosis much credence to begin with."

"Really? None of the students interviewed said anything like that to me."

"Well, I have several of them in other classes, and I've

heard rumors from the kids. They all think something connected the lecture to the deaths."

"And what do they think that connection is?"

"I don't know, Detective. That's not something I could ever get a clear answer on. But rest assured. They're all talking about it."

"Then I need to talk to them. Again. Or maybe Harvey can do that. I'll ask him. Maybe somebody saw more than they knew and either didn't realize it was important or didn't realize what they were seeing."

"That could happen too, couldn't it?"

"Way more than you think," she muttered. She scrubbed her face. "I'll take a look at that when I get home. Did you send me her lesson files? Her notes on that class?"

He shook his head. "No, they're at the university."

She thought about it. "Then I'll make a trip to the university after I get home."

He looked at her in surprise. "Tonight?"

She nodded. "Yes, tonight. It just feels like something out there is waiting to happen, that something will still happen, and I don't want to be caught unaware."

"In that case I'll drive you because you probably can't get into her office without somebody. Besides it will save a bit of time as we came in my car."

"No, probably not. That's a good idea. I'll take you up on that, thank you." She looked around and asked, "Can we leave now?"

"Sure, if you don't want any dessert."

"I don't have any room for dessert," she exclaimed.

"They do serve a mean apple pie."

She was tempted for a moment, then shook her head. "It'll have to be another time. I really want to get going."

"Fine." He stood, and, the moment he did, the waitress came right over, and they settled up the bill. As Leon led Abby outside, he asked, "Do you need to go anywhere else?"

She looked up at him in surprise. "What do you mean?"

"Just what I said. Do you need to go anywhere else or just to the university?"

"Just to the university." She frowned. "That's an odd question."

"No, it's not. I thought I heard your phone buzz, when I paid the bill, so I wasn't sure what that was about."

She pulled out her phone and frowned. "It was my phone. I didn't even look. I was too tired and hoping to not have to answer it."

"COME ON. LET'S get you home." He gently placed his arm around her shoulders.

"No," she said, shaking off his arm. "We'll go to the university."

"Are you sure?" He hated to feel so worried about her, but something was so valiant and yet at the same time so vulnerable about her, particularly tonight.

She glared at him. "Yes, I'm absolutely sure."

He raised both hands in surrender. "Fine, be a glutton for punishment."

"Too many bodies are out there," she snapped. "I won't have another one on my neck."

"And I'm not sure you should take any of them on as being your responsibility. You have to look after yourself too."

"And I am," she said. "I just had a wonderful hot meal, and I thank you for that."

He nodded. "You're welcome, but it doesn't change the fact that you're still running on fumes."

"Ha! So now you're a shrink, are you?"

"No," he replied, frustrated, "just a concerned citizen who can see somebody burning out from both ends."

"Well, that part's true enough," she admitted. "Not enough sleep and too much happening during the day. It's hard to get my mind wrapped around it all because I can follow no single thread that would get me anywhere."

"All you can do is follow whatever is in front of you."

She nodded. "First, I want to see your aunt's actual notes though."

"And that's what we're doing."

As he turned on the car's engine and headed in the direction of the university, she asked, "What made you choose this school?"

"All the good reports from my aunt as much as anything." Leon shrugged. "She'd always been a huge advocate of working there, so I figured I couldn't go wrong. Besides, teaching wasn't something that I was unaccustomed to doing. I just wasn't sure I could do it at this level. I wasn't even sure I wanted to," he acknowledged, "but there was something fresh, something lively about these students. The age factor, I think. They were all free of the parental controls. Free of the schooling they were forced to do but didn't want to do. At least they were here because they wanted to be—or at least that was the dream I would hold onto."

She smiled. "I guess it's tough when you have to teach kids who don't want to be there."

"Well, a certain number of kids don't want to be in these classes, but it's what fit into their schedule, so they were there. Some are there because they really want to be, and then some are there because they've got to have so many credits in a certain elective."

"I get it," she said, with a nod, "but it's like anything, like any job. Parts you love, and parts you don't. And you just hope …"

And here, he chimed in to finish with her. "… that the parts you love are better than the parts you don't."

She laughed. "Well, at least we can agree on that."

"I think we could agree on a lot of things," he muttered. "We just need a little more time and relaxation to find out what."

"Maybe. I don't know. I need this case to break," she stated. "It already feels like it's heading into the cold files."

He pulled into his usual parking spot. "Let's go."

"I'm surprised you left them in her office."

"No reason not to. I don't think the dean would clean out the office without notifying me."

"Maybe not, but he could."

"I have the digital copies anyway, but I was pretty sure she had everything in her files."

"Wait. So you're taking me to her office to get the paper files?"

He nodded. "Yes, I told you that."

She shook her head. "No, you told me that you saw the files beforehand."

"Sure, I saw them before in her office, and then I went to the digital copy and realized that her notes were there as well. I'm not sure they all are though, so better to have both."

"Okay, let's just get this done."

"By the way, how did you end up in foster care? Is that when you met Stefan?"

She glanced him. "What put me in foster care," she said in a harsh tone, "was the loss of my family."

He winced.

"Well, you're talking to the right person. Only, in my case," he noted, "it happened much later in life."

"Well, it's not always that easy when it happens early in life either," she said, "when you're not mature enough to handle the news or to handle the change in your circumstances. Or how much you'll hate everything around you because of what happened, to the point that you even start hating those who left you, even though they died, because you can't stand the situation you're in."

"Agreed." He nodded. "But did you ever find your way to forgiving that little girl?"

CHAPTER 17

ABBY STARED AT him in shock. "Why would I have to forgive myself?" He smiled, and the smile was so gentle and so full of life that she was immediately drawn to it, yet hated it at the same time. She tried to shut down her reaction, but it was like he'd already gotten in under her guard. "You're dangerous."

"No, I'm not dangerous at all, not to you. But I care. Whether I like it or not, I care, and I don't want to see you killing yourself over this case."

"Ha! A couple days ago you were the one pushing me to do more."

"I know, and I'm sorry," he apologized instantly. "It was wrong, I shouldn't have. I was just so afraid for my aunt."

"And now because some guy says she's dead, you're willing to walk away?"

"It's not that easy," he explained, "and certainly not just because Stefan said she's dead. I heard her voice on the phone too."

"And that totally creeps me out," she said.

"Yet, according to Stefan, you're the one who has more to do with this field than most of us."

"That's just Stefan talking."

"So, did you talk to your parents after they died?"

"You just won't let it go, will you?"

"It's important. I don't know why, and I'm not sure how, but it is."

"Well, until it becomes *more* important, we'll just drop the subject." And, with that, she stormed ahead through the university parking lot toward the building, the subject closed. She knew she wouldn't get away with it for long, not very long at all if he had his way. But she had to do something to keep her sanity, while she was dealing with Stefan hanging around. Even at that, his voice popped into her head.

You can run …

She groaned.

"What's that?" Leon asked.

"It's *your* friend, Stefan," she snapped. "He's just helpfully telling me that I can run, but I can't hide."

He grinned. "That's cool."

"Now you sound like a teenager," she said crossly.

"Sometimes I wonder if we aren't better off if we keep that part of ourselves around. Although full of anger, those years had a lot of fun times too. Adulthood can sometimes seem like everything is just one big headache, one set of rules after another, and we never really find any joy anymore."

"Being a teenager seems like more angst than anything to me. Foster care was no picnic, and headaches are a mainstay in my life."

"I've seen you struggle with these headaches," he noted quietly. "Have you got them checked out?"

"I have," she snapped. "They couldn't find anything except to tell me to let them know if they got any worse."

"And did you?" He led the way to Gertie's office.

"No, if it's something serious, I'd rather not know."

He snorted. "That's just being stubborn."

An odd look crossed her face, and he wondered if Stefan was talking to her again. That he could do so telepathically blew Leon away, yet somehow seemed normal.

AS THEY APPROACHED his aunt's office, Leon stopped and froze. She stepped in front of him. "What's the matter?" Turning, seeing the door ajar, she said, "Oh shit. I presume this isn't the way you left it."

"Hell no." He reached for the knob, but she slapped his hand away.

"Don't touch anything." She pulled gloves from her pocket and then, as an afterthought, pulled out another pair for him. Using her foot, she kicked open the door to find the room had been ransacked, at least partially. "Do you have any idea why somebody would do this to her office?"

"No," he replied quietly.

"But you said the files were here too."

"I'd already taken the hard drives home years ago," he murmured, flicking on the lights with his elbow, "but I was looking for the hard copies too."

There was just enough in his voice for it to ring true. "I get it." The room was small enough that no way somebody could hide in here, but, at the same time, who knew how long it had been since it had been ransacked? She shook her head. "This just adds another layer."

"It does, indeed, but is it a good layer or a bad layer?"

"Right now, the jury is out on that. We have to figure out what they were looking to find here." She looked around. "It's interesting though because I don't really see anything disturbed, except for her office drawers."

"No." He looked at the filing cabinet. "These are still

locked." He walked over to them. "The bottom one has been jiggered, but they couldn't get it open."

"Did you close it?"

He nodded. "And I had trouble with that lock myself. It was really hard to open."

"So maybe they couldn't get it open because it's damaged."

"Could be."

"Now the question is, did it get damaged because somebody else was trying to get into it before?"

"I hadn't considered that." He frowned. "I really don't know." He turned to her. "But this is where her lesson plans and tests are kept. You want me to get those now?"

She nodded.

"Give me just a minute to get them." He got into the drawer and grabbed two folders—one for lesson plans, one grading keys—then shut the drawer, jiggling it to prove to Abby it was locked again.

She nodded again. "I'll contact the forensics team and get them in here for this, but now I want to head straight to her house."

"You think he's gone there next?"

"I wouldn't be surprised, and, after that, we better check your place."

He froze. "Seriously?" Then spun on his heels. "Come on. Let's go."

She raced out ahead of him. "I wish I had my car."

"And, if you did have your car, what would you do?"

"I'd send you one place. and I'd go to the other."

"Well, all the information's at my place," he noted, "but the money is at hers."

"Would they know the money is there?"

"I don't know. I did move it though. So, if he's looking for it in the same place, it won't be there."

"And why did you move it?"

"Because a ton of money was just sitting in her drawer."

"Good point." They raced to the aunt's place first but found no sign of anyone having been there, and the front door didn't look to be disturbed. "Interesting," she murmured.

They immediately got back in Leon's vehicle and raced over to his place.

As they got out, she noted, "Front door's open."

He swore, and, before she could stop him, he'd barreled inside the house, calling out, "Who the hell's in here?" He heard a *thud*, then a door being slammed open, as somebody racing out the back. Leon gave chase, and she raced behind to find Leon had the perpetrator well in hand, as he brought the young man into the house.

She turned on the lights and raised her eyebrows. "You're one of the students in Gertrude's class."

He nodded. "So?"

"What are you doing breaking into this house?" she asked calmly.

"I didn't say I broke in," he said. "Besides, the door wasn't locked."

"Whether you break in or not, it's unlawful entry," she stated. "So don't sit there and get smart with me."

He glared at her and then gave her a snide look. "Obviously you're not that smart. You can't charge me with anything."

"Yes, I can, and we'll have fun matching your fingerprints to the ones you left in Professor Milligan's office too."

At that, his eyebrows rose in alarm. 'You can't pin that

break-in on me."

"Pin what?" she asked, with a smirk. When he realized that she'd already caught him on that one too, he flushed. "I'm in law school," he snapped. "No way you'll get me for any of this crap."

"Well, I'd like to know what the hell you were expecting to find," she said calmly. To Leon, she said, "Sit him down in the kitchen chair. I'm calling this in." She pulled out her phone, already asking for a squad car.

"Calling what in?" the kid asked, with a snap to his voice. "I came to visit. I checked the house. He wasn't here. It's not like he'll press any charges."

"Yeah, why not? Why is it you think I shouldn't press any charges?" Leon asked curiously.

She finished her call, all the while watching the exchange, a little curious herself. "That's a really good question."

The kid smiled. "Because he's got lots of things to hide himself. and I know all about him."

"Well, that's really interesting," she replied. "In that case I want to know too."

"Well, you're the one who's screwing around with him," the kid declared in disgust. "And you're on the case. So, we know exactly where your heart lies."

"You don't know jack shit," she said calmly. "And considering you're the one who's just pulled a B&E on a professor's office and on another prof's house, you're hardly one to talk. And I'm pretty sure, by the time we're done, your criminal record will prevent you from getting into law school."

He stared at her in alarm. "What do you mean?"

"It's not just good grades that get you into law school,

kid." She shook her head. "You need to finish your degree, and I'm guessing the guys with no criminal records get admission priority over, well, *you* now."

At that point Leon stepped in. "He could finish his degree in prison."

"Good. I'm okay with my tax dollars doing that, but I'm really not too interested in listening to him spout off his cocky bullshit right now. A cruiser's coming. They'll take him downtown, and we'll deal with him later."

"Oh, no, you don't," he cried out. "I have to go to class tomorrow."

"I don't give a crap where you have to go." She walked over, twisted his arms behind him, and stated, "I will take your ID right now though, thanks." He screamed, as if she were really hurting him, but she already had his wallet. "Nice try, buddy. That's a girly little scream for a guy, huh? What'd you do, perfect it? Sit in front of the mirror and try it on for a couple hours? I'm sure all your roommates would have loved that. I wouldn't do that in your jail cell though."

He just stared at her, dumbfounded.

"What's the matter? Has nobody ever talked to you like a real person before? Maybe you're thinking the world won't treat you like everyone else."

"And how is that?" A hard challenge was in his voice.

"Like the shit doesn't come out of your ass like everybody else's," she stated bluntly.

He flushed. "You aren't allowed to talk to me like that."

"Yeah? Who'll stop me?" She checked his ID, laid it out on the table, and quickly took photos of it all.

"Hey, that's illegal."

"Nope, it's not. And since you were caught while perpetrating a crime, we can do all kinds of shit to you." Only a matter of moments later a cruiser pulled up in the front. When the officers entered the house, she explained the situation and told them to take the kid to the station and to book him.

"You can't take me anywhere," he yelled. "My daddy will have something to say about this, and you'll regret treating me this way."

"Well, your daddy ain't going to fix jack shit," Abby replied, "but nice try."

He gave her a smirk. "You don't know my daddy."

"Yeah? I'm sure I'll find out soon enough."

The officers just rolled their eyes at him, and one added, "Every kid has to learn that lesson, don't they?"

"Yep. Daddy's protection only goes so far," Abby declared, "and, once you start breaking laws, it's not the same thing anymore."

"Sure, it is," the kid argued. "You can't do anything to me, but that's all right. Let's go through your little charade, just to make you feel better." He laughed.

She watched as they led him outside and put him in the back seat of the cruiser. "So, who the hell is that kid?" she asked Leon, sitting here quietly.

"He's the son of the dean."

"Wow, I wonder what he'll do with this."

"Up until now, he's bailed him out." He looked at her curiously. "Will you let him do that?"

"It won't be my decision," she noted. "It will be the people above me, but I'll be damn pissed if they do."

"So will I," Leon agreed. "I think it's time for a personal lawsuit, if that's the case."

"Yeah, I wouldn't doubt it at all."

"Regardless, it still doesn't tell us what he was after, and he won't talk either. He's got an attitude and is pretty much an A-plus asshole," he muttered. "Always been a pain in the ass in class too. But we tolerate a lot because of who he is."

"And that's too bad because then he thinks he can get away with everything, and so far he has." Taking a moment, she pulled out her phone. "What's the dean's number?"

He pulled out his phone and gave it to her. "What will you do?"

"I'll tell him what I did." Abby gave Leon a bright, cheerful smile. "Let's not let the kid get to daddy first." When the dean answered, Abby explained, "I'm sorry to contact you so late, but I thought you might want to know."

"Who is this?" She identified herself. "What's the matter? What happened?"

"I just arrested your son for breaking and entering into Gertrude Milligan's office and then into Leon Wellington's home," she replied. "He was caught in the act. I've had him taken down to the station to get booked in."

He blustered on the other end.

"No, sir. You know what? One time you can get him off, twice maybe," Abby said, "but that's enough of this shit. That kid needs to take his punishment like a man, something you've obviously stopped him from becoming." And, with that, she hung up. She looked over at Leon, who stared at her, amusement in his eyes. "Whatever." She shrugged. "Sometimes, you've got to get your licks in when you can. With any luck, he won't get him off, but there's no guarantee."

"If not, I'll definitely be looking into a lawsuit."

"And then you'll be looking for a new job," she noted calmly.

"Maybe. I have principles, and, if that kid walks on this

one," he said, "especially when I have a suspicion that he's got something to do with Gertie's murder, there'll be hell to pay."

"Absolutely, and that is a really good point." She phoned down to the station to make sure that he wasn't allowed out under any circumstances because he was wanted for questioning in at least one murder as well. "That'll get his father going tonight," she noted. "You want to check and see if he got anything from here?"

He nodded. "It looks like he didn't have a chance."

"So, what was he after?"

"I don't know. You want to give me a hand, and maybe we can find out. After this, I suggest we go back to Gertie's office and see what we can find. What was he after there?"

As they went through Leon's house, he said, "This is where I keep the hard drives from Gertrude's place. This is where I keep the stuff that I just brought in and scanned too. I hadn't even had a chance to print them off. As I told you earlier, I downloaded them, so we'd have a digital copy."

Abby took a look at everything. "Send me a copy of everything you've got here. I don't know who's after what, but something of interest was here, and we need to figure out what the hell's going on." She shook her head. "Punk-ass kid. What the hell is he doing involved in this crap?"

"I don't know," Leon replied, "but you can bet that dear old dad is more concerned about getting him out of it instead of fixing this."

CHAPTER 18

T HE NEXT MORNING, Abby walked into the office to hear the captain calling to her. "What's up?" she asked, as she headed to his office.

"The dean called me."

"Yeah, and what did he have to say?"

"You really caught the kid dead to rights?"

She nodded. "We really did. He was booking it out the back door of Leon's house."

"Leon?" he asked sharply.

"Yes, Leon," she replied. "No, there's no relationship, nothing untoward about it, and don't even look at me like that."

"Hey, I'm just checking."

"No, you aren't. You're digging," she replied. "I've had enough of this case. I've had enough of all this shit. I don't know why that kid was in there, and I'm pissed off that he was. Also, Gertrude Milligan's office got busted into, with paperwork and everything strewn about—which he admitted to. I don't know what he was looking for, but I damn well need to find out, and I need to do it now."

"Well, you're welcome to talk to him. He's still in a holding cell."

She nodded. "That's what I planned to do first thing this morning. I called in to make sure *Daddy* didn't get him out on a technicality because the kid's also wanted for questioning in the murders."

"Do you have anything to hold him on?"

"I don't know yet, but, if he hasn't got a damn good reason why he was busting into both places," she stated, "I have to look at him being the closest connection to the murders that we have."

"Well, I—I like the fact that we have something to hold him on," the captain added, "but do you really see him as a killer?"

"I don't know what I see him as. So far he's just a spoiled punk-ass kid, who thinks his daddy will get him out of everything."

"So far he's been right," he admitted.

"Too damn bad but he won't get out of this one," she said, as she walked out. Then she called to have the prisoner brought into the interview room.

Harvey raced in behind her. "You okay? Hell of a night last night again, huh? I missed out on all the excitement again too. Damn."

"Yeah, as always." She shook her head. "You're the one who coerced me to go on that damn date. And look what happened."

"*Look what happened* is you caught an intruder red-handed," he pointed out. "Maybe this will break the case wide open."

"What I'd like to do," she said, "is break that kid's head wide open. He was pretty lippy, spouting off insults, completely certain he could count on *Daddy* for protection."

"Is he likely to get it?" he asked, a comical look on his face.

"I don't know. I phoned his daddy myself last night and

told him what I'd done."

"Was that wise?"

"Well, I figured I should get something in there before the kid could share his version."

"That's true," Harvey muttered. "These kids. I tell you. We do all the hard work, and then they turn around and spit in our eye as they walk out of jail."

"Well, you'll get to see this one for yourself. He's coming up for questioning right now."

"Good." They watched, as he was walked down the hallway and taken into the interview room. She poured herself some coffee, then asked Harvey if he wanted some.

"Of course." He chuckled. "How long will you make him sit?"

"I don't know. How long do you think? An hour?"

He snorted at that. "You got an hour to lose?"

"Not really." Finally, after twenty minutes she got up and walked into the interview room, where he waited. She introduced herself and Harvey, then sat down.

"You took fucking long enough to get here."

She put the recorder down and turned it on, then introduced who was present and what was happening and added, "Note that witness is combative and difficult."

"I am not," he snapped. "What the hell? You made me sit here and wait."

"You waited for twenty minutes," she replied. "Deal with it."

"You could have been here earlier."

"I could have," she admitted, "but I'm busy too. So let's get on with this. First off, I have some questions to ask you."

"Well, I ain't answering shit," he sneered. "Go talk to my old man."

"Oh, I already did. Last night, in fact," she stated. "How was your night in jail, by the way?"

He glared at her. "He just couldn't get me out last night, but it's just one night. So what the hell."

"That's the spirit," she said, "one night, then two. Before you know it, you'll be racking up the years, and it'll be easy-peasy."

"No way," he argued. "Even if I were to go to jail, I didn't do anything, and it'll be a first offense, so I'll walk."

"Maybe, but I wouldn't count on it. So what is your relationship with Gertrude Milligan?"

"Who's Gertrude Milligan?"

"Interview notes. Suspect is again belligerent and unco-operative."

"Stop saying that," he cried out. "I know who you're talking about."

"Good, because I don't have time for your nonsense, so I'll go have lunch. Then, when I return, if you feel like talking, we can try again."

She stood and walked out, Harvey beside her. The kid started screaming as soon as she got to the door and slammed it closed in his face. With Harvey at her side, she looked up at him. "How long do you think?"

"What a piece of shit. Ten minutes?"

"Naw, I think his pride'll keep him going longer than that." She pulled out her phone and checked in on her emails. When the kid finally calmed down, it was twenty-two minutes later. "You owe me."

"Crap," Harvey said. "Why are you always right?"

"Because people are people, and they are shits." Something she said with some frequency in the course of her work.

Other officers were grinning at the two of them. "Got a live one in there, huh?"

"Naw, he just wants to be a live one," she replied. "He's all bluster." Through the glass in the connecting doorway, she saw his father pacing outside. "It'll be fun when *Daddy* finds out what kind of trouble he's causing too."

"You want to go tell him?"

"You know what? Maybe we should let both father and son cool their heels a little bit longer." She headed toward her office and just about made it when the dean called out her. She turned and looked at him. "Oh, hi. What can I do for you?"

"You can let my son go."

"I can't do that right now. Your son is a suspect in several murders." At that, the father's face paled completely. "And frankly he's being incredibly uncooperative and won't even talk to us," she explained. "In fact, you've been uncooperative as well and have yet to send me the threatening letters that Professor Milligan received."

He stilled, mute.

"Like father, like son. Both uncooperative. Go figure. So we're leaving him in there, until he's done with his little shit-fit. That could take, *hmm*, I don't know, maybe another twenty to twenty-five minutes. We've got a bet going on."

"What do you mean, you've got a bet going on?"

"Do you hear all the yelling?"

He nodded.

"That's your son. He's sitting in an interview room. All alone. And he's not happy."

At that, the father flushed, looked nervously toward that direction. "Did you hurt him?"

"*Right.* Of course. We all hurt him, in a room recording

both visual and audio. It's all on camera. Remember that? Everything is up for the public viewing these days, so obviously we didn't hurt him. He's just throwing a temper tantrum, like any good two-year-old."

The father stiffened and said, "A little respect goes a long way."

"Yeah, it does," she agreed, "but we are once again reaping the benefit of you getting your son out of every scrape he's ever been in by pulling as many strings as you could. He's never once faced the consequences for his crappy behavior, and now he's put himself right in the middle of our murder investigations—*three* of them, maybe a fourth where we haven't found the body yet. So I need some answers, and he can't stop running his mouthful of crap long enough to even understand the trouble he's in. So, I won't waste my time talking to him until he's ready. So he—and you—can sit here for as long as he wants to be difficult. Other than that, I really don't care. He can go back to his cell, and I can hold him for another forty-eight hours, before I even have to think about him again."

"That's hardly fair. He's just a kid."

"No, sir, that's not true. He crossed from being a kid into being a man some time ago, and a really bad example of a man at that," she noted. "Right now he's just a spoiled-rotten piece of shit." And, with that, she turned and walked away.

"Wait, wait, wait," he called out to her.

"I don't have time for this," she muttered, "so, if you've got something helpful, great. Otherwise, if you'll just start pleading for your son to walk once again, that's a no-go."

He shook his head. "No, look." He took a deep breath. "He's been really difficult. He lost his mom at a young age."

She held up a hand. "Stop. Lots of us have. We didn't all turn out to be criminals."

"Whoa! He's not a criminal."

"Do you remember me saying that he broke into Professor Milligan's office and that he broke into Professor Wellington's house? I wouldn't be surprised if Leon isn't considering a civil lawsuit right now, against the both of you."

He flushed. "Well, there's no need for that."

"I suppose he knows perfectly well that you would take his job from him, so *perhaps* that will dissuade him." The dean's face turned bright red and then pure white. "I've also contacted the university's board members, since you've got a conflict of interest here, what with your asshole son, of course, and there will likely be some bad press and all."

"No, no. Stop. Wait."

She continued to walk. He came racing behind her.

When he reached out for her, she snapped a word of warning, "Don't touch me."

"Would you please stop?" he asked, a note of desperation evident in his voice.

She turned and looked at him. "What?"

He took a long slow deep breath. "Look. I know he's got problems. I know he's difficult. It's come to my attention just recently that I have probably coddled him and made life a little too easy on him."

"You think?"

He flushed. "He's the only child I've got, and, yes, I spoiled him."

"Spoiling is one thing, but letting him walk on charges like this is a completely different issue."

"But it wasn't anything like this before."

"Yeah. So, he gets away with something small, like shop-lifting, and now he's into breaking and entering."

"Maybe, maybe, and, yes, we'll have to see what we can do about that," he admitted, "but he's not a murderer."

"Well, it depends if he was involved with anybody who is a murderer. Can you actually guarantee me that your son, that absolutely lovely example of your flesh, doesn't have an affiliation with somebody on the unsavory side who might have been involved?"

With that, the dean placed a hand to his heart, and she noted the sweat forming on his temples. Immediately recognizing the signs, she backed him up and sat him down in a chair in the hallway. "You have some things you need to think about, not the least of which is the future of this asshole child you're prepared to unleash onto the world as an adult, who appears to have a very different moral code than I would think you would want for him," she spat. "Sometimes our best efforts at parenting backfire."

"Are you a parent, Detective?"

"No, and I wouldn't wish that job on anybody."

He gave her a ghost of a smile. "He was the most beautiful baby."

"Well, he's a useless piece of shit right now."

He winced. "Could we at least be civil?"

"Maybe. At least the screaming has stopped."

"Could you please check that he's alive? I really don't think I can deal with that if he isn't." The dean still had sweat rolling down his face.

She nodded to the officer sitting outside the interview room door.

He hopped up, took a look, and turned back to her. "He's fine. Just sulking."

"Yeah, he was always good at that too." The dean pinched the bridge of his nose and then slowly got up, looking a whole lot older than when he arrived. "You know what? I think the best thing I can do is go home, contact our lawyer, and see what our rights are."

"You do that."

He looked at Abby in surprise.

"Your attorney will confirm that we haven't done anything wrong." She continued, "The problem is your son, and this behavior needs to stop. At some point in time he has to step up and take responsibility for his actions. I'm afraid that point may already be a bridge too far, as they say."

He nodded. "I can see why you would think that, but not every soul is impossible to save."

"Then I suggest that you find a way to make this work. At the moment, I don't know how far he's gotten himself into this mess. If he is involved in some way with any of the three murders I have on my docket right now, he's toast." And, with that, she turned and walked away.

This time nobody called her back.

HAVING BEEN LET back into his aunt's office, Leon put everything to rights, then sorted it out to see if anything personal needed to be taken home, basically emptying it out for the next professor. It hurt more than he had expected it to. Without a body, without any way to say goodbye, this seemed wrong and premature somehow. The dean stopped in and watched what he was doing. Leon asked, "Are you all right, sir?"

"Not particularly," he replied, his tone heavy. "Your girlfriend took quite a swipe at me today."

Leon nodded and didn't say anything. Certainly wouldn't get into a discussion about his relationship with Abby.

"You expected that?" he asked in surprise.

"She's seen a lot, and she consistently has to put criminals back in jail, which drives her crazy. Particularly if they're repeat offenders, who could have led a different life, but had parents who pulled strings to let these kids get away with murder. I've seen too much of it myself."

"Meaning, my son of course."

"No, not necessarily," he replied. "She's just seen a lot, and you know a young offender starts out that way but doesn't need to end up that way."

"No, I'm starting to realize that."

"If he didn't have anything to do with the murders, then he'll likely get off pretty light."

"And now I wonder if that's the right thing."

"You might want to look at what he would consider the worst thing and see if you can work that out for him."

The dean looked at him with interest. "What do you mean?"

"Well, your son greatly enjoys being seen as 'the man' around here, a big tough guy," he told the dean. "He hasn't yet understood that life isn't that way and that being seen as a real man comes after earning the respect of those around him. So, if you consider what would be the worst thing for him," Leon looked up at his boss and added quietly, "you might want to consider community service in a very public space."

The dean's eyes widened. "He would hate that."

"Exactly. So far, nothing has really worked to keep him on the straight and narrow. Maybe if he sees that he won't continue walking away without a punishment, a consequence that everybody will know about, then he would take a little more care next time."

"Wow." The dean shook his head. "One, I don't even know if that's something we can do. And, two, I think he would really hate me."

"He would hate you for now potentially, or he might realize he's getting off easy. Jail would *not* be a walk in the park for somebody like him at that age."

"I know," the dean admitted. "I was trying so hard to keep him out of there."

"So now he doesn't care because he thinks he can do whatever he wants. He thinks he's untouchable."

"I'll have to talk to my lawyer."

"You do that," Leon said, "but remember. All bets will be off if he's involved in anything uglier."

"The detective hinted that you might be considering a civil suit."

"Yes, I've thought about it, depending on how it all works out. Especially if there is no consequence for your son."

"Even knowing it would be the end of your job?"

"It would also be the end of yours," he stated flatly, staring at his boss.

The two of them gave equal measure to the other, and then the dean nodded. "You're quite right there," he admitted. "Let's hope it doesn't come to that. I love my job here."

"And you love your son. You've done right by one. Now it's time to do right by the other."

"You don't even have kids. What do you know?"

"No, but I work with them all the time," he said. "Your

son shows up late, if he shows up at all. He's disruptive in class. He doesn't give a crap about the subject material. He's disrespectful to staff and students alike. He's here only to put in an appearance, and then he gets to walk, probably guaranteed that he'll get his degree regardless."

"Is he really that bad?" the dean asked in astonishment. "Why does nobody say anything?"

"They can't say anything because, like you just said, it's all about our jobs. You've just told me that I'll lose mine if I sue you, so any other prof who says something about your son knows perfectly well that they're likely to get the ax as well."

"Jesus," he muttered to himself, "am I that bad?"

"When you love what you love and are prepared to defend it, even though it's well past time to do so? Yes," Leon replied. "Maybe it's time for a clean slate here too."

"Meaning, I should resign?" he challenged.

"I don't know about that. I don't think you are completely unredeemable, but I think there is an awful lot of lost faith here."

"I worked so hard to turn this around," he stated, staring at Leon. "How did it all go so wrong?"

"Honestly, anybody who's involved in the university is here because they either want the job or need the job, and they'll play nice to keep it. That's the environment you fostered, and it goes right along with the cheating problem we were trying to address."

"Your aunt was very involved in that."

"Was she?" he asked in surprise.

"Yes, as a matter of fact, she's the one who gave me the names of the culprits involved."

"And you didn't say anything to the cops?"

"Why would I?" he asked in surprise. "What's that got to do with anything?"

"Well, since she was likely just murdered," he explained, "maybe that would give the police another avenue to pursue."

"It doesn't sound like your girlfriend needs any avenues. I think she's just looking at my son."

"That's not true. Besides, if this is a legitimate lead, wouldn't you want her to unravel it and to see where it goes?"

He nodded slowly. "It honestly didn't occur to me."

"Well, now that it has, I would say that you need to let her know."

"I don't think she wants anything to do with me."

"I'll tell her if you want, but she'll come right back to you with questions."

"Yes, she will," he said morosely. "She's like a dog with a bone."

"She has to be. And trust me. If it were your son who was dead, you wouldn't want it any other way."

At that, the dean stiffened. "I'm forgetting about your aunt. I'm sorry. I really liked her."

"So did I," he replied, "and it's just one more murder in my family. Something I would never want somebody to deal with."

"That's right. I remember something about her history. I'm sorry. Here I am so upset about my son being a little shit that I forgot other people are involved with much bigger problems."

"I think that's part of life, isn't it? And we always forget because we're so busy protecting our own."

"Was I wrong to do so?" he wondered out loud.

"No. But, at some point in time, you have to let your kids sink or swim, and, right now, it's all about him needing to sink, so that he can learn some valuable lessons. Life isn't all about getting handouts. It works for a while, and then somebody comes along who kicks your ass, and not only do you not know what happened but you weren't ever given the tools to deal with it."

"Sounds like I'm a really shitty father," he muttered.

"Not at all. What you are is a caring father, just maybe not caring in the right way."

With that, the dean left, and Leon looked around at the rest of the stuff that he had to pack up. He had only a couple boxes, a couple hard drives, and some stuff that he didn't know about that he probably needed to go through. But he wondered if the dean would actually call Abby. Not taking any chances, Leon quickly dialed Abby's number.

"You again," she noted. "It's getting to become a habit."

"Yeah, a nice one," he said, with a grin on his face.

"Says you," she replied, with just enough life to let him know that she had gotten some sleep.

"You need to talk to the dean," he stated.

"And why is that?"

"He said something when he was just here. I'm at the university, clearing out my aunt's possessions," he explained, "but, in the course of our conversation, he mentioned that Gertie told him who the culprits were on the big cheating scandal that happened last year. I didn't know about that either. Yet I don't think he was surprised."

"What!" she said, her sharp voice reaching through the phone, ready to skewer him.

"Hey, hey, hey," he added, "he just told me. I told him that he needed to call you, but I'm just making sure that the information got to you. Please don't shoot the messenger."

"That would be a hell of a motive for killing your aunt."

"It would," he agreed. "Several hearings are coming up, and the scandal is likely to be pretty big, including for the university."

"What are the chances that the dean was in on it?"

"I hope not. He's the one who's gone to bat for the professors involved, which is a good thing because a lot of the students were trying to skewer them in it as well."

"Are any of those students still there?"

"No. They were all temporarily suspended, pending the outcome."

"And if a student is ultimately cleared?"

"They'll be allowed to come back with clean records and any financial aid or scholarships in place."

"And, if they are determined to be guilty, their education is history?"

"Yes, most likely," he noted. "They could apply afterward, but, if you think about it, this is a pretty prestigious university, and most people won't get back into an institution of this caliber again."

"Right. So, futures lost."

"Exactly. Rightly so, at least for some, apparently. These guys were cheaters, after all."

"Yeah, but that means they'll also do everything they can to stop this from ruining their lives."

"Maybe. I just thought you should know."

"Thank you. I'll call the dean right now."

"Good. It'd be nice if I didn't have to tell you that, and he would make the call himself, but—"

"Don't worry about it. I'll give him another few minutes, but then I'll be on it like a road rash."

"Great. He also said he'd heard I was considering litigation."

"Yeah, and that's because I suggested the arrest wasn't his only problem."

"He said that, if such a thing happened, then chances are I would lose my job."

"No doubt, though you might not want to stay there regardless."

"Well, I also put it right back in his lap and said it would likely be the same for him because, if I lost my job over it, I would make sure that he lost his too."

"Ouch, sounds like a little bit of vindictiveness is going back and forth."

"Well, if he'll cause pressure enough to get me to quit, then he's not the dean for this place."

"Let's just hope it doesn't come to that," she said.

"I agree. Did you eat today?"

"I had lunch. Why?" she asked in an absent voice.

"Just checking."

She snorted. "I do know how to look after myself, you know."

"Says you. You ate so much at dinnertime last night that you had me worried."

"Hey, I was tired, and it had been a long day. Besides, I'm a growing girl, and I have a good appetite."

"If that's all it was, I'd be more than happy," he replied, "but I highly suspect it's more a case of getting too busy and forgetting to look after yourself."

"Well, it won't be the first time for that, and I'm certainly not the only one in the world who has that problem."

"No," he agreed, "but it doesn't help you in the end, and I'd like to make sure you look after yourself. These headaches are concerning."

"Hey, we only went out once."

"Yep," he noted, "*so far*. But I really want to do it again. And do lunch and pick up coffee and walk in the park, laugh in the movies, and be moved in the art galleries."

"Why would you want that?" she asked. "My life is a mess. Dead people are all over it. I have cases that'll wake me up in the middle of the night forever. There's just … No," she said. "It's just wrong. Especially for you. You know this. You know … All cops …"

"I think it's important that they have healthy relationships," he explained. "It keeps them grounded, and that is really important."

"Maybe, but it sounds ridiculous. Every time I turn around another cop's getting a divorce."

"And I'm sorry for them," he replied, "but that's not your fault, and, if you work at it, maybe it won't be your future."

"But why do I need more work, when I've signed up for so much already?" And, on that note, she chuckled and said, "And now I have to call the dean." And she hung up on Leon.

He stared down at his phone, but he was smiling; something else that surprised him. He hadn't thought that he was dour until he met her and realized just how much she made him laugh and joke. At that, it was almost like he heard Gertie's laughter around the room.

And he whispered, "Gertie, you know that, if you have something to say, it sure would be nice if you could tell me." His phone rang at that point and groaning, he stared at it to see no number. Was it her? Could it be?

He answered it carefully. "Hello." And there was that

same static. "Gertie? What has this got to do with your lecture?"

And all he heard again was, "What if."

"What if what? What if you were murdered? I know you were murdered," he cried out in frustration. "But I don't know who killed you, and I don't know how to save you." He realized that there was absolutely no way he could save her at all. "Gertie, help me understand what happened. What are you so worried about? Why are you still here?"

The one thing he did understand from Stefan was, if the spirits were still around, such as Gertie, either she had a message or she needed to do something or to see something done. He tried hard to get Gertie to listen to him, but she hung up again. He stared at his phone, not wanting to even mention it, then realized that this couldn't go on. He picked up the phone and, without giving himself a second chance, dialed Stefan.

"Did she contact you again?" Stefan asked, without saying hello.

"Do you ever wonder that you might have the wrong person on the end of the phone when you start out a phone conversation like that?"

"No. Besides, your number is in my Contacts, so I knew it was you ahead of time."

"The phone rang again," Leon said in exasperation, "and it was Gertie again."

"She's really trying hard to get you to do something, isn't she?"

"And it's connected to the university, to that class, I think. But I can't get any further answers." Leon hesitated, and Stefan just waited. "You know what I'll ask," Leon said crossly. "You could at least say something."

"Well, you haven't asked, and I don't know exactly which way you want to do this," Stefan replied. "Can I help? Maybe. Do I want to help? Possibly," he said cautiously, "but I don't have any guarantees for you."

"No, you never do give guarantees, do you?"

"Nope," he said, "that's just life, no guarantees in this stuff."

"Did you manage to get Abby to agree to work on this at all?"

"She says she doesn't know how." He paused, then added, "Any energy work makes her headaches worse."

"Interesting. Her headaches are really ugly now, so maybe that explains her reticence," Leon noted reluctantly. "Still, she's got a hell of a mind-set when it comes to criminals. I don't know so much about the psychic stuff."

"Oh, she has an awful lot of experience in it," Stefan confirmed. "She's just been blocking it out. Which also leads to the headaches."

"Well, it would help a lot if you would explain that."

"And I can't do that," Stefan said gently. "You'll have to get her to tell you."

"Could you at least tell me in what way?"

"Her family," he answered. "Has she really not told you anything?"

"No, she's been avoiding it," he murmured.

"Well, you'll have to pin her down, if you want some answers. And it would be a good idea if you did it soon."

"Why is that?"

"Because I'm feeling the same kind of energy that she had back then. And that wall of hers is dangerous. To herself and others."

"I don't understand. You mean that the same person

who may have been involved in her family is now involved in mine?"

"Well, the cases are connected. Didn't you know that?" Stefan asked.

"What the hell?" Leon said. "How would I know that? And connected how? What case?"

"Her family and yours."

"No, no, no, no, I didn't know that at all. How does any of this relate to Gertie?"

"I'm pretty sure she uncovered something she wasn't supposed to," Stefan said.

"And he killed her?"

"It's possible," he replied in a dry tone. "But don't start going down that pathway, thinking that is the answer, because it closes you off to other revelations that could be there as well."

"I hear you," he agreed, "but we're getting to the point where Abby has other cases, and nothing here is breaking."

"Oh, it'll break," Stefan confirmed. "What you need is for her to tell you the truth."

"I'd love that, but I'm not sure how to make that happen."

"Yes, you are," he said. "You've just been playing it nice. You need to go in there with the big guns and make her talk."

"Yeah, right." Leon smirked. "You know who we're talking about here, right?"

"Yes," Stefan replied. "We have worked together in the past. What she may or may not remember is that I was also involved in her life twenty-five years ago."

"She never said anything about that."

"Well, it's time for her to start remembering that portion

of her life too," he stated, "because, whether she likes it or not, this is all related."

"And can you tell us anything about how it could be related?"

"No. I can just tell you that the energy is very similar, and somewhere along the line there has to be a connection." And, with that, Stefan rang off.

Leon groaned as he sat here. Then, with a decisive move, he stood, grabbed the boxes with his aunt's stuff, took one last look around the office, and, with a heavy sigh, closed the door. He wasn't even sure if he wanted to stay on at the university after all this, but he didn't have a whole lot of options at this point in time. He needed to make sure that he followed this through, whatever *this* turned out to be. Abby and he needed to get to the root of the matter and to find out what the hell connected the cases of his family to hers. And since when did her family even have a damn case? Frustrated and pissed off, he headed to his car, then went to pick up Chinese food and made it to her house soon afterward.

CHAPTER 19

ABBY GOT OUT of her vehicle in front of her home just in time to see Leon standing there at the sidewalk, a large bag of takeout in his arms. She frowned at him. "You can't just make a habit of feeding me," she said crossly. At the same time her stomach grumbled in anticipation. He raised an eyebrow, without saying a word. She rolled her eyes. "Fine." And she marched up, unlocked her door, and let him in. "I do know how to look after myself."

"I think most of the time you probably do," he agreed, "but you're a little off balance right now."

She shot him a look.

"Stefan," he said helpfully.

She didn't say anything but walked inside, dropped her purse and her keys, took off her jacket, and kicked off her boots. She headed straight for the fridge and pulled out a glass of red wine.

"Perfect, red wine goes with anything. Even Chinese takeout."

She smirked. "Especially Chinese takeout because it means I'm too damn tired to cook." She paused. "And thank you." Feeding Migolo first, Abby then brought out plates, sat down at the table, and asked, "To what do I owe this visit?"

"Well, you may not like this, but Stefan is on my back because he said our cases are connected."

"Yes, that is very likely. They were all in the same lecture hall, and now they are apparently all dead."

"No." He shook his head. "I don't mean the two students and Gertie."

"What are you talking about?"

"Whatever happened to your family and my family."

She stopped and stared at him, dropping her chopsticks, already perched on her chair, ready to make a getaway. "No. No way. Hell no. No," she stated, her voice rising. "I'm not going there."

"Stefan said it's connected."

"I don't care what he says," she cried out. "I do not want to believe it, so we're not going there."

"Well, maybe you need to at least tell me what happened."

She immediately picked up an egg roll and took a big bite out of it, stuffing her mouth so she couldn't talk, while she glared at him over the table. Her mind was in turmoil, and her breathing was fast. She'd known this time was coming, but, dammit, she wasn't ready for it. *Did you have to do that, Stefan?*

Do you want to find out the truth or not? he said right back at her. She closed her eyes, knowing there was no escaping Stefan. *I'll leave any time you want me to,* he said immediately.

Sure, she said, *and then you'll be back because it's* for my own good.

He started to laugh, and she glared.

Leon sat here, watching the range of emotions cross her face. "What the hell is going on inside your head?" Leon asked her curiously.

She shrugged. "It's Stefan." She immediately brought

out her phone, called him, and put him on Speakerphone. "Instead of talking to me inside my head, let's do it this way," she stated. "Leon's here with me."

"Good," Stefan said, his tone brusque. "Are you finally ready to look at this?"

"Do I have a choice?"

"No, I don't think you do."

"Fine. Just what is it that you think is connected?"

"The death of your parents and the death of his parents."

"My parents died over twenty years ago," she snapped.

"My father did too," Leon stated, staring at her.

She shrugged. "But your mother didn't."

"No," Stefan added, "his mother didn't, but she was not quite the same after the first attack, was she, Leon?"

"No, she was in and out of hospitals a lot."

"Why?" Abby asked.

"Severe brain injury," Leon stated. She stared at him in shock. He nodded. "Why? Does that make a difference somehow?"

"Yeah. Because then the killer didn't have to kill her," she replied, reaching up to scrub her face. "She couldn't identify him, and, even if she did, nobody would listen, is that it?"

"Exactly." Leon frowned.

"But why kill her ten years later?" Stefan asked.

"She was starting to come out of it," Leon said instantly. "Her memories were coming back."

Abby sat back, her chopsticks still midair. "And did she say anything about her killer?"

He shrugged. "I wasn't there, but the attendant told me that she started talking crazy about somebody she used to know."

"Somebody she used to know?"

"Yes."

"Oh, crap," she said. "Stefan, do you know who it is?"

"No. I recognize the energy signature, but I can't tell you who it is. It's blended into your energy. And it's blended into Leon's."

"So, it's somebody close to us? But I don't know that we have any people in common," Leon noted.

She studied Leon, then spoke to Stefan. "I never met Leon before this case."

"Maybe not," Stefan agreed, "but somebody is in both of your worlds. So grab some paper and figure out who it is." And, with that, Stefan hung up.

She stared at Leon. "I haven't a clue what he's talking about."

"Sounds like he has a good idea though." Leon got up and walked over to the phone table that she had up against the wall, where he found a pad of paper and pens, then brought them back, and drew a line down the center of the topmost sheet. "These will be names of people in my world, and over here you'll list the people in yours." He started making a list. He stopped after six and shrugged. "Outside of colleagues," he said, "I don't have very many people in my world."

"And it gets shorter every time, doesn't it?" she noted, her voice sober.

He looked up at her. "Right. Both parents gone, no siblings, and my aunt now gone." He also wrote down the dean and a couple profs who he knew quite well and a few other people from Gertie's life too. "I have a couple college friends I stay in touch with." He put down their names too. As well as a few from his military and law enforcement friends.

"Wives?" she asked. He shook his head. "Girlfriends?" He nodded and put down a couple.

He added, "I even made it to the altar with one."

"What happened?"

"She decided that it was too big of a decision and that she wasn't ready," he noted. "Luckily it was to be a small wedding, and we would just get married in the minister's office."

"Well, that saved a few hundred thousand dollars and hundreds of people's embarrassment."

"True enough," he agreed. "I wish she'd told me a long time earlier but, hey, whatever." He added her name too.

Helen. "Do you still have anything to do with her?"

"No," he replied, shooting her a glance. "She got married six months later."

"Wow. Okay. So what? You were a trial run to see if she was ready?"

"Something like that." He tossed down the pen and shoved the pad of paper toward her. "You know any of those names?" She went through them one by one and shook her head. "I don't know any of them."

"Fine, now you start."

"Everybody in my world," she complained, "is work." But she wrote down the detectives she worked with, her captain, and a couple friends she'd stayed in touch with from school.

"Boyfriends?"

"Well, they're there," she noted, "but I haven't had any serious relationship in a couple years." But she wrote down the two last boyfriends who had lasted the longest, but she had had no contact with them. She sat for a long moment and then wrote down one more name. "I haven't talked to this one in a long time," she explained, "but he was a good friend."

"Who's that?"

"Robin Brandt," she replied, looking at Leon intently.

He shrugged. "I don't know the name."

She nodded. "He's a songwriter slash composer. That's why I wondered if you knew who he was."

"No, never heard of him." To the kitchen air around them, she spoke. "There, Stefan. A completely useless process."

Not necessarily, Stefan replied in her head. *At least we know it's not these people.*

She laughed at that, then turned her attention back to the food, and she served herself up some more noodles. "How come I'm so hungry around you all the time?" she complained.

"Maybe it's not that you're hungry around me. Maybe it's the fact that I bring food to eat," Leon noted.

"Maybe." She shrugged, pointed her chopsticks at the notepad. "I guess it doesn't really matter though."

"Well, it does if it's important."

"I don't think so, but whatever." She reached up and stretched, then rotated her neck.

"Injuries?" he asked suddenly.

"Shot once, broken leg, couple busted ribs." Then she looked at him. "You?"

He nodded slowly. "Orthopedic surgery on one leg from a football injury, plus my wrist," he stated, holding it out. "No gunshots, thankfully." He looked at her and asked, "Where were you shot?"

"Hip." She frowned. "I spent some time in a rehab center, trying to get walking again."

"So did I."

She looked at him. "Bellevue Rehab Center?" He nodded. "Bingo." She wrote it down. "Doctors?" They had different doctors and, as far as she knew, saw different nurses. "What about therapists?"

"Honestly, I don't have a clue as to the name," he admitted. "It seems like such a long time ago."

She agreed. "I know, and it seems odd that anybody there would have anything to do with us at this point in time."

"And yet Stefan seems to be adamant." Leon paused, considering this. "Were any of your cohorts in the same rehab center?" he asked.

"Sure. Harvey. He was shot at the same time."

Leon looked at her in surprise.

She shrugged. "Yeah, we've been partners ever since." She gave Leon a big grin. "Did you know him before?"

Leon shook his head immediately.

"Well, then that shoots that down," she said, with a bigger smile and a bit of relief. She tossed down the pen. "It's useless." She picked up the red wine and took a big slug. When she slowly put it down, she asked, "Pharmacist?"

"Sure." He tilted his head. "We live fairly close to each other, so it could be that we have the same pharmacist." As it was, they did, but they didn't have the same personal pharmacist or personal doctor though.

Abby shook her head. "All of this is just coincidence."

"Maybe and maybe not," he said. "I'm not a big fan of coincidence."

"As a cop, we don't believe in them, and I know Stefan certainly doesn't," she stated.

"What did Stefan have to do with your family back

then?"

She glared at him.

"You need to tell me," he said, both frustrated and tired.

She nodded. "Home invasion gone wrong. I came home from school and found both my parents shot and lying in pools of blood," she stated succinctly. "I ended up in foster care."

"Oh my God."

She nodded. "Sucks."

"And Stefan?"

"Apparently I was found sitting in the pool of blood and half lying on my mother, screaming out into the ethers, as Stefan would say, calling for help. He's the one who heard me and mentally rushed forward to help calm my screams, and he's the one who called the police."

"Jesus. Did he come into the house?"

"He didn't need to," she stated. "Apparently I was sending—*transmitting*, as he called it. And he is a very strong receiver. He picked it up, connected with me, and, well, he's been there ever since."

LEON LOOKED OVER at her. "Can I read the details of your case file?"

She winced. "What if I don't have them?"

"Well, we can put that to rest right away," he stated, "because, just like me, you'll have full copies. You do, don't you?"

She nodded slowly. "I do, and I've never really looked into it."

"Why is that?"

"Because it hurts," she said bluntly. "It's a time of my

life that I would like to walk away from."

"I get that," he agreed. "I'm in the same boat."

"I know," she said heavily. She got up slowly. "Let me go get my files."

While she went upstairs, he did the dishes and put the leftovers in the fridge. Depending on how late they worked tonight, she may need more food. He was still puzzled by her astronomical appetite, but he was glad that he had considered it ahead of time and had brought lots. He didn't give a crap about the cost; he was more concerned about her being so worn down that it was almost impossible to fill her.

He wasn't sure if that was normal or not. But he suspected *not* was the answer. He had read enough about all things esoteric after his aunt's visit with Stefan, and he remembered something about it being normal for psychics to burn through food at a rapid rate in order to keep their energy functioning.

He had to wonder if that wasn't partly what was going on in this case. Was she actually a functioning psychic, without even knowing about it? Was that even possible? He could almost hear Stefan in his head, saying, *Of course it's possible.* Then again, almost anything seemed possible at this point. He had the kitchen cleaned up, when she came back down, carrying paper files. "I suppose you also have them digitized."

She nodded mutely. "I haven't looked at them in a very long time."

"Then maybe this is the time," he said gently.

She nodded ever-so-slowly. "Still feels wrong."

"Murder is always wrong," he said in an equally crisp tone.

She winced. "You have an answer for everything, don't

you?" she muttered.

"No, not at all. At least not for any of the questions that are superimportant."

"You mean, like, who murdered our families?"

He nodded.

"So, if we are connected," she asked, "why is it we haven't met before?"

"I don't know." He shrugged. "I'm sure Stefan would say something about things happening at the time they're meant to."

"I hate crap like that," she muttered, as she plunked herself down at the table across from him. She pushed one of the files toward him.

"Why the two files?"

"One is the evidence. The other was the detective's files—observations, things that he thought worked and didn't work in the case."

"Sounds like there was a bunch of both because both files are thick."

"Several detectives looked at the case over the years," she noted, "but nobody's ever solved it."

"Was there any DNA?"

"No, that's part of the problem."

He opened the folder and winced when he saw the crime scene photographs. "Oh my God."

"Yeah. Now you know why I don't really like to open these."

"Oh, I get it." But he resolutely turned the pages and kept on looking.

"You're really a glutton for punishment, aren't you?"

"We can't turn back the clock," he replied, "but maybe we can save somebody else."

"That's what I always said before, but it feels like we're running out of time."

"Do you really think there are other victims?"

"I don't know," she admitted. "I thought all of this centered around your aunt."

"Well, she's gone," he said, his tone raspy, as he thought about it.

"And we couldn't have stopped it because we didn't have a clue what was going on, and those two students had died just beforehand."

"Why would you think it's centered around her?"

"The private eye, the students, and the murders in her history."

"So, do you think they're all connected? Still?"

She nodded. "Yes, I do. I also think, well, I thought, that it was all connected to your aunt."

"So, what are you thinking now?"

After a long slow deep breath, she let it out very carefully, then said, "I think it's all connected to you."

CHAPTER 20

THAT WAS LOW blow to his gut. Abby watched him absorb the blow, then slowly straighten. He stared at her in shock. "What? What do I have to do with any of this?"

"Well, think about it. The same logic that applied to thinking that it was all surrounding your aunt applies to you, even more so now because your aunt's gone."

He shook his head. "I didn't have anything to do with her fiancé's murder. I didn't have anything to do with my mother's or my father's murders."

"That doesn't change the fact that more people around you have now been killed."

"The students were in her class."

"Yes, and I'm still pondering that."

"I didn't even know them."

"That's not true. You said that they were in other classes."

"Sure, but I don't know them outside of the classroom. I'm not sure that Gertie did either. And I still don't understand what the significance is of having those students die. Particularly two of them."

She nodded. "I know, and the women did look enough alike to be sisters."

"They worked on that intentionally though."

She stopped for a moment and looked up at him. "Oh,

my goodness. I wonder." She pulled out her phone and called the coroner.

"You know it's Friday night at ten o'clock," he bellowed in a blustery voice. "You'd better not be calling to bring me out to another body."

"No, I'm not. Can you run DNA between the two female students?"

"Why?" he asked bluntly.

"It's a theory I'm working on, and I need to rule it out."

"And what theory is that?"

"That they're related."

He paused for a moment. "And what good would that do?"

"It could do quite a bit," she stated. "I just don't know where this ultimately ends."

"Fine, I'll set it up." And, with that, he hung up.

When she put down her phone, she felt Leon's gaze on her.

"Why would you even think of that?"

"Because they look alike, and they've worked really hard at it. And … how much of them working hard at that is because they possibly found out they actually were related?"

"And how would they do that?" Leon asked.

"I'll tell you how. Those genealogy sites," she said. "They're pretty popular right now."

He slumped back. "*Huh.* I never even considered that."

She watched in amusement as Migolo hopped up onto his lap and sprawled across his lap. His hand automatically stroked Migolo's sleek back, as if it were as natural as breathing.

"No, it just hit me. We assumed that the resemblance was because of surgery, but what if they already had that basic structure?" She looked at her phone. "Do you think the mothers will answer any questions?"

"I don't know, but, if they do, and we find out differently, you've sure got some more ammunition. The problem is, what about the father?"

"Which one? Ah, that's a good point too."

"And the one has a temper, doesn't he?"

"Yes," she murmured, "and in a big way. Things were pretty tense in that home."

"Well, you could always give them a call."

She winced at that but picked up her phone, and, when she got a hold of Sammie's mother, Abby stated, "I need to ask you a couple more questions."

"When will this end?" she wailed.

"It's hard to say, but something I don't know. Is your husband within earshot?"

"No, he's in the shower right now. Why?"

"Because the question I have to ask is a little delicate. I need to know if there's any chance those two women could be related."

The mother gasped. "Oh my, I really don't like to hear that."

"No, but it's something that I need to know. They did look alike."

"Yes. Yes," she agreed, "they did." Her voice was hesitant, just enough to set Abby's instincts alight.

"Did you adopt your daughter?"

"No," she stated, "I didn't. Sammie's mine. You can check her birth records."

"Unfortunately I will have to do that," she replied, "but, so far, you haven't answered my question."

"I don't know," she said, "maybe."

"Did you have another child?"

There was silence on the other end of the phone, and then she whispered, "Yes," and started to sob.

"And did you put that child up for adoption?"

There was a broken "Yes" coming through the phone.

"What adoption agency?" she asked. She provided the name to Abby, who thanked the mother and said goodbye. It took only a few minutes afterward to find it online. But it was late Friday night, and nobody would be open. She groaned at that. "I'll have to call the other mother to make sure Aimee was adopted."

"And you realize of course that Sammie's mother, if this is how it plays out," he noted, "she's now lost two children."

"Yes, I realize that. And that brings me back to the question of what the hell is going on here?"

"True, what of Aimee's mother?" Leon asked.

Abby hesitated. "I'll have to call her too."

"No time like the present," Leon noted, "and you really have no option right now."

She nodded and dialed Aimee's mother. When the woman answered the phone, her voice was hesitant, as though somehow afraid of the call. "I don't have any more information for you."

Abby replied, "That's fine, and you need to know that we're working hard on your daughter's case. But I do have a personal question I need to have answered."

"What is it?" she asked.

"Was your daughter adopted?"

The woman sucked in her breath. "Yes," she whispered.

"Did she know that?"

"Yes," she said.

"Did she have anything to do with one of these genealogy websites?"

The woman bawled.

Abby winced and looked over at Leon, who nodded. He pushed the notepad and pen toward her. She nodded. "And what did it tell her?" she asked, when the woman could finally speak.

"You'll find out sooner or later," she murmured.

"Yes, I will, and it would have saved us a lot of time if someone would have said something about this earlier."

"Well, it was relatively new," she explained. "We were still adjusting to the news."

"The news being?"

"They were sisters," she replied brokenly.

"And they knew it?"

"Yes, they recently found out, and I think they hated us for it."

"Well, I think that might be a fairly common reaction, if you find out you're adopted and that the best friend you've had all this time is actually your sister. Who else knew about this?"

"I don't know," she said. "I don't know who they told. We were all a bit out of sorts, and then—what a terrible way for this to end up."

"Yes, that is terrible, and I'm so sorry for that. Did Aimee find out anything else that upset her?"

"Like what?"

"I don't know. Were there other siblings?"

"I don't think so," she replied. "There was something about cousins, and she would look into it, but I don't know if she did or not."

"Was she looking to connect with her family? With her birth family?"

"It was discussed, but Sammie didn't seem to think her mother would take it too kindly. Her stepfather didn't know about it."

"Right, that makes it difficult, doesn't it? And it also depends who the birth father is," Abby added.

"Aimee was put up for adoption, and we adopted her because we knew she needed a home. We did it in good faith, and everything blew up in our faces."

"Unfortunately that can happen," Abby said. "You gave her a good life, and that's what you need to hang on to."

"Thank you," the other woman said, as she hung up the phone.

Abby looked over at him. "Okay, so now we have two women who were sisters, who didn't know they were sisters. They found out, probably after taking a closer look at each other and then doing a genealogy test, only to find out what they suspected was true. There was anger at both families. Sammie's stepfather apparently does not know." Just then her phone rang. She winced. "It's Sammie's mother." She answered, "Hello." Instead of the mother, it was the father.

"What did you say to her?" he snapped. "She's crying like a crazy woman and won't stop."

"I'm sorry," she said, "we only spoke for a few minutes."

"Well, it's that damn bitch of a daughter of hers, isn't it?"

"You mean, *your* daughter?"

"Yeah, my stepdaughter," he snapped. "That girl was nothing but trouble."

Abby put it on Speakerphone, so that Leon heard the details. "I'm sorry you feel that way. She's dead now. She won't be a problem to you anymore now, will she?"

"Oh, she'll be a problem right through the next ten years

at this rate. I just wanted a little peace from her. All she did was make trouble."

"In what way?"

"She kept bugging her mother about other family. I told her there was no other family, but she wouldn't listen to me."

"Where did she get the idea there was?"

"I don't know. She'd been on this kick for a while."

"So not just from somebody at university?"

"Well, that friend of hers was bad news too. I forbade Samantha from having anything to do with that Aimee person, but Samantha kept ignoring me. What are you supposed to do in this day and age when your kids won't listen anymore?"

"Well, she was an adult," Abby noted gently. "At some point in time kids have to make their own decisions."

"Well, she made the wrong fucking decision," he snapped. "Now stop calling us. The next time you call us, you better have a killer." And, with that, he hung up.

"Don't you just love how everybody is not responsible for anything in life?" she asked, looking at Leon.

He shook his head and shifted slightly, sending Migolo off his lap. The cat shot him a look and sauntered away. "Obviously, somewhere along the line, the daughter—Sammie—found out something, heard something, found something of her mother's, suspected something, and went a little further to find out."

"Well, when you consider the close resemblance to her friend, that alone might have been enough. They were both at the university for a few years."

"So this curiosity might have started a couple years ago."

He nodded. "It would make sense. But it still doesn't

explain the killings."

"Neither does it explain that they were killed in Gertrude's class. Do you know where she got the idea for the What If class?"

"Yes, from her sister, my mother."

"What?"

He shrugged. "They used to play a what-if game all the time."

She sagged back in her chair. "Like the lecture she was doing?"

"Yes. She did it as a dedication to her."

"Gertrude was really obsessed about her sister, wasn't she?"

"Yes, particularly after talking to Stefan."

"Sounds like Stefan didn't help much."

"It gives you a perverse sense of satisfaction to say that, doesn't it?"

"I'm just frustrated," she admitted. "Honestly, he's also been a huge help. But, at some point in time, you wonder if that help is of value."

"That's only because you don't want to look deep within yourself."

She glared at him. "This isn't about me."

"It's always about you," he stated. "When people say it isn't about them, they're lying."

"That's not fair," she protested. "I'm trying to solve these cases."

"Yes, you are, but you already know—from somebody you apparently trust enough to help you with these cases—that you need to open up some walls."

"What's the point of opening up walls," she said, "and letting all that hurt in?"

"What if you could let all that hurt *out?*" he asked. "You surely can't believe that you've dealt with any of this, when you've keep it all locked up like you do."

"I've dealt with as much as I can," she said quietly. "And you don't need to judge me for that."

"Ah, I'm not judging you," he replied gently. "I'm trying to help you open up. Because you'll never be fulfilled or even begin to heal if you can't let out all this pain."

"No"—she shook her head—"you don't understand."

"What don't I understand?"

"I was there when they were murdered."

LEON STARED AT Abby in shock. "Seriously?"

She nodded.

"Well, who did it?"

She gave him a bitter smile. "Do you really think I haven't tried to figure that out? Do you really think there is any way I would still be living like this if I had a way to solve it?" she asked. "I have no idea who killed them. Especially if the cases are connected to the killer who could be watching you right now."

He nodded. "Which is why Stefan's telling you that you need to open up and to be aware," he said, with a decisive nod.

"Not as though I want to consider it," she snapped bitterly. "You also have to understand this is a hell of a big wall in my head. Bringing it down won't be easy."

"Of course," he agreed. "You saw something shocking and horrifying and painful, and you were too young to process any of it."

"I'm not sure age has anything to do with it," she argued

tiredly. "Just think about what you said. Does anybody ever get to process any of this stuff?"

"I don't know," he noted. "It seems like there's no end to it, doesn't it?"

"There isn't any end," she agreed. "I did the best I could. Then I walked away and tried to rebuild my life, but I was fully aware it would only work if I could get this completely out of my head."

"So, you stomped on it?"

"No, metaphorically speaking, I put a large concrete lid on top and sealed it with great big massive bolts that I screwed down tightly, so I would never get into that memory again. Stefan would say I need to take down that barrier, how it's served its purpose and now is hurting me, like with the headaches," she noted thoughtfully, staring out in the distance behind Leon. "But that is what's coming across my mind right now."

"Which is why you won't go back to the doctors. You know what needs to be done already," he declared. "What if your parents' killer was telling you to shut all this down and to not ever open it again?"

"Well, that would be really great if he had that ability," she argued, "but who the hell can do that? Besides Stefan?"

"I don't know. You were a young, impressionable child, so, in theory, it might not have been all that hard to do. You would have done anything to make this all go away."

"It's not like I'll just lift that concrete lid," she stated dismissively. "Especially after all this time."

"I bet you could," he replied. "You're not that child anymore. You could just blow that lid right off."

"And then what?" she asked. "Have all that pain and horror come crashing through? I'll put myself in a coma."

"Not likely. Stefan would help. Wouldn't that be better than having all of it hidden away, right along with the identity of the killer, hidden where you can't even access the information? How is the cop in you happy to allow that to happen?"

"The little child in me is happier to avoid touching this," she murmured. "I just don't want to deal with it."

"I get that." He reached across the table, held her hand in his, and cradled it gently. "You're not alone this time, you know?"

"Sure, I am," she retorted. "I'm alone in my head."

"No, not at all," he argued. "Instead of actually having the good and happy memories of your mother and father, you have the memory of whoever it is who killed them. Do you remember anything around that time?"

"No," she snapped, trying to pull her hand from his. "I told you that I came home from school to find them dead."

"Ah, but you also said you were there, so already there's a conflict. So did you find them dying instead?"

"Maybe," she said, staring at him, "I don't have any memories of that day."

"Of course not. The shock and trauma would have washed it all away, but they're in there. They're in there somewhere in your psyche."

"So what?" she asked. "It still doesn't have anything to do with these current cases. Or why these two students and your aunt had to die."

He nodded. "Maybe not but, if Stefan says this is all connected ..."

She looked up at him. "Did you have any other family?"

He frowned. "Not that I know of."

"What about Gertie and your mother? Being sisters ..."

He stopped, and a funny look came to his face. "You

know what? There *was* a brother."

"I believe so, yes. In my research. A brother? Wait," she asked in amazement. "Dead?"

"He was like the black sheep of the family, walked away when they were kids. I doubt he's even alive." He added, "He took off a long time ago. I don't remember my mother ever speaking about him much."

"But, if your mother had a brother, then Gertrude did too. Did he have any family of his own?"

"I don't think so." He stared around at the kitchen, an odd look on his face. "How absolutely bizarre to remember that you actually have family, only to find out that maybe he's the one who wiped out the rest of your family. Jesus." He pushed back his chair, got up, and walked around the kitchen. "This is just way too much of a mind-bender. The two students were actually sisters. And my aunt was potentially meeting my uncle, a man I've never met and barely remembered his existence. So a family theme is repeated right there."

"*Siblings.* I need to find out who he is," she said, bringing up her laptop. "Well, look at that. One brother, his name is Henkel. He was eight years older than Gertrude."

"Henkel," Leon repeated. "That's not a name I know."

"No. But that's what's on his birth certificate." She did check through a few databases to see where he was and then whistled. "And the reason you didn't know anything about him," she said, with a shake of her head, looking at Leon, "and why she likely told you that he was dead ..."

He raised his eyebrows. "What? Don't keep me in suspense."

"He's been in prison. He got out three months ago."

"Jesus, what for?"

"Murder."

CHAPTER 21

ABBY HAD SENT off a flurry of emails last night, as they tried to dig up information on the whereabouts of Gertrude's brother. Leon had gone home soon afterward, oddly disquieted over the news. She warned him, "If anybody contacts you—"

"Yeah, I get it," he said. "It's the first time there's actually been any relevance to your comment about me being the center of it. I don't know if it's to torture me or whether he's just trying to wipe everybody out, including me."

"I don't know," she said, "but, until we find him and have a talk with him, we won't get any answers."

He looked at her, gave a quirky smile, and added, "You need to take care of yourself."

"I'm working on it," she replied. "You helped a lot tonight by bringing in food. I hadn't realized just how hungry I was." She yawned, wishing the damn headaches would ease back. Instead they were getting worse. Just the thought of the testing she'd likely have to go through to sort it out and then finding out what it could be… well, it was enough to keep her from the doctor altogether.

"And you need to deal with that block in your head," he declared, reaching out lightly and tapping her temple. "It could be serious. The sooner you figure it out, the better."

She rolled her eyes at him. "Yes, *Daddy.*"

"Oh hell." He groaned. "That's the last thing a guy wants to hear."

She snorted at that. "I don't have time for a relationship."

"Not right now you don't," he added, "but you will when this is over." And, with that, he left, leaving her standing in the doorway behind him.

"I wonder," she muttered to herself as she closed the door and locked up.

But sleep had come hard and fast, and she'd gone into the deep zone very quickly.

SHE WOKE UP at 6:00 a.m., groggy, knowing today would be the day, feeling like she'd turned a corner on something, and then remembered all the news gathered last night. Hopping out of bed, she had a quick shower and even now barreled into the office an hour early. She tagged Harvey on her way. Surely they could do something now.

He met her at the office. "Sounds like we've got something positive happening."

"Well, Gertrude's long-lost brother is just out of prison apparently, and even Leon didn't know anything about his existence."

"And he was in for murder, did you say?"

She nodded. "Apparently he shot up a gas station attendant."

"Not exactly the same kind of a crime as any of these woo-woo ones."

"Right," she agreed. "I know it's an odd thing, but he seems to be very involved in the esoteric."

"Meaning?"

"I don't know." She just threw out that info to him. "Maybe I'm just worried that there is some way to kill somebody without leaving any evidence."

"I'm sure there is. We have cases that go unsolved all the time."

"Yeah, but not mine," she snapped. "I don't want this one to be one of those." At her desk she pulled up Henkel's file. "We have his probation officer." She quickly got him on the phone and asked about his whereabouts.

"He's checking in once a week," he noted.

"What was he like in prison?"

"A model prisoner. They had no trouble with him at all."

"Interesting."

"Why is that?"

"Well, let's just say that somebody in his family was murdered a couple days ago, and we're looking at him to see if there's any connection."

"I'd be really surprised if there were," the officer replied. "I've met with him a couple times. He seems really well adjusted."

"And he's not angry, not hating his family, not looking for revenge or something?"

"No, he studied metaphysics and astrology." He chuckled. "Not exactly things to get him a job, but getting that degree held his attention the whole time and helped to straighten him out."

"A degree in what?"

"Metaphysics," he said.

"I didn't even know you could get a degree in that." She gasped in surprise.

"Well, he found a way to do it. And it's for real. He

spent a lot of years studying in jail."

"Good enough. I still need his contact information."

She got it from him, and then she hung up the phone. "As far as his probation officer is concerned, he wouldn't be involved in anything like this. Turned a corner, studied in school, seems to be a completely different character."

"Anything that works to get themselves out of there."

"I agree with you, but you know what? It's also easy to go into this assuming he's the killer."

"Well, we can't assume anything. Nothing about this case is straightforward," Harvey replied.

"No," she agreed. "The other interesting thing, and I hate to say it, but there hasn't been another killing."

He looked at her and said, "Shut up. You know what happens when you say something like that."

"I know. I know. I know. Take back, take back," she said.

"No, it's too late," he replied glumly, staring at her. "You know we'll get a call now."

"Well, I sure hope not," she stated. "I know that the PI's wife wants the body released. I'm sure the students' parents are looking to have those funerals arranged as well. I don't know what Leon's plans are, considering there's no body for his aunt." Just then the phone rang. She looked at it and groaned. "Dispatch."

"We have a dead body," the dispatcher said, and she gave the address. "In the back of a Dumpster."

"Do we have any ID on it?"

"Not yet. Victim is an older lady." And, with that, the dispatcher hung up.

Abby looked over at Harvey. "Well, that came faster than I thought."

"I told you," he said. "You can't say shit like that."

"I got it, and I do know better. But maybe this is one who we're looking for."

"And why is that?" he asked, hopping to his feet and grabbing his jacket.

"An older woman."

"You thinking it's her?"

"I don't know, but we need her body to show up somehow."

"Well, let's go find out."

By the time they reached the crime scene, it had already been cordoned off, and the coroner was there. He took one look at Abby and glared.

She raised both hands, palms out. "Wow, did you get out of the bed on the wrong side this morning?"

"I didn't need another body. Which one of you started this?"

"Hey, it wasn't us," she protested.

He just gave a loud groan. "Sure."

But it was a well-known fact that when things go downhill, everybody started looking to see who was making things difficult. "Do we have an ID?" she asked.

"Yep, it's your missing Gertrude Milligan."

"Well, I don't know if I should be happy or sad over that," she muttered.

"Well, the fact that she's dead ..."

"No, you're right," she agreed. "I guess I had already assumed that, and it was only a matter of time until she turned up."

"Don't assume anything," he scolded her.

She winced. "Got it." Of course she got it. As she stood here, looking around, it was hard to see how the aunt had even gotten here. "Is this a dump site?"

"Looks like it," the coroner agreed. "She's in the Dumpster at least. No signs of trauma at all."

Abby groaned. "Not another one."

"Yes, another one."

"Dammit," she swore. "We need to find out how these people are dying. They can't die by fright, can they?"

"Well, it's not unheard of but, in this case, no."

"Why in this case, no?" she snapped.

"Because they didn't." He glared at her. "And don't get snippy with me."

She threw up her hands. "You're always snippy with me."

"That's fine," he said. "I'm allowed to."

And that left her standing here, sputtering.

Harvey hauled her away. "Leave him alone. When he's cranky, you know you can do nothing about it."

"Sure there is… Be cranky right back."

"You saw how well that worked for you."

She snorted. "Normally he's pretty good to work with."

"He's got a lot of bodies that he can't find a cause of death for, just like you've got a lot of bodies and absolutely no suspects," he explained. "It's the same thing. We're all under pressure to solve this. The media is getting wind of some of it, and that's just bad news."

"I know, and they won't be fair about it either."

"What is there to be fair about?" he asked in exasperation. "We have all these bodies and no idea what's going on."

"Well, that's fine. We'll process the scene and hopefully get some forensic evidence for the first time, and then we'll go talk to a parolee."

"Hey, I can get behind that," Harvey agreed. "Let's get

through this, and then you'll have to make a death notification."

She stopped, looked at him. "Ah, crap."

He nodded. "Leon deserves to know."

"I know he does, but, even though, you know, he suspected …"

"Suspecting a death is not the same thing as knowing and having that finality that says, *This is the way it is, and there's no coming back from it.*"

"No, there really isn't," she muttered. But making a call about his aunt wasn't something she got to very quickly. It was actually noon before she realized what time it was. She dropped Harvey off at the station and said, "I'll go to the university and tell Leon."

He nodded. "Good luck with that."

"Yeah, I know. He'll be devastated."

"And you should understand. Even you were holding out hope."

"There's always hope," she said sadly.

She drove to the university and pulled into the parking lot. As she walked up, she realized that she still hadn't questioned the dean's kid. She didn't even know if he was still in holding or if he had been granted bail and gotten out. She hoped he was still there. Either way, she would have to talk to him soon. And he was a live one, but now they had found another live one, and they had still another on the loose.

At times like this she wished she had help. Sure, she could call in more people, but she knew that they were all busy too. Everybody was overwhelmed. It'd be nice if the damn criminals would take a holiday for once, but, for whatever reason, they were in a hot spot right now. And, like everything, there was an ebb and flow. Some days were worse; some days were better. And right now she was just caught up in a really ugly one.

She headed up to Leon's office, not surprised to see a lineup of students outside. She took a seat, as if she were a student herself, and just waited. Everybody seemed to treat him with respect, and she was quite surprised at the camaraderie he had with them. Finally the line had cleared. He turned to her, and his eyebrows shot up. "How long have you been waiting?"

"Long enough," she said, hopping to her feet.

"Wow, don't you look beat … again."

"Thanks," she said. "You're supposed to say I look great."

"You always look great," he noted, "but you're looking great in a really beat-up way."

"It's been a hell of a morning." She motioned at his office. "Can we go in?"

He nodded and waited until she stepped in front of him, then he closed the door. "What's the matter?"

She just took a deep breath and said, "We found your aunt."

He froze, studied her face, and then slowly sank into the chair beside his desk. "You mean, her body?"

She nodded. "Yes. I'm so sorry."

"Me too." He covered his face for a moment with both hands, before looking up and asking, "Do you know what happened?"

She winced and shook her head. "Same as the two students and the private detective."

"No sign of trauma?"

"Nothing."

"Jesus," he muttered.

"I know. In this case though, her body was left in a Dumpster on Dexter Ave N."

"Really?" Leon stared at Abby. "Like somebody just threw her away, like she was garbage?"

"I know. It seems so intentional, and I'm wondering if there is some sort of metaphor you can relate it to."

"I don't know." He sighed. "Maybe it'll come to me later but, right now, no."

"Good enough. We also haven't run your uncle down."

"Is he in hiding?"

"Not necessarily. I did talk to his parole officer, and apparently he was a model prisoner, no problems in any way. He earned a degree while he was in prison ... in metaphysics."

"What? You're kidding!"

"I know. Not exactly your run-of-the-mill degree to help a guy get a job straight out of the penitentiary. Then again given his age when released he'd be getting social security."

"No, not at all. And it kind of goes along with the woo-woo stuff we've been talking about."

"Exactly, but I don't have any answers yet. We're out looking for him now."

"Good enough. What about the dean's son?"

"I was actually just thinking about that, when I came in. I'm not even positive if he's still at the station or not, though I haven't been notified otherwise. I hope he's still in custody because it'd be good for him. I'm headed there to talk to him now. I just wanted to come here first to let you know about your aunt."

"I appreciate it."

And she saw the waves of grief on his face. She hesitated,

then walked over and gave him a hug. "I'm sorry." He reached up with strong arms and held her tight. Nothing was more vulnerable than a big man taken to his knees with grief. "You two were really close, weren't you?"

He nodded. "So close," he whispered. "As you would have been, if you had anybody left after your family was massacred."

"Mine happened so fast, I didn't really have much chance to deal with it. I was shipped off to a foster family right away, and I had no time to process it all. Just slammed down the lid and put one foot in front of the other."

"I get it," he said.

She nodded. "I'll go back to the office. I'll talk to the dean's son and see what that little shit's been up to."

At that, he cracked a smile. "Remember. Judge not in case you be judged."

"If that's a biblical verse, it doesn't really fit. Because somebody judged me a long time ago, when I was just a child, and took everything from me."

"Maybe, but you can lose still more."

She looked at him. "I only have a cat now."

"And you could lose Migolo too," he noted, "but, in my experience, when you start saying it can't get much worse, it usually does."

"I won't say that"—she shook her head—"because you're right. It can get a lot worse. I'm just hoping it doesn't."

He smiled. "Good luck with that."

She left him, feeling like she was deserting a puppy. And it was stupid because he was a hell of a man. Strong and capable. And this was not something that would bring him to his knees. It was just confirmation of something they already knew and, at the same time, hadn't really wanted to acknowledge. Nothing was so final as finding the body.

Abby snagged a coffee as she walked back into the station and headed down to the cell blocks. Sure enough, the kid was there. She stopped in front of the cell.

He looked up, resentful. "When am I getting out of here?"

"I don't know. Are you ready to come talk to me?" He stood and walked toward the cell door. She had him brought to the interview room and asked, "Have you seen your dad?"

"He says he's talking to his lawyers, but last time I was out way faster."

"Last time was a first offense," she noted, giving his father kudos for taking his time.

"Apparently," he said, looking around a little nervously.

"Now, let's talk about your break-ins."

He stopped, looked down at her notepad. "Are you recording this?"

"Yes, I am. Every interview room has audio and video feeds." She asked, "Why?"

He just shrugged.

"It helps me when you're lying. I can go back to this and confirm what you've said and didn't say."

He winced at that. "Do you like your job?"

"I love my job." She lifted her head and stared at him. "Why?"

"I don't know." He shrugged. "Just trying to figure out what I'm supposed to do with my life."

"Well, you can get it straight for once," she said, "and then you can decide."

"I haven't gone down the pathway too badly yet," he protested.

"Well, why don't you tell me just how far down you've come," she said, "and we can figure it out from there."

"It's not like you give a shit."

"You might be surprised," she replied. "I don't want to see you going to jail with the hardcore criminals. They'll eat you for breakfast and smile while they're doing it. Jail's not pleasant for young men."

"I've heard," he said. "I was talking to a couple guys in the holding cell. One is terrified he's going back in again."

"Well, I'm not sure what he did, but, if he's in jail here, he could very well be headed back," she muttered. "Maybe he should have chosen the straight and narrow."

"He says he didn't have anything to do with it."

"And maybe that's true. In which case, he should walk out of here, no problem."

"But it won't happen. You know that," he scoffed. "You'll set him up for failure."

"You know, honest to God, that's never been my thing," she stated. "I'd rather set you guys up for success."

"How does that work?" he asked. "I'm here in a cell. That's hardly a success."

"You haven't told me jack shit yet." She put down her pencil, stared at him, and just waited. He looked like he would hesitate, and she just waited him out.

Finally he said, "I was paid."

"You were paid to ransack her office?"

"I was paid to find something," he added in a rush, "and I needed the money."

"Why did you need the money?"

"Because my dad cut back my allowance."

"Sounds like he needed to."

He winced at that. He looked around the room to see if

anybody was listening. "I needed the money for drugs. And I knew he wouldn't give me a break on that, particularly if I told him why I wanted it."

"How did this guy approach you?"

"At the school. I think he was one of the other profs."

"Why would one of the other profs want you to go into Professor Milligan's office and get something?"

"I don't know. I didn't care why he wanted it. He just did."

"What was it he wanted?"

"Some family photos in her office—he wanted them."

"Isn't that a little weird? Somebody wanted a dead woman's family photos?"

He looked at her in surprise. "I didn't know she was dead. I thought it was more of a lark."

"And yet it was an adult?"

"Yes, a man."

"Did you know him?"

"No. I assumed it was one of the profs, as there's a lot of them I don't know."

"Okay, so you have no idea who it was, and he didn't identify himself?"

"No."

"How much money would he pay you for this?"

"Five hundred bucks."

"Wow, five hundred bucks to retrieve a couple family photos."

"Yes, so I didn't do anything wrong."

"But you still busted into a locked office, and then you went into Leon's house."

"Well, he wasn't happy with the photos. He wanted more, figured her nephew would have them."

"Interesting." She rapped her fingers on the table in front of him. "And did he pay you more to go to her house?"

"Not her house, his house."

"And why was that?" she asked, deliberately having led him in this direction.

"Because he said there were more."

"So, you didn't mind going and breaking in to get these photos?"

"I knew she wasn't around, so it was pretty safe. As long as Professor Wellington didn't find me. But, of course, you both did."

"Yeah, we did. And did you find the photos?"

"No, they weren't there. And I haven't talked to him since."

"Did you consider that maybe he sent you on a wild goose chase, then called the cops to say somebody was breaking and entering into Professor Wellington's house?"

He stared at her in shock and then outrage. "Do you think he did that?" he cried out. "What a dickhead."

"Well, hey, you're the one who took money to break into an office at the university and then a private residence. He just set you up perfectly."

"But I'll just rat him out."

"Yeah? Did he pay you cash?"

He nodded.

"Anything on paper?"

He shook his head.

"Any photos of this guy?"

He shook his head.

"So, as far as I'm concerned, you're making it all up."

He stared at her, and his jaw dropped. "What? You don't believe me?"

"Why would I?" she said, pushing his buttons to make him spill a little more.

"Because I'm telling the truth," he replied.

"Are you? And you're the same kid who was throwing your little shit fit and screaming in here for how many hours the last time?"

He flushed at that. "Well, I didn't realize that I would be stuck here." He looked around. "I really don't want to stay here."

"Maybe not," she said, "but, until I can corroborate this story of yours, for which you've given me no proof—"

"I have the five hundred bucks in my wallet," he said.

She looked at him in surprise. "Show me." He stood up and then realized that he didn't have his wallet. He glared at her. "They took my wallet."

"Well, I'll go check. Hopefully you're telling the truth." She stepped out into the hallway and walked down to holding, where they would have secured all his personal belongings. There she asked for a list of what was in his possession at the time of his arrest. When she got the list, she looked at it and whistled. "Look at that? Five hundred bucks," she said. "I need that money sent to forensics." The evidence officer looked at her in surprise. She added, "It might have been touched by our killer."

"There'll be a ton of fingerprints on it."

"Maybe not," she noted, "if they were right out of an ATM machine."

He got up and found the bag with the kid's belongings and brought it back. With gloves on, she carefully checked through the wallet, and, sure enough, they were all crisp one-hundred-dollar bills. She pulled out all five of them, put them in an evidence bag, and had them sent up for fingerprints. Then she put the rest of his belongings back into the evidence bag and then returned to the interview room.

He watched her come in and asked, "Did they steal it?"

"Nope, they sure didn't," she said, still wearing her gloves. "I've sent them up to get fingerprinted."

His eyes sharpened. "That's right. Maybe his prints are on it."

"Depends on how much you rolled around in them in the meantime," she noted drily.

He flushed. "I'm used to having a lot of money. That five hundred bucks is nothing to me."

"Yet you were willing to break the law for it."

He sagged in place. "Okay, so it was a stupid thing to do."

"Yeah, it was. And remember. There are consequences for your actions."

"It's my father's fault."

She stopped in the act of getting up; then she sat back down again and looked at him. "What did you just say?"

"If he hadn't cut back my allowance, I wouldn't have had to find money elsewhere."

She just sat here and stared at him.

It took a few minutes, but finally he sagged in place. "Fine. All right. All right. It wasn't his fault. It was my fault."

"Why did he cut back your allowance?" He wouldn't look at her. "Come on. Tell me."

"It's none of your business."

"In that case you can stay here until you're ready to answer my questions." She got up to walk to the doorway, and, as if he finally realized she would pull the same trick she had pulled the other day, he sat straight up.

"Hey, you don't have to be mean."

"You don't have to be naïve," she replied immediately. "You didn't have to go on a breaking-and-entering spree. I mean, think about it… Was it worth all this? And what's still to come?"

"All right, I'm sorry."

"*Sorry* doesn't really cut it," she said. "Not only that, the woman is dead, and you stole family photos that I'm sure the family wants back."

He looked at her in shock. "I didn't even think of that."

"I don't think you did much thinking at all," she snapped. She shook her head. "Can you describe what these photos look like?"

"Yeah, it was picture of her and a guy."

"Yeah, what guy?"

"I don't know, just a guy."

"And that's all he wanted?"

"Yeah, and he told me exactly where they were."

"Interesting. And yet in Leon's house you didn't find any?"

"He wasn't so sure there was any, but he wanted me to go check. I think he might have looked in her house already." He shrugged. "But I don't know that."

"Well, I guess you didn't find any then, did you?"

"No, I didn't. But that doesn't mean there aren't any. You guys showed up before I could finish the job."

At that, she sent him back to the jail cell, contacted Leon, filled him in, and said, "I'm heading to your aunt's to take a look for any photos like that."

"I'm coming," he said immediately.

"I don't know if that's wise," she muttered.

"Doesn't matter if it is or not. I'll meet you there." And he hung up.

She groaned.

Harvey looked at her. "You want me to come?"

"No, he's meeting me there," she muttered, as she made her way to her vehicle and headed over to Gertrude's brownstone. As she exited her car at the front of the house, Leon pulled up in front of Abby, parking the wrong way.

She glared at him. "You could park the right way."

"Yeah, and you could go in on me and leave me locked out."

She laughed. "You know what? I hadn't even thought of that."

He grinned. "Did the kid say anything else about the photos?"

"No, just that he was paid five hundred bucks to get them."

"And I can't even remember what photos he's talking about."

"And that's one of the reasons why I want to see if there are others. The kid said he didn't get a chance to finish the job."

"Interesting. Are you still thinking it's my uncle?"

"I don't know," she admitted. "Maybe it's your uncle or maybe it's this other man who she was excited about seeing."

"Or maybe they're one and the same."

"Exactly. I don't know about the colleague and whether she actually understood your aunt's reaction, but, if this is the first time she has had a chance to see her brother in all these years, you know, maybe she didn't really register how her reaction would look."

"And I don't know how good a friend Prof Tristen was to Gertie," he noted quietly. "It could have been more a judgment call on Emelia's part."

"Or trying to cause trouble. Or be relevant herself some-how, or, or …"

"Right. Exactly, because, as you know …"

And they both finished their sentence together. "People will be people."

He chuckled. "You're really good at that saying."

"No, nobody's really good at that saying. That's just the way people are."

As they walked inside, she stopped and took a look around. "If it's not on the wall, which is what we should check first, we also need to look at where else she might have kept something like that."

"That would likely be in her bedroom," Leon suggested. They wandered through the house, studying all the photos, not that there were many, and, by the time they were through checking the downstairs, she shrugged. "I didn't see anything."

"Neither did I." They made their way upstairs into Ger-trude's bedroom. A perfectly made bed with everything in its space.

She sighed. "You'll have a heyday cleaning this place out."

"Ha! It's damn near clean," he noted. "I'll have to move the personal belongings, but other than that, I just—I don't know what I'm supposed to do with it."

"You'll figure it out, presuming you're inheriting it."

"Yeah, I am. The lawyer contacted me already."

"Good. At least you know that much. Considering her brother is actually alive, I did wonder."

"I figured that Gertie's Will put me back on the suspect list."

"No, I'd already figured you would be the heir. It would

have been more suspicious if you weren't."

He shrugged. "We've always been close."

"And that's what you'll keep in mind, as you deal with all the problems going forward."

Upstairs in the bedroom, she walked around the walls of the master bedroom, through the bathroom, looking for anything, but not finding any photographs. Finally she ended up at the night table and said, "Sorry, Gertrude, but it's part of the job."

And she rooted through the night table. She'd already gone through it once, looking for anything to help them find out where she may have gone and hadn't come up with anything, so she wasn't expecting this to reveal anything either. When she was done, she stood and turned to him. "Anything?"

He shrugged. "No, I can't find anything."

They turned and double-checked the bedroom, and finally she said, "You know what? It still feels like something's hidden here."

"Something hidden? Like what?"

"I'm not exactly sure," she said thoughtfully. She walked back to the headboard and pulled the bed out ever-so-slightly. And behind it was an envelope. She leaned forward but couldn't quite reach it. Leon came up and moved the bed further out for her, and she pulled it out. "What about this envelope?" she asked. "Have you ever seen it before?"

He shrugged. "It's just an envelope. Who the hell knows what's in it?"

"Good point." She upended everything atop the bed and whistled. "Who the hell is this?"

"I don't know." In the photo, an obviously much younger Gertrude had her arms wrapped around a guy and appeared to be blissfully happy.

"Maybe it's the fiancé," Leon suggested quietly. "It would be nice to think that she was happy at some point in her life."

"I know. They don't really look like family, do they?"

"No, I don't think so, but I'm not exactly sure. It's an old photograph, and it's pretty grainy."

Then a man spoke from the doorway. "It makes no difference because they are mine."

Abby turned to see a tall scruffy-looking man, holding a pistol on them. "Whoa," she said, raising her hands slowly to show him that she wasn't armed. "Who the hell are you?"

"More to the point, who the hell are you?"

She replied, "Well, if you'd let me get my badge, I can tell you."

He winced. "Of course you're a cop."

"Gertrude's been murdered," she said, "so we're investigating her place."

"I know, but I didn't kill her."

"I'm glad to hear that, but I sure as hell would like to know who the hell you are."

"Her brother."

Of course it was her brother. "Did you see her since you got out of prison?" Now that they knew he was alive, he'd jumped to the top of the suspect list. Convenient that he was here now. Although nothing was convenient about the pistol. "You only got out of prison three months ago, right?"

"Yes." He studied her closely but did not lower his weapon. "No, I didn't look her up right away, though I did tell her that I was out of jail."

"Okay. And why didn't you go see her?"

"I was trying to adjust to the world on the outside. I

didn't want to be quite so crippled and ignorant about everything going on here," he said. "The world moved a whole lot faster than prison did."

There was a lot of truth to that. She looked over at Leon to see him studying the stranger closely.

"So why the gun?" she asked.

"Hey, you're the intruders, not me," he snapped.

"And yet now that you know I'm a cop and this is Leon, your nephew, not an intruder, you still haven't put it away."

"I'm thinking about it," he said, "but I have to believe your story. My sister is missing, murdered according to you. One thing about being in jail, it makes you doubt everything. And you don't trust anymore."

"True. I'm standing here wondering if you killed her yourself. After all, you spent a lot of years in jail for murder."

"I didn't kill her. But she killed someone. She killed her fiancé."

Leon gave a start at Abby's side.

But she'd heard a lot of lies in her short lifetime and this sounded like another. She risked a quick look at his energy. He was definitely lying but just that one look made her head want to implode in pain.

"She was pregnant. He didn't want it. They fought. She killed him. I took the fall. She got the insurance money and his house. She was supposed to share, but she let me rot in prison. Now she's dead, just as I came to collect."

"She killed him? And you took the fall?" Somehow that didn't sound like the Gertrude she'd come to understand, and, from the growing anger on Leon's face, he wasn't appreciating this twist either. And then there was the pregnancy. No, this was all just more lies ... "So?"

"It was still planned between us. Now I want my money."

In her heart of hearts, she knew no way in hell Gertie did that. In fact, something about this still stank. "I feel like we're not getting the whole story. You've been locked up for a long time. Are you sure you don't want to tell us all about it? The truth this time."

"You mean, just keep me talking," he said in a lazy tone of voice, "and maybe you'll find a way to get out of here."

"Are you really planning on killing us?" she asked blandly. "That will make for interesting news headlines. Killer gets out of jail, then turns around and kills three more people in order to be sent back to prison because he missed it so much."

He snorted at that. "No way in hell anybody could miss that. But there's only two of you. I already told you I didn't kill my sister."

"Yet it happens all the time," she said, with half a smile, as she studied his position and the way he was holding the gun. Way too much experience and casualness in that. He was used to holding weapons. She wasn't sure exactly how the truth would come down here. But one thing she did understand was whether Gertrude got the insurance money or not, she hadn't done so illegally. There was just too much righteousness about her to have sunken to that depth. "You know she was really happy and looking forward to seeing you, right?"

"Maybe, and maybe not." He suddenly looked sad. "I missed her a lot. I was looking forward to seeing her again. Yet it was hard. That's partly why I didn't come earlier."

Leon suddenly snapped out, "No way my aunt killed her fiancé. I don't believe you. You're lying."

"Too damn bad," the stranger yelled, suddenly losing his

temper. "Move over closer to the cop."

"Ah!" Abby crossed her arms over her chest and stepped farther from Leon, while she studied Henkel calmly. He looked unsure of how to handle the two of them. "So now what will you do? What good will shooting us do? And why are you here? What the hell is this now?"

"Why aren't you scared?" he asked.

"Well, if this is all about Gertrude, she's gone. We came here to get the pictures. I gather that's what you're after."

"Did you find them?" His eager gaze landed on the bed beside her. "Well, there they are," he crowed. "Damn good thing."

"Damn good thing what?"

"I was looking all over the place for those things."

"Why?" She tossed a glance at them. "What difference does it make?"

"It's kind of nice to see because it shows Gertrude had a happier life at one time."

"Says you," Leon said, with a snort. "Gertie was a lot of things, but happy was not one of them. She suffered through terrible traumas. She deserved to be happy."

"Why did you kill her?" Abby asked again.

"I wanted information, but I didn't kill her. Can't get information from a dead woman."

"And did she give it to you?"

"No," he snapped. "She wouldn't say any more than she would in all the years I was incarcerated. Neither would she give me my money."

"Yet you came here for these photos. Why?"

"They'll tell me all kinds of things," he said, "and, from here, I'll find out what I need."

"You're looking for someone," she guessed, making a

stab in the dark.

He glared at her. "Just shut the fuck up."

"Yes, you are. The question is why. And who?" she added thoughtfully. She looked over at Leon. "Nothing here is ringing a bell, huh?"

Leon slowly shook his head. "I haven't a clue what's going on," he admitted, "but I sure would like to."

"Of course you would," Henkel said, looking at him. "You're just another dumb fuck. You don't understand anything."

"Then explain it to me," Leon snapped. "She was my aunt, and I loved her."

At that, the gunman laughed. "You still don't get it. She wasn't your aunt. She was your mother."

LEON'S HEART SQUEEZED tight. "What?"

"You heard me. She was your mother. You were raised by her sister because Gertie wasn't married and didn't have a firm foundation anywhere around her after losing her fiancé and didn't think she'd make a good parent. So, her sister took over your care, and you became hers."

"My God," Leon said, feeling his very foundation rock and yet steady in some odd way. He had no trouble believing that. Most of everything else this asshole said didn't ring true, but that Gertie was his mother? … Yeah, he felt that connection between them. But why hadn't she said anything to him? Especially after his mother/her sister died. "Why was that even kept a secret?"

"What do you mean, why?" he snapped. "In this day and age you should understand perfectly. Back then Gertie couldn't stand the thought of being pregnant and unwed."

And, of course, he did, but he didn't.

"Besides, it doesn't matter," Henkel said, "they're both gone anyway."

"Yep, very true."

And Leon gave a half smile. "Was I the only child she had?"

"Oh, aren't you a smart one," he said. "Full marks to you because the answer is no. She gave up the first son for adoption. The second one went to her sister. After that she had her tubes tied."

"And who did she give up the first one for adoption to?" Leon was still thunderstruck over the revelation. But was it true? An older brother? … Dear God. After all this time, thinking it was just the two of them… now to find out he had more family than he could have even guessed. An uncle and a brother.

"Don't know," Henkel said, "but I was sure hoping to get a hold of him. I want to see the boy."

"Right, and that's who's supposedly in the pictures," Abby noted curiously. "And I notice you say *boy*. Why him and not Leon?"

Henkel just gave her a hard glance.

And she made a stab in the dark. One that would have Leon reeling. "Unless it's your son too."

And, at that, his uncle smiled.

"Jesus," Leon whispered at her side.

This was getting worse with every new reveal.

Henkel looked over at Leon, shrugged. "You're not mine, so don't get your panties in a twist over that. She fucking had an affair on me." The gun waved at both of them. "So tell me where my son is."

"We have no idea," Abby said in bewilderment. "This is

the first we're learning about him."

"Well, that's pretty strange because it went through an adoption agency."

And, at that, she winced. "Right. And then it'll be the same one as the students. The Bellevue one, right?"

"Yes, of course," Henkel said, with that same eagerness, which had Leon staring at him in surprise. "So you do know."

"Oh, I know how something else connects," she said, "sadly enough."

"I need to find my son."

"I can't help you while I'm here, with you holding a gun on me," she snapped.

He motioned at her to head down toward the doorway. "We'll just go down and see what you can do to find out for me."

"And how will I do that?" she asked him, her hands out calmly in front of her.

"I don't know," he said, "but I spent an awful lot of time trying to get the damn answer from her, and she'd never tell me."

"Did you go to the adoption agency?'

"They wouldn't even talk to me," he snapped. "I tried everything ..."

"And you know you're not allowed to possess a firearm as a parolee, right?"

"I don't give a fuck what you say," he snapped. "My son is out there somewhere, and he doesn't even know that I exist. How the hell is that even okay? She got rid of him and never even told me until it was too late."

"I'm sorry if she did that," she said. "Still, being her brother... that your son is the result of incest... that you abused your sister, likely for years, I totally understand Gertrude refusing to tell you. She had a terrible life. You likely killed her fiancé too. No wonder she never married. You were always a threat out there."

He glared and stiffened. "Don't talk to me like that."

"Why not? You're not denying it. You sexually assaulted her for years. What about the other sister?"

He shrugged. "I didn't like her much. Gertie was mine. She had no business going with another man. Especially not getting pregnant. But I took care of him."

"Shit," Leon said. "So, you really did kill him. Poor Gertie."

"Absolutely and it's nothing less than he deserved. But that's not the murder I went to jail for. I went out that night, and I ended up shooting the gas station attendant. I was still high from killing the first one and got a little carried away. I deserved to go to jail for that. But I didn't deserve to have my son taken away from me."

"Maybe not, but no way in hell that boy wants to have anything to do with you, then or now." She stared at the man in front of her. "Did you expect her to keep a baby, the result of rape and incest?"

"Of course I did. She never loved that other asshole. She loved me."

"I don't think that's quite the right term," she said quietly. "Maybe she was dependent on you. Maybe she was a prisoner to you. Maybe she was already dealing with some kind of Stockholm Syndrome. Maybe she came to hate you honestly. But I don't think love was her dominant emotion."

Henkel glared at Abby. "That's enough out of your mouth. I want to know where my son is, and you'll find out for me."

"Yeah, and how do you expect me to do that? I need access to my computers at the station." He hesitated. She shrugged. "I have to get into the station to do the research. No guarantee I can get that information at my fingertips either. But I definitely can't do anything anywhere but at my desk."

Leon was quiet, and it was all he could do to keep from reacting to that news. But there were still so many unanswered questions.

"Did you kill the students in her class?" Abby asked.

He looked at her in surprise. "I didn't kill anybody but that gas station attendant and her fiancé, but you got no proof of that second one."

She frowned, shaking her head. "Seriously? You didn't kill the two students? What about the private investigator she hired?"

"Well, I didn't kill anyone in the last many decades. My sister deserved killing for hiding my son, but she died before I got the answers I wanted," he said. "Why do you think I'm standing here waiting for you to get them for me?"

"Ah. Well, that's a problem then because we've got an awful lot of bodies."

"I don't give a shit," he said. "You should see the prison where I was. A ton of bodies were there too. People die all the time. Not my deal. I just want my son."

"I don't even know if he's alive. Did you consider that?"

"Not for long. It was the one thing that Gertrude always held over me," he snapped, "his location."

"Well, I don't know anything about it," Abby said, "and it'll take some time, and these adoption records are not something I can just turn around and get unsealed."

"Well, if a parent wants to find out, isn't it law that they can?"

"No, it isn't. Some states allow it, but it also depends on the paperwork that was filed at the time and whether Gertrude wanted anything to do with the child afterward. I guess it would depend on how much she loved you."

And there was just enough of a dig in her voice that Leon turned to look at her. "Will egging him on really help?" he muttered.

"Maybe not," she said, "but I'm a little fed up with being held hostage here. I'm tired, and I'm cranky, and I want to get some sleep."

The gun slowly lowered.

She nodded. "That's good. Be smart," she said. "All I can tell you is, when I go into work tomorrow, I'll find out as much as I can."

"Shit," he said. "I want to know where my son is now."

"Yeah, and I want to know who killed all these people," she snapped. "I was really hoping you were my gunman." She motioned at the gun in his hand. "You look like a great suspect."

"I'm not your killer. And I was really hoping you would know where my son is." Henkel looked at her, as if assessing her honesty.

"As I've said repeatedly, I don't have the answers. And I can't get them here. So, we're at a stalemate. What'll it be?"

He lowered the handgun all the way. "You might as well go home. I know where you live anyway."

"Yep, you sure do." And then she smiled, looking behind the gunman, and added, "It doesn't matter if you do or not." *Thank you, Stefan.*

Leon started at the appearance of the two officers, standing behind Henkel with their guns up.

"Drop the weapon and hands over your head. Now."

He glared at her. "How the hell did you know? How did you get a message out to them?"

She shrugged. "It's not all that hard," she said, with a smirk. "I suggest you listen to the officers, if you want to get answers."

He slowly lowered the weapon to the floor and stared at her. "You'll find out where he is?"

"I promise. I'll find out. At least I'll find out what I can. I don't guarantee that it's good news."

"No," he muttered, "but, after all this time, he needs to be alive."

"And why is that?"

He looked at her, haunted. "I have no one else. I was obsessed with finding him. Just knowing that I had a son out there somewhere kept me going."

She winced at that. "You know something? That's a theme that seems to be going on around here right now."

"You would have had Gertie," Leon added, "if you hadn't treated her so badly."

"I loved her, but she didn't love me back."

"No," he admitted, "but why would she? You abused her for years, and she never even told anyone."

"No, she was like that. She wanted me to get help," he said, "but I thought I was doing okay."

"Looks to me like a work in progress," Abby said kindly. She watched as the two police officers led Henkel away in handcuffs.

As he got into the vehicle, he turned and looked at her standing on the porch. "You'll find him, right?"

"I'll do what I can," she promised.

And finally they drove Henkel away. She turned toward

Leon. "Holy crap." He opened his arms, and she walked into them, grateful when they closed securely around her.

Against her ear, he whispered, "Come on. We're going back to my place. I've had more than enough of this place today." Picking up the pictures, he led her to his car and drove them both home.

CHAPTER 22

ABBY LET HERSELF be led into Leon's house and ushered straight up to the bedroom. She stood in the middle of the room, shaking her head. "I should go home."

"Screw that. Maybe you want to be alone, but I don't."

He quickly stripped down to his boxers, pulled back the sheets, and said, "Come on. You need some rest. You look like I feel."

"You mean, shell-shocked?" She sat down on the side of the bed, still fully dressed.

"Yes, shell-shocked."

"Why does everybody make up all these intricate lies instead of just being straight and saying, 'Hey, I'm looking for my son. I raped my sister. I thought she loved me. I was an idiot. Whatever, I want my son.' Better, right?"

"Do you really think that's any better than what he did?" Leon asked, looking at her with a puzzled expression.

"No, I hate what he did, and I'm glad that he served time for the one murder. But, by his confession alone, he killed her fiancé for the sheer bliss of killing somebody she loved."

"Yes, that was my take on it too," he agreed. "Not so much that her fiancé loved Gertrude, but that Gertrude loved her fiancé. In Henkel's eyes, she committed the greatest sin by loving somebody else."

"Yes, and she was forced to live with that."

"And yet she had two kids."

"And you could be one of them."

"I know." Leon paused. "It was a bit of a bombshell, and I'm not sure I believe it even now. There was something about Gertrude though that was very close but standoffish, as if she felt she had no right."

"Protecting you from her brother. The whole thing's a mess." Abby plunked herself back down onto the pillow and said, "I'll just sleep now for ten hours."

"Not in those clothes." Leon came around, quickly stripped off her shoes and socks, pulled her jeans off her body and treated her like a child. Afterward he pulled her shirt over her head, even unclipping her bra and tossing it onto the pile of clothes on the floor. "Now, you can tuck up under the covers."

She murmured something, but it wasn't enough for him to figure out what it was. But she rolled over, and he pulled the covers over her shoulders, and he said, "Sleep."

"If I can only get my mind to shut down," she muttered.

"To think that he's out of jail, and he spent all this time looking for his son."

"Do you have any idea about the son?"

"No, but it all comes back to the stupid adoption agency." Then Leon asked her, "Were you ever adopted out?"

"I was later, yes. Which is kind of a miracle, as I was eight when I was first put in the system. The older kids don't usually get a permanent home." She frowned and continued, "I wonder if that was done through the same agency?"

"Probably," he said. "And I wonder if my mother adopted me from my aunt."

"Well, that could put all of us in the same agency," she

guessed. "Not sure if that's of any value. Though it certainly doesn't explain how the private detective fits into it."

"No," Leon replied. "That one is still a bit of a conundrum, isn't it?"

"What about your mother and your father?"

"I don't know," he said quietly. "A part of me is scared to find out."

"You know that we need to find the son, possibly your older brother, right?"

"I know, but sleep first."

She closed her eyes and willed her mind to drift off. She felt him relaxing deeply into sleep beside her. She was jealous of that skill, that ability, because all she wanted to do was the same. But every time she would drop off to sleep, she'd jolt awake. Finally his hand reached over and tucked her up against his warm chest. "Forget about it all. Just sleep."

"I can't. My mind is just racing from one thing to another."

"What's the biggest thing?"

"How they died."

"And do you think that may have had anything to do with what Stefan was saying?"

"I'm afraid it has everything to do with it, but, if there's a psychic out there who can kill without leaving any sign of what he's done, we need to stop him."

"And who do you think that is?"

"I have no clue. None at all."

"Yes, you do." His voice was very quiet against her ear. "So do I, but we can't do anything about it today. Close your eyes." And he reached up a hand and gently massaged her shoulder.

She felt some of her tension relaxing, and she whispered,

"I shouldn't be here."

"It's exactly where you should be," he said. "This is where you belong."

She snorted at that, but it was too much effort to even protest. And, as his magical fingers worked their way down her spine and across her other shoulder, she fell into a deep sleep. But it wasn't restful in any way, shape or form. There were demons and bullets and dead people popping up alive all of a sudden and then crashing dead again. She came awake with a start, sitting upright, completely disoriented.

Beside her, Leon whispered, "It's all right. Just relax."

She looked down at him and rubbed the sleep from her eyes. "What time is it?"

"It's two o'clock."

"Is that all?"

"Yes. Time to get more sleep."

She sank back down onto the bed, positive that she wouldn't sleep again, but, when she opened her eyes the next time, she rolled over to see that he was already sitting up.

He smiled at her. "It's six-fifteen."

She groaned. "I feel like I've been run over by a truck."

"In some ways you have," he said, laughing. "It's called the train of life."

"Oh, it's my job too."

"And you wouldn't change it for the world."

"That depends. If I can get out of this successfully, then maybe." She looked across at him, both still in the bed, and smiled at him. "Thank you."

"For what?" he asked in surprise.

"For letting me sleep here."

"Since I basically brought you here when you were too exhausted to do anything in the way of protesting," he said,

"I guess you're welcome, but I'm thinking maybe it was fate." He gave her a comical look.

She rolled her eyes at him. "And for not taking advantage."

"Wow. Contrary to popular opinion," he said, "I like my women fully awake and lucid in whatever activities we're involved in at any given moment."

"Well, last night was crazy," she added, "but you did give a hell of a massage."

He gave her one of the gentlest of smiles she had seen. "I'm glad it worked. I just got out of the shower. Do you want one?"

"Oh, hell yes." She jumped up, wrapping the sheet around her. "And I would also love a change of clothes."

"Well, we're not to the point of keeping clothes at each other's places yet," he said, with a laugh in his voice. "But if you think anything in my drawers would fit you—"

"Not likely. You're twice the size I am."

"Hey, don't make it sound like that. On the other hand, you're half the size of me."

"That makes me feel like I'm tiny, which I'm not. I'm five-eight and one-forty."

"And a wonderful one-forty at that," he said, laughing.

She closed the bathroom door on him and stepped into a hot shower. It felt absolutely divine. By the time she was done, she had made peace with the fact that her only real option was to wear her clothes from yesterday, which was too bad, but whatever. She dressed, hoping that nobody from yesterday would notice, and maybe she would get a chance to swing by her place, check on her cat and change at some point. She could do that maybe, if she got out of here fast enough.

As she headed downstairs, she was met by the smell of coffee and toast. "Now toast would be heavenly. Wow, okay. I was expecting plain toast."

"Nope, not around here," he said. "Sausage and eggs to go with it. Sit at the table."

She obeyed immediately. "Usually I just grab a coffee."

"Yeah, I know," he said, "and again that doesn't cut it around here."

She smiled. "I feel like a child being taken care of by a parent."

"Well, get over that in a hurry because there is absolutely nothing parental in the way I view you."

She didn't say anything, but, as she mumbled her way through the sausages and eggs, she asked, "Are we really doing this?"

"What?"

"Having a relationship."

He looked hurt. "You know what? It really looks to me like we're already there."

"Maybe. I'm still not sure it's wise though."

"Am I still on your suspect list?"

She shrugged. "No."

"Then it doesn't matter in the least," he replied. "And now, just relax, eat up, and then, if you're lucky, you'll have time to go to your place and change your shirt."

She groaned. "My car's not even here. It's still at Gertrude's."

"No matter. I'll drive you," he said. "It's not very far from here."

"Good. It'll be a hell of a busy day."

"You've got this," he said.

His words were ringing in her ears as she climbed into

his car, and he drove her to Gertrude's. She picked up her car and drove home. She quickly changed her clothes, fed Migolo and headed to the office. There was a smile on her face and a spring in her walk, and, damn, all she'd done was sleep with the man. And, in this case, she meant *sleep*. And that was something.

She didn't know the last time she had actually had a night's rest with a man beside her, equally happy to just sleep. It wouldn't last; she knew that. Hell, she didn't want it to. She wanted to jump his bones as much as he wanted to jump hers, at least she hoped so. But she was all about timing, and this case needed her attention. As she walked into her office, Harvey was there.

He looked up, smiled. "Hey, I hear we got another prisoner."

"Yeah, somebody who pulled a gun on me last night," she said, scowling.

His smile dropped away. "Seriously?"

She nodded. "Yeah, seriously."

"You want him brought down to interrogation first?"

"Is the kid still here?"

"No, his dad got him out last night."

"Good enough, and, yeah, let's bring the new guy down for questioning. Turns out Gertrude had a son, and the father is her brother, who just got out of prison. He abused her while they were growing up. She had a child out of wedlock, and it was given up for adoption."

And Harvey's eyebrows shot up.

She nodded. "That apparently is why this Henkel guy came to Gertrude's place last night, finding Leon and me searching for the photos that the kid had been paid five hundred dollars to find for him. Henkel's been looking for

Gertrude and her photos for the last few days. He contacted her a few days ago and, according to what the other prof was saying, Gertrude was really excited to see him, but, according to Henkel, all he wanted was to know where in hell she had stashed his son."

"Good God." Harvey stared at her in shock.

"I know, right? This case is just getting more and more stupid."

"But it sounds like you're actually getting somewhere," he said in surprise.

"Wow, is that a vote of confidence?"

"But it's not even woo-woo stuff," he added, laughing.

"We'll get to that," she said darkly. "There still has to be something here to explain those deaths. Maybe there's a poison nobody knows about."

"Something so fast-acting?" he asked curiously.

"I don't know."

"And how does any of that relate to Gertrude's question in the philosophy course? The whole *what if* angle?" She turned on him in frustration, and he held up both hands in surrender. "Hey, I'm just asking."

"Well, maybe what you should be asking," she said, "are questions I can answer, or, even better, why don't you go find the answers to all those questions yourself. Great questions by the way. I'll expect the answers by the time I get back from the interview."

"Do you want me to come to the interview?"

"No, I somehow got a bit of a rapport with him last night. Let me go in and see how it is."

"How's Leon doing?"

"I imagine he's doing just fine," she replied nonchalantly.

But Harvey's laughter followed her down the hallway. She allowed herself a brief grin, before she walked in. And, sure enough, there was the gunman. "So a new day. New questions. For starters. Leon's father? Who was he?"

"The fiancé. And you know something? I can't even remember his name." Henkel shrugged. "Our youngest sister, Mary, adopted Leon."

"And Gertrude was okay with that?"

"Apparently. They had kept it really quiet. So I have no idea. Now, where is my son?" he snapped.

"We're looking. I've got a call in to the agency for access to the adoption records, and we have to get special permission to get the information released."

"Well, get at it because I'm not talking until then."

"It could take days," she said.

"Doesn't matter. I've been locked up a long time, so what's a few more days?"

"Well, you did kill a man. According to what you said last night, you killed two men."

"Yeah, and they both deserved it."

"The gas station attendant deserved it?"

"Yeah, he gave me the finger," he replied, "and I just wasn't in the mood to deal with that shit."

"Ah." She shook her head. "And did Gertrude's fiancé deserve it?"

"He shouldn't have fucking touched her," he said, his voice low and mean.

"Got it. What's yours is yours."

"Exactly, and don't you forget it."

"Have you had any contact with your son? Do you know his name? Do you know anything?"

Immediately he turned into a concerned father again.

"No, I don't have a clue, and I wish Gertrude was here, so I could talk to her."

Matter of fact, even as she watched, his eyes filled with tears, his bottom lip trembled. She didn't know if he was a hell of an actor or if he sincerely was grieving over Gertrude's demise. All the years and times he abused his sister is probably what kept him smiling in jail.

She shook her head. "I'm looking up all the information on your son, but it'll take some time. Now, tell me why you hired that kid to get the photographs."

"Well, that's obvious." He stared at her in surprise. "Even you should work that out."

"I'm trying to work it out. I figured that you were hoping there was a picture of the two of you."

"I figured there was a picture of two of us, and I was hoping there was a picture of her and the baby."

"But would it have been Leon or the other one?"

"I was hoping it was the other one," he snapped, getting angry again.

She stood. "Okay, good enough. Now let me see what I can find out."

And, at that, he calmed down.

"And that kid I hired," he asked, "is he okay?" He looked over at her. "I wouldn't want another man's son to get injured over this."

She stopped and stared at him. "You killed two men, who were sons to other men," she stated, "but you don't want *this* kid to get injured or hurt because of your actions?"

"No, he's just a kid."

"Well, you do understand that your son is no longer a young boy, right?"

He snorted. "I'm not an idiot. It was a long time ago."

"It sure was," she said. "The kid's got to be what, twenty, thirty, forty or more?" She was testing him.

He just blurted out the answer. "Well, the fiancé was a whole twenty-two, and I figured that my son was born about five years before that."

"Where were you that you didn't know he was born?"

He shrugged. "I took off for a while to make a fortune. When I came back, it was all over with."

With a nod in his direction, she headed out.

As she got back to Harvey, he was waiting in the observation room, having listened in on the interview.

"Interesting and a bit of a mess, isn't he?"

"You think? How the hell his parole officer thinks he's just fine and not capable of murder is beyond me. Henkel's a huge mess. He runs hot and cold. He runs calm and angry. He sounds normal, and then he sounds like he's completely off his rocker. But, when he goes superquiet, then I figure he's most dangerous of all. He'll be charged over the gun incident of course but it won't stop this."

Just as she and Harvey walked back to her desk, her phone rang. It was the Bellevue Adoption Center.

"You'd need a court order," the woman on the phone said. "I'm sorry. We can't just turn over this confidential information."

"It was a long time ago," Abby replied carefully. "And we're now worried about his life."

"Well, that's just too bad. The rules are the rules."

"So, neither of the parents can ask for this information, is that correct?"

"Yes, that's correct. As a matter of fact, the mother even signed forms to say the child is not allowed to search her out."

That was a surprise. But given who the father is and what Gertrude went through, maybe not. "So I'll need to get a judge involved in this, huh?" Abby asked sadly. "That'll just push everything back, and then we'll have to make all your records available to me."

The woman hesitated.

"And be prepared, of course, since it will be quite a show as the police move in and collect all your records."

"What? Why would they do that?"

"Oh, when someone is not being cooperative," Abby explained, "we find there is usually a reason, so we would need to have a close look at *all* your adoption cases, just to make sure nothing is illegal."

"All of our adoption cases are perfectly above the law."

"Then why are you not willing to help? A man's life is in danger."

"Yes, and, as you already explained, his mother has been murdered, and his father is barely out of prison."

"He's a parolee."

"Well, that's hardly a step above."

"Oh, wow," Abby replied, though she wouldn't argue with the woman. "All I need is to find out is if this guy is even alive and how I can contact him."

"Well, we don't have those records, but I can tell you that he was adopted locally to a good family."

"And I need a last name."

"The last name I have on file is Doe, as in John Doe."

Abby sat back, pinched the bridge of her nose, and asked, "Seriously?"

"Seriously," she replied in a pained tone. "It's not unusual for people to not want anybody to know that they've done this."

"And why is that?"

"Shame, more often than not," she stated. "You'd be surprised how many people think it reflects badly on them that they can't have children."

"Surely there was another name on the paperwork."

"We did do a check," she said, suddenly relenting. "On the second set of paperwork he did sign as John Doen. D-O-E-N."

"Ah, so he just left off the *N*. Possibly a mistake or just the person entering the information couldn't read his writing."

"Maybe, I don't have his current address, just the original one."

"Give it to me, please."

The woman searched for that and gave it to her, over the phone.

"Thank you."

"I need your badge number, so, if anybody contacts me about this, I have somebody to go back to."

"Perfectly understandable." Abby provided her name, badge number, the precinct she worked at, and her work phone number.

"Okay, thank you," the woman said with relief. "I have to watch my back too."

"Absolutely. Not a problem."

At her desk for the first time in what seemed like a while, she felt some of that big wall around her starting to crumble. Maybe it was the fact that she was getting closer; she didn't know what it was, but she heard this weird sound, like somebody climbing steps. She expected to hear a knocking sound after that.

She looked around her, but nothing was here. It sounded almost familiar, but she had no idea why. She frowned as she sat here, until Harvey walked over, looking at her with concern.

"Wow. What's wrong?"

She shook her head. "Sorry, I'm just lost in thought."

"Well, now you can be found again," he said, with a comical grin. "Where are you at on this kid?"

"I need to check into this. I've got a name and an old address, but I don't expect that it'll be current."

"You want to run by there?"

"Maybe, yeah, that'd be a good idea. I wouldn't mind getting out of here."

"I'll drive," he said.

She thought about it and realized there was no reason not to. "As long as you don't kill me on the way," she quipped.

"Hey, I've never had an accident yet."

"I know. I know, but there's always a first time for every-thing."

And she followed him out to the car, her notes in hand, that weird sound of somebody climbing stairs still echoing around her. She shrugged and whispered, "I don't know who the hell or what the hell that is, but it sucks. Knock it off."

And, sure enough, it stopped.

LEON MADE IT through the day with a smile on his face. At lunchtime he called Abby and left a message, when he couldn't get through. He hated the fact that she would be so busy that this would be a common occurrence, but he would get used to it. Because the alternative was to live without her. The fact that he'd gotten her home to his place last night had felt so damn right and so good. Just holding her was perfect. He couldn't imagine what making love would be like, but he was looking forward to finding out. He also knew it would have to happen when this case was over because she wouldn't allow herself a few moments of pleasure or tension-relieving activity at any other time. Her focus was all-encompassing.

Of course he was doing a little bit of research himself. He'd contacted the same adoption agency to see if there was anything on record for him. When they couldn't find his identity or who his mother was, it also confirmed that he had been illegally adopted by his mother. He sat in his office, wondering.

"Gertie, why would you do that? Why? When my mother was long gone, could you not have even told me then?"

Protecting him maybe from Henkel? That made sense. It went along with her strange obsession with trying to find her sister's killer too. Leon could only hope that, when they finally did get answers, they would get *all* the answers, not just part of them. But it did sound like things were breaking open. It's just that they were getting more and more confusing at the same time. He imagined this was the darkness before the dawn and that, by the time dawn broke, they would have what they needed—the answers to all these questions.

Leon figured, if he managed to get through all of the secret documents that Gertie had left him, he'd probably find some paperwork with some answers. And, if he was lucky, a letter of explanation. But, in order to do that, he had to be in the right frame of mind, and then he realized that he could do his part and find out who the killer was. He shook his head, pulled out one of the hard drives, and started searching through it.

It wasn't long before he found a note addressed to him. When he opened it, his heart sank and then swelled, as he realized that she had finally confessed. And there it was… all laid out before him.

Her fiancé had been killed by her brother—the brother who had sexually abused her for years. She'd gotten pregnant and had given up the baby for adoption. And then, when she had finally found love and had gotten pregnant, her fiancé had been murdered by her brother too. She found out about the pregnancy after her fiancé was gone.

She gave him, her beautiful boy, to her sister, who had been desperate to have children and never could. Maybe it was a huge gift to them all, as Leon had been well-loved throughout his years.

She went on to write:

I still don't know who killed my sister and her husband—who you knew to be your mother and your father. You know as well as I do what Stefan said. That it was someone close to us, but I don't know who it could be. I can tell you that your uncle was in prison and that's where he should stay. Not only did he kill the love of my life, which I could never prove, he also killed a gas station attendant.

As for your half brother, I don't know anything about him, and I don't want to know. Maybe that's not fair, but I spent enough time in pain and torment at his father's hands. I couldn't bring myself to do anything for him. He needed a mother who would love him completely, without reservation, and that wouldn't be me. Forgive me.

As always, everything is yours. It always has been, including my heart. Yet it broke my heart all the time to know that Mary was so thoroughly loving every moment with you, when I couldn't have the same.

I could have told you after Mary died, but then it felt like a betrayal in some way, and I couldn't do that to her. I just focused as much as I could on solving the crimes against our family, and I haven't managed to do that either. It breaks my heart to think about it, but maybe one day we'll have answers.

Leon sat down and sent an email, with bits and pieces of the letter to Abby, so she would know:

She called her firstborn Drew, short for Andrew. Not that I think that helps much. Surely his name changed when he was adopted. And I'm surprised she even named him, considering she didn't want anything to do with him. Maybe she named him afterward, just to have something to call him, like for purposes of her letter to me.

Then he signed off on the email and sent it. He quickly did a follow-up email.

Dinner tonight at six. I'm cooking, so make sure you are at my house.

He knew that she would probably call it off and say that she couldn't because of work, but maybe, with any luck, they could have something of a normal life today. At least that was his hope.

By the time he finished at the university in the afternoon and headed home, he still hadn't heard from her. He headed to his place, checked out the groceries situation at his house, and decided that he would do spaghetti. As he started in on the sauce, he called her yet again, but, so far, he got no answer. As he picked up the phone to call her this time, Stefan called him, his voice irritable and sounding cranky.

"When will you actually listen?"

"Stefan?" It was really hard to concentrate when he was talking with Stefan, so he shut off the burner on the stove and asked, "What's going on?"

"She's not answering, and there's a reason."

"Yeah, I get it. She's busy."

"No," Stefan said, his tone worried. "I think it's much worse than that."

His heart froze. "What do you mean?"

"Something's wrong. I've been getting mixed signals for the last fifteen minutes."

"Like what?"

"I don't know,"

Then Leon's phone rang, another call coming in.

He hung up on Stefan to answer it.

"Hey, this is Harvey, Abby's partner. She collapsed when we were at the old address for your half brother. She's in the hospital right now."

"Collapsed from what?"

"Well, the doctors know what she had to eat today and anything you might have given her last night," he said, "but so far they haven't found any reasons why."

"Oh God," Leon said, "please let it not be the same as the rest of the victims."

"I'm afraid it is," Harvey said, his voice terrified. "She's at the hospital. You can come see her. I know that you have a special relationship."

He reached for his wallet and keys. "I'll be there in ten." He ended the call, raced to his car, and headed to the hospital.

Harvey was waiting for him at the entrance. "She's in here," he said and took him to a private room. And, damn it, if she didn't look like she was sound asleep. He walked over, picked up her hand, and checked for a pulse.

"She's still alive," Harvey said. "I'm just not sure why."

At that, he turned to look at Harvey. "What do you mean, *why?*"

"The doctors don't know what's wrong. Let me put it that way. So it's like her body just hit overload and shut down."

"Yet it's not shut down. It's like she's asleep."

"More like in a coma," he said. "I've been sitting here, waiting for somebody to come back with tests, but, so far, nothing."

Leon nodded. "Look. If you need to go off and do something, I'll stay here with her." Harvey hesitated, and Leon said, "I'm not leaving her side. It's okay."

"Fine, but, if there's any change, let me know." He handed him his card.

"Will do. By the way, did you guys find out anything?"

"We got an address from the adoption place and went there. It was an old busted-down home. We talked to the neighbors and canvassed all around, but the family apparently moved away a long time ago, and the place has just been there like that ever since. We went into the house, and that's when she dropped like a rock."

"Crap," he said. "So a dead end?"

"Yeah, a dead end. There was some talk about the boy going into the military, so we're checking records."

"Right." He shook his head. "What a mess."

With that, Harvey left.

Leon sat down beside her on the bed, hating the icy coolness of her skin, then picked up his phone and called Stefan. "Can you do anything for her?"

"Yeah, that's why she's still alive," he said bluntly. "We're keeping her alive. Just call us a life support system."

"We?"

Stefan chuckled. "I have a helper."

"Is it the same as the last time, with Gertie?" Leon asked.

"Yes," he said, "and, in this case, because she's still alive, we're finding something we've never seen before."

"Well, I know that already," he said, "but what is it?"

"It's a psychic block," he explained. "Somebody's put an energy block inside her mind, shutting down the blood to the brain. Just long enough for her to go unconscious, and then another block spot controls the oxygen, the aorta out of the heart. Just long enough to shut down the oxygen. And then it releases."

"So, it's like something's there for a short time and then it dissolves. Leaving no trace."

"Exactly," Stefan said.

"So, what are you doing right now?"

"Always looking for new blocks," he replied, "because this energy is alive."

"Alive?" Leon asked in alarm.

"Yes, alive. As in whoever is doing this to her is still trying to kill her."

CHAPTER 23

*C*LIP-CLOP, CLIP-CLOP,* THE footsteps ran up the stairs. But a voice at the top said, *Stop, don't enter.* She recognized the voice, but the dream kept going, first to a man's voice, then to another man's voice, then yet another man, and finally a woman's voice. Chaos in her own brain, her dreams, her nightmares.

She struggled to find a way out. Even when she had bad dreams, normally her bladder would wake her up, and she could get out of the nightmares. But this time she was stuck. Whatever this was, she was going around and around in circles. No, she was going up and down the stairs. Through it all, she thought she heard another voice that she recognized. *Stefan.*

Yes, you know me, he confirmed. *I've been here before. I've been here with you many times. We've solved cases. Your name is Abby,* he said. *You're a police detective. You are thirty-three years old, and you have just found somebody you can trust in your life, Leon.*

Her mind grabbed that name. *Leon. Leon. Leon.* And, sure enough, his face popped up in front of her in spirit form. She smiled, reaching up a hand, only to have the face dissolve under her fingers.

That's right, Stefan said, *hold that image.*

Stefan? she asked.

Yes, it's me, he said. *You need to stay around and to stay conscious. Focus on my voice. Focus on me. Focus on Leon,* he added with emphasis.

Why? Is Leon in danger? And, with that, she rose up one more level out of the darkness.

I don't think he's in any danger, at least not at the moment, he shared. *But you're in danger.*

I am? she asked. *What do you mean?*

I mean, you're in literal danger, he explained. *We're trying to keep you alive, but someone is actively trying to kill you. Even as we speak.*

She struggled to compute the information.

Remember the wall in your psyche? Remember that staircase?

Yes, she replied, *it's been bugging me for a while now, so much going up and down the damn stairs in my brain. The headaches have been godawful too and getting worse.*

Yes, the staircase is an old meditation technique, he stated. *At one point in time, you used it to get to sleep.*

You showed me all kinds of things. The staircase was one of them.

Yes, and honestly there's still some of my energy in here. His voice was a little chagrined, as if his energy wasn't supposed to be here. *We kept that bit there in case you needed help again.*

Maybe that's a good thing. Maybe that's why I'm still alive. On the other hand, after all these years, maybe that's why the headaches …

It could be, he realized in surprise. *I hadn't thought about that, but you could be right.*

I can't quite pull out of this, she murmured. *It's just so heavy. I feel like I have no oxygen, like I've no blood flow, like I'm dying.*

That's because you are, he said, his voice sharp. *Remember Leon.*

Leon, Leon. And there he was in her mind again.

Focus on his face, Stefan said. *And remember. Somebody is trying to kill you, and you can't let it happen.*

No, I don't want to let it happen. But everything is just so hard to pull into clarity.

Your parents were already murdered, Stefan said. *Remember.*

Yes, and I was in foster care until I was adopted.

Yes, and that could be the connection to whoever is doing this.

Sure, but there were thousands of children.

And maybe he was in foster care or worked in the system?

Maybe, she said, searching through her memory banks. *I really don't know. I can't sense anyone else in here.*

Think, Stefan said. *The energy is here. Look.* He pointed to what looked like a big concrete block, sitting atop one of her arteries.

As soon as she saw it, she said, *Oh my God, that hurts so much.*

Then lift it, Stefan ordered. *Right now, lift it.*

She reached down and picked it up, surprised at how heavy it was, even in her dream. *I can barely do anything.*

But Stefan did something, and the next thing she knew the block was up and off. *Good*, Stefan said, the relief in his voice overwhelming her. *I wasn't sure we would lift that one.*

Was it really blocking my artery?

Yes, it was. Somebody has been playing with your mind, he said. *Somebody who's a very strong energy worker, but who's determined to use energy for his own purposes. And I think he's had his hook into you a very long time ago. I just don't know why we didn't see it.*

Yeah, remember. People will be people, she said bitterly. *And likely the wall … I kept fortifying it, so I wouldn't have to deal with what was behind it. Getting rid of that block is helping… I'm feeling a little bit better, but I still don't understand who's doing this.*

That's the problem, Stefan said. *We have to figure it out, and fast. Somehow he has access to your mind.*

What does that mean?

That wall that you've put in there, I think that wall is keeping him in your mind.

How is that possible? I built it, with you, as a way to block out the awful memories of my parents' murders.

Yes, Stefan said. *Your mind's always been very strong, and plus I've stepped in now and again to help, and I can only think that's why you aren't dead right now.*

Would he need access to me physically?

Not after the first time. No, not if you were particularly vulnerable. I believe, in Gertrude's case, he must have known her but had to have known her at a time when she was most vulnerable. Same for the others. I'm not sure about the two students. But, if there was any time that they were vulnerable, he could have somehow gained access to their minds and waited until he wanted to make his move. In the case of the private eye, I don't know what to say.

He was a drunk. A workaholic and an alcoholic. Maybe that out-of-control state made him vulnerable… but we still don't know who or why.

I don't know, Stefan said, *but you'll find there's one person with a connection to them all.*

The two women in that classroom?

I know. Did Gertrude ever tell you if she really liked them?

Yes, she thought they were really sweet, and she loved having them in her class.

So, they may have been targeted just for that reason.

So, this is really about Gertrude, not Leon, isn't it?

Yes, Stefan said, *it is. But right now, it's about you, and keeping you alive. Now, I need you to lift one more block.* And he pointed to it.

She groaned. *My God.* It was over her brain stem. *It's massive.*

But it's only energy, Stefan reminded her. *I need you to take the thing that you're most proud of in your life and warm yourself up with it.*

The cases I've closed, she said. *The people I've helped.*

Well, that's a good thing. What about your parents?

Yes, I loved them so much. Tears rolled down her face.

And yet you've denied yourself of all the good memories of them.

That damn wall, she said.

Look at the block.

As she looked at it, she saw that it was part of her wall.

Yes, he's using that wall that you have kept rigidly in your mind, repressing all your bad memories. He's using that against you. He's taking the power from that wall, and it'll kill you.

She felt another energy there too. A feminine energy. A familiar feminine energy. *Dr. Maddy?*

Yes, I'm here.

Can you help?

Yes, I can, but you have to be ready to let that wall go. We've told you over and over again that it's got to go.

I know. I know. Now I can't put it off any longer. But I don't know how I'm supposed to do that.

Take a bomb to it. Drive a car through it. I don't care what you do, she said. *Pulverize it somehow.*

And, as soon as Dr. Maddy said that, a big huge hammer came out of Abby's imagination and down onto the wall, shattering it instantly.

Immediately memories flooded her psyche, memories of pain, grief, and loss. Finding her mother on the floor, already cold and dead, lying in a pool of blood, throwing herself on top of the woman she loved. Then sitting up at the sound of a voice and seeing a man standing there, staring at her in shock. He was covered in blood, standing right in front of her. He was young, long-haired, lean.

And a complete stranger.

"Did you do this to my mommy?" she'd cried out.

"Yes, I did," he'd said. "That's all right, little girl, I'll fix you so you won't remember this anymore either."

Just then she'd felt something reaching inside her head and shutting off everything in her mind.

Stefan, he was there, she cried out. *He did something so I wouldn't remember. He was already inside my head. We walled him up with the memories.*

I see that, he said, his voice grim. *A wall you were supposed to take down when you were ready.*

I didn't get very ready, did I? she snapped.

He chuckled. *How about now?*

Yeah, it's gone.

Good, Stefan said, *now take a look at the face. Take a long look at the face of the man who killed your family. He was young back then. He's much older now. Age that face and see if you recognize him. Because that same man is killing all of these other victims.*

She stepped inside her memories to face the stranger. She stared up at him; he was young, younger than she expected.

Who are you? The memory didn't answer her, but he smiled at something he'd been thinking back then. Only that particular smile … was the same as someone she recognized.

And, with that, she snapped awake.

LEON STOOD STIFFLY. "I don't understand." Unfortunately he understood more than he cared to, but his mind was still grappling with what happened. He'd been sitting, his eyes closed, thinking on all the information they knew up to now and trying to understand what had happened to Abby.

Harvey hadn't offered much in the way of details. She'd collapsed, but nothing remarkable was given in the way of details surrounding her collapse. He'd called for an ambulance, then had called Leon.

And that was about it.

Even the doctor couldn't tell Leon anything new. But he'd asked Leon multiple questions himself, and having no answers made it all seem so much worse.

He'd been sitting, mentally going over her day, wondering what would have brought on the collapse, when Harvey returned.

"How is she?"

"No change."

"Damn."

"Look. I won't leave her, so if you want, I'll just let you know if there's any improvement."

Harvey frowned. "I hate to leave her." He walked over to the edge of the bed.

"That's why I'm staying."

The two men eyed each other, and it's the first inkling

Leon had of Harvey's relationship to Abby. He'd thought they were best-friends types of partners. It's obvious he cared a lot for Abby, but Leon just wasn't sure in what way. Emotions shifted rapidly across the older cop's face.

"Why did you go to that house?" Leon asked suddenly.

Harvey looked at him in surprise. "It's the last known address that the adoption center gave us."

"Ah, did you guys run down the adoptive parents?"

Harvey nodded. "They are both deceased."

"Shit. Way too many deaths in this case," Leon snapped. "We definitely need to find my half brother."

At that, Harvey stiffened. "We're doing what we can."

"I know. I'm sorry. I didn't mean to be critical, but surely all that information is readily available now."

"Not if he changed his name or left the country or even if he's stayed under the radar. All kinds of possibilities are here." He shifted to stare down at Abby.

And that's when Leon saw it. He stared at Harvey's profile. Surely he was wrong. He had to be. Why would Harvey stick close to Abby, if the horrible suspicion inside Leon's head was correct?

But he already knew the answer. How else did one keep track of what the cops knew about the murders, except to become one and stick close to the cases?

Leon slowly stood, but Harvey sensed something.

He spun and stared at Leon. "What?"

Leon shifted closer to the door. "It's you, isn't it? You're Gertie's oldest son?" He tried for calm, but his tone came out accusing and harsh.

Harvey didn't bother answering. He moved so fast, Leon wasn't prepared. Still cursing his much slower instincts, Leon felt Harvey's hands on him much faster than he was prepared for. Still, Leon had been a cop for a long time, but, after ten minutes of wrestling for control, he felt the cold steel against his throat.

And Abby's voice calling out, "Harvey?"

CHAPTER 24

ABBY BOLTED UPRIGHT in the hospital bed and stared at the tableau in front of her. Shock slammed into her, as her mind grappled with what her eyes saw. Harvey, her long-time partner, holding a knife against Leon's throat.

"Is this how you want to go?" Harvey asked Leon.

Leon's body was stiff, and he asked, "Why would you kill me like this and not the way you killed everybody else?"

"Because it would be more fun this way," he replied. "More personal. I really love the feel of blood."

Abby stared at her partner, but spoke to Leon's mind. *He's lying. He has no way to get into your head. Keep your mind closed to him.* When she felt Leon had received her message, she spoke. "Harvey?" And her voice broke.

He turned to look at her in shock and in horror. "No, no, no," he said, racing to her side. "You're not supposed to be awake."

And he lifted the knife to stab her, only Leon was right beside him, snatching his arm back and slamming him hard against the wall.

"No," Harvey cried out, "she's not supposed to know. That ruins everything."

She slowly slid out of the hospital bed, her movements tired and heavy, as if just no life were left in there. She reached for Harvey, her hand grabbing his, the knife now safely on the floor and under her bed. "Why?" she cried out.

He looked at her and said, "Gertrude was my mother."

"What?" She stared at him in confused horror. "And you killed her? Your own mother?"

He nodded slowly. "I had to. She couldn't be allowed to live, after what she did."

"What did she do?" Abby cried out, desperate to understand. She stared at her beloved partner, who knew everything about her life and about the murders that had crushed her. And something else hit her. "Oh my God, you killed my parents. You are the one who killed my parents. Why?"

"Your mother worked at the adoption agency. She wouldn't give me the information that I wanted to know, even after I tortured her for the information. So I had to kill her to stop her from telling anyone."

"And my father? Was he just collateral damage?"

He nodded slowly. "He walked into the house, when I'd just finished her off. I had no choice," he said, almost pleading for understanding at the end. "But I didn't walk away from you. I helped you block it all out, so you could live a normal life. I just had to keep checking on you to make sure those memories didn't surface."

Betrayal. Pain. Loss. So many emotions she could barely breathe.

"You're special," he said, looking at her in appeal.

"Special?" she cried out. "What are you talking about?"

"Because I set up a mind block only. I didn't know that's what I was doing. I was still new to it all. My adoptive mom taught me. She used them on my adoptive father and her boss at work to make her life easier. Once she realized what she could do, she tried to teach her husband, but he laughed at her, so she put one in his head and killed him. I knew she could do this. And I wanted to learn, but it's not easy," he admitted. "I didn't finally get to do one successfully until you. Then I had to stay close to see if it would keep working. You've been so strong all these years. I did try a couple times to remove it, and, even once to kill you, but I couldn't." He shook his head. "I don't know why you are so strong. I've been desperate to figure it out."

She didn't dare tell him that it was because of Stefan and that damn wall she'd been refusing to pull down. "Oh my God." She stared at him, tears rolling down her face. "You're like the big brother I never had."

"I am your big brother," he said in surprise.

"No, you're not. Not at all. You're Leon's big brother, but you didn't care about *that* relationship. What about your mother? Your adoptive mom?"

"She's dead. She was my first success in killing this way. The doctors didn't even look at her for long. She had an existing heart condition, so that made it easy for them to close her case. I knew she'd be proud of me." He frowned. "But there are limitations I can't seem to overcome. I can't do it with everyone." He reluctantly looked over at Leon.

"And Gertie?" Leon asked.

"What can I say? She's dead. She should never have been allowed to live as long as she did. Same for my father. Of course he's dead now too. You've been out cold and haven't caught up on the news."

"What news?"

"Well, of course it's not a surprise, but the guards are about to find Henkel, my real father, at any moment," he said, laughing. "He was easy. I went on the pretense of asking him questions. Obviously I had some questions for him, but he was pretty easy to access. We were blood after all. That gives me a built-in pathway. So he was easy. I walked out with him screaming behind me, and then I killed him. I'm sure the doctor will say he collapsed and died from shock." At that he started to laugh robustly.

"Why kill him? All he wanted was to find you."

"Well, he's too damn late," Harvey snapped. "He should never have let me go. And he should have killed my bitch of a mother as soon as he found out how she betrayed him."

Abby and Leon shared a look. Abby spoke telepathically to Leon. *Let me see if I can handle this. Stay back, please.*

"You don't have to fucking hurt me," Harvey said to them, picking up on their intentions.

"No," Abby argued. "We do. We really do. And somehow we have to stop you from using that mind of yours to hurt everyone."

"Well, that you'll never do," he stated, taking a step closer to Abby.

When Leon took a step closer to Harvey, Abby sent out another message. *No. Not yet. Please, Leon. Stay back.*

"Now that I know what to do, everybody around me will die," he promised, "and I'll start with you, Abby. And I'll find a way to take out your boyfriend after that."

Harvey glared at Abby, but that gaze focused into almost a laser beam.

She felt the force driving into her brain. She smiled at him. "Oh hell no." And she pushed him back out.

Harvey jerked back and stared at her in shock. "No, no, no," he said, clearly agitated. "You can't do that."

"I can. I really can."

Leon relaxed a bit, relieved, but on edge still.

Harvey immediately tried to refocus his strength against

her.

Abby felt the blast hitting inside her brain, filling her, and yet surrounding outside her body at the same time, and she cried out in shock, falling backward against the bed.

"Stop it," Leon cried out. "You're hurting her."

"I plan on it," Harvey snarled, "and so much more."

"No," she yelled, both to Harvey and Leon, but Leon got a little hand wave to stay back. Inside her mind she called out, *Stefan!*

He responded in that always calm voice. *I'm here.*

I need help. He's so strong, she cried out. *The pain is killing me.*

Remember. Focus on Leon's face.

Why is Leon the answer? she cried out, still in pain.

Simple, Dr. Maddy whispered, her voice soft and gentle. *It's love—the answer to all the hate in the world, all the darkness, all the evil. There is only one answer, and that is love. And, for you, that is Leon.*

With the last of her waning energy, she focused on Leon's face, as he screamed, lunging at Harvey, hitting Harvey on the head, trying to get him to stop hurting her.

And she smiled, speaking out loud this time. "Leon."

He turned, looked at her. "What? Are you okay? What's going on? You look weird."

"Step aside," she whispered.

He shook his head. "No way, he'll come after you."

"He's coming after me now," she said quietly. "Just step away. I don't want you to get hurt." She watched the confusion and then the acceptance, as Leon stepped back, trusting in her. That was worth so much.

Harvey stood up to his full height and laughed, his laughter getting louder, louder, hysterical. "You can't beat me," he yelled. "I'm strong, way stronger than you."

"No," she said, "before, I was young. I was untrained. I didn't really know, but I do know now, and I'm so sorry, Harvey, because I loved you like a friend. I loved you like a brother. But it's not the same now, not when I know you're a killer, not when I know what you've done. So, I'm so sorry but—"

And he screamed, "No, no, no," and he jumped toward Leon, as if intent on taking one last victim with him.

In one powerful move Abby poured an icy-cold blast of energy into Harvey's brain—Stefan and Dr. Maddy aiding her with their energy as an extra power source—surrounding his brain in ice and draining away all the heat, until there was nothing left.

Harvey crashed to the floor. Dead.

Released from the energy highway they'd created, Abby crashed onto the bed immediately. Her mind bereft, empty. Stefan was gone. Dr. Maddy was gone. And Abby could only hope they were fine. She felt their energies smiling at her, so she knew they were. She looked up at Leon, as he raced to her side, picked her up, placing her on his lap, as he sat down on the bed.

"What the hell just happened?" he asked.

"Maybe when I'm old and gray, and I'm recovered from this, I'll explain, but, until then, I'm not sure I have an answer."

"My God." Leon looked at Harvey on the floor. "Is he dead?"

"I think so," she said. "What I know for sure is that his energy, that brain energy, is gone. We blasted it to smithereens. And you can't tell anyone."

"Tell anyone what?" he asked, staring at her in shock. "I

don't understand any of this."

"Good." She sagged against him. "Any chance we could go home now?"

He picked her up and carried her toward the door. "I'm walking out of here right now with you."

"Well, we need to call the cops first."

"You can call the cops later," he said.

"I don't have to. Stefan already did." And, sure enough, at that moment the hospital security guards came racing in. They looked at her, cradled in Leon's arms.

"What the hell happened?"

"I don't know," Abby said. "Harvey started to scream, and it's like something popped inside of him, and he collapsed. I was just waking up. I don't even know what happened."

The doctor came in. "Well, I'm sure glad to see you awake, young lady." When he looked at the cop on the floor, he asked, "But what the hell?"

"Look. I don't know what's going on," Abby said, "but I'm not feeling all that great."

"No, you need to stay here." He tried to usher her back to bed.

"No, I really don't. I'll go home to my place, where I can rest and cuddle Migolo, my cat. If anything gets worse, I promise I'll come back." She motioned to Harvey. "I've got officers coming to handle this."

And, with that, Leon carried her outside to his car. He didn't say a word as he pulled up in front of her house. She tried to get out and walk, and he said, "No, let me."

He scooped her into his arms and carried her inside. She realized this big strong man was trembling, the aftermath of what happened in that hospital room hitting him. He didn't stop at the front door, but he did shut and lock it behind him, then carried her upstairs to her bed, where he stripped her down to the skin. Then he followed suit seconds later and tucked her into bed, before he joined her. He just held her tight, spooning them together, Abby wrapped up in his arms and his legs, before covering them up.

Migolo joined them almost immediately and curled up in her arms.

Abby laid like that for what seemed like forever, and finally she felt her body starting to relax. She tilted her head back and said, "It'll be okay, you know."

"It may never be okay."

Well, it would, but getting over these events and having that flood of memories to deal with as well would take time. A lot of time. "Yes, it will," she repeated.

He looked down at her. "I gather that the wall came down?"

She nodded. "Harvey killed my parents," she said. "Such a betrayal. I really loved that man. He was everything in a partner I could wish for."

"Well, maybe now that you don't have a police partner," he said, "how do you feel about getting another kind of partner?"

She smiled. "You know what? I can't think of a better idea. I'll replace him with you any day." She turned to face him, taking Migolo with her.

"Good, because I don't think I'll ever let you go again." And he lowered his head and kissed her with deep drugging kisses, from one side of her mouth to the other, before sliding his tongue between her lips and warring with hers.

And it was too much for Migolo. He quickly disappeared.

Leon lifted his head. "Never letting you go." He kissed her again hard, deep, plundering her to her very soul.

She felt her body responding, almost shakily, but she certainly wasn't arguing; if anything, she was giving as good as she got. She pulled him harder and closer to her, holding him tight, whispering, "I promise," she said, "nothing like that will ever happen again."

He shuddered, the emotions exposed on his face plunging deep into her heart, her soul, her being. She smiled, sliding her hands up to hold his face still. "Close your eyes." He did and relaxed gently against her, as she whispered, "Now, open your inner eyes."

He opened his mind's eye, only to realize that she was there in his mind—with him—sitting on a cloud, staring at him. "What the hell?" he asked.

She held a finger to her lips and whispered, "It's okay," she said. "After I smashed that wall, I opened up another wall, as a way to keep you alive, while Stefan and Dr. Maddy and I blasted Harvey with icy energy because he was trying to take you down." She hesitated, then rushed to add, "So I hope it's okay, but you and I now share this walkway between us."

He stared at her in shock, and then slowly a smile crept out. "If there was ever someone I wanted a walkway with," he said, "it would be you."

She smiled, wrapped her arms around him. "Glad to hear that because once we're joined—"

He nodded, and they spoke in unison. "We're joined forever."

And, at that, he aligned his body with hers, right at the heart of her, and slowly entered, pulled back, then moving his body, rising and falling in a motion as old as time, taking them both on a long journey to a cliff's edge, but then promptly sent her over, screaming out loud in joy, releasing and receiving love. When he joined her on the other side, he gathered her up in his arms, and he said, "That is one hell of a walkway."

She burst out laughing.

He grinned and held her close. "Now let's hope that our lives are full of laughter and love from now on."

"They will be. We'll make sure of it."

EPILOGUE

"**A**LL THIS PAPERWORK will take me weeks," Abby muttered to Leon, as she readied to head off to work the next morning.

"Did you get all your questions answered?" He kissed her.

"Yeah, I did, when I accessed Harvey's brain."

Leon seemed impressed, surprised, maybe a little skeptical. "At least you have answers."

"Yeah, but not answers I can give to the students' parents."

"No," he agreed, "and, for that, I'm sorry, since they'll always wonder just what happened. On the other hand, they don't have to get into any ugly discussions about adoptions or anything else."

"No, but they won't get closure."

"At least the private detective's body can be released, and we can bury my aunt," he said quietly. "But what of my adoptive parents and my half brother and Henkel?" He looked at her, and she nodded.

"I'm sorry," she said. "When I was in Harvey's mind, I saw his memories, heard his thoughts, understood his motivations. Once he realized that Gertrude had had a second child and gave you to Mary, he decided against killing you, and he went and killed Mary and her husband, just to torment Gertrude more. Harvey hated her for giving him up. That became his obsession, and I didn't even know." She shook her head. "Once he left his adopted family's house, for a while Harvey just drifted. He was in the military, and then he joined law enforcement, and the rest is history," She paused. "Until he saw Gertrude again. And it all came flooding back."

"Where the hell would he have seen Gertrude again?"

"Oddly enough, he was sitting in on her What If? class," she replied quietly. "I didn't realize it, but he had been working on a degree on the side, picking up some philosophy courses to go with it. I'll have to go through the university tapes again, and I think I saw him, with his face down, a cap over his head, as he left her class.

"He'd heard a lot about her class and had decided to sit in. When he saw her, he knew, and, when he saw how Gertrude interacted with her two students, Harvey couldn't stand it, and he killed them in that last class. Several students talked about how the two women were like teacher's pets. It drove him crazy. But Harvey had no way to get into their minds—until they had their last surgeries.

"He realized they were in a weakened state when they came back, as they were still healing, but it was enough to gain access, to put in his hook or his block or whatever the hell he did. Then he just waited for the right time. It's why he didn't kill the third girl. She didn't have the same surgical weakness, so he had no access. He'd stewed about it for the whole term, watching them interact, knowing Gertrude had not cared enough about him to keep him, yet she loved these women."

Leon stared at her. "To have so much potential …" Leon shook his head. "Wow, that's ugly. And the PI? Because of the alcohol, Harvey got access to him?"

"Yes, any addict is vulnerable," she confirmed. "In your case, you're his blood relative. So I'm not sure why he couldn't kill you. He should have had a direct access, like with Gertrude, like with Henkel, his birth father."

"I felt some pressure at the end there, in the hospital, but I've always been very good at focusing on what I want, so I just told the pressure that I had no time, that I was trying to figure out something important—like, saving you."

"And that's likely all it took. Remember. This stuff really only needs you to have control over yourself. Harvey couldn't take over, if you were already in control."

"Got it."

"So much potential and he wasted it all," she said. "A shame, isn't it?"

"That's not quite the word I'd use, but it gets the meaning across, yes."

She smiled at him. "It's all good now. I don't know how I'll explain any of this to the captain. It may just stay open as unsolved woo-woo cases. Or I can get Stefan's help to explain."

"And I'm okay with that too." He shook his head.

"Then I'll be happy to never open that case again." She hesitated.

He looked at her and asked, "What?"

"Just because of the very nature of what I can do," she said hesitatingly, "I will likely be doing a bunch of work for Stefan, as we go after other killers, like Harvey."

Leon nodded slowly. "I guess you have to, don't you?"

"Since there are so very few of us energy workers, who can do anything about it," she explained quietly, "I feel dutybound to help others get away from similar killers."

"Well, I'm definitely in your corner on that," he confirmed. "Let's hope that there aren't very many out there."

She winced. "According to Stefan, there's a lot."

"Oh God, that's horrible, but it doesn't matter," he said firmly, as he pulled her into his arms, gave her a goodbye kiss, and added, "Remember. As long as we're together, nothing else matters."

This concludes Book 20 of Psychic Visions: What If….

Read about Talking Bones: Psychic Visions, Book 21

Talking Bones: Psychic Visions
(Book #21)

Hiding out in the French Quarter of New Orleans only made sense for someone like Skylar Livingston. Owning a voodoo shop was just an added touch for fun. It also helped with her cover, plus gave space to the multitude of ghosts in her family. And her shop was close to the cemeteries, ... a very necessary part of her ... hobby.

Gage Hawkins was tracking his uncle's last movements before his disappearance—hunting a special set of tarot cards—which led to Skylar's shop, Talking Bones. After a bad head injury that brought weird sights into his view, Gage could see this Talking Bones place and Skylar were special. He could only hope she had answers because he had a lot of questions …

Skylar preferred the dead to the living most times, but Gage had her reconsidering. Until she realizes something is wrong in his world, and it's quickly overtaking hers.

When Gage's uncle turns up dead, more than the undead are in Skylar's world. … A killer is too …

Find Book 21 here!
To find out more visit Dale Mayer's website.
https://geni.us/DMTalkingUniversal

Sneak Peek from Talking Bones

S KYLAR LIVINGSTON UNLOCKED the connecting door between her upstairs apartment and that of her ground-level New Orleans shop, Skylar's Heaven, and stepped inside her store that Friday morning. She walked rapidly to the back room and shut off the alarm. With that done, she entered her shop and opened the blinds to the front windows, letting light into her store. Taking off her sweater, she proceeded to the counter, where she flicked on the lights throughout, and only then did she fully open her eyes.

With the shop fully lit, the spirits were much less prevalent.

She called out, "Good morning, guys."

There was a weird wavering of the air, as multiple personalities greeted her. Every morning when she arrived, the ghostly apparitions were so bright that it was hard for Skylar to see where she walked, as she headed to the alarm system. The ghosts were an alarm system as well, but Skylar still felt the need to have a more traditional system in place.

"Going to be a crazy day today," Thomas said, by way of his greeting. He was one of many resident ghosts here.

Checking around, she noted that nothing appeared to be wrong or different with the energy or the ambience in the store. No sign of an intruder. No sign of any problems, but she hadn't fully checked in the back yet. She made a quick walk through to the rear area, where she put on a pot of coffee, relieved to see absolutely nothing new or different.

In her world, boring and normal were perfect.

With all of that in place and the coffee dripping, she headed back out to the main store area, unlocked the front door, and peered out the window. She still had fifteen minutes until opening, but the streets were already filling with tourists. That was both good and bad. She needed the income that the tourists provided, but she didn't like some of the energy that they brought with them. As a matter of fact, she didn't like anything about the commercialism or the necessity of making a living.

But she hadn't won the lottery and neither had she been born rich. So she worked.

She yawned and quickly covered her mouth with her hand, wishing she could sleep in later in the mornings. But that would mean hiring somebody to open up the store for her and giving her those extra few hours. Then again, if she didn't spend so much of her nights in the damn cemeteries, it wouldn't be as big of a problem.

Skylar brushed her long black hair off her face, noting that in her hurry she hadn't brought a clip. She looked around, found a wooden stick and a hair pin from the olden days that she had marked at two bucks, then quickly twisted her hair up and fixed it firmly in place. Noting just how quick and efficient that was, not to mention stylish, she looked at the price on the rest of them and quickly changed it to seven dollars instead. She often found that, with things for sale in the store, if she doubled the price or made it even higher, the items sometimes took on a life of their own.

Then her ghostly friends helped too.

She knew that she could count on the effect of the spirits

and their energy to set the mood inside, which was perfect for a voodoo shop, although it took a lot from Skylar to keep it energized high enough to bring in people.

Whenever she recognized that some people were looking for a spooky experience, she would quickly lower her energy shield, so that the store had the ambience of something darker. She could cheerfully blame the ghosts for that, if any tourist was so interested.

As she looked around, she saw all her regular ghostly crew.

"You know that you can go home anytime," she stated, something that she shared probably thirty to forty times a day. At least when the store was empty. The ghosts all just nodded, and not one moved.

The frustration was crippling at times. "You all do that, seemingly agreeing with me, yet you're all still here. Even though you have options."

Thomas whispered in her ear, "We are here because we want to be."

"You're not connected to me though," she murmured. "So you don't need to stand watch, although it is appreciated."

"We *are* connected to you," he argued, crossing his arms. He looked like somebody from Abraham Lincoln's era, with a top hat and a black suit. He was tall and almost gaunt.

She sighed. "Just because I rescued some bones—"

"Yes, but we're also here because we want to be," he noted, "so you can't chase us away."

She rolled her eyes at that. "My shop is getting more crowded all the time."

"That's all right," replied Dodi, a pale-faced woman on the other side of the counter. "We'll just move to your apartment then."

Immediately Skylar shook her head. "No, no, no, please don't do that."

The woman looked at her in surprise. "Why not?"

"Because it's nice to have a place that is only mine." Although it wasn't only hers. No way to explain that to this group of ghosts though.

Dodi looked at Skylar for a moment and then gave a complacent nod. "I can see that for you, it's true. I had nine children, so I wouldn't know what that is like. But I'm happy to give it to you."

"Nine children?" Skylar almost gasped at that. When she heard a noise from the front door, she turned toward it. One of the ghost kids, Chucky, called out in excitement, "They're coming."

She groaned, plastered a smile on her face, and waited, while the door opened fully. Then her smile became real. "Hey, Tomo," she greeted the tall, spare man walking toward her with a sheepish smile. "How are you doing?"

He held up a plate. "My latest offering. I'm hoping you would try some."

She looked at the plate avariciously. "More beignets?"

"More beignets," he confirmed. "You know that they have to be absolutely perfect in order to compete with everybody else around here."

"You keep trying all you want," she murmured, as she stared at the plate with three fat treats, "particularly if that will keep the samples coming my way."

He burst out laughing, his beautiful caramel-colored skin glowing, as his face split wide into a big grin. "You know that you'll get all the beignets you want from my restaurant, when I finally get there—and for free."

She shook her head. "You can't do it for free. You'll have to play the game and charge for your goods, just like the rest of us."

"I wish I could hand them out for free though," he replied in all seriousness.

"I know you do," she added gently, "but somehow we're caught up in this commercial lifestyle, where I must have people actually pay for my products, so I can turn around and pay you for beignets."

"But, if I just gave them to you," he started, "you wouldn't—"

"Then how will you pay your rent?" she asked, with an understanding smile. He really was a wonderful soul, just not the most realistic when it came to business. He wanted to believe in a world of sunshine and roses, where everybody loved everybody else and where they all took care of each other. Well, she wanted to believe in that too, but her life experiences had confirmed a whole different reality was out there.

"I wish I had enough money," he noted, "where I could just do it by donation."

"I wish you did too because I know that system does work in some places." He looked at her with interest, as she shrugged. "I've heard of pilot programs that have popped up in different areas with that structure, but I would presume that you still need to have enough income on a regular basis to pay the rent."

He winced. "I don't understand why that rent money thing keeps coming around every month." She burst out laughing, and he shot her a quick, bright grin.

Skylar continued. "See? Now that's what I love about you—that humor, with a completely deadpan face, while you crack a joke like that."

He nodded sagely. "And you're always happy to see me because I bring along the sunshine."

She gazed at him affectionately. "That is very true. The world will be a sadder place when you choose to leave it." He looked at her in surprise, but she shrugged. "Don't ask me. It's just the way the words came out."

"Are you, like, sensing anything?" There was hesitation and worry in his voice.

She stared. "Hell no," she said out loud. "You know that's not a part of what I do."

He nodded. "But I think you probably could if you tried. At least my grandma says so."

"Your grandma would accept anybody in the business if she thought she could get them to help with her clients and could make money off them," she teased.

That grin flashed again. "You do know her, don't you?"

"I know her very well," she stated, with a smile. "You guys have been very good to me since I've been here."

"Too bad you haven't been here longer," he added cheerfully. "We would have been nice to you since then."

Skylar nodded. Nothing she could really say to that, but it was such a typical comment from him, and, thinking back, she wished the same thing.

He looked around. "Well, here we go. Looks like the tourists are filling up the streets once again. You'll have a wild and crazy day, from the looks of things. Good thing I brought you some fortification," he noted, with one raised eyebrow.

"Tourists are a blessed evil." She shook her head.

"I have to admit I do like to be with them, but then, at some point, it gets very draining, and I need my own space.

That's when I go bury myself in the kitchen and come up with new recipes."

"You go do that all you want," she agreed. "I'm always happy to try out your experiments."

"Even the failures?" He groaned, with an eye roll. "That says something."

"Hey, I don't get that much to eat these days," she murmured.

"If you'd ever get some sleep," he admonished her, "you could get up earlier, in time to actually eat before you have to open."

"I *could*," she noted, "but now you've saved me from starving yet another day." When he frowned at her, she laughed. "Don't worry about it. I'm fine."

"Have you really not eaten?" he asked.

"Not yet, no, but the coffee's still dripping."

He continued to frown, tapping his fingers on the front counter, as he glared at her.

"I'm fine," she murmured. "I really am."

"I'm not so sure that you're fine, as much as you're trying to convince me that you're fine."

Again, another astute comment from him that she hadn't expected. She patted his hand. "I get it, but it's all good."

His response was stifled, as a crowd moved into her shop. She smiled at the crowd and greeted them. "Good morning."

As if sensing that he was preventing her sales, Tomo immediately left, so she could get to work.

She was sad to see him leave. He was one of the few *real* friends she had here, among all her ghostly ones. She knew perfectly well that Tomo wouldn't remain in this world much longer. Life, then death. It was the normal cycle of life, and she saw it time and time again. It was hard when they were young, and, just because she knew Tomo's fate, she had no ability to change it. Therefore, she kept him happy, doing the things that he loved. Meanwhile, maybe he'd find a new treatment for the cancer eating away in his system.

She hadn't changed fate one bit over the last twenty years and highly doubted that she could manage to do it now. Her own grandmother would have told her to stop wasting time and energy on something she can't fix or stop, stating that the spirits had their own reasons for what they were doing, and it wasn't for Skylar to know.

She'd even asked several of the ghosts in her shop for advice on how to help Tomo, but not one of her ghosts had a word of advice on how to postpone that final date with destiny.

For that reason alone, she tried to keep Tomo focused on what was happening in his world, all to make him smile. Surely smiling had to be worth something.

The smell of the beignets, still warm on her counter, tantalized her, even as she studied the customers who had just entered. "May I help you find anything?" she asked, casting another longing glance at the treats in front of her.

"We're just looking," a woman replied, her voice upbeat.

Skylar nodded and picked up a beignet, then quickly took a bite.

Almost immediately came a gasp from one of her potential customers. "Oh my," the woman told her, "we just came from that famous café down the road. Their beignets were absolutely wonderful."

Skylar immediately nodded. "Yes, they are."

"Do they deliver too?"

"A friend of mine picked these up," she explained.

"Nice friend," the woman stated jealously.

Skylar kept her voice and smile soft, as she waited for them to peruse the store to see if they wanted to buy anything. Usually the early morning crowds were heading out for long days of sightseeing and rarely bought anything right off the bat because they were carrying everything they had with them. When they all tripped out with a smile, calling out for her to have a happy day, Skylar's forecast had proven out because no one had bought a thing.

She immediately walked to the back room, then grabbed her first cup of coffee and returned to the counter, lifting a beignet and taking a big bite. As she stood here, wiping the powdered sugar off her face, her front door opened with an odd surge of air. She froze.

Only a few things would cause the wind to blow into her store like that.

With buildings across from her shop and around on all sides, the wind ran down the street. It rarely came into her store. And, sure enough, her curious gaze followed the gust of air all the way from the front to the back of her store and again to the front, as a man stepped over the threshold of her entrance. She stared at him, and her heart sank. "May I help you?" she asked, forcing a smile she didn't feel, while she studied the strong energy in front of her.

"I'm looking for Skylar," replied the man in a deep voice, his gaze intently studying her.

She nodded. "Well, you found her. What can I do for you?"

He observed her for a long moment, but she refused to give in to the uneasiness in her gut telling her to run, even though the power radiating off his frame was unbelievable.

She didn't dare make a comment or even let him know that she registered that something powerful filled him, because surely he already knew.

"I need you to help me with something."

She raised her eyebrows. "I'm sorry. I don't know what you're looking for, but I just run this little shop here."

He burst out laughing. "That's hardly all you do."

She frowned and replied in a much different tone, not liking anything about his. "I'm sorry. I don't understand what you're implying."

"I'm implying that you're very talented in many other areas," he stated, "and I don't have time for the facade."

"That's nice," she noted. "And I don't really have time for anything you have to say, with an attitude like that."

He nodded. "No? I can see that. Apparently I'm being more abrupt than usual."

"Really?" She smirked. "I hadn't noticed."

"I don't think much of anything gets by you, and I do not suffer fools either," he stated in a silky voice.

She stared at him and asked quietly, "Are you calling me a fool?"

He shook his head. "No, and I can see that your defense mechanisms are already standing at full attention. I'm really not here to harm you."

"Interesting, yet you say the darndest things."

He frowned, as he studied her again. "Can we drop the pretense?"

"Please do," she agreed patiently, not sure where he was going with this, but afraid she wouldn't like it.

"I need help finding my uncle."

"And what has that got to do with me?" she asked, a frown crossing her brows in bewilderment.

He scowled, as if finally realizing it was possible that he had the wrong person. "My uncle, I am afraid he's missing."

"Have you gone to the police?" No way would she try to find a lost uncle. What gossip had he listened to?

He sighed impatiently. "Of course I have. And, having exhausted all leads, I'm here, looking for assistance from you."

"And whatever would possess you to come to me for help?"

"Well, you're the one who talks to all these ghosts in here, aren't you?" he asked, with a negligent hand movement.

Her heart clamped down tightly, and she stared at him in shock, her breath frozen in her chest.

"I could see them when I came in, at least some of them," he explained. "I have a very general ability, not a full slate like you do."

"I don't get it," she admitted, covertly gasping for air.

"And I don't have the time or the patience for this," he snapped. "My uncle might be dying, and I need help finding him."

Find Book 21 here!
To find out more visit Dale Mayer's website.
https://geni.us/DMTalkingUniversal

Simon Says... Hide: Kate Morgan (Book #1)

Welcome to a new thriller series from *USA Today* Best-Selling Author Dale Mayer. Set in Vancouver, BC, the team of Detective Kate Morgan and Simon St. Laurant, an unwilling psychic, marries all the elements of Dale's work that you've come to love, plus so much more.

Detective Kate Morgan, newly promoted to the Vancouver PD Homicide Department, stands for the victims in her world. She was once a victim herself, just as her mother had been a victim, and then her brother—an unsolved missing child's case—was yet another victim. She can't stand those who take advantage of others, and the worst ones are those who prey on the hopes of desperate people to line their own pockets.

So, when she finds a connection between more than a half-dozen cold cases to a current case, where a child's life hangs in the balance, Kate would make a deal with the devil himself to find the culprit and to save the child.

Simon St. Laurant's grandmother had the Sight and had warned him that, once he used it, he could never walk away. Until now, her caution had made it easy to avoid that first step. But, when nightmares of his own past are triggered, Simon can't stand back and watch child after child be abused. Not without offering his help to those chasing the monsters.

Even if it means dealing with the cranky and critical Detective Kate Morgan …

Find Simon Says… Hide here!
To find out more visit Dale Mayer's website.
https://geni.us/DMSSHideUniversal

Author's Note

Thank you for reading What If...: Psychic Visions, Book 20! If you enjoyed the book, please take a moment and leave a short review.

Dear reader,

I love to hear from readers, and you can contact me at my website: www.dalemayer.com or at my Facebook author page. To be informed of new releases and special offers, sign up for my newsletter or follow me on BookBub. And if you are interested in joining Dale Mayer's Reader Group, here is the Facebook sign up page. http://geni.us/DaleMayerFBGroup

Cheers,
Dale Mayer

About the Author

Dale Mayer is a *USA Today* best-selling author, best known for her SEALs military romances, her Psychic Visions series, and her Lovely Lethal Garden cozy series. Her contemporary romances are raw and full of passion and emotion (Broken But ... Mending, Hathaway House series). Her thrillers will keep you guessing (Kate Morgan, By Death series), and her romantic comedies will keep you giggling (*It's a Dog's Life*, a stand-alone novella; and the Broken Protocols series, starring Charming Marvin, the cat).

Dale honors the stories that come to her—and some of them are crazy, break all the rules and cross multiple genres!

To go with her fiction, she also writes nonfiction in many different fields, with books available on résumé writing, companion gardening, and the US mortgage system. All her books are available in print and ebook format.

Connect with Dale Mayer Online

Dale's Website – www.dalemayer.com
Twitter – @DaleMayer
Facebook Page – geni.us/DaleMayerFBFanPage
Facebook Group – geni.us/DaleMayerFBGroup
BookBub – geni.us/DaleMayerBookbub
Instagram – geni.us/DaleMayerInstagram
Goodreads – geni.us/DaleMayerGoodreads
Newsletter – geni.us/DaleNews

Also by Dale Mayer

Published Adult Books:

Bullard's Battle
Ryland's Reach, Book 1

Cain's Cross, Book 2

Eton's Escape, Book 3

Garret's Gambit, Book 4

Kano's Keep, Book 5

Fallon's Flaw, Book 6

Quinn's Quest, Book 7

Bullard's Beauty, Book 8

Bullard's Best, Book 9

Terkel's Team
Damon's Deal, Book 1

Kate Morgan
Simon Says… Hide, Book 1

Simon Says… Jump, Book 2

Hathaway House
Aaron, Book 1

Brock, Book 2

Cole, Book 3

The K9 Files

Kurt, Book 12

Tucker, Book 13

Harley, Book 14

Kyron, Book 15

The K9 Files, Books 1–2

The K9 Files, Books 3–4

The K9 Files, Books 5–6

The K9 Files, Books 7–8

The K9 Files, Books 9–10

The K9 Files, Books 11–12

Lovely Lethal Gardens

Arsenic in the Azaleas, Book 1

Bones in the Begonias, Book 2

Corpse in the Carnations, Book 3

Daggers in the Dahlias, Book 4

Evidence in the Echinacea, Book 5

Footprints in the Ferns, Book 6

Gun in the Gardenias, Book 7

Handcuffs in the Heather, Book 8

Ice Pick in the Ivy, Book 9

Jewels in the Juniper, Book 10

Killer in the Kiwis, Book 11

Lifeless in the Lilies, Book 12

Murder in the Marigolds, Book 13

Nabbed in the Nasturtiums, Book 14

Offed in the Orchids, Book 15

Lovely Lethal Gardens, Books 1–2

Lovely Lethal Gardens, Books 3–4

Lovely Lethal Gardens, Books 5–6
Lovely Lethal Gardens, Books 7–8
Lovely Lethal Gardens, Books 9–10

Psychic Vision Series

Tuesday's Child
Hide 'n Go Seek
Maddy's Floor
Garden of Sorrow
Knock Knock…
Rare Find
Eyes to the Soul
Now You See Her
Shattered
Into the Abyss
Seeds of Malice
Eye of the Falcon
Itsy-Bitsy Spider
Unmasked
Deep Beneath
From the Ashes
Stroke of Death
Ice Maiden
Snap, Crackle…
What If…
Talking Bones
Psychic Visions Books 1–3
Psychic Visions Books 4–6
Psychic Visions Books 7–9

By Death Series

Touched by Death

Haunted by Death

Chilled by Death

By Death Books 1–3

Broken Protocols – Romantic Comedy Series

Cat's Meow

Cat's Pajamas

Cat's Cradle

Cat's Claus

Broken Protocols 1-4

Broken and... Mending

Skin

Scars

Scales (of Justice)

Broken but... Mending 1-3

Glory

Genesis

Tori

Celeste

Glory Trilogy

Biker Blues

Morgan: Biker Blues, Volume 1

Cash: Biker Blues, Volume 2

SEALs of Honor

Mason: SEALs of Honor, Book 1

Hawk: SEALs of Honor, Book 2

Dane: SEALs of Honor, Book 3

Swede: SEALs of Honor, Book 4

Shadow: SEALs of Honor, Book 5

Cooper: SEALs of Honor, Book 6

Markus: SEALs of Honor, Book 7

Evan: SEALs of Honor, Book 8

Mason's Wish: SEALs of Honor, Book 9

Chase: SEALs of Honor, Book 10

Brett: SEALs of Honor, Book 11

Devlin: SEALs of Honor, Book 12

Easton: SEALs of Honor, Book 13

Ryder: SEALs of Honor, Book 14

Macklin: SEALs of Honor, Book 15

Corey: SEALs of Honor, Book 16

Warrick: SEALs of Honor, Book 17

Tanner: SEALs of Honor, Book 18

Jackson: SEALs of Honor, Book 19

Kanen: SEALs of Honor, Book 20

Nelson: SEALs of Honor, Book 21

Taylor: SEALs of Honor, Book 22

Colton: SEALs of Honor, Book 23

Troy: SEALs of Honor, Book 24

Axel: SEALs of Honor, Book 25

Baylor: SEALs of Honor, Book 26

Hudson: SEALs of Honor, Book 27

Heroes for Hire

Vince's Vixen: Heroes for Hire, Book 19

Ice's Icing: Heroes for Hire, Book 20

Johan's Joy: Heroes for Hire, Book 21

Galen's Gemma: Heroes for Hire, Book 22

Zack's Zest: Heroes for Hire, Book 23

Bonaparte's Belle: Heroes for Hire, Book 24

Noah's Nemesis: Heroes for Hire, Book 25

Tomas's Trials: Heroes for Hire, Book 26

Heroes for Hire, Books 1–3

Heroes for Hire, Books 4–6

Heroes for Hire, Books 7–9

Heroes for Hire, Books 10–12

Heroes for Hire, Books 13–15

Heroes for Hire, Books 16–18

Heroes for Hire, Books 19–21

Heroes for Hire, Books 22–24

SEALs of Steel

Badger: SEALs of Steel, Book 1

Erick: SEALs of Steel, Book 2

Cade: SEALs of Steel, Book 3

Talon: SEALs of Steel, Book 4

Laszlo: SEALs of Steel, Book 5

Geir: SEALs of Steel, Book 6

Jager: SEALs of Steel, Book 7

The Final Reveal: SEALs of Steel, Book 8

SEALs of Steel, Books 1–4

SEALs of Steel, Books 5–8

SEALs of Steel, Books 1–8

The Mavericks

Kerrick, Book 1

Griffin, Book 2

Jax, Book 3

Beau, Book 4

Asher, Book 5

Ryker, Book 6

Miles, Book 7

Nico, Book 8

Keane, Book 9

Lennox, Book 10

Gavin, Book 11

Shane, Book 12

Diesel, Book 13

Jerricho, Book 14

Killian, Book 15

Hatch, Book 16

The Mavericks, Books 1–2

The Mavericks, Books 3–4

The Mavericks, Books 5–6

The Mavericks, Books 7–8

The Mavericks, Books 9–10

The Mavericks, Books 11–12

Collections

Dare to Be You...

Dare to Love...

Dare to be Strong...

RomanceX3

Standalone Novellas

It's a Dog's Life

Riana's Revenge

Second Chances

Published Young Adult Books:

Family Blood Ties Series

Vampire in Denial

Vampire in Distress

Vampire in Design

Vampire in Deceit

Vampire in Defiance

Vampire in Conflict

Vampire in Chaos

Vampire in Crisis

Vampire in Control

Vampire in Charge

Family Blood Ties Set 1–3

Family Blood Ties Set 1–5

Family Blood Ties Set 4–6

Family Blood Ties Set 7–9

Sian's Solution, A Family Blood Ties Series Prequel
Novelette

Design series

Dangerous Designs

Deadly Designs

Darkest Designs

Design Series Trilogy

Standalone
In Cassie's Corner

Gem Stone (a Gemma Stone Mystery)

Time Thieves

Published Non-Fiction Books:

Career Essentials
Career Essentials: The Résumé

Career Essentials: The Cover Letter

Career Essentials: The Interview

Career Essentials: 3 in 1